A SUNCASTLE KNIGHTS STORY

A GAME LIKE Ours

MARISSA J. GRAMOLL

Editors:

Deanna Young

Karin Salisbury

Proofreader:

Eris Marriott

Logo Designer:

Eleanor Aldrick

Cover Design and Formatting:

L. Steinworth www.theartofliz.com

Models:

Ashley and Scott Knapp

ISBN Paperback: 978-1-7366277-1-6

ISBN Hardcover: 978-1-7366277-2-3

TRIGGER WARNING

A Game Like Ours is a New Adult, Queer, College Literary Fiction with strong romantic themes about coming to terms with loss and identity.

This book contains content that may be triggering–including death of a loved one, suicidal ideation, eating disorder, homosexual persecution, physical abuse (off page), and other intense situations.

Not recommended for younger audiences.

AUTHOR'S NOTE

I wrote about some very sensitive topics and did my best to handle them with the utmost care. Some of these topics and situations are very close to my heart and were things that brought tears to my eyes as I wrote them. This is the story I needed to tell, the book I needed to write. I hope that the way I depict these scenes in A Game Like Ours shows respect and thoughtfulness to those in similar situations. Much of this book was drawn from my personal experience and the experiences of those close to me. Our culture has a long way to go toward acceptance. I hope that in a small way, this book can help. For all my bisexual readers, I hope you feel seen. You matter to me.

———

A NOTE ABOUT EATING DISORDERS:

In preparation for this novel, I researched Eating Disorders both inside and outside of athletics, doing all I could to represent this subject with care and consideration. Please know that this is a work of fiction and may or may not feel real or reasonable to some individuals. Bobby's story is authentic to his character. The struggles he felt are very close to my heart and I hope that it provides a message of hope in the way it is represented. Eating Disorders are unique to the individual. If you or a loved one is challenged with this, there is help available.

For more information, visit:
  https://www.nationaleatingdisorders.org/

For everyone who has lost someone they love and had to keep on living.

For everyone who has had to love in the dark.
I see you.
I'm with you.
This book is for you.

1

BOBBY

I wish feelings had an on-and-off switch.

They say that you go *through* stages of grief. But that ain't true. You don't go through grief. You get stuck in it. Like mud after a rainy game that sticks to your cleats, this shit doesn't go anywhere. It's a part of you, even though all you want is to be washed clean of it. Washed clean of it all.

I need to focus. Especially here at work. These little guys need me.

"It's hot today," I say. "Hydrate, hydrate, hydrate." I clap my hands while they grab their water bottles. Ice-cold sugar-free Powerade rushes down my throat.

I stretch my neck from side to side and watch as the Tiny Knights line up. My group of nine little-leaguers wait to bat. Some of 'em are chewing Big League Chew bubblegum. Dangling from the dugout. Reminding me of the cast from *The Sandlot*.

I crouch near home plate with my palms digging into my knees. My teammate Briar's group takes their position in the outfield.

One of my littlest players, Blake, is up first. I check his helmet and bat. "Okay, ready to go?" I step over so I'm close enough to help but not in the way.

Pitcher sends the ball our way. Blake chokes, standing still. Scared shitless. Poor kid.

"Strike one!" Rodney calls as the ball bounces against clay in the catcher's box. Blake didn't swing. I watch his face. He's been having a rough day. He needs a hit.

Second pitch with perfect potential flies through the air.

"Strike two!" Rodney yells.

"I can't do it." Blake throws his bat on the ground.

"Hey, now." I hop over to him. "Sure you can. Let's just try it this way, alright?" I keep my smile encouraging, handing him his bat. "Elbow here. Yep, like that. Okay." I look at him. "You got this. I promise."

"No, I don't." His face turns red as he huffs his frustration. "I just don't even know what I'm doin' here. I'm the worst player there is." He kicks his cleat into the clay, dust flying.

"Do you remember yesterday?" I raise my eyebrows. "Who hit a beautiful home run on our mornin' game? It wasn't Cal, was it?"

Cal's standing by us and he chuckles. He's wearing his purple jersey and gray pinstripe pants. They're rolled up below his knees, showing his purple stirrups and cleats. Kid's got confidence in droves, so I know he can take the joke. After just a sec of watching Blake, he catches on that we need to lift some spirits. "Not this time, Coach."

I tsk. "Well, you just told me I was lookin' at the worst player there is. But seems to me that's not really possible."

"Sure it is, Coach. I don't know how to do this." Blake hangs his head. "First missin' all those throws this mornin'. Now I just can't even hit. I wanna go home."

"It's just a rough day. We all have 'em. I mean, I miss a lot of hits too." I pat his shoulder.

"Hey, Coach Briar!" I cup my hand to shout across the field. "You miss a lot of hits, dontcha?"

"Blake's seen me play." Briar hollers. "I miss hits all the time."

"Last game we played in the championship a few weeks ago, I was at bat. Struck out. Cost the team a lot. But you know what?" I have Blake's attention. I can feel it. Can't let that go before I drive in some inner strength. "I gave it my best. And that's all any of us can do. Good days, rough days, we keep playin'."

He's hearing me, I hope. Please, let these words sink in. He needs it, today.

"You know how to do this. You've done it before. You've just gotta give it your best. Even if you miss, you just gotta give it your best." I bend so I'm at eye level with him. "I have total faith in you."

"You do?" Blake's eyes find mine.

"Sure I do. And so does your whole team. You're not alone, alright. Never alone."

I take my spot off to the side. Pitcher sends the ball our way. Blake swings. He *swings*. I breathe in relief. Ball connects with his bat. A line drive between second and third. It's enough time for him to run to first.

Thank God.

When the game's over, Blake seems better.

"Proud of you." I pat his shoulder while he shuffles into the dugout. "You gave it your best."

"Thanks, Coach." He smiles.

After the game, we run Catch, Tag and Throw drills.

"Coach Bobby, you gonna get drafted this year?" Cal runs up beside me to take his spot in the rotation. Blonde hair sticks out of his cap. I had Cal last summer, too.

"You could be the next Dansby Swanson." Cal throws the ball to Larry, on third base. "Or Jose Ramirez."

"We'll see." I smile, flattered that they think I'm going somewhere.

———

THE KIDS GET PICKED UP, LEAVING ME STANDING ON THE EMPTY FIELD. The past pulls me in again. I'm forever its prisoner.

For a second, it's like Cody's here. Standing on the mound, spitting sunflower seeds. I remember him everywhere.

"Did you see that? Bobby? Did you see that?" Cody grabs me by the shoulders. He's jumping up and down. "I've never thrown that fast! Oh my gosh, did you see that?"

"I saw! Of course I saw. Are you kiddin'?"

He smiles so wide at the radar reading 67 MPH. Most kids our age throw 60 or less. "I can do this."

"Told ya you were gettin' better." I bring him in for a huge hug.

"You're comin' with me, Bobby. Both of us, playin' for the majors! I can see it now." Cody's hand stretches with the horizon like he's looking into the future.

I swallow hard. Being at camp brings memories. Everything does. The dead aren't really the ones that die. It's the living. My insides have rotted like his corpse in Happy Memorial Cemetery.

I miss ya. I feel hollow and heavy. *Shit, I miss ya so much.*

I don't want to live on. I don't want to be the survivor. I don't want to keep breathing. Cody just slipped away. One minute he was here. The next he was gone.

Someday, will we all just slip away? If I hold my breath long enough, will I melt into the universe connecting everything to nothing, all at once? Will I get back to him? Can I please just get back to him?

I need to lock up the field and head to meet Sam, but my feet won't move. I'm stuck here. No, not stuck here, stuck in the past.

Life feels so futile now. I know it's not. Hell, I just helped Blake hit the goddamn ball. But it feels like there's nothing here for me now that Cody's gone.

Am I anything without him?

Was I ever?

Not knowing stirs up all the wrong kind of fear.

My eyes burn, making me want to close them and never open them up again. I bend down to pick up the bag of gear. Can't stay here. Can't stay lost in the past. Can't stay on this field that just reminds me of him.

I press my eyes closed tightly against the summer sun. Sweat drips from brow to cheek. The back of my hand swats it away like tears.

I grip the cross necklace Cody gave me and hold on tight. *Why'd you let him die, God? Why?*

"You okay, man?" Briar runs over to me and I shake out of my thoughts. "We gotta get locked up and I got work in half an hour."

"Yeah, yeah. Sorry." I lock up the gate. "I'm okay," I lie.

Not sure I'm ever gonna be.

Loss takes everything away. It clouds over what was once beautiful, leaving something dark and hazy in its wake. True for anyone who has lost someone. A fallout. A divorce.

A death.

———

THANK GOD, I GET TO BE WITH SAM TONIGHT. SINCE HIGH SCHOOL, I've been with both men and women. Sam is non-binary.

When I met Sam at a baseball tournament a few years ago, they joined me and Cody for an extra practice. We became fast friends, evolving into something more or less like friends with benefits after they graduated.

I drive the two hours to downtown Columbia. They travel here for work quite often and we meet up. Always worth the drive. I park my truck a couple blocks away and walk to the Marriott. Sam texted me their room number.

Once I'm in front of the hotel room, I delete our string of texts. No paper trail. I'm paranoid, I know. But I don't want word getting out.

Word *can't* get out.

The door opens, and I take them in. Dark hair and a trimmed beard. A coy smile plays on their face. Straight white teeth. Thick eyebrows. Very tan skin. Wearing a tailored suit and tie after a long day of business meetings. A little shorter than I am. Delicious muscles covering every inch of them.

"You made it, mate." They smile, latching the bolt on the hotel room. "I've missed you."

"Missed you, too." I bring them in for a hug. "How've you been?"

"Besides these stupid meetings, fantastic. How about you?"

"Good." I nod.

"Get settled." They gesture to the deluxe suite with drawn curtains and six bottles of sugar-free grape Powerade sitting on the coffee table, my favorite.

I plop my backpack in one of the armchairs. Take off my hoodie and set it down.

"You're losing weight." They look at me, concern in their eyes.

"It's nothin'." I choke. Shit, I wish they didn't notice. Need to cover it up. "Just stressed," I assure them as they look longer at my thinning frame. Untucking my shirt, I hope it looks better.

"What is this? You shouldn't be dieting this hard."

"I'm fine." I shrug.

"You're not low on cash, are you? Because I'll write you a check."

"No, no. I'm alright. I swear." I bring them in for a kiss, my lips melting into theirs, tasting the remnants of their spearmint gum.

"I know your body so well. This isn't alright." They put a little pressure against my stomach, a gasp coming at how little of me there is. "Let's go get a bite to eat. Now. You feel like you've been starving for weeks."

"No." I take their hand, intertwining our fingers. "I want you. Then we can get food."

"No. Food now, play later." They wink.

———

WE RELAX ON THE BED, ENJOYING THE AFTERGLOW. ALL WEEKEND, we've ordered room service, fucked and talked. The "Do Not Disturb" sign has stayed on the handle.

Their head rests on my chest, against my pounding heart. They play with my cross necklace in their hand. "I'm so sad you carry this, all the pain on your shoulders about what happened." Sam and I kept in touch, after that tournament where we met. Eventually, we shared our attraction for each other and the secrets. Sam is the only safe space I've had to really be who I am.

"Cody was a great player. I know you blame yourself a lot about what happened." Sam runs their finger along the baseball design engraved in the cross.

"I hate that he's gone." My throat is thick. I haven't really talked to anyone about this. There's so much brewing inside of me. Who I want to talk to is Lexie, Cody's surviving fiancée. I haven't seen her since the day of his funeral.

"Damn that truck." Sam's face is full of care and I'm more thankful than ever to have someone to talk to.

"Damn that truck." I agree, running my hand through my hair.

"I'm glad you're still here." They kiss me, coming on top. Their skin melts into mine as I stroke their back.

"Think you'll ever come out?" they ask.

I sigh. "After retirement, maybe."

"Wish it wasn't such a big announcement." Their voice is hopeful. I dare to dream with them. For even just a second. A world where it won't matter anymore. A world that learns it never should've mattered at all.

"I'm just me. I've always just been me. You don't pick who you love or how you feel. You just do. But I'm preachin' to the choir. I know, I know." I cup their chin in my hand, their beard against my palm. "Will you come out?"

They close their eyes, masking the pain behind them. "I don't know that I ever can." Their throat bobs with a harsh swallow. "Just to you, at least for now." They lay beside me, letting out a deep sigh. We stare at the ceiling, broken. "Thank you for accepting me." They run their hand across my cheek.

"Of course." My lips form a line. There's a heaviness that rests in my chest while I think about all they've been through. If I came out, I'd risk drama with my baseball career. My parents would be okay. My friends would adjust. But Sam? They'd lose so much.

"I think about it sometimes. Maybe if I announced it would do some good." I feel so jumbled inside. "Maybe it would help the others. There's this guy on the team. Somehow we got to talkin' one day." I smile thinking about Briar. "He came over one night and told me he's gay. Tellin' me he knew he could trust me somehow. But he won't tell anyone else on the team."

"And how could he?" Sam rolls toward the nightstand, handing me the sugar-free Powerade. "Maybe if you both came out at the same time. But then what?"

"Then what?" I take a drink, then slip off the bed and into my jeans. "Yeah that's not gonna happen. It'd risk the draft." I grind my teeth. "The world is more accepting today than it was. But it's not where it needs to be. Not yet. Conversion therapy is still legal, for fuck's sake." I feel sick thinking about it. Thinking about people, like some of my extended relatives, that would make a huge deal if they knew I'm bi. Most of the team I play on now would be fine. *Most* being the operative word. There are some that wouldn't treat me the same if they knew. Briar only came out to *me*.

"Maybe one day it'll be safe for you." Sam goes to their suitcase for some casual clothes. They toss me their shirt and I put it on, tossing them mine. It's a cute little thing we do every time. Exchange shirts.

I like smelling like them when I drive home. "Maybe one day. I hope it's headin' in that direction."

"I hope so, too." They come close to me and I feel a shift in the energy of the room. They have something important to say. "As nice as this weekend has been, I have something to tell you."

I brace myself, my stomach doing somersaults as I await whatever news is coming.

"This is the last time I'll be able to see you, at least for a while." Sam's eyes are sad. This was always a possibility. Nothing owed. Nothing expected. "I'm worried about telling you because I know you're already going through a lot." They eye my stomach and I tense. Wish they didn't notice. Wish there wasn't anything to notice.

"It's alright." I force my mouth into a line. "Casual can only last so long, right?"

"I am taking a new job back in Sydney. If you find yourself there, look me up." They sigh.

"Oh, Sam, that's great." I smile as big as I can, despite how hard it is to hear.

"Promise me you'll take better care of yourself." They lean in close to me. "You deserve better than starving over stress." The words sink in deep. I don't want to be this way. I don't want to be so hard on myself.

I grip them tight, holding them close. "We've had a lot of good times."

"Some of the best." Sam gives me a kiss filled with all the passion we've shared over the years.

I head out the door, wondering if I'll ever see them again.

My baseball cap is pulled down tight, and I slip my sunglasses on before the elevator doors open, tucking my chin, head down while I exit the lobby. There's an ache in my chest that spreads the longer I walk. Sydney fucking Australia. Across the world from me. Clenching my fists, I steel myself against this change. I'll get over it. I have to.

But as I drive all those miles to my apartment, it hits me why this is so hard.

It's another goodbye I wasn't ready for.

Do we all just slip away?

2

LEXIE

*T*he sign reads *Welcome to Suncastle South Carolina.* Red and white lights flash in my mind. The ambulance—a trigger from my broken past. My foot presses harder on the pedal, hoping that if I drive faster I can get away from this torment. Pressure in my chest makes it hard to inhale, so I turn the radio louder to escape.

Am I really coming back here?

Driving toward the beach house, I notice this town looks the same as it did when I left it. The exit off the freeway, leading to town, passes in my car window like a glimpse of the past calling me. The little shops and bars. The best pizza place, The Splat. The bookstores advertising half-priced textbooks. The McDonalds and an Olive Garden in the parking lot beside a strip mall with Kohl's and Ross. The billiards bar and rows of run-down sorority houses. Feeling more and more like a college town the longer I drive.

Nothing's changed, except that Cody's not here.

Our house comes into view and my eyes burn.

As the radio switches to a commercial break, I put the car in park. I've already been idling for ten minutes in the driveway, dreading going in.

"You have to finish school, Lexie. You've already done three years

in the program." Mom made it clear she was only paying for school if I continued at Suncastle College. So I have to finish, no matter how hard that is.

"Cody would want you to keep livin' your life," My sister, Charlene, told me. I wrap my arms around my body pretending it's her hug. Yeah, easy for them to say. They aren't the ones who lost their whole world in a split second.

I shoulda run off forever. Instead of walking, I feel I'm floating—like I'm not really here. The eight-hour drive was just the same: drifting, like clouds shifting over the Atlantic. I'm in some alternate reality. Lost in another time.

Turning my house key, I walk through the front door. Shimmers of dust dance in the sunlight, coming through the floor-to-ceiling windows. A thin film coats everything. The sofa, lamps, tables, and even my easel in the corner.

The longer I stand here staring at a space that used to be ours, I know I shouldn't be here. My throat swells so much it isn't a throat anymore, it's a blob of muscle and tissue that has no passageway for air. Not that my chest would allow that anyway.

"Take the time you need. Feel what you need to feel," my therapist's voice reminds me. I shake out my hands, doing little jumps on the porch, forcing myself farther inside.

This house.

Our house.

The house where Cody and I lived. The house where we had our last fight. The house where I heard about the car wreck.

Those flashing lights....

My phone buzzes. It's Charlene.

Charlene: Make it back ok?
Me: If you count suffocating where I stand as "ok," then, yes.

It isn't good for me to be confined within these walls. When I tried to explain that to Mom, my words fell on deaf ears. She says Dad told her it's too much of an investment to lose. It doesn't make sense for me to pay rent somewhere else when there's a perfectly good house to live in.

Maybe if I was his biological daughter he would've done that for me. The thought stings. Some part of him must love me or I would've been left to fend for myself a long time ago.

I hold a dusty breath, trying to stop worrying about things that will never change, like Dad. Be thankful. I have the life others dream about. So much good.

Until I lost Cody...

A wave of grief crashes over me, because now that I'm standing in *our* home, I see Cody everywhere. Our engagement photos, printed on canvas, all over the walls. His framed baseball jerseys in the front office, behind the desk. The gray paint he picked for our walls. His shadows surround me until there is nothing but darkness left.

I shouldn't be here.

My backpack thuds on the white and black checkered tile. I kick my shoes off, plopping on the white sofa in our front room. Papers are scattered on the coffee table, because when I left, I didn't have enough brain power to think about going through them.

This wasn't a good idea. I swallow saliva that feels like lava, drowning in heartache.

He's gone and I'm here.

I'll never accept that.

My phone buzzes, the distraction a frail tether between me and the real world.

Mickey: You here yet, sugar?

I hear his southern drawl through the text.

Me: Yep. Here.
Mickey: Be right over. Bobby's comin too.
Me: Oh, ok.

Bobby? I rub my temples. Seeing him is the last thing I want right now. I thought it would just be Mickey, but that's fine. It's fine. It'll be fine.

Focus on the good.

Bobby's been my friend since junior high. Seeing him will help me feel at home here. This is fine.

Then why are my hands shaking?

Distraction. Now. That is what I need. Keep moving. Shifting. Thinking about what matters in this moment, instead of all the moments of the past.

Fresh sheets. That matters.

I go upstairs, gripping the railing for dear life, knowing that being here is stirring up all sorts of things I wish I didn't feel.

I see Cody's smile.

"Babe, you forgot this!" I throw his hoodie down the stairs. "It's gonna be chilly!"

He stands on the third step and I rush down to kiss him. His lips on mine, his arms around me. "Love you." He taps my nose with his.

I try to feel him close, but I can't. Not that I deserve him close.

The bed is a heap of our unmade sheets. I freeze, tears stinging my eyes that I blink away. Keep busy, keep busy. Stripping them, I remember the first time we made love here.

And then I remember the last time I tried to.

The air thickens around me. Keep going, keep moving. Don't think about that. Think about anything besides that. Please, God, Jesus, and the Universe, help me forget. My eyes burn as I send a prayer into heaven, making sure I cover all my bases with whomever or whatever is out there.

Flicking the ceiling fan on and cracking open the windows, sea air finds its way in and out of my lungs. I try to stream Pandora on my computer, but I have no internet connection. Of course. Something I meant to think of, but didn't. Mental note...figure out internet.

Going downstairs with the sheets, I remember that there is no laundry soap. I throw them on the railing and grab my keys. Someone's knocking, their silhouettes coming through the window.

Bobby and Mickey stand in front of me, Mickey pushing open the unlocked door.

Fuck.

I knew I wasn't ready. Not ready to see them. Not ready to be home. Not ready to live another goddamn moment without Cody.

Startled, I step back. "Oh, hey."

They're wearing button ups and jeans and baseball caps. Mickey's is a grey and purple Suncastle Knights cap and Bobby's is a Yankees classic: navy with white embroidery. Their cologne is so strong that I smell it from here. They look nice. Too nice. My heart rate increases, knowing Mickey well enough to gather that he has something big planned.

My attention falls on Bobby. Time has been good to him. He is tall and chiseled with those broad shoulders, good for playing third base. His dark brown hair is short, whiskers a day or two past the last shave framing his defined jaw.

Mickey is a little shorter than Bobby, much tanner and with shaggy brown hair that curls haphazardly. Good looking guy, too. Mickey topples me backward in the biggest hug that only a best friend is capable of bestowing. "Darlin, it has been too fuckin' long." He holds me for a minute, then looks around the beach house like I'm a realtor and he is interested in buying. Running his finger over the dust on the entry table, it turns his print gray. "What's all this?"

"Like no one has been here in a year or somethin'." I roll my eyes. "You know what it is."

Mickey flicks the dust off his finger. "You stayin' here tonight?"

"Yep." I rock from my heels to my toes.

"Then I'm cleanin' it up for you. Your mama should've called. I woulda helped already."

"It's fine. I was just goin' to get some laundry soap." I swallow. Mickey has always been too good to me. Even when we were kids.

"Bobby'll take you while I start cleanin' up." Mickey shrugs his shoulders. "Right, Bobby?"

"It's really okay. I have plenty of time to clean on my own." I hold my purse close to my chest. Mental note: find a way to keep Mickey from ruling my life.

Mickey gives me a serious look, reserved for when he's not getting his way. "Doll baby, I'm cleanin' this place up, and that's the last I'm gonna hear about it." He points out the door. "Get goin', now. Bobby, take her out to the truck."

I roll my eyes. Mickey has a knight in shining armor complex, I swear. Always bossing his friends around under the rouse of taking care of us.

Bobby stands in front of the door, leaning casually, hands in his dark wash jean pockets. "Hey, Lex."

"Hey, Bobby."

We stand there for a long while as I notice the kind smile on his face.

"Shall we?" He opens my front door, waiting until I go first. Walking to his blue souped up truck–with giant tires and a really nice sound system, Bobby opens up the door for me.

"Thanks." I step in and close the door.

He shrugs and climbs into the driver's seat. As he pulls out of the driveway, I can't stop looking at him. His blue and white checkered button up hugs his muscled form in all the right places. In high school, everyone and their pet fish had a crush on him. All the girls and some of the guys. Willardson High's most eligible. Only he looks better now. I can't imagine how many are fighting over him today.

"How you been?" He breaks the silence, his deep and silky voice mixing with the sound of Brad Paisley's "Old Alabama" playing on the radio. Drumming his fingers on the steering wheel at the red light, he exudes a sort of comfort all the time. Cool and casual, no pressure when you're with him. No pressure at all.

Despite all his good looks, he hasn't gone out much with anyone. He slept around, sure. But nothing serious. Mickey told me a week ago that Bobby isn't in a relationship. Don't know that he has ever been in one. I'm kinda surprised he doesn't have a girlfriend. Or boyfriend, maybe? I bet if he is gay he won't come out because of baseball. Cody said some things that made me think that, but I've never asked Bobby.

"Good, good." I say the same line to him that I tell everyone else, because, well, it's easier to hide behind the walls of what I wish were there than to face the reality of what is. "How you been?"

"Great." His lips turn up in a smile, but I see something underneath, a layer of all that I feel. For as long as I can remember, Bobby was Cody's best friend. It's hard to see that he lost someone, too.

A while ago, he sent me several texts. They weren't drunk texts either. They were genuine, *how you doin' with everythin'*, kind of texts. I never replied. Should I tell him why? No. Not right now. One step at a time. I'm here. Back in Suncastle. I can't do it all in one day. Everything inside me burned the night Cody died and I feel like I'm carrying all the lumber I can, trying to build over this heartache, one plank at a time.

"Glad to hear it." I swallow the lump in my throat. I'll play along with this delusion—for now.

"Quickie's alright?" He offers the small grocery store across town.

"Yep, sounds great." My breath comes out in a hot, shaky moan. Bobby looks over, those blue eyes dancing beneath long eyelashes. His gaze shifts abruptly.

He's tense.

Cody's death changed me a hell of a freaking ton. It changed him, too, but what's with this *happy-go-lucky Bobby is tense* vibe? Not sure what to make of it, we continue without another word all the way across town.

He parks and I open my door before he has a chance to get it for me. I know he's a gentleman. Born and bred by a *Better Homes and Gardens*-loving mama, like I was. But I'm not about to wait for him to help me out of the car when he's doing me a favor. This is already awkward enough.

Bobby grabs a handbasket and waits for me as I pull a cart from the corral. "You went out to help your sister, right?"

"Yeah, up in Tennessee." I wheel forward, starting down the cleaning aisle.

"How was it?"

I add a jug of detergent and fabric softener. "It was good to see her.

My niece is so adorable." I pull out my phone and show him a picture of Paisley at her second birthday party.

Bobby tilts the phone closer and smiles. "Aw, ain't she a little cutie. Looks just like your sister."

As soon as he releases, I shove my phone in my pocket, blushing that I'm showing it to him. I'm not usually this random. Why am I feeling nervous? I load in other necessities and follow Bobby to the produce section. He puts a bag of spinach in his basket while I add an assortment of fruit into my cart. I stock up on all the staples: milk, bread, eggs, tortillas and a bunch of frozen stuff I can reheat on busy days. We get to the candy aisle and he puts a big bag of Peanut M&Ms in his basket. Peanut M&Ms were Cody's favorite.

"You don't buy what I thought you would," I say before I think better of it. Shit. I close my eyes for a long time, gripping the shopping cart until my knuckles burn. "Sorry, I shouldn't bring him up or poke at you for somethin' that mattered to him. I'm sorry."

Bobby's hand comes on mine and I gasp, the connection so intimate a warm shiver works through my spine. It's unexpected and somehow needed.

"You're okay." His smile is genuine when I venture a look. "It's okay."

We linger until I force down the rock in my throat. "Anyway. We probably should get back before Mickey gets high on Windex."

"He has before." Bobby chuckles, lightening the moment.

"Oh, I know." I rush to the register and we check out. All paid for, we silently return to his truck, not saying a word all the way home. I can't stop thinking about his hand on mine.

Why did my body respond to him?

It's just Bobby.

3

BOBBY

*B*right red waves tumble out of her ponytail, fair skin of her forehead pressing against the window. Her eyelashes are long and without a touch of makeup, she's breathtakingly gorgeous. Full lips and a small adorable nose. Everything I haven't been able to stop thinking about.

I hoped that I could let go of my fantasies. But now that she's beside me, I know that everything I've felt still burns deep inside.

She's hurting. Her eyes are closed and her posture exhausted. I know what that feels like. It must be too much to be back in Suncastle. This pain is familiar, because it hasn't let up–not for one second–for me either.

"How are you, really?" I keep my tone soft and gentle, knowing that she hasn't replied when I've asked before.

She looks at me like she's wondering what to say. "You know." She shrugs, looking out the window again. "It's hell."

"In every way." I'm doing all I can not to wrap her in my arms and hold her like I did the day of his funeral. My dream is to offer her escape to a beautiful, safe place where it doesn't weigh so heavy. I know what it feels like for me, so I can't imagine what it is for her. Cody was my best friend. Up until a year and a half ago, there wasn't any part of my past without him in it. But he was her future. He promised her that when he never fucking should have.

I swallow the lump in my throat and focus on driving, deflecting the things I refuse to think about. Feeling a need to take care of her, I go five under the limit when I normally speed. I've never been able to make sense of the way I feel. She was always untouchable.

Is untouchable.

Only I touched her and I swear that she felt something.

I've daydreamed of touching her a million times, shoving it to the back of my head where it belongs. It's too hard to cling onto some pipe dream.

But I felt too much.

I touched her, letting go faster than it takes to call a strike. There was so much connection in that moment that I'm already craving more.

No.

I shake my head. This isn't a good idea. I can't. I won't do that to myself.

I won't do that to Cody.

My eyes sting knowing what it'd do to him to see me and Lex together. He'd go fucking mad. I squint, halting my emotions right there. He would've thrown punches if he knew how I felt when he was alive.

In fact, he did.

A few times when I showed up for Lexie while Cody bailed on her. He always gave me shit for it. The worst time ended with my nose bloodied at senior prom. The last thing I need is his ghost coming after me. God, he would do it, too. Probably castrate me in my sleep for thinking about Lex as anything more than a friend.

Friend. That's what she is. That's what she'll stay. Just like Mick, and Zac, and Briar.

The last time I saw her before she left, she cried in my arms. It felt *right* to have her there. But it's all fallacious. I need to get a grip and a good lay to take my mind off this. I wish Sam was in town. Or Charli...I guess I could text Charli. We've gone out a few times over the summer. Nothing serious, but nice when it happens.

I feel sick to my stomach thinking about it. It was one thing to sleep around when it was just me. But now that Lexie is back? It's making me want to try something with her when I know I can't. Which means I do need to message Sam or Charli. Don't let this take root.

Only, it already has.

I pull up at the beach house, and before I can say anything she hops out.

Hurrying to the backseat, I take all the bags. I'm here, she doesn't need to be burdened. Looping each plastic handle through my arms, I leave her just the jug of detergent and an open hand. I gesture to the house. "So you can get the door?"

Lexie tilts her head to the side, a playful smile on her face. "You're not the only one who works out, ya know." She grips a bag from my hand and we play a game of tug of war until I win. Her hand brushes mine and she smiles. That personality of hers makes me dizzy.

Shit.

Her voice lingers in my mind. She's so smart. So sweet. Oh how I've missed being around her. I wanna know everything she has to say.

I stare as she saunters away. Her body is toned and tall. Long legs in grey leggings and a cute shirt with billowy sleeves that flow in the gentle sea breeze. The round tight ball of her ass flexes with each step while my breath hangs in my lungs. What I feel about Lexie isn't going to go away, is it?

Double shit.

It hasn't even been two years since Cody died. But God, it feels like a lifetime. I follow, breathing in the deep scent of Lysol once I'm over the threshold. Eminem blares through the house and I almost trip on the full garbage can in the middle of the hall.

"Wow, this place looks amazin'!" Lexie sets the detergent on the counter, putting her hands on her hips.

Mick walks from the bathroom, throwing away a paper towel covered in gunk. He peaks inside one of the bags I set on the counter. "Quickies? On the other side of town? No wonder it took so long."

I sneer. The real reason I took her to Quickie's–the worst grocery store in the area–is because I wanted to avoid Oak Street. I drive twenty minutes out of the way to avoid it. That road gets me. Memories of the accident attack me every time I drive on it. The road is nothing more than a grief trap for me. It would demolish her.

"One day we will have to move on," the preacher said at Cody's funeral. But I don't know that we will. If that truck driver could've seen him. If he could've been paying more attention. If I'd talked to him for two more seconds so the universe didn't align for his demise.

If.

If.

If.

The worst word leaving everything open. I can't handle the *ifs*.

If I would've driven him home.

Shit, that *if* hurts me the worst. He shouldn't have been alone and I knew it. If I would've had him stay over, or called Lexie to come get him, or put him in my truck. If there hadn't been a rain storm. If he hadn't been such a mess when he left my place. If I would've listened to my gut to not let him go. If he wouldn't have told me every fucking thing that I wasn't ready to hear.

My heart aches, wishing I never had to bear his secret. Wishing he never had one so hard to keep.

"Lexie, go get ready. We're goin' out to Garrison's tonight." Mick brings me back to earth and away from the void of ifs.

"No." She puts her fingers to her mouth, dancing them over her lips like she's playing out a beat, her little quirk that drives me wild.

I plant my feet to keep from getting closer to her.

"It's your first night back in South Carolina," Mick pouts. "We're goin' and that's final, young lady." He shakes his finger at her like he's her mom. God, he's ridiculous.

"I have a lot of laundry to do. My sheets are all dusty from sittin' here so long." She heads to the stairs.

"We're goin'!" Mick calls.

"If she doesn't wanna go, she doesn't wanna go." I plop my spinach on a shelf in her fridge next to the Peanut M&Ms. Mick won't like what I'm saying, but I'm standing up for her and he can shove it.

"They taste better cold." Cody tosses back a mouthful of M&Ms and chomps in a way that implies everything besides good manners.

Lex's laugh lights up. "Stop it, baby. You'll choke." She puts her hand on his chest and grabs the bag away. "Slow down, slugger."

"The hell are you talkin' about? We're goin' to get her good and wasted. It's karaoke night and you saw how stressed she is. Needs to take her mind off everythin'." Mick's voice is raised. His temper is the shortest fuse I've ever seen.

"I mean, she drove all day to get here. Tennessee's what, eight hours away? She might want pizza and a movie or somethin'."

"Bobby's right. I do, actually." Lex leans on the doorway. Her hair is pulled out of its ponytail, gorgeous bright red waves falling below her chest. She's got a laundry basket at her hips, tats peaking out from under her shirt sleeve.

"Order us some pineapple deep dish from The Splat. Oh, or that chicken bacon ranch one, whatever it's called. Hannibal? Cannibal? I don't remember." She does that adorable head shake, and goodness, I can't breathe.

Friends, just friends.

"But we'll have to go to your place. I still don't have internet set up." She frowns.

"You got it." I pull out my phone.

"No, no, no. We're goin' to Garrison's." Mick stands between me and Lex, close enough that my chin knicks the fabric covered button at the top of his baseball cap. "I just cleaned up the whole beach house. You haven't been here in a year and a half. I'm takin' you out proper like."

"We'll do whatever the fuck she wants." My tone is rude, but I'm fighting for this one. Mick will deal with it. He has to. I clear my throat, because apparently I can't talk anymore, and press my lips in a line. "Garrison's will be open next weekend, when Lex has had a chance to settle in."

"You're a sweetheart, Bobby." Lex walks down the hall toward the laundry room, not giving a fuck about Mick's opinion. His surprised face makes me chuckle. He slams his shoulder into mine, annoyed. I push him back.

"I have to work next weekend." He's so pissed at me.

"Then we'll go the weekend after that." I shrug.

"Right after classes start?"

"We are taking care of *her.*" I raise my eyebrows, my voice soft so that Lex doesn't blush. She's not a project or anything. I just want to support her, especially on her first day back. "This is about what *she* needs."

"Since when did you become an expert on Lexie?" Jealousy laces his tone. He gets all weird about Lex. Like because he's known her the longest he has some claim on her. *You don't own her, and you never will.*

Cody constantly told me about how her parents would put her in a box and she would just break free like the phoenix she is. No one controls her. I won't let Mick pretend he can.

"I'm not an expert on Lexie, but I fuckin' know what she's goin' through. A night out is not gonna help." My eyes catch a glimpse of her hair as she leans into the hallway to pick up a dropped pillowcase. Every part of my body responds. I lick my teeth, annoyed with myself. She's here for an hour and already it's like when we were fifteen and I was playing spin the bottle, wishing it would land on her just so I could taste those lips. My mind wanders to my hand on hers. The heat of her skin beneath mine. The way she laughs. The thoughtful things she says.

My cock throbs against my jeans. Fuck. This has to stop. It has to. I focus on anything that isn't her. Pulling at my brain, I hope for anything else to think about. My grocery list–nope, was just at the store with Lex. My calendar–yes. There we go. Tiny Knights Training Camp. God, I love those kids, even if it is just a community building thing to make the university look good. "You goin' to be at Tiny Knights Training Camp tomorrow?"

Mick rolls his eyes. "In my abundant spare time."

"Whatever." My eyes go to the laundry soap sitting on her counter. I grab it and find her in the laundry room. "You're gonna need this."

"Thank you."

I can't tell if she's talking about the laundry soap or that I told off Mick, but I don't care. I'm so close her shampoo scent fills my senses as I fumble with the measuring cup, pouring detergent into her machine.

"I'm glad you're back." I suck in a harsh breath, at war with myself. She doesn't need this. Doesn't need me flirting with her, talking with her, helping her.

What does she need?

I retreat back into the hallway before she has a chance to respond. Stepping out the front door, in the ruse of calling the pizza place, I sit on the concrete step hoping to gather some semblance of control.

Raking hands through my hair, my Yankee's cap falls behind my head. Goddammit. I can't handle all this. It's not supposed to be me here, it's supposed to be him. Just like old times. But I know the truth. The real, honest truth. No, no, no. We are not gonna go there. I'm not gonna think about that.

My eyes burn as I focus on my breath. Clearing my head, I imagine a baseball. The way it feels in my hand. The weight. The seams against my fingers. The smell of the field. I let out a long breath. Find my center. Find my control.

Get a fucking grip.

I pull out my phone to order the pizza and those cheese sticks she likes. My feet tap against the sidewalk, so much nervous energy running through me without any place to go.

"My birthday girl gets whatever she wants!" Cody's standing on a chair at The Splat, announcing to the whole restaurant that it's her birthday.

"Cody, get down." Lexie pulls at his hand.

"Not yet, baby doll." He looks around. "Get my girl some more cheese sticks!" He waves down a waitress, then leads everyone in singing "Happy Birthday" until Lexie's face is the color of her hair.

My eyes are hotter than the sidewalk. Because every moment with him was like that. Spectacular. Larger than life. Until the brightest star among us was snuffed out too soon.

Fuck, Cody. Why'd you go and die like that?

A car stops in front of the beach house. Claudia gets out and waves goodbye to whoever's driving. Fuck. My teeth clench, wishing to God that it wasn't her materializing in front of me. As if this evening wasn't complicated enough.

I care about Claudia, I do. We've talked enough that I know she's been used a ton. Life has not dealt her a kind hand. She's got PTSD because her dad was shit. Now, she uses sex as a way to cope. It's not healthy.

Like I have room to talk.

I don't.

She's wearing a cute outfit, short jean skirt and a lace tank top. Long brown waves reach her mid back. Her perfume surrounds me the closer she gets, burning my nostrils like the Lysol did a moment ago.

Her eyes meet mine. "Didn't know you were here."

Fuck. Fuckity, fuckity, fuck. And I have fucked her, *twice* in the same night. Shouldn't have. Not even the first time. She's had eyes on Mick for a while and there's probably more history there than I'm aware of. That night when I brought her back to my truck is one I wish I could rewrite. We were both drunk. She was going through hell. Asked me to take it all away. So I did. I hate to think that I added to the list of people who used her. But I'm not feeling anything more between us. Especially since Mick wants to be with her.

"What are *you* doin' here?" I don't fake a smile. I've told her we're done and yet she still texts several times a week asking to do stuff. Or she slyly shows up places where she knows I'll be.

"Just stopping by, Bobby." She puts so much sweetness into my name it's like she's talking about syrup. *Go back to iHop babycakes. I ain't serving you a damn thing.*

"Why?"

"Mickey told me to come over."

I pull my hair, looking over my shoulder to make sure he's not leering behind me. "He's inside."

"Come with me." She makes it sound sexy. *Why? Why Claudia?*

Why? You want another one night stand with me? No. Just go figure things out with Mick.

"I'm good." I'm not good. I'm never good when she's around. I feel like I'm navigating a mine-field, waiting for the one miss-step that ends up with me flat on my back and a huge mess to clean up. Jeez. I don't need this. Not on top of everything else.

"Okay then." She clicks her tongue, strutting by me in her boots. My empty stomach roils. I wait for a bit on the porch. When I do go inside, I want to make sure she knows it has nothing to do with her.

I sigh, walking into the beach house.

Mick sits on the countertop with Claudia and they're giggling about some shit.

The laundry machines thrash against the wall. Can't see Lexie. My feet go up the stairs, to their bedroom. It will never be hers. This was theirs.

The windows are open, and the room is clean. My heart pounds in my chest seeing Cody's bedside table. His cap. His wallet and keys. His Bible and spiral-bound notebook he always used as a journal.

Lexie sits on the mattress cover, hunched over, shoulders shaking. Her hand is a fist against her nose and mouth, cheeks red and wet. Sniffles register in my ear.

Oh, God, she's crying.

I ease backward, but the wood creaks beneath my Chuck Taylor's.

"Oh," she gasps, wiping tears away like they are poisonous. "Sorry, Bobby. I didn't see you." The next wave hits. She cries into her hands.

Part of me wants to get outta here. Leave her alone to mourn. Afraid I'll do something stupid.

Swallowing hard, I observe her, my pain inside intensifying as she cries. How can I leave her now? How, when I know how bad this hurts? How, when I've felt so alone? Grief is worse when there's no one to feel it with. Energy pulls me to her like a magnet. I sit next to her on the bed and before I know it, I'm scooping her into a hug. "It's so hard," I whisper, my own grief coming up.

One hand brings her head against my chest while the other strokes down the length of her hair. Her body shakes against mine. I hold her tighter, gripping for dear life.

For Cody's life.

"I know." My throat is scalding, the air so heavy I don't think I can breathe. I hurt for her. I hurt *with* her.

I wish I could take it all away.

She pulls back, an embarrassed, forced smile on her face. I put space between us, swallowing the baseball in my throat. Her hands wipe away more tears. I have to look elsewhere because I can't keep my eyes on her.

Can't get too close.

Won't get too close.

"Goddamnit." She brushes my shoulder where tears fell onto my shirt. "I shouldn't have come back."

"Don't say that." My heart lurches, afraid she may turn tail and run. I can't watch her leave again.

"It's too much." She closes her eyes for a very long time, like she did over at Quickies. "I don't think I can stay."

Pain erupts in my chest, catching me off guard. I've always been empathetic, but this is more. It physically hurts. A throbbing that worries me. Whoever coined the term *heartache* wasn't kidding.

"What do you need?" I take her hand in mine. Soft warm skin meets my cold, calloused fingers.

She looks out the window where a handful of people walk the beach. Wind blows past us from the open window. Her hair moves out of her face. She's beautiful when she cries—when I see her soul.

"I think I need to get out of this house."

"Yeah." My answer is quick, because I'd do absolutely anything she asked.

"Without Mickey and Claudia."

"K." I stand, taking her hand, helping her off the bed. "You wanna get some of your stuff together? Stay at my place tonight?" I see so much pain inside her.

"I haven't taken my luggage out of my car. I've got clothes in there."

I shut the windows and latch them, helping her secure the house. We go downstairs where Claudia pulls her hands out of Mick's pants.

It seems like Mick is two different guys. He's the helpful guy that cleans the house from top to bottom in an hour. Then there's this guy who's thinking with his dick in the middle of Lexie's place.

"Y'all go to Garrison's. Have fun." I toss Mick my keys as he awkwardly buckles his belt up. "At least one of you make sure you drive my baby home sober. If there is so much as a scratch on that truck, so help you, Jesus."

"You got it, Bobby." Claudia's face is red.

Lex and I get into her car. I'll take care of her. It's the most important thing I can do.

For Cody.

4

LEXIE

*B*obby turns his key in the lock at the same apartment he had freshman year. He walks in first, setting the pizza on the counter. "Make yourself at home." He smiles.

I take off my shoes and drop them on the thin carpet by the front door. His place is nice–a small apartment close to the baseball field. Leather couches back up against the walls in an L shape around a coffee table, facing a decent sized flat screen mounted on the wall. "Mickey still livin' with you?"

"If you can call it that. He's rarely here. Works a lot." Bobby grabs a few things and puts them somewhere else–tidying up, as if I care.

I scan the room for some sort of stereo and find it on a cabinet against the far wall, tucked away where you can't see if from the window. "Mind if I turn on some music?"

"Go ahead." He's still moving stuff.

Music fills the room while I meet him in the kitchen. He's got this adorable frazzled look while he's shuffling things around.

"It's fine. Don't bother cleanin'." My words stop him and he looks at me like he's nervous, a look I've rarely seen on him.

"Yeah, um, here." He pulls out a plate from the dishwasher, looking at it as if he's worried it's not clean. Why didn't he grab two?

The smell of pizza lures me into the boxes, stomach growling, mouth watering as I remember the sweet sauce and fluffy crust. I've missed The Splat. He bought me cheese sticks. Can't wait for us to dive in. Only, he plops down at the table with some sort of Tupperware filled with chicken and vegetables.

"You're eatin' that when we have this?" I eye the pizza.

"Yeah." He shrugs, a piece of broccoli going to his mouth.

I glance at the cluttered kitchen counters, protein powder, a huge bag of jasmine rice, jars of trailmix-looking stuff. "So you bought two large pizzas and cheese sticks for me?"

"It's not cheat day." He shrugs again, so matter-of-fact that I stifle a chuckle. "But you could leave enough leftovers for when it is." That smile of his brightens up his whole face. That hasn't changed. He's always been funny.

Salty goodness saturates my throat, and I go to the fridge. "You got Coke?" There's three cartons of almond milk, a shit-ton of eggs and dozens of those Tupperware containers. Food Prep, maybe?

He's dedicated, I'll give him that. I don't eat crap everyday. But I also don't make a huge deal about my diet, so the fact that his place is devoid of junk food surprises me. There isn't a can of Pringles or any hint of chocolate milk. Cody made sure we always had those things; I thought Bobby liked them, too. Wait, he just bought those M&Ms. Don't know where he stashed them, though.

"Shit, um, I don't have much. I'll make you a smoothie." Before I can say no, he's fiddling with his blender, going to the freezer for some frozen fruit.

"Oh, it's alright." I pour a glass of water.

"No trouble, you like creamy stuff, don'tcha?" He sets a bag of frozen peaches on the counter, going to the fridge for the almond milk.

"You sure?"

"Oh, yeah. I'll get some Coke for next time." He winks, putting a bunch of stuff in the blender like he does this everyday–as he probably does.

My heart warms because I know how much he loves peaches and

was willing to share with me. Bobby rinses the blender and sets the smoothie in front of me, returning to his place at the table.

"These from your parents' trees?" I expect it to taste like the health food store, and it does. Not very sweet and grainy because he put a scoop of protein powder in it–likely out of habit–but the peach flavor is really good.

"Yeah, I went home last week and brought some back. Mom's tryin' to clear out the freezer for the new crop."

"I feel special." I smile, licking some smoothie off my lips.

"You are." His eyes hold mine until he looks like he regrets it.

He just called me special and it's like the grocery all over again, a warm shiver working through me.

"You go home often?" I dip my cheese stick in the ranch.

"No, not really. Every few months. You?" His Tupperware is half empty. Damn, he eats quick.

"Not except for Christmas." I eat my weight in pizza, the nostalgia welcome on my tongue. "The Splat, man. We used to go there every weekend."

"I remember." His smile does something to me, and I flutter through sensations like I'm a mix of cold and warm at the same time. There's something here, between us…isn't there? No, there can't be. I clench my nails into my palms under the table, not sure why I'm reading into anything.

It's just Bobby.

"Cody'd dump the sugar packets in a cup of water with lemons like he wanted homemade lemonade." Bobby charades the action as if he's doing it here and now.

I chuckle. "And I'd tell him to just drink my actual lemonade, shovin' it in his face."

"No use tryin' to get him to do a damn thing. Stubborn ass." Bobby leans back in his chair, stretching his neck side to side.

"About everythin'." I roll my eyes, laughing to myself about how many stupid things he'd do, no matter how much you tried to tell him not to.

"God, I miss him." Bobby's voice is so deep it's like I'm covered in a dense fog. Weight that never seems to go away pushes me down. I knew it'd be hard to return to Suncastle–and it is–but I can make it. I need to make it through this last year. I'm too close to getting my athletic training degree to just quit now.

While I put the pizza in his fridge, Bobby rinses out his container and fetches the bag of spinach, popping the leaves in his mouth like they're potato chips.

"Your pick." Bobby clicks off the stereo and hands me the TV remote while we sit on the couch with Netflix pulled up. His user has a bunch of crime investigation shows and a dozen dramas in the watch again section.

"I would've thought you were more the comedy type."

His face drops and that ever-present weight intensifies. "Oh, um, haven't felt like it." He lets out a long breath like he's trying to cover his pained expression. Cody's death has changed him so much. I tap my nails against my leggings, trying to think of how to shake us both out of this funk.

"Isn't there a game on?" I click through and pull up the Yankees game but it's commercials so I sink into the couch looking for shapes in the popcorn ceiling. "Thanks. Ya know, you didn't have to let me come over."

"Oh, it's nothin'." He smiles in such a tender way that I wonder what is behind those eyes and going through his mind. "I'm glad you're here."

"No, I mean, it was sweet of you. Standin' up to Mickey and takin' my side and all. Felt like I was suffocatin' up in our bedroom. I don't think I would've been much fun at Garrison's tonight. Not that I wanted to be at home, either."

"You don't wanna live at the beach house, do you?"

I suppose my actions are making that pretty obvious. "I wish my parents would sell it and I could move somewhere else. Or they didn't insist on payin' my way through college as long as I do it their way." The words come out of my mouth and I feel icky for not being grateful. "I sound like some spoiled rich girl right now." I pull at my hair, looping the ends around my finger and twirling.

"Some spoiled rich girl?" His blue eyes are kind, brows wrinkling down like we both know that isn't me.

"Here I am, livin' off 'Daddy's money' and complainin' about it when I've got a whole beautiful home to live in." I huff out my frustration, years of wishing for something different dripping from my words. "I didn't want to, ya know."

"Didn't want to..." Bobby waits for me to finish and I find it adorably validating that he is so present in this conversation.

"I never wanted to just live off them. I don't like it one little bit. Tried to get a job in high school several times. Mom wouldn't have it. I worked when I lived at Charlene's house, but it isn't enough to live on all year. Now I'm back and dependin' on them writin' my tuition check. Bein' a senior in the athletic trainin' program could allow for part time work until season but nothin' significant."

"Yeah, bein' involved with the teams takes a lot of time. I'm takin' twenty credit hours this semester."

"Twenty?" I gasp, my fingers coming over my lips. I couldn't possibly keep good grades with that many classes.

"That way I can drop to twelve in the spring and still graduate before the draft." He crosses his fingers on both hands with a quirky smile, flaring the dimple on the left side of his mouth with a wink.

"You take this many classes every fall?" I can't imagine being that busy.

"The engineering program usually takes an extra year. I'm just lucky it worked out with baseball so I can still be playin'. Would've sucked if I had to stick around without playin' ball." He shrugs, settling back into a comfortable position on the couch. "But yes, most fall semesters I take on a heavy course load. Just tryin' to get all my requirements in."

"Oh yeah. I remember you bein' Red-shirted sophomore year. You blew your elbow out, wasn't it?" I heard about it after one of their practices.

"Yeah, it was stupid. Ended up in surgery too close to season." He massages his elbow. "It's all good now, though. Mindy is one hell of an athletic trainer."

"Oh, she's amazing." I shake my head, still thinking about his schedule. I don't know how I would juggle all that *and* be on the baseball team. More than that, Bobby is one of the best players. I'm amazed at how hard he must work to keep up. I think he has a job, too. "Jesus, I can't believe you're takin' twenty credit hours. Maybe I should be doin' the same thing. I'm only takin' fifteen."

"You did some summer classes though." Damn, he has a good memory.

"Yeah. I'll do fifteen hours this semester and then fifteen more. Right on track to take my certification exam after graduation." I hold my breath, knowing this isn't really where my heart is. I loved athletic training when it meant seeing Cody a lot but now that he's not here, I don't know how to feel.

"Do you still want to study athletic trainin'?" It's like he can read my vibes better than anyone else. He's so focused on me I can't breathe. At home, I didn't get attention, and if I would've said this, they would've told me how selfish and unreasonable I was. If they did notice me, I was an imposition–better when I stayed out of sight and out of mind. But Bobby is hanging on my every word, perceptive enough he's catching what I'm not saying.

"Oh, sure. Don't get me wrong, there's a lot I do like about it. Sports medicine has always been fascinating to me. And it's *reputable* enough for my parents, who think art is anythin' but a career. I guess it's just not my passion, ya know?" I sag deeper into the couch, hating that all I've ever wanted is their blessing while I attend art school. I've tried so hard to show them that painting is more than just a hobby to me.

"Okay, so athletic trainin' works. But what about this? If nothing else mattered, what would you be doin'? Like if you could do *anythin'* what would it be?"

"Anythin'?" I fiddle with my hands.

"Whatever the hell you want." He grins, and I see those nice, straight teeth from when we had braces at the same time. We'd often commiserate about the appointments to get them tightened. But man, it worked for him. The Universe had better go and make him famous because he's got the smile for it. "Anythin'."

My heart warms because I know exactly what I would do, no question.

"Come on now, sweets. I see it on your face. You've got that big ass dream playin' out like your favorite memory. It's about bein' an artist, ain't it?"

Aww, he remembers. A warm shiver travels up my spine and heat rises in my cheeks. Holy hell, what is getting into me? "Yeah, I'd go to art school."

"So do it."

My eyes go wide at the absurd way he makes this sound completely possible.

His hand finds mine and my body hiccups from the connection. "I wouldn't wanna stay at that beach house either. Too much hauntin' your every breath when you don't need reminders. I get it, I really do," he tsks. "You said your parents are against it? Can you finish your degree and then get your own place? Go to art school after you've saved up for a bit?" He looks at his hand like he just realized he's holding mine and pulls it back, taking off his cap and running fingers through his hair, leaning back so we are both cozy but not touching. His body language tells me he wants to be close, and I shake away the thought. That isn't what this is. Is it? My heart pounds in my chest because Holy God Above, he can't be hitting on me, can he? We've been friends forever, and all that time I've been ninety-percent sure he only played for the other team.

Only, what if he is interested in me?

"Come on Lex, I've seen your art. It would be a disservice to the world if you stopped now."

"I've just got to figure out how to endure life until I can really be on my own."

"You need a place that can be yours." He stretches his shoulders, repositioning to face me. The fabric of his shirt draws tight across his muscled chest, and I feast on just how good he looks. "And I don't mind if you stay here in the meantime. Seriously." We look at each other for several heartbeats, and I'm looking for any indication that my suspicions are real or fabricated. We've all been close, our group of friends doing everything together through junior high and high school. This may just be him showing up for me as a friend. But there's something in his eyes, and I have to know what it is.

Our gazes lock while I'm still searching for that something more. "Does it feel like you're dead inside?" He shakes his head like he can't believe he said that. "Nevermind—"

"It does," I whisper, taking in those enchanting eyes of his. Did I notice how blue they were in high school? Have we ever looked at each other this long?

"I hate it." He looks sad, and I know I've never seen this side of him—only the life of the party, star of the baseball team, the popular kid, the funny guy. There's nothing funny right now and hurt spreads through my chest, catching his contagious pain.

I'm bringing up bad memories, proving that I shouldn't be here. That I should go. "You know what, thanks, Bobby, for dinner. For everythin'. I'll just—" I'm off the couch and heading for the door like the only thing I know how to do is run far and fast from anything we may be to each other.

"Hey, wait." He looks shocked, following me. "We don't have to talk about all this if you don't wanna. We don't have to watch anythin'. I have cards too. Diablo, if you like playin' video games. Or um, just call it an early night. Whatever you want."

"No, no, it's not that." I look away from his eyes, feeling them linger on me.

"What is it then?" He's so close and something about it feels *right*, more than the warm shivers—something with depth and longing and *love*?

My heart pounds harder in my chest. "I'm makin' all this worse and I don't want to do that to you," I squeeze my eyes tight, "and to me, and...fuck." I rub my fists on my eyes. "It's just so much to be back here and I am makin' every goddamn bit of it worse." I slap the door.

"How?"

Heat rises to my face and I wonder if I can ever regulate my temperature again. "I'm clearly makin' you miss him. Makin' it all feel worse." I hold my breath, hold my purse, hold the doorknob.

"I miss him all the time. You're not makin' anythin' worse." He waits until he has my eyes while I timidly meet his. "You can't make Hell worse, Lex. It's already Hell and I know we've both been trapped there for four hundred and seventy-two days."

Four hundred and seventy-two? I count backward, closing my eyes as the realization hits: the number of days since Cody's death.

"You keep track?"

"Yeah." He sighs, and it's so heavy that I tense every muscle in my body. "And no, I don't want to. Every day without him just feels wrong."

My insides are ablaze, that familiar tinge of emotion working from my throat to the back of my mouth. So much for building planks around my heart, I've just burned them all away with my anguish. Eyes stinging, I blink hard, hoping to stay the waterworks–I've already cried with Bobby more than enough.

"We don't have to do anythin'." He leans against the wall, silently pleading with me not to walk out this door, his somber smile pulling at his cheeks but not reaching his eyes. "You look tired. Let's get you some rest."

"I haven't slept in a long time." My comment does something to him that I can't quite read while I press against the closed door, mirroring his posture. Looking at his bloodshot eyes shoots pain through my stomach because he doesn't sleep either. I don't know what to make of him... or any of this. Too much change at once isn't good for anyone, and my gosh he's changed a hell of a freaking ton. This is not the Bobby I knew in high school–not even a little bit.

"What would help you?" His brows raise and I know he's sincere and that he wants to be there for me. This realization flutters my heart, and my breath catches, knowing he genuinely cares about me.

"I'll sleep on your couch. I just don't wanna go back to the beach house."

"Don't be ridiculous." He walks down the hall, stopping halfway, looking back at me, frozen in the doorway. "Come on, now." His accent is thick and *sexy* making me swallow hard. What the fuck is happening right now?

His room is crowded with a queen-sized bed up against the wall, black sheets and a blanket in a heap on the unmade bed. It smells nice in here, like Hollister cologne. Twenty or more Yankees caps hang on his wall and this breaks me because Cody was gonna play for the Yankees. Before all this, Bobby was a White Sox fan. And seeing that he changed his allegiance makes me want to crawl into a secluded cave and cry in the cold, pouring rain from now until eternity.

Cody meant the world to both of us, and for the first time, I'm not alone in my grief.

Bobby lifts the blanket, throwing it over the bed, smoothing the edges like a maid at a hotel. "I'll get your bag outta the car."

"Thanks." I hand him my keys out of my pocket and sit on his bed when a yawn stretches over my face until my cheeks burn.

"Does it feel like you're dead inside?" His question plays in my head while I think about all the times I've felt that way.

The thud of my duffle bag brings me back to the moment.

"Bathroom is that door." He tilts his head into the hallway. "And here's a towel if you wanna shower?"

"A shower sounds heavenly." I stand near him, observing his presence, acknowledging that he's really grown up…have I?

"Whatever you need. I mean it."

"Well, I think I'm gonna need some more pizza. You didn't order near enough," I tease, thinking about telling him I need a Coke. Knowing he would drop everything to go get me one, I stay silent.

"What was I thinkin'? Shoudda bought six more orders of cheese sticks." A half smile shines on his face. "I'm glad you're back." He places his arms around me in a hug. My body melts into his muscular frame, cautious at first and then relaxed–like I was always meant to be there. His arms hold me with a gentle strength that makes breath hang in my lungs. He smells like laundry soap and subtle hints of that cologne that fills his room. His grasp is so consoling and for the first time in a long time, I am safe and at peace. When he releases, my body remembers the feel of him against it, wanting more.

I pull him back in close to me and hold, pretending for a second that nothing is wrong, escaping inside his embrace the way I need. He gasps as I bury my head into his chest, and then he softens, those arms enveloping me while the heavy thud of his heart pounds against my cheek.

"You're great, Bobby, do you know that?" I pull back. "Hope I'm not gettin' in your way by bein' here."

He shakes his head. "You're not an imposition or anythin' so don't even think that, alright?"

And he's gone, leaving me to do whatever I need.

———

THE WATER RUNS OVER ME, A FOG FILLING THE TINY BATHROOM. HEAD and Shoulders shampoo, a bar of Lever 2000, and lots of soap scum buildup like he and Mickey haven't cleaned the shower for a long time. Something about his apartment is welcoming. The bit of reality that exists in this not quite perfect bathroom calms me. I feel relaxed, almost, the memory of his hug lingering on my skin.

I'm here with Bobby and his presence soothes me in a way I didn't expect. Shaking my head, I wonder why on earth I'm associating the word *soothing* with *Bobby*. He's always been my friend, but he and Cody were like blood. That's why he gets it even better than my therapist did.

I feel queasy, wondering if I'm subconsciously trying to replace Cody with Bobby. They are a lot alike, in some ways. But that wouldn't be right. I can't betray Cody like that and I shouldn't mislead Bobby into thinking *he* is what I'm after.

I'm even more confused at these thoughts running through my head. Am I into Bobby? Didn't think I was.

His bed is the ideal combination of firm and soft, just like his body was mere minutes ago. The moment I hit the pillow, I'm in a deep sleep–so deep I don't realize I've slept in until I look at my phone and it's almost noon. Good heavens, I haven't slept through the night in so long I can't even remember the last time it happened.

Throwing on some jeans, I go to the kitchen and notice immediately that Bobby has cleaned up the clutter and junk from the night before. Something else is missing. Him. He's not here. I look around for a note, but there isn't one. And Mickey isn't home either.

Okay, Bobby....

I gather my stuff, make up his bed and head to my car to get out of here. It's time to face campus. The night of real sleep will help. Maybe one day I won't be so dead inside.

5

BOBBY

I didn't want to leave her. She looked peaceful for the first time since she returned to Suncastle. When Briar and I got back from our morning run, I tapped her shoulder. She didn't even stir. Made me happy to see her passed out in my bed.

I watched for a second, scolding myself with each heartbeat until I pulled away. I wanted to climb in beside her, feel her body against mine. Just like when she held me so close last night. It was like everything I've hungered for was filled. I don't know how she makes me feel so much. But she always has. Every casual hug or bumped shoulder our whole life. Being with her does something to me. I don't want this feeling to end. Ever.

I shake my head. This is not going to work.

Walking to my car, I wonder if Lex is still at my place. I wanna see her again. Hell, I wanna spend all my time with her.

Get a grip, yeesh.

I need some distance from her, before I do something. If I go too far, I'll regret it and hell, so will Cody's ghost. She needed someone last night. Who she needs is my best friend and some fucking closure from the death that left us both wide open.

My stomach drops like a fly ball that shoulda been caught.

God, Cody, I wish you were still here. Every day I wish you were still here.

My throat tightens as if my guts are trying to climb out. I can hardly breathe. It's not like the usual retching sensation that would come next. It's replaced something else.

A sort of visceral hope. A connection. A tear in the fabric of reality. An otherworldly tremor.

Like whatever is beyond hiccups long enough that Cody and I are together.

This millisecond burns me with the knowledge that there's an afterlife, even if it's just the energy of a person that lives on. Call me crazy, I know. But there has to be *somethin'*. Or else I wouldn't feel this at all. I wasn't trying to.

Good to feel you close.

Losing him usually makes me hollow inside, but sometimes it's this connection. I know he's close right now. Like if I had immortal eyes, I could see him. *What do you think about all this with me and Lex, hm? I know, I know, that's not what you want.*

Because I *am* in love with her.

How do I know this? Because I haven't felt a real connection with anyone else. Believe me, I've tried.

I get around. Open-minded as long as word doesn't get out in a way that would hurt baseball. Tons of practice, experiments, kinky stuff, good times. I've had casual girlfriends. Drunk fucks–like Claudia. One-night stands with hot guys that don't know my real name.

Sam is the only one who knows my identity. We respect that we're both closeted. They have as much on the line if I tell their secret as if they tell mine. Not that either of us would. It's nice to have a safe place with them. But at the end of the day, it's just a hookup.

The last several years, I've done a little bit of everything. They're people to have fun with. Get laid. But even though I feel things deeply, I can't feel much for any of them. Not like what I've felt for Lexie since the first time we hung out right after one of our games back in junior high. They don't do it for me.

I try.

Really, I do.

Lexie, though...well, she's different. I know, I know. Sounds ridiculously cliché. Hey, you went out with her. I don't have to tell you how amazin' she is, Cody.

I sigh. Everything is so different with her. Despite my constant effort to ignore it. Whether she knows or not, my being lives within her. Companion souls. A link I've felt since we were kids. My mind can't make any sense of it.

Trust me Cody, I didn't ask for it to be like this.

I'm dying to know if she has felt any of it. May just be me and my out-of-control feelings. No. It's something. I know it's something.

I wish I knew you'd be okay with this.

He doesn't reply. I just get feelings. Or memories of what he used to say popping into my head. The tremor is gone, and I'm hollow again. Grief is like riding rapids. Unsure territory in constant shift and flow.

How do I snap out of it?

I drive to the gym and spend two hours pumping iron to my AC/DC playlist with Briar. The news plays on the TV. A car crash. Fuck.

I shouldn't look. I know what it'll do to me. But I'm glued to the screen like I couldn't move if my life depended on it.

"That's too bad." Briar's voice is heavy, his hand on my shoulder. "Let's go." He gets it. His brother passed in a motorcycle crash several years back.

Vomit comes up my throat as the memories overtake me. Running to the hospital. Seeing him dead on the gurney. I knew he was gone. We all knew he was gone.

Can you hear me, Cody? Because I'm mad. I'm fuckin' mad at you for leavin' us behind.

Because every time I remember, it's not just Cody's body covered by a steril white sheet, too wrecked for us to see him. It's not just a cold, antiseptic smelling emergency room. It's not just the somber face of a nurse, eyes trying to convey how sorry she is that there was nothing to be done.

It's Lexie's by his side, in so much pain. Slamming the hospital bed and then crumbling into my arms with her tears. Like it was yesterday, her shouts of *no* again and again ring in my ears. She was left so broken. Destroyed.

Just like I am.

6

LEXIE

*G*etting books for classes shouldn't be this hard when I'm a senior and I've done this a dozen times.

Regina comes up beside me. "Oh, hey!" She has a stack of books in her hands. "When did you get back?"

"Yesterday." I shrug. "I thought you graduated last fall."

"Oh, I'm doing the grad program now."

"Really? That's great!"

"MATC." She smiles and sourness fills my gut because I could be there now, done with my undergrad, getting my masters in Sports Nutrition...or heading to art school.

"What team you workin'?" She grips her books to her chest.

"Baseball."

"No shit." She beams. "You've been waitin' for that."

"I know." This does little to make me feel better about all the delays. But hey, college isn't a race, I'll get through when I do. "The last team I need to work." I'm referring to the requirements for my athletic training degree, but it holds double meaning. Baseball is the last place I want to be, now that all I'll think about is Cody. And I'll have to work with Mindy. I'm not looking forward to that after the way she acted when I told her I wasn't coming back after Cody passed.

"That's amazin'. Mindy is gonna love havin' you. You gone to see her yet?"

"Heading there next." I pretend to be happy. Really, I love Mindy to death–but she didn't take it well when I left.

I can't put this off forever, and maybe she doesn't hate me as much as I think. Maybe,maybe, maybe. I hope….

On the short trip from the campus bookstore, I walk past several athletes I know. We smile and wave. I go from the Underbelly–the prime campus hangout spot with the smoothie place and the Redbox–to the crosswalk, passing the soccer fields where the team is running two-a-days. I remember the hell it was to work two-a-days with them.

Baseball here is the biggest deal. So much revolves around this sport it's not even funny. Scouts and reporters come to the games. I can count on one hand the games we've lost. These boys are good. Coach Conners and Coach Denson run a tight ship and Mindy is one hell of an athletic trainer.

Sandy, the head professor of the athletic training program, steps out of her office. "Lexie?" Her face lights up, looking over a handful of notebooks. "Oh my God!" She pushes the notebooks aside, trying to give me a hug while I inhale her pleasant perfume.

"Hey, Sandy. How you been?"

"Great! I'm thrilled to see you back. I saw the note from administration." She gives me another hug. I've always loved Sandy. She really is the mother of the athletic training program. I met her as a freshman, and I always felt that, under her wings, I could learn to fly. I'm so torn because I do love so much about this program and so much about the people here. I wish there was a better way for me to pursue my art *and* be involved in athletics. I used to run myself raw trying to make it work, but there's not enough time for both. Not with how much I'd like to spend on my art...if I can ever bring myself to paint again.

"It's great to see you, too."

"I'm so glad you came back."

The word *back* makes my throat thick.

I am back. Without Cody. He doesn't get to finish school. He doesn't get to go play for the Yankees. He doesn't get to wait for me to walk down the aisle in his old church in Willardson. I swallow, holding my breath and hoping the look on my face doesn't betray my thoughts.

"I gotta run, Lexie, I'll see you in class." She heads on her way and I'm thankful she doesn't see the tear sneaking out of my eyes. Deep breaths. Keep going, keep moving, keep shifting. Mental note: watch a Nicholas Sparks movie so I can get all of this crying out of my system in the privacy of my own home.

I walk past the baseball coaches' offices and they are there, always working, even way before season. Coach Conners smiles at me through the glass with an enthusiastic wave.

The team photos are in the display case. My Cody, right there for all the world to see, his eyes so bright. So full of life.

Anything can change in a moment.

A second.

"Hey, Lex." My friend Jae comes in front of me, wearing an athletic training t-shirt and khaki shorts, his thick English accent lacing his words.

"Good to see you." I give him a hug, welcoming the distraction from my pain.

He's one of my best friends. We worked together in the training room a lot before I left. "Looks like we're going to have baseball together."

"I know." I smile, genuinely happy for something to look forward to.

"Have you seen Mindy yet?"

It's the million dollar question. No, and I don't want to. "Heading there now."

"That makes two of us."

Thank fuck I won't have to do this one alone.

He opens the door and the smell wafts up my nose: a mix of sweat, lemon-scented cleaner to make sure no one gets MRSA, and bandaids. Ice baths are churning with players submerged, discomfort playing across their faces. Nine of the twelve tables have athletes on them.

This is more my home than the beach house. I doubt that place will ever be home again. I love that Bobby was supportive of me getting out of there. He's being so nice to me. My skin tingles with the memory of him holding me last night, and it brings a small comfort as I anticipate the reckoning that's about to occur.

The track team shuffles in like a stampede of zebras in their striped uniforms, waiting in line for ice bags and heat packs. A few of them talk about classes while others talk about their summers.

I jump in motion, helping suck the air out of the ice bags and tying a knot. The giant roll of plastic wrap screeches, wrapping one bag of ice after another against overworked thighs and shins.

"Thanks." Bryce Woudermilk says with that goofy, toothy smile of his. He's holding a banana. He usually carries a banana. Funny thing to remember, but hey some things never change.

"You ready for the meet on Saturday?" I suck the air out of his second ice bag.

"As ready as I can be." He props his leg up so I can wrap the ice on his shin.

"That's fair." I'm glad he doesn't ask me how I've been–I'm sick of all the attention. Yes, I left and yes, I'm back. I wish everyone would stop making such a big deal about it.

"See ya around, Lexie." Bryce follows his team toward the locker room.

"See ya, Bryce. Good luck this weekend!"

Right after the track team disperses, the soccer team arrives. We're running low on ice. A freshman stands here looking like we've been invaded by vampires, waiting to suck all the blood out of her neck.

"You know where Tony's room is?" I ask her.

"No." Of course she doesn't. It's preseason and this girl is as new as any fresh-born. It's what we call all the wide-eyed, innocent freshmen. Like little newborn babies, caught up in the real world for the first time.

"I'll take her." Jae ties off another wrap, then endearingly shows the new girl the ropes. He's joking around with her, trying to make her feel comfortable with a bright smile on his face. It really is a family here. This program is everything I've missed about Suncastle College. Athletic training isn't art school, but it's a worthy second choice. I do love the environment and the people. Being here brings an unexpected familiar comfort.

It's good to be home.

We finish the rush, athletes dispersing and going back to what they need to do next. I head into the office. Jae takes it upon himself to show the freshman around the athletic building, so I guess I am doing this alone after all.

Deep breaths.

My heart pounds in my chest while I remind myself I can do this.

Mindy is at her computer and doesn't look up when I approach. She's busy because she would've helped with the rush if she wasn't. Good thing Jae and I happened to show up.

No athletic trainer is too good to make an ice bag.

I swallow my judgement because I know that's not being fair. Mindy isn't above anyone, she just has a lot on her plate. Baseball means the world to this school and this town. It means the world to the thousands of people that watch the boys play on television.

"Oh, hey Lexie." She looks up from her work with a smile, and I start to relax.

"I'm back if you need me."

"Don't yet." Her coffee cup tips the last sip into her mouth, and she sets it on the desk.

"Can I get you another coffee?"

"Oh, no. You're not my ball-boy, Hawthorne. Not anymore." She winks and I remember being new here and trying to prove myself by going above and beyond. Mindy loved to tease me that I was acting like a ball-boy when I didn't need to. It's sweet she remembers.

This is going better than I hoped, but it still feels like something is off. Back before Cody died, she would have jumped up and given me a hug when I walked into her office. Even though she's joking around, it's like she doesn't want to see me. I hope by the end of working baseball together, I can convince her to change her mind.

A couple email notifications ding on her computer screen and she clicks the first message. "It's kinda crazy right now, but I do want to catch up soon, okay?"

The look on her face tells me we're done talking, and I don't push. I want to ask her what day practices start or have a few minutes of small talk, but I won't. She doesn't look up when I walk through the offices to get to the other side, and I am relieved that this wasn't more confrontational.

Stepping into the hallway of the athletic building, my chest burns.

"You ready to go, babe? Cody stands in the doorway, like he always does. He's planned his schedule around my training room shifts so he can walk me to my car every day. It's such a small thing, but man it means the world to me.

I wrap my arms around him. "Guess who got to tape her first athlete's ankle for practice today? As a freshman, when most of the athletic trainin' students aren't allowed to touch them until they pass all the taping labs." I tilt my chin up to see his reaction.

"I told you that you could do it." He kisses me long and slow. "You've got the best taping skills of all the freshmen combined."

Taking his hand in mine, I lead us out of the building. "Guess I need to thank my boyfriend for all those hours of lettin' me practice on him."

"Your boyfriend, huh? Dang, I was wishin' I could have a shot with you." He winks.

I stop, looking at his shining eyes and plant a kiss on his lips. I wiggle my nose around his. "You have all the shots, honey. You always will."

I swallow the lump in my throat. Cody's not here in this hallway waiting for me. He will never walk me back to my car or give me a kiss. Loneliness encapsulates every inch of my skin. I feel empty inside.

Or maybe all I feel is dead.

7

BOBBY

My bed is made. Pizza is in the fridge. Lexie isn't here. I'll bring her the pizza.

What part of putting distance between us includes seeing her two days in a row, hm? I don't know. But I also don't know if she wants to stay here tonight. The crick in my neck, from sleeping on the couch, screams I shouldn't offer. But I'll let her move in today if it means easing a morsel of her pain.

I drive to her beach house, thankful that Mick returned my truck in fine working condition. He and Claudia were out all night. I think I heard them slink in around four a.m. I should've slept on his bed until he got back.

In front of her house is a Merry Maid's van. Lexie's car isn't in the driveway. Her mom must've hired the cleaner. I get my phone out.

Me: Coming home soon?

Thinking about Lexie has me feeling lighter than I have in a while. I've always felt this way around her. I feel lucky she's back in town and I can just stop by. She's such a caring human being.

One day we lost a game and I was feeling like shit. She knew just what to say to make me feel better.

I'm still fuming while I drive us to Shakey's. Our group of friends all meet up here after every game.

"I'm gonna go check in with Mama." Cody leans down to kiss Lexie. "I'll be back in a few." He leaves us at our booth in the back corner so he can go see his mom in the kitchen.

"Shit, that game sucked." I collapse into the bench across from her.

"You'll get them next time, I know it." She smiles.

"No, I shoulda played better." I tilt my head down, my frown glued to my face.

"Shoulda played better? Are you kiddin'?" She gives me an incredulous look. "Bobby, you had three base hits and caught two outs. It wasn't you that needed to play better." She's not making a joke or hurting me worse like some people might. No, not Lexie. She's both honest and caring. A smile pulls at the corner of my lips. Just like that, she diffused my pain, like when I put ice on my sore shoulder.

Jeez, I hate that Cody's with her and not me.

I stare at the screen knowing full well that she won't reply. She couldn't return any of my messages over the last several months. I'm sure as hell she won't reply today. But the screen lights up. I reread three times to make sure it's real.

Lexie: Yep.

My heart smiles. That link between us tightens around me. False hope blooms in my chest. I need to tell her how much she means to me.

No.

That's literally the worst thing I could do. *Get a fuckin' grip, man.*

On her ass. Her boobs. Her body dripping wet, coming all over my face.

No. No. No!

Good Lord, is this really going through my mind right now?

Pursuing Lexie is a dark road I won't go down. Cody would never forgive me. I would never forgive myself. If it was meant to be, we would've dated a long time ago. Only I don't believe that rational thought one bit. I wanna be with her. For real. Give us a chance. I can't think of anything I want more.

She pulls into the driveway and fumbles into the backseat to get a bunch of text books.

I drown.

Short jean shorts and a white tank top with a gray bralette peeking out. On her left arm is a large tattoo of a spiraling snake coiling around succulents from her mid bicep toward her elbow. When she bends over I see the bottom of her butt cheeks, toned and delicious.

I bite my finger while heat rolls through me. Damn, she's so gorgeous and doesn't even know it. A sloppy bun sits on the top of her head. Bright red, sweeping bangs flutter over her green eyes.

I stand outside my car looking like a pizza delivery boy with the boxes balanced in one hand.

"Oh." She gasps.

"Didn't mean to sneak up on you."

"Oh, no, you didn't. I thought you were comin' later."

"I can circle the block."

She busts up laughing. Shit, I've missed her laughing at my jokes. She does that little finger over her mouth thing. "No." She plays stern with a scolding look, then laughs at herself. "No, come on inside."

Yes, please.

My mouth waters. I swallow it down, trying to block the desire rushing from head to toe. If grief is riding rapids, loving Lexie is sending me down Niagra Falls.

I need to be inside of *her*. Beach house. I need to be inside of her beach house. Because that is the closest I'm gonna get.

Friends. Just. Friends.

Cody's pictures assault me as punishment for my filthy thoughts. His large crucifix hangs right by the door. *Jesus, save me now.*

As much as it pains me, it's good to see Cody's face. Our friend Trish loves photography, so she took lots of photos. I count ten pictures hanging on the walls. Engagement photos from the same weekend he popped the question. I purse my lips, not knowing if it's better to look or pretend he isn't there. It hurts both ways. There's a ton of old photos that I keep in a box at my parents' place. Trying to leave the past in the past since it already follows me around everywhere.

I put the pizza in her fridge, seeing all the stuff I took her to get at Quickies.

"You left the M&Ms." She sits that perfect ass against the countertop.

"They were for you," I stammer, searching the kitchen for something to focus on that isn't her.

"You bought me M&Ms?" She raises her eyebrows.

"Yeah." I stay behind the island, trying not to look at her adorable body. Does she know what she does to me? I'm going fucking insane. Would she like it if she knew? Can I ask her that?

No. No. No….

She'll always be Cody's girl. If I said that, she'd never want to see me again.

"You didn't need to buy me M&Ms."

"It's not about need." Only, it is. It's about how much I need *her*.

You'd be so mad, wouldn't you, Cody?

If the roles were reversed, what would I want? If I'd been the one to date her. The one to die. And this was Cody in our kitchen. Would I want her to be alone? Would I want her hurting? Would I mind if he looked at her like this?

I need some air. I turn on her sink and run cold water over my hands, sudsing up with some vanilla hand soap.

"We're all finished." The Merry Maid smiles at Lexie.

"Thank you so much." She hops off the counter and I let out the breath I've been holding for far too long. I follow the maids out the door. They continue while I stop. It's like my shoes stick to wet cement on her front step. I'm melting into the floor, unable to move.

"Lex?" My body is near her, heart surging. I know what it wants. If only I could let myself ask her.

No. No. No.

"Yeah, Bobby?" Her breath is warm against my neck because I'm standing so goddamn close to her. It's like personal space doesn't exist. She looks up at me with the most tender expression. I thought I was drowning before. Fuck me now.

"Did you...well *do* you wanna stay at my place tonight?" I can't read her response and don't know what to make of that. Usually I can. Her eyes are cloudy. I don't know if that's from emotion or being tired. I think she's considering my offer, but I can't tell. This is confusion in every way, shape and form.

"I dunno." She finally says. "Hey, you brought over a lot of pizza. Is it cheat day yet? Maybe you wanna come eat some?"

I smile. "Yeah." Only I oughta say no. Being around her is so intoxicating. I can't breathe. My mouth is like a desert. Forget control. I've already lost it.

We go to the kitchen. She puts a few slices of pizza on a cookie sheet. "I think Mindy hates me."

"What?" I lean against the countertop. "No, I'm sure she doesn't hate you. I don't think Mindy hates anyone. Least of all you."

"Oh, she does. I saw her today." She grabs the M&Ms, going to the couch. Her legs cross under her so she sits on her feet. I sit beside her and her knee brushes mine. Tingles go from my knee up to my hip and into my groin.

No.

No.

No!

My breath stops in my lungs. I'm a million degrees. Usually, I'm freezing cold.

"You alright?"

"Yeah, I'm fine." I search her eyes for any bit of what I'm feeling. The longing that devours me more the longer I'm with her. All these years I've held back. But today, it's like a volcano of feelings erupts, releasing a love I can't withhold.

Maybe I'm an idiot. She doesn't want me. Doesn't feel this. What's that thing people say? Blind in love? Well I'm outta my mind, whatever's happening.

She pops some M&Ms into her mouth, offering the bag to me. "I forgot how good these are."

I eat a blue one and a green one.

"I got internet again." She clicks on the TV.

"Oh, good."

"Just Netflix, though. Debating on gettin' some channels." She and Cody used to host big baseball watch parties with every ESPN variety coming through their flatscreen. Didn't matter who was playing. We all got together. Half the team and all their girls crowding around the TV with all kinds of food and beer.

We watch an episode of *Arrested Development*. I've never seen it, but apparently she's binged the show four times. It's funny and we laugh, but really all I'm thinking about is how to calm my pounding heart. The show has no hope for distracting me.

"Why didn't you leave a note?" She clicks the TV off.

"Hm?" My eyebrows wrinkle.

"It's not common for me to wake up in some guy's apartment all alone and not know how to lock up or anythin'."

"I hope I'm not just some guy to you, Lex." The words come out before I think them through. My voice is deep, heavy. So much feeling escaping–that fucking valcano *again*–while I basically put my whole damn heart on my sleeve.

What's wrong with me?

Her face is in shock. Dammit. Not what I was hoping for. I imagine her leaning toward me, those lips so close I can taste the peanut M&M on them.

"I didn't mean it like that." Her words zing me out of my fantasy.

"What did you mean?" Anger sizzles the way her touch did moments ago. I grit my teeth reaching for some level of calm. I have none. I'm not just some fucking guy. I want to be so much more than that. "Forget it." In autopilot, I do the only thing that makes sense right now. If anything makes sense.

I'm almost to the door when she comes up in front of me, stopping my exit. This must be what she was feeling last night. I rake my hands through my hair.

"What the fuck, Bobby?" She's looking from my eyes to my shirt to my eyes again. This moment is intense. But not in the way I want us to be intense.

"I don't know. I just–" I rake my fingers through my hair again, pulling strands until my scalp aches. "I don't know what to do here."

"What do you wanna do here?" Her face mesmerizes me. I'm at a loss.

Wishing to have any hint–any clue–that it's not just me that feels, I stare into those green eyes and notice the hazel accents as if she painted them herself. My heart thunders in my chest, wanting to confess but knowing I shouldn't.

"This isn't about Cody, is it?"

"God, no," I huff. But maybe it is. Everything is. Every fucking second of the day is wrapped around him and what he left behind. I'll never outrun it, even if I was the fastest player on the team.

She licks her lips. Hands go to her hips. Feet away from me. Looking up to keep eye contact. "Because you're acting fuckin' nuts."

I am.

"Tell me what's going through that head of yours so I can stop guessin'. It *is* about Cody, isn't it?"

"Yes. Maybe. I don't know." Am I really being vulnerable with her right now? This is all she'll get out of me. I'm here for her. Not the other way around.

"If you need to go, you can go." She moves away from the door. "The last thing I want is for you to feel trapped." For a moment we hold each other's eyes. "But, I'd like you to stay."

"I don't feel trapped." I relax. My insides reach for her. Wanting to grasp her. I melt into these hazel-green eyes. Wanting to hold her. To have her. To love her. "And I'd like to stay."

8

LEXIE

I'm pretty sure Bobby has something he needs to say but can't figure out how. So much pain radiates from him, and seeing this brings up something inside of me that I can't identify. There *is* more here, between us.

Is this new?

The thought punches me in the gut as I look at the past through a different lens. I'm such an idiot; he clearly has feelings for me. That little moment proved what I was wondering about last night.

I'm dancing around so many thoughts as I pull the cookie sheet out of the oven and set it on the island, nervous energy keeping me moving. There's enough food to feed me all week still left in the boxes. He bought them for me even though he didn't need to. Southern gentleman buying me dinner–buying me M&Ms–letting me sleep in his bed, claiming he doesn't want to be *just some guy*. I sigh, feeling naive for missing every one of the hints he's dropping.

Fuck, he *likes* me.

I don't know what just happened, but I don't want to drive him away, which makes me wonder what is going on inside of me.

A framed picture of Cody and me catches my eye.

"We'll always be us, right?" Cody brushes hair out of my face, smiling on the beach.

"I'd like that."

"There's no one else you wanna be with?" He looks a little worried. "I mean, I'm goin' to play for the Yankees in a couple months. I wouldn't hate you if you wanted to break up."

"No, of course not. Do you wanna break up?" My heart races.

"Hell, no. Lexie, you're the one I want."

"You're the one I want, too."

"Forever?"

"Forever."

"Marry me?" His voice is choked up, the sun melting on the beach in deep reds and pinks.

"There's nothin' I want more." I kiss him hard, knocking us into the sand. Holding him. Gripping him. Longing for everything he just promised me.

Grief knocks me off balance, and I brace myself against the countertop while I ride the waves of memory. My heart burns, my throat swells, my head spins, my fingers run along the spot where an engagement ring used to be.

"Can I help?" Bobby leans against the counter, hands stuffed in his pockets.

"Got it." The hint of a whine comes out of my throat, and I swallow it back, getting a drink of water.

"I'm sorry I'm actin' so weird. I just–" He shakes his head. "I'm sorry." Bobby feeling so much and sharing so little makes me ache for all that's inside of him. He needs me, I realize. All the years we've known each other, I've never seen him this broken. But he's lost and shattered–just like I am.

"Oh, it's okay, I get it. Really." My mouth raises in a smile until he nods. We need each other–and it isn't one sided because that hug last night has me craving his comfort. I need him as much as he needs me, and there's something beautiful about that. Cody was Bobby's best friend, and I know it's because he felt accepted with him. Of everybody in our friend group, Cody had this ability to make everyone feel valued and important–even when they were different. That's why I loved dating him so much. Maybe it's because his life was so shitty, or maybe it's just because he cared about all of us so much. Cody's death hit Bobby and me so hard, and fuck, we *need* each other. The thought of Bobby going out that front door tore into me, and my heart is still somersaulting in my chest.

Neither of us eat with the air so heavy that we don't say a word. So much for getting his side of the story.

"Wine?" I sigh.

"Please."

I go to the fridge and pull out a bottle of chardonnay.

"So, now that I'm gonna try to stop actin' all crazy and shit." Bobby shakes his head. "How about let's talk about somethin'. You got any fun art projects you're workin' on? Like remember that blue butterfly paintin' you did for the senior year exhibit? Doin' anythin' like that?"

I smile that he remembered that piece. It's one of my favorites I've ever done. His eyes are waiting while I focus on the sinking feeling in the pit of my stomach.

"I've stopped painting." My glass clinks against the granite countertop. "It's stupid."

"Why?"

"I just don't know how to paint now. Holding the brushes makes me think about all the times I painted while Cody read. Reminds me of how much he loved my art. How when we first started dating my parents were shitty about it but he convinced me not to give it up." I lick my lips, the chardonnay lingering on my tongue. "I just can't seem to paint without him. My heart is what attaches to the canvas. And right now, it's like I don't have a heart at all." I grimace. I've shared too much. "That sounds pathetic."

"Pathetic? No. That's the saddest thing I've ever heard." His words sink deeper into me the longer we sit.

"I don't think I'll ever want to again. It's one of my biggest fears, that I won't get over the grief, and for the rest of my life I'll be a broken version of myself."

"No. You will." His eyes are kind. "One day you will." His eyebrows wrinkle. "You can't stop, Lex." He takes my hand in his and there's so much depth in those eyes. "He wouldn't want that. Not one bit."

"I know." I sigh, watching the pale yellow swish in the flute.

"It was hard to play ball again." His voice is thick.

"It was?" I hadn't thought about it, but it makes perfect sense.

"Course it was. Shit, not even was. Is. *Is* hard every fuckin' day." He looks away and I see that struggle painted all over his face as if I was working on a canvas right now. My heart stirs. Until this moment, I haven't wanted to paint. But I want to capture this pain on his face. I want to share that intensity with the world. *Fuck, Bobby, how'd you go and inspire me so quick?*

"You've gotta paint. Where's your paint? Let's get it."

"Soon, okay?" I chuckle. "I just haven't felt like it."

"Well, I do hope you reconsider. Because the world is missing out on a lot without your art in it." Bobby's lips look so kissable. Wow, I'm getting drunk.

Swirling my almost empty glass, my gut clenches. "I haven't kissed anyone in a year and a half. My last kiss was on Cody's dead lips and do you know what kissin' a dead person is like? It's like kissin' a frozen bowlin' ball, I'm not kiddin'." I stare blankly at the wall in front of me.

"A frozen bowlin' ball, huh?" His response makes me aware I just said all that out loud.

Fuck, I bring my fingers to my lips, so embarrassing.

"It's from all the formaldehyde." He shrugs. "That's why they're cold. You could just pretend you were kissin' Edward Cullen."

I choke on my wine. "It's not the formaldehyde. It's 'cause they put the bodies in a freezer."

"No, I think it's the formaldehyde." He shakes his head, and I see a bit of a smile. "Google it."

"I cannot believe I just told you that."

"What? That I'm wrong about dead bodies?"

"No, that I kissed his corpse."

"No, you told me you kissed Edward Cullen. We are rewritin' this memory right now." He points in the air like a playful scolding. "He'd be honored. He was always a huge fan of Robert Pattinson." Bobby's making light of this, and I love him for it. Death is always so depressing and heavy, but he's saying things that take away a bit of that pain, leaving something much better in its place.

"Team Edward, huh?"

"Oh yeah." Bobby smiles. "Jacob never had a chance at winnin' his heart."

I smile into my wine, wanting to drink all I have in the house. "Do you talk to Cody's family much?"

"Never. Do you?" Bobby downs his glass and I pour him another.

"Not since the funeral." I look at the kitchen cabinets, remember the flowers lining the countertop. Flowers for my loss, as if they could make it any better. There is no *better* about death. There's only the torment you live with as you become the survivor, the victim of tragedy.

"I should. Check in on Mama Jones at least. Make sure she's doin' alright." He's looking at his shoes, Chuck Taylors on those long feet. I'm surprised he makes a style choice in favor of arch support–he's full of surprises, isn't he?

What else will I learn about you, Bobby?

"It's not exactly easy to talk about it with anyone, much less his mom. Like what? Do I call her for Mother's Day? Christmas? Oh, hey, I'm sad he died, still sad he died, op, yep, I can't go a fuckin' day without missin' him like crazy. What do you even say?" My entire body hurts the more I speak. I cannot handle that I was basically her adopted daughter and now I don't ever want to talk to her again. It's too much.

But I'm sitting here with his best friend, and I find myself feeling guilty because I feel more comfortable here than I think I should.

Bobby's presence soothes me.

Why do I keep thinking that? I swallow everything back, because I don't know how much pain I can take. Cody is gone. *Gone.* And no amount of feeling like shit over it will bring him back. I need a distraction from everything that is Cody's death in a big, bad, ugly way—just like Bobby does—so here we are.

I pull another bottle of chardonnay, popping the cork and filling our glasses. The pizza sits on our tray as undisturbed as a graveyard. Bobby has taken maybe three bites while I've yet to eat my first. All we do is drink and stare at the kitchen walls like they are reading our minds, recording this story of loss and longing.

He pours another glass of wine, so much that I won't let him drive home with this level of intoxication. I can't handle the thought of him leaving me alone in this house anyway.

We keep drinking, the wine winding down my pain, dulling my senses as I recall a yesteryear I barely believe I lived. "Cody loved this house. It could've fit his childhood home four times over in the square footage."

"I hate that stupid little house. If Cody's dad didn't spend so much on himself he could actually take care of their family. Give 'em a proper place to live instead of that dump." Bobby isn't hiding the anger in his tone, though what he is angry about, I don't know. Seems to go beyond the sad excuse for a home Cody grew up in. Something else must be on his mind. "I miss Cody all the time. But I don't miss their house."

"You know what I miss?" If we're diving into the past, I'm going to go all the way. No, not all the way, just most of it.

"Tell me?" Bobby genuinely wants to know.

"I miss watchin' him play. I miss him readin' his favorite parts of books out loud with no context whatsoever." Everything I say gets louder, like a release of what is dark inside of me. Record this, kitchen cabinets—tell the story Cody doesn't get to anymore. "I miss sleepin' with him." The way he would touch me when I begged for it. That the first time, our first time, was together.

I've never been with anyone else, but I think I could be one day. With the right person. My eyes trace the outlines of Bobby's pecs through his tight shirt.

I shake my head knowing it must be the alcohol making me think this way.

My heart throbs in my chest, the familiar flame in between my legs begging for my attention. Am I getting turned on because I'm thinking about Cody or because I feel something for Bobby?

This is confusing in all the wrong ways.

"I miss playin' with him. It's not the same. Team's not the same." Bobby shakes his head. "I mean, he was movin' on anyway. I just thought I'd still get to watch."

Wine flows down my throat, and I go and get *another* bottle. I don't know why we're drinking into oblivion, but it feels like the right thing to do. As my inhibitions lower, I go with it, thankful I don't have to be responsible tonight.

"I'm amazed by your strength," Bobby says.

"Strength?" I scoff and some wine sprays out of my mouth, onto his face. "Whoops, you just got Chardonn-rained on."

He chuckles, and his laugh is the sound of heaven, I swear. It's the best thing I've ever heard. Bobby is the funny one–the one that makes other people laugh. It's rare to hear *him* chuckling, so rare that it feels like I've won the Oscars or something. Bobby doesn't give out those laughs for just anything. They're earned.

His t-shirt wipes the wine off his face and when his shirt comes up I see those muscles on his tan skin. Fuck, he's so chiseled my mouth waters as I stare at that human perfection. The heat in between my legs intensifying.

Bobby *is* turning me on. Jesus, what am I supposed to do now?

"They say that wine exfoliates better than any acne cream, so you may wanna leave that on those pores of yours." I pull my fingers to my lips, realizing it probably sounded like I was insulting his skin. My eyes linger on his face, free of any blemishes or scarring so many of us have leftover from high school.

"Bullshit. Wine is not exfoliating at all." He full on laughs, and I swear to God I've never heard anything so everlasting. I laugh with him while he says something funny, but I don't register what it is because I'm too giddy from the wine.

"Not that you need it. Your skin is astounding, really. I'm envious."

"Then maybe you need to get Chardonn-rained on, hm?" He splashes his almost empty wine glass at my face.

"Ah!" I push his glass away, taking both of his wrists in mine and he almost falls off the barstool. With quick reflexes, he recovers.

"Bottoms up." I giggle the whole way through refilling. Full glasses pour, dumping into our mouths–forget savoring–we're getting hammered, and I'm here for it.

His knee brushes mine and just like when we were on the couch, I feel *somethin'*. Not knowing what that something is, I lean closer. My hand touches his arm, the connection catching my breath in my throat. Heat surging in my chest, I get closer.

"You feel it?" His eyes beg me and I think about how he rushed away a little bit ago.

You're scared of this, aren't you? We're both terrified, I feel that terror spreading from his soul to mine. It's an unusual thing to share, and I need to understand why.

"Somethin'." My eyes find his and it's a sea of longing. For me? For what may be happening? Like I'm on the Titanic about to sink, I plunge in, icy worry surrounding me because who knows where the fuck this will go?

His face comes close, so close his cheek brushes against mine. Warm, soft, welcoming. It's like he's the rescue boat pulling me out of the Titanic just before I drown, lost in the icy depths forever.

He is the heat when I've been living in the frigid cold. Like fire and ice, we collide.

"Lexie?" Our noses brush, his hand framing my jaw.

"Yeah?" I choke.

"I'm goin' to...I'm goin' to kiss you." It's so fucking cute that he said that. His mouth hovers ever so close and the suspense gets me as I search those shining eyes. Lost in time and space, I plead for more.

Heat rises through my middle while his hand moves behind my neck, cradling me like I'm the most valuable thing on this earth.

I breathe, bracing myself as I lean in.

His lips merge with mine, feasting like I'm better than his favorite peach ice cream. Like he's dying and I'm the medicine that will cure him. Like there's nothing that could stop him from sharing his passion with me.

And I want him to share every goddamn piece of himself with me from now until the end of forever.

"Like it?" He's hardly pulled back, so much that the words chafe his mouth against mine.

"Mmm hmm." I shake my head, a moan escaping as he presses his chest against my perky nipples.

"You *want*...." His eyes are the deepest blue, hypnotizing me as I struggle to hear his words from the buzzing in my head. "...more?" It's just this heat between us, his teasing driving me into a frenzy when his lips take me again, tongue flowing with mine to explore.

Fucking hell, this is amazing.

I don't know if I'm starved for loving or I'm too drunk, but he's fantastic. His kiss is delectable, forcing me into pleasure I didn't know was possible. Tantalizing tingles swarm my body while I press closer, my hand teasing his erection under his jeans. He fills my hand and I moan, the lush connection of all he wants and all I need. He's so fucking hard, for *me*. I leap off my barstool and onto his lap, his hands going under my ass, bringing me against him.

"Still want?" Sexy silk in his voice makes my lady clench so tight that she's ready to come.

"Please." I whisper against his ear while he works away at my shorts with careful attention. His middle finger wraps that perfect part of me and wiggles, the bud of my clit as happy as she's ever been.

Holy God, is this what it's supposed to feel like?

A harsh intake of breath has me holding it, my head rearing back. He follows my face with his, touching me, kisses in rhythm with his writhing touch. Oh God above, I didn't know it could feel so good.

"You're so fuckin' wet for me," he whispers against my ear.

Oh, yes, accurate observation. I'm a river, fully and completely drenched.

"I knew you had to feel this. I knew it. I kept talkin' myself out of it, but man, it was here. It's always been here." He repositions to bounce me against his cock and my walls clench, imagining how his tip would feel inside of me.

With a stronger urge than I've ever felt, I want him to take me here and now.

I shove the pizza pan aside and he lifts my ass against the counter top. There's a confident smile on his lips as he slides a finger into my core. My body sings under his touch, like he's my favorite song and I'll always be singing.

I kiss him back, deeper, harder, all mine.

What are we doing?

Bobby realizes the moment I do that this isn't alright. We drank too much. He pulls back, looking away and leaving me starved for his connection the moment he withdraws. Like the Titanic broke in half, launching debris, shattering our rescue boat, and I'm sinking into a frozen ocean.

"Fuck." He shoves his hands in his pockets while his body slams against the wall, hard enough to really hurt. "Fuck, Lexie, I'm drunk. I'm sorry." He rakes his hands through his hair, pulling tight on those immaculate, deep brown locks.

I hop off the counter–so dizzy I couldn't pass a concussion test. We didn't even fuck and I can't walk straight. What's he like when he goes all the way?

I need to find out, aftershocks pulsing through me, feeling *so* good.

My soul deflates when I see his face. Like I'm a balloon and he's holding a needle, I pop.

His palms press his eyeballs like he wants to push them out of the back of his head. He looks up, showing me everything I don't want to see.

We've just shared something that the only word for is *magical*. But Bobby isn't looking magical. Instead I see a mix of pain, torment and regret.

Oh, God.

As much as it felt good to kiss, it now feels just as bad to see what it did to him.

We have to keep this together, because I'm already attached. My teeth chatter, ice flowing from my anxious heart while air goes in, holds, releases.

He's staring at the wall behind me, swimming in something deep and terrible. I know that look because it looks like how I feel inside, most of the time.

"It's okay, Bobby. Really." I zip my shorts, tossing the cold pizza into the garbage. "If it wasn't alright, I would've stopped you."

"We shouldn't."

"No." Although I don't like that word coming off my lips when I mean the reverse, seeing as everything about how he touched me makes me crave him with a longing I've never known. I worried it would feel like a betrayal and maybe I'm just drunk, but that felt so much better than anything I've ever shared with anyone.

That couldn't have been a mistake.

Keep surprisin' me, Bobby.

9

BOBBY

*W*hat have I done?

I walk to her fridge, filling my wine flute with water. I chug. Another glass. Water is healing. We both need healing for the shit I pulled. A third glass rushes down my throat.

What was I thinking getting drunk? I have work tomorrow. Some spontaneous cheat day. Seven hundred calories per bottle of Chardonnay.

My hand was *inside* of her. I still feel that warm, wet, tight sensation tattooed forever on my fingers. Forever on my soul.

Oh, shit she was so tight.

And *wet*.

And every kind of perfect I expected her to be.

Shit.

My hand has been inside more than a dozen people. Probably less than twenty, but more than a dozen. I'm not going to sit here and count, even though my stupid brain keeps track of how many days it's been since my best friend died. Four hundred and seventy seven.

Double shit.

What the hell have I done?

I'm pacing her kitchen. Lexie stands by the counter, looking into my broken soul. Is she okay? I sure as hell am not.

All I can think about is her black silky panties and the amazing way her skin felt against me.

"Slow down, big guy. You don't need to fill up a fish tank." Her eyes are wide. Adorable bangs hide eyebrows I know are raised in concern.

Protein.

That will curb the hangover as much as I can. Vision a little nebulous, I open up her fridge. Get the eggs. I already had a fuck ton of calories. It's okay. Eat what I need to. It will be okay.

"You have a fryin' pan?"

"Yeah." She bends over. I look away. Jeez, my hand was in between those perfect legs.

Lex sprays the pan with cooking spray. Starts up the stove. I crack eggs, scrambling them up.

"Protein and hydration for staving off a hangover."

Of course she knows. She's fucking brilliant. I shrug. "I'll buy ya more eggs."

"I don't care about the eggs." Her eyes hold mine. There's space between us. Keep that space. I have to.

We go back to the bar. The same seat where I first felt her. My heart beats faster. I'm fucking sweating. "Have some." I force half the eggs down, wondering if I'll vomit.

"You make good eggs."

I'm pretty sure my voice would stall in my throat if I tried saying anything. Can't trust it. Can't trust me.

For years, I've wanted to touch her. Wanted to feel her. Wanted to explore her. But not drunk. Lexie deserves so much more. Guilt grips my sternum like a prison cell, not letting breath in or out of my lungs.

I wash the pan. Dry it. Return it to her cabinet. She hasn't stopped looking at me.

"I should go." The alcohol is fading. I've always tolerated it pretty well, ever since parties in high school. My metabolism is fast and I'm shaking out of it. Doesn't matter. I'm walking home.

She comes to where I stand. I pull at my t-shirt collar, because I can't get any fucking air. Her nipples tease my chest, hard through the layers of clothing. My cock perks, begging to finish what I never should've started.

Triple shit.

The room spins as she tilts my chin to look at her. Those green eyes command my attention. Like I'm melting into the floor, I lose all resolve to leave.

"What are you runnin' from?" She gives me a look that makes me fall harder for her.

How is it that she's calling me on this? I am running. I am fucking running from this.

My hand grips the back of my neck. I'm not ready. *What'd you think would happen when you went fingers deep inside her, Bobby?*

Her eyes are kind, waiting for my answer. Wanting my answer.

"Fuck, Lexie, I dunno how to do this." My nails dig into my skin.

"Do what?"

"You know exactly what," I scoff.

"I wanna hear you say it." Her eyes haven't left mine. My cock throbs and I'm sure she feels it against her belly because she leans into it.

You tease....

My body hums. I'm drunk on her touch more than the lingering wine.

"Lexie, I'm not doing this to him." Moving to a place neither one of us wants to go, the mood shifts. Energy drops. I shouldn't have said that.

Her body withdraws like I'm oil popping out of a pan, scalding her skin on contact. Anguish fills her eyes.

No, no, no...This isn't what I want. This isn't what she needs.

"Excuse me, for a minute." She hurries away. The hall bathroom door clicks shut, reminding me of another door that shut me out a long time ago. Reminding me of another time when I felt utterly rejected. A time when I never should've gone that far.

I sink to the ground and hug my knees.

How could I do this to her?

10

LEXIE

*H*e's gone before I get out of the bathroom. Bobby restraining himself because of Cody, hit me like a typhoon. It's been hard enough to come back to Suncastle. Now, this.

Forget the Nicholas Sparks movie. I've cleansed all the tears out of me that my tear ducts are capable of producing.

Not because I wanted it to. I didn't want any of this. Except his kisses. I wanted those.

The realization shakes me up in all kinds of ways. I want Bobby? He turned me on faster and harder than anyone else ever has.

What if it's just me needing someone to touch? Cody and I were together for so long and I've been alone since. In some ways, I was alone when we were together. Couldn't let our carnal desires get in the way of his faith...except on rare occasions.

Cody was so weird about sex and I think it was all those Sunday School lessons getting to him. A constant conflict of him wanting to be with me intimately and wanting to stay pure. He couldn't have both–according to religion–but he sure as fuck tried. After the wedding, it was supposed to be fine. Like God could sanctify sex within the bonds of marriage. I had no problem with him wanting to wait, but it sure as fuck confused me when we did have sex and then he'd pull an abrupt change. Hot and cold all the time, giving me constant whiplash.

But tonight, Bobby giving me so much pleasure made it feel good to be wanted. It felt good to be *touched*, even though he ran away like a scared little boy.

I stare at the kitchen, missing that soothing presence of Bobby. Holy God Above, I don't think I've ever been kissed like *that.*

My legs, giant blobs of jelly, ascend the stairs. Keep going, keep going, keep going. In a way, I want to punch him for leaving me here alone after I asked him to stay.

My struggles aren't consuming me. Instead, I feel a lightness, a twitterpation, a curious jolt of wondering where Bobby and I could go. I didn't even know being with him was an option. But man, he's got quite the attraction to me, regardless of my previous assumptions. His eager fingers made that perfectly clear, and I doubt it was *only* the alcohol.

One of these days, I was going to have to sleep here alone. Checking in with myself, I realize that all the horror I thought would grip me isn't present.

Flopping on the bed, birds on both hands aim at the ceiling. *Fuck you, Bobby.*

Heat fills my core as I tighten in pure pleasure at the memory of him.

I want *to fuck you, Bobby.*

The biggest part I dreaded about coming back here was to sleep alone in *our* bed. I thought it'd be a bunch of tears and pain, but I already got that out of my system. Bobby inadvertently replaced all my inner shit with a blessed distraction. Guilt should be what I'm feeling right now, but it's faded away since the moment we kissed. I must be in shock.

I know I have to move on without Cody even though I don't want to. I've told myself I need to move on a thousand times, but tonight is the first time I felt that *may* be a possibility for me.

The last several months have been filled with grief and a lot of loss. God, Jesus and the Universe, please forgive me, but I'm done feeling

all that. Tonight gave me a glimpse of what moving on can feel like–
and kill me now, or let me really live.

Bobby has feelings for me. I have feelings for him.

Grabbing my phone I pull up his number and compose a text.

Me: Did you get home ok?

My mind pulls up so many memories of the times we were always
together. Cody, Bobby, Mickey, Trish and I. At baseball games, out to
eat, going to movies, parties on the weekend. Best friends since junior
high when we all went out for burgers and shakes at Shakey's after a
baseball game. We all got along like we were meant to be together.

We will never *all* be together again.

Awaiting Bobby's reply, I text Trish.

Me: At my place...alone.

She's back home, working as a photographer, and I know if I'm not
ready to be back in Suncastle, I sure as fuck am not ready to go back to
our hometown, Willardson.

Trish: There with you. You know, virtually. I'll come visit soon, just
got to get through all these photo edits.
Me: Bobby and I just made out.
Trish: Say what now?
Me: Probably nothing… we were really drunk.
Trish: ha...Bobby and his drunk fucks.

I roll my eyes. Trish has always seen Bobby as a huge player. I
don't know, maybe he is. But tonight felt different. I mean, we didn't
go all the way, and he left. That has to mean I'm not just one of those
casual lays he's been rumored to have. Right?

Another text floats above my current thread.

Bobby: Yeah, I'm home. Sorry about tonight.
Me: I'm not.

For a while I look at the screen for a reply that doesn't come. The extra long pillow wraps my body. I like to pretend it's Cody because, fuck, I miss his hugs the most. The way he loved to hold me in bed, our bodies sticking together, talking about anything and everything we wanted to. I swear I didn't have a clue what love was until he came into my life. He knew me better than I know myself and accepted every bit of me. Could Bobby ever know me that well?

Snuggling into the pillow, I'm not imagining Cody anymore–I'm imagining his best friend. Those brown locks gripped in my fingers, his hips flush with mine.

I've never thought twice about Bobby this way, and it's apparent I've been missing out.

11

BOBBY

*I*t's been a week since I saw her.

Felt her.

Tasted her.

I caused her more harm. All I wanted to do was take the pain away.

Serves me right for wishing for the impossible. Walking the miles home was my punishment to myself. Enduring the hell of a hangover. Trying to stay focused in the hot sun of Tiny Knights Training Camp.

I haven't really eaten since Lexie's house. It's a bad idea to start this up again. I know, I know. But I can't. Too stressed to force any food down my throat. Worrying that when I do, I'll make myself sick. Only I *am* making myself sick. I'm functioning on sugar-free Powerade and black coffee. The perfect picture of health...not.

The boys run their last set of drills before pickup time.

"Makin' great progress," I tell Larry. "You did awesome with your throws today."

"Thanks, Coach."

"Remember your gear." I clap my hands and the boys disperse.

"Gym after this? I got an hour til my shift starts." Briar puts his arm around my shoulder, walking to the dugout.

"You know it." I nod.

I feel a little lightheaded and hold my breath while Briar high fives some of the players.

I hoped I was getting over this. But fuck, I've been starving myself more than not lately. That's why Sam noticed. It's been bad.

High school drove me to dangerous lows when I couldn't snap out of it. Mom pushed me hard to train for baseball. I guess I took it too far, getting obsessed with caloric intake and the easy way I could rid myself of everything in a few minutes. On the cold tile floor of the bathroom with my finger down my throat. I knew I shouldn't.

By graduation, I was doing okay. Determined to keep my parents from finding out what I was doing.

Right after Cody died, I spiraled into horrible patterns that I'd worked hard to leave behind. Life was too out of control to do a goddamn thing to stop it. Purging was my control.

Having this eating disorder is the farthest thing from what I want. It can get in the way of my shot at playing major league. Because of this, I am determined to not let it go too far. It took a long time before I tapered it back to just a temptation, instead of a way of life. I'm proud of myself for doing that while I've never breathed a word of it to another person. But now I feel like hell for letting it take control again.

"Cal, good work today." I pat his back as we walk out of the dugout.

"Thanks." He shrugs while we exit the practice fields. Cal's dad waits in the parking lot. He looks a lot like my dad, making me miss my old man.

I swallow. It's been a long time since Dad and I have talked. That weekend I went home for the peaches he had to work, so I only saw him for a minute at the hospital cafeteria on my way out of town. Barely saw Mom either. They have a lot going on with Dad's surgery schedule. Mom was really busy tending to our neighbor, Mrs. Harris, who broke her hip. I think it's taking a lot of their time because I haven't heard much from them since.

"Ready to go, sport?" Cal's dad's hand is on his shoulder.

"Thanks, Coach." Cal says.

I smile. "You're doin' great."

"Born for greatness. We'll see you at the awards tonight," his dad says as they head to their car. You can always tell when someone has a good support system at home. Though my dad was rarely present himself, he made an effort to show up for me when he could. He bought me top-of-the-line gear. Private lessons. The best summer camps. Doing stuff for me, even when his schedule was hectic at the hospital. I knew his heart was there with me on the field on the days he wasn't.

Cody's family was dirt poor, so Dad had us both work in the peach orchard in exchange for gear. It always meant a lot to me that he took care of my best friend.

In many ways, I had the perfect home life growing up. My parents have that passionate marriage I dream about. The happily ever after. Mom stepped up to make up the difference when Dad couldn't be there. She was that adorable baseball mom, baking a hundred white and red baseball sugar cookies for the team. Throwing beginning and ending season parties worthy of being on Pinterest before Pinterest existed.

Cody didn't have that. His dad was a truck driver and his mom was stretched thin with their million and three children and the two jobs she juggled. She came to a game once, with all the kids. Once. Cody had a parent at one game. Ever. Even though he was the star of the team, making headlines in the local papers often. Makes my chest hurt thinking about it. And he was still amazing. So much of who I am is because of him. His friendship shaped my life. I wish I could've told him more.

Life is talking. Sharing. So when Cody died, a big part of why it hurt was because I couldn't talk to him like I used to. It'll never be what it was. I can't tell him how much he meant to me or how much I love him. Not like I could. My answer to this? Tell the people still living before I can't tell them anymore.

I pull out my phone and get Dad's number ready.

Should I talk to him about the eating disorder? I swallow against the pain in my throat. It'd only disappoint him. He'd probably lecture me that I need to have more faith or go see a doctor. I squint my eyes tight, wishing I had someone to talk to. It's hard to bear alone.

Maybe I could tell Lexie?

No. I am staying away.

Because Lexie and I cannot be anything. Not even friends. It's too hard. I'm not strong enough.

Dad's phone goes to voicemail, like I figured it would.

"Hey Dad, wondering how it's goin'. Call me back." Click. Park. Work out with Briar for a while, until he heads to work. The machines feel good. I perform under the strain. My body is a fine-oiled machine.

Mick plops beside me.

"How's Claudia?" I snark. We haven't exactly been on speaking terms since things got unusually tense.

"Why?" He adjusts the weight setting.

"Seemed you two were havin' a nice time." I shake my head.

"None of your goddamn business."

"Fuck, man." I glare at him. "I'm just makin' conversation."

"Conversation? Well I have one for you, then."

And here it comes.

"What's gotten into you about Lexie?"

"Nothin'." It's one hundred percent my plan to keep this to myself. I'll take it to my grave. Just like my other secrets. Because nothing else is going to come of it. Not one more kiss. Hell, not even another look. I tried to be there for her but obviously can't keep my hands to myself.

But man, do I miss her.

I never have missed Sam like this. Or anyone. It's so different with Lexie. Different and awesome and a million kinds of things I cannot have.

"You know she's workin' baseball, right?" Mick watches for my reaction.

I didn't.

"Yeah." I shrug, but he picks up on the way my face falls before I get a chance to hide it.

"You gonna get your head out of your ass and ask her out? Or are you gonna string her around like the other dozen?"

"Oh, I see. So you can have as many girls as you want but I can't even look at Lex, is that right?" I give him an incredulous look. "Did I miss the part where you own her?"

"Are you gonna ask her out?" He growls.

"You know what? Fine. I'll tell ya. In another reality? I'd ask her out. Sure. In this one we are livin' in? No chance in hell."

"Good. Because it's not what she needs."

"What does she need?" I set my jaw, huffing out frustration while I wait.

"Not you."

"Oh, and are you interested in askin' her out? Because it seemed you made quite the impression with Claudia."

"You leave Claudia outta this." He clenches his fists.

"Then you leave Lexie outta all of it," I stand up from my machine, done with this conversation. Mick can keep all his judgement to himself. Why is he so upset about this? About everything? We used to be close but something is up and neither of us is trying to fix it. I've got enough to worry about that I don't have time to deal with his drama.

Back home, protein powder sloshes in my blender bottle. I have a constant headache from not eating. I drink it and hop in my shower. *Keep it down, Bobby. Keep it down.* I wring my hands, determined to ignore my urge to heave.

I make it out of the shower with the shake still down.

A small victory.

In the mirror, I realize I need to shave before tonight's award cere-mony for Tiny Knights Training Camp.

Lathering my face in shaving cream, the doorbell rings. While I'm wearing nothing but a towel? Of course. I hurry with my face while the bell rings a second time. Then a third.

It's probably my box of supplements that they have me sign for. Or Mick leaving his keys in his room and getting locked out again. I'll grab it real quick, then finish with my face.

"Hey." Lexie stands at my door holding a big box of peaches. Lexie? Here? Now? At my door when I'm in nothing but a towel?

Dammit.

"A highschooler came by sellin' these. Thought you'd like some." Her hair is in a long bright red braid down one side. She's wearing a Suncastle Knights baseball cap. A black tank top hugs her curves above her short khaki shorts. My heart races. Shit, if I haven't missed her like crazy.

"Oh, thanks." I go to take the box. My towel drops from my hips to my ankles.

Shit.

Her eyes are glued to me, naked, for a little longer than a breath.

Double shit.

My heart beats out of control while I set the box of peaches aside. "Whoops."

She and I lean down to grab the towel off my cheap apartment carpet. Her hat bumps into my chin, getting caked in shaving cream.

Triple fucking shit.

"Uh, sorry about that." I point to her cap, gather up my towel, and sling it around my hips. "Come on in, let's get your hat cleaned up." I head toward my bedroom.

She follows me, acting like me in nothing but my birthday suit is a normal occurrence. Turning on the sink, she gets a washcloth wet and works away the shaving cream. I duck into my room to get some damn clothes on.

When I come back into the hallway. She's holding my razor in one hand, leaning her body against the doorframe with a sexy smile tugging on her lips.

"I'm glad you're enjoyin' this." I roll my eyes.

"Didn't know I'd get a show." She hands me the razor.

I work off several days of scruff.

"Oh? I thought the show was the exchange for a big ol' box of peaches."

"No, that's not what I came for." She giggles.

"Well what did you come for?"

"An explanation."

I close my eyes for several heartbeats. It's erratically surging in my chest. "I told you."

"You barely told me anythin'. Are we gonna dance around this forever?"

"No, I'm gonna change the beat." I play off her verbs the way I wish I played off her body. "You and I both know this ain't a good idea." I gesture between her and me. Water splashes away the shaving cream. I wipe my face with my towel. She sits on my bed like she belongs there. Why the fuck is she being so casual?

Most girls would be raging at me for leaving abruptly. Hell, even Sam didn't like how short I got with them. Lexie is acting normal. Like it was no big deal that I vanished and haven't called her since.

We were both drunk. Part of me hoped she was drunk enough not to remember what we did. But the fact that she is comfy on my sheets makes me think otherwise.

I crave the way she feels. That touch I had of her body has driven me mad ever since I withdrew. I want nothing more than to jump on this bed right now and take her to the highest level of heaven there is.

But I won't. I can't.

Never again.

Grabbing a shirt, I walk to my couch. She follows, sitting too close. Just looking at her ignites my feelings. It's hard enough to shove the thoughts out of my head. Being here with her, it's impossible to ignore them.

"I've gotta know what's goin' on with you." She holds my attention for a long while. I feel heavy. Like I'm stuck in a pool of quicksand. No way out. Drowning. Swallowed whole.

"Lexie, I don't think I can be what you need, alright?" Every word makes my stomach churn that protein shake. Don't throw it up. Can't throw it up. Won't throw it up. Not with Lexie here. Not at all. Shit, I've gotta stop this shit.

"He's been gone more than a year." Her eyes are kind, but I sense her nerves. She doesn't know how I'm going to take her words. Based on our previous encounters, I don't have a record for being smooth or understanding. Or anything other than a walking, talking, over-reaction.

"I know."

"I know that you know." She takes my hands in hers and it's familiar and warm. Like coming home. "Bobby, I didn't see you then. Back when we were in junior high or high school, or any of those times we hung out. But I see you now. And I don't know everythin' goin' on inside of you, but I want to know. Ever since the other night–"

"The other night never should've happened." I shake my head, pulling my hands from hers.

"Who says?"

"Me."

"Well open your goddamn eyes because I don't see anythin' wrong with what happened."

I raise my eyebrows waiting for her to drop some joke. To take it all back. Because it was a mistake. The longer I look at her, the more I'm surprised. Because this is no joke. She means it. My thoughts gloss over what she just said. *"I don't see anythin' wrong with what happened."* New awareness dawns in my soul.

"You don't?" This feels more like a dream than what is actually taking place in my living room. Staring at that horrible part of carpet in front of my door, I hold my breath in my lungs.

"No." She shakes her head, bright red braid bouncing with each move. My mouth waters, wanting to watch that hair as I throw her onto my bed.

You're already in too deep, Bobby.

"Do you know what I think?" She leans in closer.

"What?" I clear my throat, all kinds of clogged up by her presence.

"That we all have our own versions of the truth. Two people can experience the same event and have a totally different truth." She sits a little straighter. "My truth is that I feel somethin' for you and even though it scares the fuck out of me, I want to know what we can be. Now." She holds her hands in mine. Those soft fingers send sizzles of electricity straight to my heart. "I need to know your truth."

Several seconds pass in the most excruciating silence. I leave her hands, running my fingers through damp hair and pulling tight. "Lex, I care about you enough to know that I can't be with you. I'll only make this worse. I'll drive deeper the heartache we both feel every hour of the day. I can't do that." The words make my throat ablaze, but they are my honest reality. Though I lie to some, she deserves the truth. My truth…I like that. "I care about you, okay?"

"Okay." She purses her lips and looks at me for a long time, as if she thinks I'll say more.

My heart is at war with my head. Her wanting me is the ending of so many of my fantasies. But I know this isn't what we need. I have to stay strong when all I want to do is scoop her in my arms and kiss her.

Please Lex, just know that this is the hardest favor I can give you. Because she doesn't need to be with me. I'm too broken to love her the way she deserves. I'll stay single forever if I need to. But I won't hurt her this way. I can't.

We get off the couch and go to the door.

"I'm hopin' sometime we can revisit this." She stands on her toes and kisses my freshly shaved cheek. A shiver works through me as she walks away.

Because all I can think is that I'm making a huge mistake by letting her go.

12

LEXIE

*P*reseason Physicals are the worst time of year, I swear. We've been getting ready all day, making sure the freshmen can take blood pressure and temperatures worth shit. Got tons of files, one for each team member of each sport. It's a fucking administrative nightmare.

Mindy gave us strict orders, and I'm going out of my way to do the best I can. I'll show her that I can do this. Things have still been awkward with her, and I hope it's just a stressful time or something. Why she is so upset, I may never know. But I want to fix it. I really do.

My eyes search the room for people I know, while there's only one person I want to find.

Bobby.

His name brings a warmth to my heart and that ache I've had, worrying I've lost him before anything really began. If I can talk to him again, I'll convince him he needs me. That I need him. That it would be okay with Cody, because why wouldn't it be? Cody was so protective of me. If there's anyone he'd trust me with, it's Bobby.

Continually scanning the room, a crushing reality sinks in the longer I'm here. We should've run into each other on campus by now, but we haven't.

Bobby doesn't want to be found.

He's the one that ran off when he thought we went too far. But he's the one who moved so fast. The one that wanted *something* with me. That sliver of faith is all I have to hold onto. Because fuck, I want to know what we could be.

Athletes wait impatiently in lines out the door. I wish we had more than one night to get through all the student athletes–the paperwork alone takes so much time. Even with every ATC and student working, we're understaffed.

"And the next set." Jae brings me a fresh stack of paperwork. "Two hours down, six more to go." It'll be at least midnight before any of us think about going home.

"Pizza!" Jessica yells, but I don't have time to look up.

The hours buzz by.

By the end of the night, my hand throbs from filling out so many forms. We clean up the training room, and I stuff a slice of cold pizza into my mouth before my insides gnaw a hole through my belly.

Jae and I walk to the parking lot and I give him a ride to his dorm across campus.

"This is the last year we have to run physicals as students." He smiles.

"Thank fuck." I roll my eyes. There's a heaviness in my chest, wondering if Bobby is avoiding me.

"You alright?" Jae's eyebrows wrinkle as my car idles outside his dorm.

"Did you see Bobby tonight?" My head leans against my headrest. This is the first time I've mentioned him to anyone in the department. "I kept wishin' I'd see him."

"Bobby, eh? He *is* nice looking."

"He's so much more than that." I kill the engine, knowing I need to talk and Jae is probably the only safe person, besides Charlene or Trish. Mickey has been avoiding me, and I think Bobby may be the reason.

Have I been reading everything wrong? Have I screwed everything up with Bobby and Mickey forever? Fuck, these guys are supposed to be my friends. I sigh, wondering what hope I'm holding on to. Bobby and I got drunk and made out. He's clearly moved on and I'm an idiot to think anything more of that night. He's always been a player. I just thought maybe with me, it was different.

"Do you think I'm stupid?" I sigh, sinking into the seat, gripping the wheel 'til my knuckles blanche.

"Why would *you* be stupid, love?" He waits until I look at him. Jae always builds me up. Just a genuinely good human. "I can't imagine what you've been through. I really can't. But I don't think stupid is a word I'd ever use in reference to you."

A smile tugs at my lips. "You always make me feel better."

"Do you think Bobby wants to be with you?"

"I think he does, but I don't think he'll let himself."

"Sounds like Bobby, doesn't it?" He laughs, shaking his head.

"What would you do if you were me?" I need a glimpse of wisdom because all that runs through my head is crazy levels of doubt that I'm being stupid and that it's silly for me to hold onto any bit of hope. There isn't a more down-to-earth person than Jae. He's one of the best people I know, and that's why I can trust him with this. If only it weren't all so complicated.

"It's not like I've been lookin' for anythin'. I just wanted to come back here and finish school."

"And, I'm glad you did." He brushes his hair out of his face, readjusting his glasses.

"Me, too."

"If I were you, I'd wait and see if anything comes of it," he sighs. "Bobby's been through a lot, too."

"I know." My mouth is hot while I spend a moment trying to breathe. How is it that I am still hoping? Thinking about him soothes me, fills my being. He's worth waiting for and fighting for, and worth whatever it takes just to know if we can ever be *more.*

An ache spreads through my chest as I realize how much I miss him. He's become a home to me, filling that hollow void inside of me that no one has been able to touch since Cody died. It's changed everything about how I feel, given me comfort to know that I'm not alone.

Even though I haven't seen him, I've drawn from his strength, and it's helped me be in Suncastle, helped me make it through one more day and then do it all again and again until maybe one day it won't hurt so much.

"Maybe you need each other." Jae's hand is on mine, a smile on his lips. "I wouldn't be hard on either one of you, though. The road you walk upon is not one anyone would ever desire."

His words ring true, and I swallow the knot in my throat.

"You'll figure it out though, my dear. I've no doubt of that." He clicks open the door and goes to his dorm. I feel a little lighter as I drive home.

My pictures with Cody hang on every wall in the beach house. One day soon, I'm going to make this beach house my own. If I have to live here, it's time to make some room for new memories. I'll never forget Cody, and as hard as it is to trust myself that I won't, it's time to move forward.

"You need a place that can be yours." Bobby couldn't have been more right.

It's time for me to live, instead of pretend I'm dead. Only a part of me died with Cody, not all of me. I can't waste the life I still have left.

I don't know everything, but I know that.

Cody would want me to move on.

It's time.

13

BOBBY
NOVEMBER

*G*rief won't leave me the fuck alone.

I'm depressed constantly.

Sitting in class, my head pounds. I left my backpack in the training room. Shit. I'm so out of it today. *Get in the game, Bobby.*

If I thought things got bad when Lexie first came back to Suncastle, it's a million times worse now. I'm avoiding her to keep myself away. But this doesn't feel right, either. I am so lost I don't know which way is up.

I toss and turn all night, battling nightmares or insomnia. Or both. By the time I fall asleep, it's way later than it should be. But I can't seem to keep my eyes open when my alarm clock goes off. Can't seem to get out of bed.

It's never been this bad.

Sleeping through my first few classes every day. Not even running with Briar in the mornings. My grades aren't slipping yet, but they will be if I don't watch it. I've got piles of assignments due.

Feeling this way is shit. Stuck in the past and afraid of the future. I'm sinking low and don't know how to get help.

I need my best friend.

God, are you listenin'? Cause I swear you made a mistake with this one. Just go back and make that car wreck not happen, would ya? Please? I don't ask for much. But could you do that? Please? Maybe? Or just help me figure out some fuckin' way to cope with it all?

No peace comes. No answer. It's just me. Alone.

"Promise me you'll take better care of yourself." Sam's plea to me from the last time I saw them haunts me. They knew the direction I was heading, even then. I'm on a slippery slope, like sliding to home plate in a rainstorm. There's no way to get through this without getting covered in mud.

I miss Cody. I miss Sam. I miss Mick actually being my goddamn friend and roommate instead of treating me like I'm the reason for all his misery.

I miss Lexie most. I feel completely alone.

Class ends. I walk into the athletic building and fill up my water bottle. This will tide me over until I decide to eat. Not that I deserve any food. I don't deserve to take care of myself.

I change into my uniform, some of the guys coming and going from their lockers.

"Bobby!" Zac greets me when I walk in the waiting area for team photos. He's a first baseman and a good friend. Mick doesn't look up, even though he's sitting next to Zac. God, I wish I knew what the fuck was going on between us.

"Hey." I nod.

Most of the guys are horsing around. Some glued to their phones.

"Haven't seen you much," Zac says. "Whatchu been up to?"

"Been busy. Classes and shit." Nausea bubbles up my throat, competing with my headache for attention.

"Oh, that's right. You're takin' a million credit hours." Zac crosses his arms.

"Tryin' to graduate." I narrow my eyes, feeling unusually defensive.

"I don't get that, though. Somebody's gonna draft ya. What's the point? I mean some of us need that backup plan, but not you." Zac nudges my shoulder.

"The point is I'm four and a half years into an engineering degree and one bad injury could ruin my career. It's somethin' to fall back on."

"Why'd an injury mess you up? That doesn't sound like you. Your elbow was fine. You're the star of this team. Someone is gonna pick you up. Maybe drop some classes and come hang out with us more."

"I still hang out." I stretch my neck, rubbing at the tight muscles, trying to get some relief from this goddamn headache.

Conrad and Dexter walk past us. I overhear them coordinating plans. They both have wives and babies about the same age so they get together on the weekends.

"I know you do. Just looks like you're workin' yourself too much. Maybe you need a break or somethin'. You certainly don't need an engineering degree as much as you think." Zac shakes his head.

"Quit givin' me shit, alright? You just never know." Jeez, do I feel like hell-warmed-over. Maybe Zac is right. I'm working too hard.

I should've stopped sooner at the gym. Didn't want to. Pumping iron offered some distraction from the oppressive black cloud hanging over me. So I did a double workout before class. Then I didn't eat after. Haven't eaten much all week. Again. This is happening too much. I feel awful. But it's nothing. I'll get through it. I always do.

Briar walks in and we nod at each other. I'm glad he's been cool about me ditching him for the morning runs. I don't think I could handle more drama right now.

"You wanna go to the field after this?" Zac offers. "Maybe it'd be good to toss the old ball around."

"I got a shit ton of studyin' to do. Maybe Sunday?"

"Yeah, okay."

I sit on the arm of the old couch beside Mick. He looks worse than I feel with dark circles under his eyes.

"What's the matter? You fail McGibbon's test again?" I knock his shoulder.

"Lay off." His tone is harsh. He struggles with school, so that's probably the last thing I should say. Batting a thousand.

"God. Take a joke already."

He's pissed. Gets off the couch. I sit where he was, massaging my temples. We've been roommates since freshman year. Never been like this. I don't know what the hell is wrong. Not that I've been much company.

"What's up with him?" Zac's gaze follows Mick across the room where he sulks in the corner, crouched on his ankles.

"Haven't a clue." I roll my eyes. "Speakin' of hangin' out, what're you doin' tomorrow night?"

"The Splat."

My mouth waters thinking about it.

Dennis and Ethan crowd next to our couch, laughing about some shit.

"You're welcome to join. I think Mickey's comin' if he doesn't still hate you." Zac looks at Mick sulking in the corner. Jeez, Mick's making it so obvious to the whole team.

"I'll think about it."

The door to the gym opens. A bunch of people come out. My vision is so hazy I don't notice what team it was.

The guys start heading in. I stand from the couch. The room fades in and out, then goes completely dark. For several seconds, I can't see my hand in front of my face. Fuck.

"You alright, man?" Briar grabs my elbow as I sway.

Forcing a breath, I blink it out. "Just stood up too fast." I shrug. "Thanks."

He appraises my statement for a moment. "You sure you're okay?"

"Yep." I plaster on my brightest smile and open the door for us.

"Cool." He nods.

I take my place for the photo, feeling sicker by the moment. Just a little longer.

After I change out of my uniform, I sit on the locker room bench for several heartbeats. I'm not okay. Just need to get home.

I stumble into the training room, to retrieve my backpack from Mindy's office. My knuckles drum the frame by the door.

"Oh, hey, Bobby. Come on in." She pulls her long brown hair out of her face.

I take a seat in one of the empty office chairs. Feel like I'm gonna fucking pass out.

"How were pictures?" Mindy sips her coffee, turning her chair away from her computer to give me full attention.

"Good. Just came for my backpack. Is it here?" I lick my dry lips, clearing my throat.

"Oh yeah, Jessica saw it in the exam room after y'all were all hangin' out this mornin'." She holds out my backpack. I stand to get it. The world turns dark. I grip the chair to keep from falling over.

"Ho, there." She holds my shoulders and after a second lowers me into the chair. "What's wrong?" Her eyes look me over, scanning for symptoms.

"I'm fine."

"Don't look fine." Mindy always knows when something's up. I mean, it's her job, but she's damn good at it.

"Just a blackout." I shrug.

"How long you been blackin' out?" She gives me a serious look. Shit. I've said too much already. Shit. Shit. Shit. She can't know about this. But how am I supposed to get out of it now? Goddamnit.

"Just today. I got a headache. Haven't been sleepin' well this week." A weight settles in the room. The frustration eats away at me the longer I look at her concerned expression. I'm so fucking sick of it. Sick of not taking care of myself.

"Headache, not sleepin'." She lists off what I said. "What have you had to eat in the last few hours?" And there it is. The question, clear as day, that I can't answer.

I stay silent, wishing I had the strength to come up with a lie. But I don't. It's gone too far. I do need her help. Fuck. I don't want to need her help. I don't want to do this at all.

She looks at her watch. "Did you have lunch? Breakfast?"

Nothing. Jeez, why can't I think of some excuse?

"How long you not been eatin'?" Her eyes hold mine for several heartbeats.

Balling fists at my side, I clench my teeth. I swallow hard. Wish I was better at lying. Wish my brain wasn't as starved as my body, then I could come up with a good reason to calm the fear I see in her eyes. Wish this wasn't happening at all.

Mindy has done everything since my first day at Suncastle College. Gone above and beyond to take care of me. I can't lie to her. I just can't. "I gotta go."

"No, Bobby."

Feels like getting caught. Like I'm in trouble. But it's all in my head. Mindy would never scold me for anything. Not even this.

Her eyes hold mine. "Somethin's goin' on. If you're not eatin', we need to talk about it, okay? Can you tell me?"

My throat closes up on itself. I feel worse the longer I sit here. Like a lost little boy. Fucking shit. I've done it now.

She goes to a little cabinet and pulls out some fruit snacks and a protein bar, then to the little fridge for a Gatorade. It's not sugar-free. None of this is sugar-free. I can't have it.

"How long since you've eaten?" She asks again.

"Um…" I rub my forehead with my thumb and forefinger. "I'm not sure." Wrong answer. Batting a thousand, again.

"Does this happen a lot?" She sets the food on the desk in front of me. "Whatever it is, you can tell me. I'm here to help."

I'm looking at the ground. If there's a feeling stronger than embarrassment, that's where I'm at. Senior year. Still not over it. Won't ever get over it. Won't ever be good enough for Lexie. Or a draft. Or anything. Not good enough for anything.

"Hey, now." She pulls my chin up. "We'll figure this out, alright?"

"I don't know how." I squint my eyes tight, rubbing my eyebrows. Can't believe I'm telling her this. The pounding in my head won't stop. The torment won't stop. So out of control. I try to imagine a black abyss and focus on a baseball. But it's like it's gone. Like I can't reach the deep cleansing breaths. Or meditation. Or any of those things that usually help.

The foil crinkles while she tears open the fruit snacks. "Here."

"Can't have 'em."

Her face is concerned. I've crossed a line and she knows it. She holds out one fruit snack. "Come on, let's start here."

One. I can eat one. Start with one. My finger trembles while I put it in my mouth.

"When was your last good meal?"

I strain to remember. "Sunday...?" Sounds terrible. "I've snacked though," I add quickly. Not totally starving myself. Just skating that line a little too close. "I'm eatin', okay? I'm eatin'."

"But you haven't had a meal since Sunday." Standing at the file cabinet, she pulls my medical chart. I suck on the fruit snack. Takes all my power to keep it in my mouth. I can eat one fruit snack. I have to. She won't let me leave until I do.

I can throw it up later.

My stomach knots with how heavy this moment is. I don't wanna do that. I don't wanna be like this anymore.

I'm sick of the fight. The constant battle in my head. Being in such a dark place.

My heart drops to my stomach. I was thin before the semester started. So thin that Sam noticed. Now, well, now I'm dwindling into nothing.

"Hey." She puts her hand on my shoulder. "We can get you some help."

I open my eyes, worried about what the *help* might look like.

"I've seen you low before, Bobby. But not this low." Her face is serious.

"I'm just stressed."

"You're stressed, have stopped eating and it looks like you're droppin' weight." Her eyes linger on my body. Pants falling down. Hoodie fitting loose.

A couple people come and go from the exam room behind us. I turn in my chair, throwing my hoodie over my head, not wanting them to see me.

"Now that I'm aware, we are gonna put a plan together." She glances at her watch. "Dr. Brown will be here soon for Thursday night visits. We need to have him do a checkup and make sure everything's okay. He'll probably send you to the lab for some bloodwork. You can wait here until it's time. I'll order in some food for when you're finished with this." She gestures to the snacks. "Am I gettin' you a salad or a smoothie?"

"I have food at home." I lick the sugar off my teeth, disgusted this is happening.

"Smoothie or salad?"

I close my eyes. "Salad."

"Okay." She calls in a takeout order from the campus cafe and sends one of her students to go pick it up.

"So sometimes you're not eatin'. This been goin' on for a while?" She's given me a few minutes to swallow these snacks. I don't want to talk about it, but I know she will keep asking.

I shiver, biting my chapped lip until it hurts. "Yeah."

"Laxatives? Weight loss pills? Diuretics? Excessive workouts?"

"No. I just don't eat. And sometimes I purge." I sigh, this is so goddamn heavy. I wasn't supposed to let this all slip out. Been keeping it a secret for years.

Why tell her now?

But shit, I have to tell her since I've opened my stupid mouth. "Mostly, it's just the starvin'. But if I do eat, I'll heave it up. I'll double up on workouts. Goes on for a few weeks, then I snap out of it. Just takin' a long time to snap out of it right now." I fold my arms over the desk and rest my head on them. "This sounds horrible outloud."

"We are gonna get you some help." Her hand is on my shoulder. A moment later, Mindy rummages through her drawer until she fetches a business card.

My stomach drops as I read the words on the card. The fruit snack makes me choke as it goes down wrong. *Dr. Simon Rogers, Psy. D.*

She's sending me to the team psychologist. The letters fade as I stare at the black ink against the white card.

"I think Dr. Rogers will be a good fit. If he's not, we can try someone else. You want me to make an appointment for you?"

"I got it." I close my eyes, clenching my jaw tighter. The air in this room suffocates me. It's that feeling of impending doom mixing with low blood sugar and dehydration. The only reason I will agree to go is because I need to play this season. I need to prove that I deserve to be drafted.

"It's okay to need help." Her hand rests on my shoulder again, her tone kind. "We all need help sometimes."

"You're not gonna tell Coach about this, are you?" My mouth feels covered in sand. Senior year. My last season of collegiate baseball. The last chance I have to get drafted out of school. If he thinks something's up, I won't play as much. I know it. *Oh, we can't have Bobby out there when he's not taking care of himself.* I can hear it now.

I thought I was over this. Disappointment covers me like a cloak; I want to use it to disappear, but I can't.

"Everything we talk about is confidential, but I think it's a good idea for you to let Coach Conners and Coach Denson know about this."

I swallow. Shit. No way am I telling them.

"They care about you a lot. It would help to make them aware of what you're going through." Her smile is kind. "Have you talked to your parents at all?"

"They are barely talkin' to me." I grind my teeth. Is this "tell Mindy every goddamn thing" day? May as well tell her I'm bi. Jeez.

"I would see if you can let them know."

"No," I sigh. "My dad's a fuckin' heart surgeon, Mindy. He's not gonna handle this well. You and I both know. That's enough."

"I hope you think about it. There are people in your life that can help support you." She tilts her head to the snacks, wanting me to finish before the salad arrives. I've still only eaten maybe three.

She pretends to be busy, watching from the corner of her eye. Like I can't be trusted to be alone.

"You gonna make the appointment, or you want me to?"

Has it really come to this?

A student brings Mindy my bag of takeout and then leaves. I force down the food and rest my head on the desk for a few minutes, each heartbeat pounding against my temples.

The team doc comes and gives me a checkup. Orders a fuck ton of bloodwork. He and Mindy talk about next steps. Nutritionist. Food plan. Accountability. Weekly visits with the team psychologist. Weekly visits with team doc. Weekly visits I'll have to fit into my schedule. A written contract that promises I'll comply.

"I don't have time for this. I'm taking so many credit hours. Working out so much. I don't have time for all these appointments. It's almost the season," I tell Mindy, but it sounds like a little boy throwing a fit.

"I know it's a big commitment, but we have to get you healthy again so you can play. Just like we did with your elbow."

"This is not the same thing." I lick my teeth, fucking sugar covering them.

"It's important, Bobby. I can help. We'll lump the appointments together as much as possible so that you have time for classes and everything. I don't want you working out as much until we get you through some of this."

I agree because I don't have much of a choice if I wanna keep playing.

Apprehension works through me; I worry that Lexie could walk in on me like this. I still haven't called her. Haven't gone to visit her. All I've done is left her out to dry like yesterday's laundry. She deserves so much more than that.

"You wanna let some of that stress out?" Mindy closes a folder she put together with all my appointment information and some printouts on nutrition.

"No." I pull my backpack over my shoulder.

"You'll eat again when you get home?"

"Yeah." I blow air out of clenched teeth.

————

AT THE APARTMENT, I POP SOME TYLENOL AND SLEEP FOR A COUPLE hours. A reminder text appears on my phone to eat. I mix a protein shake. I'd love the peaches in the freezer or a piece of toast with jam on it.

Peaches from our tree.

No. I don't get to have that. Just the shake. Only the shake. It's not much, but I think I can handle it. Maybe. *Please, just let me. Fuck. Just let me.*

My chest is heavy as I swish my blender bottle and go on my couch, forcing one torturous sip after another down my throat.

Mick isn't here. The asshole is never here. Wish I wasn't alone right now. Probably shouldn't be. Thoughts are getting darker. So dark I'm frightened. Need someone to help. Briar's parking in front of the complex. I see him from the window. He'd come over. I can call him.

No. I rub my forehead, debating more pain pills. Probably won't feel good if I puke them up, though. No more pain pills. Just the shake.

Wanna call Lexie. Her number is pulled up on my phone. No matter how much I want to, I can't bring myself to press the button.

The desire to heave up everything takes over. Sugar. Can't have the sugar. Can't have the calories. That salad from Mindy was drenched in dressing. I go into my bathroom and kneel in front of the toilet. My finger goes down my throat, the same way it has countless times before.

What would Lexie say if she watched me do this?

My mind is a freefall, tunneling into oblivion. I couldn't do this in front of her. If I ever want to be with her, I can't. This has to quit.

She'd tell me to stop. Even though she's not here, I feel her support. *"Don't do this Bobby."* It's like I can hear her voice. Like she's right here with me.

That thought is my saving grace. She is my saving grace.

My arm braces the toilet seat. I rest my throbbing head on top of it. Hot tears fall into the bowl, instead of the sugar and calories that wanna come up. My traumatized mind wants them to come up. I can't have them. It's not cheat day. I can't have sugar and calories when it's not cheat day. I've gotta get rid of them.

"No. Don't do this, Bobby." Sam's voice. Lexie's voice. Dad's voice.

Cody's voice.

They don't want me to keep hurting myself. Fuck....

I can't do this anymore.

I won't.

I can't.

Not right now.

Not today.

Mindy can help. She made me see the doctor and is sending me to the psychologist.

Memories of the first time I gagged myself come to my mind. Cody's birthday, right after he started dating Lex. Lots of treats. Too much sugar. Too many calories. He came to check on me. I faked a stomach flu. It was so easy. Shoulda faked one with Mindy today.

Shit, I wish I never started.

I splash water on my face and go lay down, though I have tons of assignments to finish. On my nightstand is Cody's journal. The one he gave me a long time ago. My eyes find the page that I read most. Wish it made me feel better, instead of worse.

My phone buzzes in my pocket. I want it to be Lexie. It's Mindy, asking if I ate.

Me: Just had a protein shake.

Mindy: Good. I'll check in tomorrow morning. You got this.

Gripping my knees to my chest, I wonder if she's right. Can I get this under control? In a way that it doesn't just keep coming back when my life goes to shit?

Soon, I need to talk to Lexie. I don't know when or how, but I need to. Keeping my dinner down tonight is the first step.

14

LEXIE

"*Y*ou're doing the right thing." Trish holds a box on her hip. Her light brown hair rests on her shoulders under her black fedora. Red lipstick and lots of eyeliner accent her features.

"It doesn't feel right."

"I know, but it is." Her half smile gives me courage to close the last box. Everything is changing and I wish I knew how to feel.

We repainted the hallway blue and all the pictures are down. If I have to stay here, all of this belongs in a box–not because I don't want to remember him, but because every photo stirs up my insides.

It's hard to do this, but I need to.

"You have to do what you need. Because you are the one that's still alive." My counselor's voice plays, reminding me of the coping skills I learned right after Cody's death. I don't find that comforting, at least not yet, but I'm trying.

"We puttin' all of this upstairs?" Trish wraps up another of the canvas prints, nestling it safely in a plastic bin.

"Maybe I should give some of these pictures to his mom, or maybe some of his old stuff. How much would she want?"

Trish considers my question. "I don't know, Lex. Their place is so small it doesn't have room for the stuff they have."

"Do you ever see them?"

"Yeah, sometimes." Trish lives in the apartments pretty close to Cody's parent's place. "Mama Jones goes on walks down Holland Road while I'm drivin' and I'll catch her at Publix."

"She still workin' there?"

"Yeah and at Shakey's."

I'm not surprised she's still working two jobs. They barely made ends meet before, and the kids are only bigger now. "Man, I miss their strawberry banana shake."

Trish points at the air. "And the onion rings."

"I never thought we wouldn't talk." My saliva is thick as I look at the canvas print in my hands.

"I'd be surprised if I was you, too. Y'all seemed real close."

"Thought she was the mom I never had but I couldn't have been more wrong. Maybe it just hurts too much to talk to me when she can never talk to Cody. I don't know."

The ache in my heart that happened the moment I heard about the accident grows with things like this. Lack of closure burns at my soul like eroding acid.

"Let's go to Kohl's and get you some new decor." Trish carries the last box to my bedroom closet where we're storing everything until I can think of a better place. "Then let's get pizza."

"Okay." I check my wallet to make sure I have my credit card. Dad pays the balance, no matter what I put on it. It's a nice thing that I bet will stop after I finish school. He's been more than kind about putting me through college.

We get to Kohl's and it feels good to be somewhere like this, not on campus where I live and breathe.

"Home stuff is in the back."

"I know that." I shake my head while she leads the way through the women's clothing and the baby toys.

In homewares, a wall of towels invites me to buy them. "I dunno what I want." The decisions perplex me, likely a result of my controlling mother. She made all the decisions growing up–everything big and small. How am I supposed to pick any goddamn thing for myself?

"That's what you have me for!" Trish picks out several nice pieces that go well together. We smell candles, throw around throw pillows and dance in the aisles when "Show Me the Meaning of Being Lonely" by The Backstreet Boys comes on.

"I've missed you, girl." My smile reaches my eyes, my artistic side reawakening. I haven't felt creative since, well, since he died.

"Course you have, sweetheart." She pops her bubblegum bubble like it's still as cool as when we were ten.

"Maybe somethin' like this." I hold up a soft throw blanket.

"Would look good with your big butterfly painting. You know, the blue one? We can put it on the front wall and have these on the table." She examines a large maroon vase.

My stomach drops. "Am I really replacing all of our stuff?"

Replacing *him*?

"I know it's hard." Trish puts her arms around my shoulders. "I miss him too." The air feels cold, and I shiver. Keep going, keep moving, get through this.

"How're classes going?" Trish offers a blessed change of subject.

"Going a'right. I help out in the trainin' room a lot, giving tips to the freshmen, waiting for baseball to start up. I'm thrilled for this season."

"Um, duh. You've always been a cleat chaser." She winks.

"Yeah, and well, I guess I'm doin' it again." Nerves riddle my system as I recall the horrible dance that is Bobby and me at the moment. Trish may or may not approve.

"No shit." She wrinkles her eyebrow. "That new kid? The one that's supposed to start as shortstop? Or Zac? He's lookin' real good this year. Ugh, I need to experience his home run," her eyes turn dreamy, "but I'll stay far away if he's the one you're after." Trish may be done with school, but she keeps up with the players.

"No, um, I don't know how to tell you this." I tap my foot against the cart wheel.

"Well spit it out girl. Who is it?" She holds a pillow that would look good with the throw blanket in the cart.

"Bobby."

She drops the pillow to the floor and chokes on her bubble gum. "Wait, wait, wait. Let me get this straight. Bobby–third fuckin' baseman, used to be Cody's best friend–Anderson? That Bobby?"

"He's the one."

"The one." Her eyes are wide, holding mine like she's waiting for me to correct her. "No shit?"

"No shit." I'll ease into it, because she may be pissed that I didn't call and tell her every goddamn bit of it before. "Remember when Bobby and I made out."

"You said you were drunk." She references our texting convo.

"Well we may have started out that way, but I think there's more." My stomach flutters.

"Well spill woman, have you, uh, you know?" She winks. "Bobby is good at that sorta thing, so I've heard."

"No." I bring my fingers to my lips, trying to ignore the judgement she may have if I am just hooking up with him. "Well, almost, I mean. The night we were drunk, we coulda." When I think about that night with the wine, my body tingles, remembering the feel of his fingers.

"Why on earth didn't you? Because that boy is f-iiii-neee." She drags out every letter and I relax a bit, realizing she isn't totally against the idea of me crushing on him.

"Bobby? The one that was always as obnoxious as fuck when he wasn't just a quiet wallflower. You think he's f-iii-nnnnnneeeee?" I overemphasize her overemphasis.

"Girl, you and I both know he was never *that* obnoxious, and that he has grown up to be someone you'd find on the cover of a magazine. He looks as good as Zac Efron. And I don't mean cheesy Troy Boulton from *High School Musical* Zac Efron. I mean Teddy from *Neighbors* Zac Efron."

I'm pulled into a daydream. His perfect skin, perfect bod, perfect smile. "Yeah, I can see a little bit of Zac Efron."

"Somebody call the swoon police. Jesus Christ, are you drenched where you stand?" She chuckles while I shake my head.

"Damn, girl, why didn't you tell me sooner?"

"Well, we aren't anythin'." I put the pillow in our shopping cart and head toward the front of the store.

"Honey, I'm sorry. You two would've been cute together." She shrugs. "But Bobby is just the king of casual sex. He has a higher hookup percentage than his batting average."

"No, I don't think he was looking for a hookup." I pull my lips in a line.

"Of course he was. You know Bobby. He's only in it for the moment. I don't think he's ever had a girlfriend. Ask anyone we went to high school with. Want me to call them up?" Trish pulls out her phone. "Sue Taraway, Vanessa Hodge, Anna Smith. The list goes on and on...."

"I don't care who he hooked up with in high school. Cody told me stuff that made me think Bobby was gay. Maybe those girls were just him figurin' things out. Who knows?"

"Oh, I don't think he's gay." She waves her hand like she's clearing the idea out of the air. "But I'm not just talkin' about high school. What about every Friday night at Garrison's? The man keeps condoms in his wallet *and* his glove box. He's not serious with anyone. I doubt he's capable of really bein' with you for more than a night or two. Well, maybe three. I think Vanessa said she had three different hookups with him. Was always runnin' her mouth about how good he was in the back of his truck. Jesus she doesn't ever stop talkin'. Bobby does a fine job of lettin' his reputation get around."

My face heats up while I dig my nails into my hand, sorry I even brought it up. Trish is ticking me off with how shallow she thinks Bobby is. I bite my lip to keep from yelling at her.

"I mean, if you wanna ride his disco stick, go ahead. Enjoy yourself." She puts her hands on my shoulder while we wait in the checkout line. "But please, honey, don't get too attached."

Too late for that.

I force a breath, working to relax. Trish has my best interests at heart, and I know she wants to look out for me.

"Tons of people sleep around in college. I don't think he's gonna be like that forever." I'm not sure why I'm defending his behavior, but I'm not okay with Trish thinking less of Bobby. I need to help her see that he's more than just a shallow player.

"To be fair, I haven't talked to him much since I left Suncastle." Trish puts the items on the counter while I pull out my credit card.

Maybe Bobby has never been in a relationship because he hasn't found the right one yet, not because he isn't capable or doesn't want to.

I could be the right one.

I flick hair out of my face and pluck the electronic pen from the card reader, signing for the total. This is silly. I'm just fooling myself. Everything Trish has said *is* true. It's no secret Bobby has had many more one-night-stands than grand slams.

A bit of longing pulls at me. If he wanted to just hook up he wouldn't have slept on the couch when I stayed at his place and he wouldn't have stopped finger fucking me just because we were drunk and he was thinking about Cody.

"But what if he is wanting somethin' with me?" I look to Trish as we load up her car, not sure what she will say or if I will agree.

"Then let me reiterate, that boy is f-iiii-neee. If he wants somethin' with you then good for you girl." She applauds, but it's more like she's patronizing me. "But, he *is* a player and you need to keep that in mind."

"I will…but we aren't even anythin'."

"Whadda mean you aren't anythin'?" Trish gets in the car. "You sound like you care about him an awful lot. How are y'all not an item? I am so confused."

"He ran the fuck away." I sigh. "He acted super interested, didn't seal the deal like we know is his normal course of action, and quit fuckin' talkin' to me."

Trish takes a moment to digest the information. "No shit?"

"Why do you keep sayin' that? Of course, 'no shit'. This is the real shit story, girl. I wish it was different, but it's the truth." My heart hurts a little more with each word. "Every day I hope I'll run into him. Campus isn't that big, and we run in the same circles. But I haven't seen him since that day when he was wearing nothin' but a towel."

"You saw him in nothin' but a towel?"

"Yeah, and then he dropped it."

"Wait, you saw Bobby Anderson *naked* already, but you haven't slammed him?" Her jaw drops. "God, woman, that's some self control. Definitely. He is sexy as fuck, I'm assumin' in all places?"

"Sexy as fuck. And duh, what kind of question is that?"

"So he ran away, then what?" Trish pops more gum in her mouth and chews until she can blow a bubble.

"Nothin'," I huff. "God, I wish he would talk to me."

Trish messes with the radio stations while we wait at a red light. "To be honest, I thought if you'd go out with anyone else from our little group, it would've been Mickey."

"Speakin' of Mickey, he's been nothin' but an ass. I try to talk to him all the time and he's always runnin' off without any real conversation." I am so frustrated with the way he won't even chat when I see him in class or around campus.

"Do you think he's jealous of Bobby?"

"No, somethin's up, but he won't tell me what." ...not that I haven't tried to get him to talk.

"I haven't talked to Mickey in a long time. But you don't have anythin' with Mickey?" Trish adjusts her hat.

"No. I didn't think I had anythin' with Bobby either, but here we are." I raise my hands up with a shrug.

"Yeah, here we are." Trish rubs her chin. "Well, why'd he run away?"

"He says he can't do this to Cody."

"Aw, how loyal," Trish smiles and I can tell she's *trying* to be supportive of me wanting to be with Bobby. "Gotta respect that guy code. Can't date your bro's fiancée."

"Somethin' like that." Only after my last fight with Cody, I doubt we would've stayed engaged. How was I supposed to know that we weren't really happy? That in some ways I'm glad he's not here.

Fuck. What am I thinking? That is so wrong. I shouldn't even think that way. I clench my nails into my palms, mad at myself for admitting this. It's something I've tried not to think about. Tried not to even get close to thinking. "I'm not happy he died, but I am happy we aren't together."

Trish hardcore stares at me.

I pinch my eyes shut and dig my nails deeper into my palms. "Fuck, I didn't mean to say that out loud."

She purses her lips. "Things weren't quite there for you, huh?"

"No," I whisper.

"You know, I figured as much."

I swallow what feels like acid burning my throat. "You did?"

"Have you tried tellin' that to B?"

My insides swirl like the wrong combination of paint that you can't quite get right no matter how hard you try. "I can't."

"Maybe if he knew what *really* happened with you and Codester then y'all can wash away the guy code and shit. Not that I agree with all that, anyway. I mean, it's definitely not the typical circumstance. Maybe if B knows you and Cody weren't the happily ever after everyone thought, it'll help him be okay with goin' out with you. And maybe you're right. Maybe he does want something more than a hookup with you."

"No. I can't. You're my bestie and I didn't even tell you about the half of it. How the fuck am I supposed to tell Bobby?" My head hurts thinking through all of this.

"Um, you have feelings for him. B deserves to at least know that, don't you think?" Trish stretches her neck.

"I can't." I swallow. "If Bobby wanted somethin' here we would already be doin' it."

Trish gives me that half smile that says *I have a lot of advice, but I'll spare my thoughts for now,* driving toward The Splat.

"The fact that our friend group all used to be inseparable and now hardly see each other gets to me." I press my head into the seat. "It's so hard to think you'll be friends with these people and then wake up one day to realize you rarely talk. Why does everythin' have to change?"

"I don't know, but you're right. After Cody died, it just hasn't been the same." Trish's tone is sad, adding to that ache in my chest that never goes away. "Cody meant so much to all of us. It's like our little group forgot how to be a group without him."

"He was the glue that held us all together." Guilt wraps tendrils around me for telling Trish that I'm happy without Cody. "I hoped if I never told anyone, then maybe it wasn't real–maybe it was all just in my head and I haven't been coping with the accident and that's why it all seems fucked up. Part of me has always wondered about us, even when we were boyfriend and girlfriend, even when we moved in together. I love him more than heaven and earth and everything in between, but I don't know if we were really meant to be together. Because one night with Bobby was filled with so much more than I ever knew was possible."

"Oh, fuck." Trish stares at me.

"What?"

"You're completely in love." Her words ring true, like even my heart knows it. "Okay, you *have* to tell B about Cody, or I'm gonna do it for you. Stop feelin' bad for how you feel, girl. It's okay that Cody wasn't your forever."

"Cody was always givin' me whiplash. We'd make out and go crazy and then he'd just stop and pull out all the *we have to stay pure* shit. I never knew what was goin' on between us."

"I'm not surprised that neither one of you had a clue." Trish rests her hand on my shoulder. "His family's intense about religion."

"They're intense about everythin'." I swallow the lump in my throat, remembering his whole existence was a dumpster fire and everyone in our small town knew it.

"And so was Cody." Trish's eyes are kind, and I wish I felt some of that compassion toward myself.

"And I loved that about him." Memories come in shreds of infinity pulling me toward all the happy moments we shared between the drama. "We chose to be together. I hate that I have so many regrets."

There will never be closure for what happened.

Trish parks at The Splat.

"I don't blame Cody, ya know," I force a breath, trying to explain what I never meant to say. "We were both so young. He'd never been with anyone before me, and you know I hadn't either."

"Honey, I'm not judgin' you at all. What happened in your relationship happens all the time to people. Yours just has a tragic ending." She squeezes my shoulder as we pull into a parking spot.

"I wish I could talk to him about this."

"That's the worst part, I think. You can't talk now, when you have so much to say."

"And I'll never be able to." Weight encapsulates my chest until I'm unable to breathe. Trish opens her car door and the chilly air hits my face.

Sharpie marker fills the brick walls, signatures covered over and over again, every college student making their mark on the walls. We order and sit in the corner. Basketball plays on the TV, because it's November.

November means I missed Bobby's birthday. Fuck, I meant to at least text him.

The cheese sticks come out. "I could live off these things."

"You practically do," Trish teases.

"Bobby bought me some my first night back."

"See, he's a sweetheart. Cody was the obnoxious one. I'm pretty sure the only time B was obnoxious was when Cody was egging him on." Trish is softening up to the idea now that she knows how I feel.

"Good point." I shake my head.

"Well, look what the cat dragged in. It may just be your lucky night, my love." Trish raises her eyebrow toward the front door. "Must be fate or somethin'." She smiles. "It's my lucky night, too. Zac is with him. Good thing I brought my big purse with all my hair stuff and a change of clothes." She winks.

I'm afraid to look. Oh fuck. I'm afraid to see if she's not just playing some cruel joke.

A shiver works through me as I hear *him*. No, it couldn't be. His laugh carries into my ear and my heart pounds.

Blood drains from my face, because fucking hell, he's here and I can only hope he doesn't keep avoiding me. The moment I hoped would happen–but had no clue when or how–it's here.

Mustering up all my courage, I risk a glance at the order line–I could be wrong–it could be anyone. Trish could be teasing.

But there's no mistaking that tall, shaggy haired baseball star who took my heart even if he didn't mean to.

Bobby is *here*.

15

BOBBY

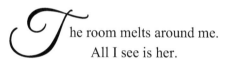he room melts around me.

All I see is her.

Lexie.

I want her to be mine so much I can't breathe. The time without her, knowing she offered us a chance to be together, has torn asunder my very soul. I don't know how to be what she deserves. This burden weighs down my every decision, knowing I must keep some level of valor in order to become someone she deserves.

All I feel is broken inside.

But you weren't broken, Cody. No matter what fuckin' happened to you, you weren't broken. One tragedy happens in my life, and I fall apart.

Cody had the kind of strength people dream about. He came from literally nothing and worked his ass off. Once he got out of that hell of his childhood home, he only got better at baseball. Everyone noticed. First, a full-ride scholarship; then, first-round draft pick for the Yankees promised at the end of season.

I force a breath through my rattling lungs. My heart pounds in my ears.

God, Cody. What would you do if you were me?

That tremor in reality comes. I feel Cody close. His energy is like a life source, taking the broken pieces inside of me and mending them. *"You're not as broken as you think,"* he seems to say through the void.

Lexie is here. Like a message. A sign. A symbol.

Do you want me to be with her?

My throat burns.

"Cheese sticks or no?" Mick shoves my shoulder. He must've already asked. I told him that I'm sick of the shit between us. Time to move on from whatever he's pissed about.

"Yeah, sure, whatever."

I leave twenty bucks in his hand and walk out of the line.

She's looking right at me. "Must be cheat day." Her voice is like a big fly winning the game.

"Hey, Bobby." Trish smiles.

"Oh, hey, Trish." I go around the table and give her a half hug. "It's been a while."

"Sit with us?" She looks at the two empty chairs at their table.

"Yeah, thanks."

Lexie is so perfect in front of me that I stumble into the chair opposite her. My memories go to that night. Feeling her skin. Her silky panties.

I swallow. This is exactly what I'm afraid of. I'm so fucking attracted to her. I need to stay away. I can't do this to us.

But, I want to. The look on her face tells me Lexie wants this, too.

"I'm gonna get some more lemonade," Trish excuses herself.

It's just us. Me and Lex. Her smile is even better than I remembered it. She looks so nice, like she's handling life alright. I hope so. I've been worried maybe I've made things worse for her. But it looks like she's taken it in stride. She's such a strong person. I'm constantly inspired by her. Always have been.

My hands burn, the memory of her skin beneath my fingers swallowing me. I can't handle the torment knowing I did that to her. To Cody. I shouldn't have given in to all that.

"You can have some pizza if you want." Lexie leans her elbows on the table and props her chin in her hands.

"Oh, thanks. Um, Zac's gettin' some." My eyes hold hers. Those sweet green eyes in the low light. Shit, have I missed her.

"How was your birthday?" she asks.

"My birthday?" I forgot about it. That's a first. Looking at my phone screen, I see the date. Mom forgot about it too. My stomach drops. I know she's been really busy with Mrs. Harris, but this is the first time she hasn't come to Suncastle for a fun birthday dinner. That isn't like her. I pick at my nails, wondering if Mom is okay. She said they'd been busy, but that was months ago. It feels funny that I'm the one trying to get in touch with them when it's usually reversed.

I pull out my phone and text Mom.

Me: hey, mom.

Nothing. No response. Why is this starting to be the new normal?

"Did you do anythin' fun?" Lexie pulls me from my phone.

"Oh, yeah just studied all night on my birthday. I'm drowning in classes. Jeez, enough about me. How you been?" I ask her, trying to get out of my own head.

"Missin' you."

My heart sinks into my gut, a place with no return. I freefall through my feelings, sucking in a hard breath.

"Look, I've gotta be crazy about you or somethin' because even though you've been avoidin' me–"

"Avoidin' you?" I wrinkle my eyebrows, leaning closer.

"You gonna pretend we're *never* in the athletic buildin' at the same time?" She gives me an *I'm-calling-your-bullshit* glare and I chuckle.

"Okay, okay, but hey, I did tell you what I was thinkin' that day you came to my place." I look at her hands, close enough to touch.

"When are you gonna believe me that this," she points between the two of us, "would be okay with him?"

Her words scald a hole in my soul like a bullet came from her lips and shot straight through my heart.

"You need to heal and I think I can help."

I need her help.

But I don't deserve it.

I don't deserve her.

Not right now. I'm in a flare with my eating disorder. Mindy just found out about it for heaven's sake. Lexie's the last person I want to bring into this. I need some time to make myself better.

Lexie's hand comes to mine, rubbing shapes into my knuckles. A heart....

Her touch is like satin. Her essence soothes me. Her soul cares for me. I don't know how or why she gives a damn. But it's all over her face. It's all over her heart, the one she's drawing on my skin like she wants to give hers to me. Like maybe, in some ways, she already has.

"We can try this, ya know. Just see what it'd be like." Her smile is hopeful.

"I donno, Lex. I'm a mess right now." Breath hangs in my chest. My eyes instill every bit of my truth that I can.

"I dated Cody for years. I think I can handle a mess."

I laugh, because she's right. How is it that she sees anything good in me?

"I'm sayin' we'll never know a damn thing if we don't give it a try." Her face comes close to mine. I smell her sweet perfume. Like cinnamon apples or fall or home. "You wanna try?"

My heart leaps in my chest. Because as much as I'm not ready to go into this relationship, I know I want to. Maybe time isn't what I need.

Maybe she is.

I want to love her the best I can. Show her all of me, even my hidden and secret parts. Learn what she loves. Give her that.

Every last day of my fucking life.

But it's too much. I'm going to suffocate in my own disaster before I have a chance to learn all about hers.

16

LEXIE

I am on an emotional rollercoaster sitting at The Splat. One moment, I'm holding onto so much hope that he's wanting to talk. But then, it's like a light switch, feeling connected to him–then being shoved away. Cody did something like this and it always bothered me. But it's different here. I can tell that Bobby is fighting a battle in his head.

Instead of being annoyed, I'd like to help.

"I don't know, Lex. I want to, but–" He looks at the TV, the wall behind me, our hands. Opening his mouth, it's like he wants to say something but can't. He's withdrawn from this moment, like he's too deep in his own thoughts. I lean back in my chair, recovering from the shift.

That night at my house, I was convinced something was there, something I never knew before. That wonder and power struck me, and I haven't thought of much else.

Trish is right, I *am* in love with him.

But this isn't easy. He sat with us, so he *wants* to be here. I see something else in his eyes and I really want him to tell me what it is.

Why does something so beautiful have to be so difficult?

How am I *still* holding onto hope for this man? My heart scuttles in my chest the longer I stare, because fuck me, I cannot believe my eyes.

Tonight?

Here?

I guzzle more beer. "Want some?"

He takes a swig and fills a cup from the pitcher sitting on our table. I want to talk, to be with him, to fix his broken parts with the shattered pieces of my own.

Our hearts are both destroyed; we need each other to fix them.

Tell me what's on your mind. Tell me how long you've had a thing for me, Bobby.

I think back to the day of Cody's funeral, when Bobby held me and we both sobbed.

Did it start then? So soon after Cody's death? I don't know, but I remember him holding me. Sitting across from him at the table, I feel that same comfort–that same bit of soothing that his presence always provides, even when I'm confused.

Why does he soothe me?

Mickey pulls up a chair.

"Hey, shitface." I greet him while Zac sits between Mickey and Bobby.

"Shitface?" Mickey feigns pain in his chest.

"Oh yeah, I texted you ten times about study group." I roll my eyes.

"I don't always have my phone, you know that." He taps his knuckles on the table.

"Uh, huh. Convenient excuse." I shake my head.

I'm back to focusing on Bobby. He and Zac are carrying on about the game.

Trish disappeared, so I go to the bathroom to find her. "Why the fuck did you leave me out there with him?"

"You didn't want that?" Trish plays innocent, reapplying her lipstick. Her crush on Zac sent her in here to push up her push-up bra even more. "Thought maybe you could actually have a conversation if I gave y'all a minute." She pops her cherry red lips, turning in the mirror, giving herself a once-over. "I am havin' a good butt day. Look at this."

"You're always havin' a good butt day." I take her purse and fish out the clear lip gloss. "And about Bobby, I have no fuckin' clue."

Trish teases her hair with her finger nails, fluffing at the tall body of her curls. I look at the outlet on the sink seeing that she brought her curling iron with her.

"You want him."

I think about how I felt when I saw him, how much I've missed him. For weeks I've just wanted to talk, to figure out what is between us.

"I want him?" I smooth the lip gloss, looking at Trish in the mirror.

"I see the way you look at each other. Fuck, Lex. He's always looked at you like that, hasn't he?" Her words ring truer than I'm ready for. "Now that we're here, I am realizin' that he's always been lookin' at you. I think he's wanted to be with you for a long time."

The world spins around me. "You're not sayin' what I think you're sayin', are you?"

"Remember that night when Cody punched him?" She puts a grin on her face and nods until I catch up with all she's insinuating.

At prom, Bobby and I were dancing because Cody had stood me up–again–and Bobby didn't have a date. It was completely innocent, just dancing as friends. Cody had been having a bad day, and I thought he just lost his shit over nothing, because, well, he did that sort of thing quite often. Cody punched Bobby so hard that it made blood gush all down Bobby's tux. We went back to my place to get the stains out and they were laughing and joking like nothing had happened. Because, well, Cody lost his shit sometimes, and we all knew that. He never hurt me, but he'd throw punches at Bobby.

"Fuck." I close my eyes for several heartbeats. "I thought that Cody was just bein' a dick."

"He was." Trish puts on lotion, her unplugged curling iron cooling while we chat. "Typical intense Cody for ya."

God above, the boys will be gone from the table if we stay in here for her entire beauty routine.

"But what if *you* are what they were fightin' about?" Trish angles her head toward me.

I reach out for the counter, hoping to get a grip on reality. "You're tellin' me that all this time, there was somethin'?"

"Look, sweetheart, I dunno." She puts her purse on her shoulder. "But I saw how he was lookin' at you tonight, and it seems there's a lot goin' on here that you need to ask him about."

My throat burns when I realize how much I want this, how much I want *him,* how much I hope Trish is right about everything.

What are these feelings? I never in a million years planned to return to Suncastle and find Bobby, but here he is in front of me.

I understand that his soul is wounded, damaged, because I've felt my own destroyed soul every moment of every day since Cody passed. We can come together with our broken pieces.

Can two shattered halves make a whole? I hope so. I can be the one to give him redemption from the pain that rests within those mesmerizing blue eyes.

"I just know that everyone is clamorin' for his attention and seems you're the one who gets it." Trish pops her lips again. "So, I'd at least see what it could be."

"I don't know. He's so in his own world, like he's ignorin' me."

"Ignorin' you? Bullshit." Trish pins a little flower into her hair and stuffs her fedora into her purse. "He sat at *your* table. He'd glance at me, but it was *you* he was lookin' at. Not the TV. Not the guys. Not me. You, Lexie. Bobby Anderson was lookin' at you." She adjusts her shirt. "And I see what you were sayin' earlier. It does seem like there's more goin' on here than just the hookup."

My body is a mix of excitement and apprehension at her words. I think over the evening, how happy I am to see him. How he coulda just gotten take-out and left without another word. I know he's been avoiding me, but tonight he chose not to. I have to take advantage of this moment.

"You're right." I pull open the bathroom door.

"We were wonderin' if you locked yourself in there." Mickey

teases as we return to the table. "Was about to call the goddamn fire department."

Trish rolls her eyes at Mickey. "Some of us care what we look like."

"What's your name again?" Zac asks, falling perfectly into Trish's plan to win him over tonight.

"Trish." She extends her vanilla lotion covered hand to shake his.

As I take my seat, it's like Bobby's looking into my soul, and I feel a deeper connection, like I've never felt before. A yearning scorches through me like the time his tongue danced in my mouth. My legs swell beneath my hips, craving his touch, his body against mine. That glowing warmth fills my very being.

Let me in Bobby...let me show you what we can be.

The basketball game on television ends, and the guys cheer and Bobby is swept up in the energy of the guys cheering–laughing, making fun of the fumbled plays on the screen, and joking with each other.

I love seeing Bobby light up the crowd this way. He's funny, cracking joke after joke, making it hard for anyone to breathe because they're laughing so hard.

I remember the way his laugh echoed in my ears in my kitchen. How can my mind hold on to every detail of that night in perfect clarity?

If this were any other guy I'd be furious, not giving him a second thought–but it's not like that with Bobby. With Bobby it's real. His motives are as pure as fresh canvas ready to paint all that we can be. He isn't doing this to hurt me. He's doing it to protect me.

But I'm not the one that needs protection.

All at once, everything snaps into focus. I've wanted to help him through his pain, but he needs more than that. He needs me to protect him from his torment. *You don't have to carry this alone, Bobby. Not anymore. I'm here.*

His eyes meet mine and hold, like he senses every vibe I'm sending. He tilts his head toward the back door. As he gets up to go to the back of the restaurant, I follow him, without a second thought.

17

BOBBY

I'm sorry. I'm sorry for everythin'. I'm sorry for not trustin' you. For hurtin' you. I've hurt you so much. I'm sorry I'm not good enough to be with you. I'm sorry that I keep fuckin' up.

These thoughts have been on autoplay since I saw her last. Every time I've thought about her, I've wanted her. If only I could let myself.

When she walked away from the table, it became perfectly clear to me. I'm not in a place to let her go. My heart stopped beating when she left. My soul shattered. My being stalled in time and space. Like there was nothing left without her.

I need her.

No more being stubborn. No more being stupid. No more convincing myself this is a bad idea.

That tremor, that ripple in this world and the afterlife comes. *Twice in one night?* Cody wants me to be there for her. He does. He wants both of us to be happy.

You do, don'tcha?

Warmth spreads through me like his hug. *"'Course I do, ya idiot."* Memory of his voice makes me smile. *"Took you long enough to figure it out."*

I know, I know.

It feels so good I can't believe it. Maybe this is it. Maybe this is our chance. Maybe he's okay with us moving on. Why wouldn't he be? He loved us both.

Is this for real? I close my eyes, so much pressure behind my lids, stinging as tears fill but don't spill out.

"Love her right, Bobby. Take even better care of her than I did. I can't be there anymore, but you sure can."

I imagine his expression, a mix of teasing encouragement. He's the one that made me try harder. The one that made me push farther. The one who made me be more.

He's still making me live my dreams.

Lexie follows me to the end of the hallway, outside the exit. We stand in the cold air behind The Splat.

Her body is close. She looks amazing. I swallow, taking in the nearness of her. That perfect round nose kissed by the cold air, starting to speckle red like she has freckles. There's a longing in her eyes that fills me with all I never knew I needed.

"Can we talk?" I face her in the alleyway. "Can I say I'm sorry–" my words get cut off as her lips slam into mine, taking me fully and completely in a way that I've never been kissed. She presses into me. I think about all I've wanted. All I've kept us from.

I know here and now I won't be the reason we can't be together. Never again. I need her. She needs me. The kiss fills every part of my being. That tremor is replaced with the feeling of eternity. The moment of two souls in utter bliss. Not needing anything or anyone else.

Having each other.

18

LEXIE

*R*isking everything, I go for it. I go for him.

When he opens that sorry mouth, I shut him up because I don't care if he apologizes; all I care is he gives us a fucking chance.

The taste of his lips melt into mine, resisting at first and then unrestrained. The universe aligns, energy matches energy, desire fuses with desire.

He's kissing me back.

His body shakes as he grips me closer, pulling me against him, kissing harder. Our tongues collide while everything melts away until I'm in another dimension. The passion he plays baseball with erupts in my mouth. He's breathless as he edges back, cheeks pink, bright blue eyes shining in awe.

I wrap my arms around his neck, those toned shoulders welcoming my touch. "I think we need each other."

"I think you're fuckin' right." He kisses me long and slow, gripping my ass and bringing me close to his erection–already hard and wanting. My heart pounds against his chest as I lean into his grasp.

"And, I am sorry." He licks his lips. "That I keep tryin' to leave you alone." His hands shift and he lifts me up, bracing my back against the brick wall. My soaking center is against his abs, so fucking firm even through his clothes. One hand holds me up while the other pulls my hair, a messy wad in his strong hands, keeping my head close to his. "That I keep tryin' to stop thinkin' about you." He rubs his nose against mine, his lips working toward my ear until in a whisper, he says, "but baby, do you know what I'm not sorry for?"

My core tightens, ringing with unadulterated desire. "What?" I manage to gasp as he runs his tongue along the inside of my ear.

"What I'm about to do to you." The way he talks is so sexy I swear I'm on the cusp of orgasm. My body sags against him, warm and wanting. God, how does he do *this* to me? My heart is ecstatic that we're here, now, kissing, holding.

I want you so bad.

"Care to find out what that is?" His breath is hot against my ear.

A worker from The Splat comes out with an armload of garbage. Bobby lowers me to the ground and takes a step back, now that we have an audience. His rosy cheeks and the way he bites his lower lip makes my knees weak.

"Let's walk." Taking his hand, we go down the cobblestone alley, historic downtown, lit by street lamps. The air tickles my face and I shiver, goosebumps present as I withdraw from his warmth. In a fluid motion, his hoodie is off and wrapped around me.

"Thanks, Bobby."

"How'd you know?" He pauses to look at me.

"Know what?"

"That I wanted you?"

I shrug my shoulders. "Haven't thought about much else."

His thumb glides over my cheek, my body hungering for more of his touch. "But I shut you down. Didn't give you anythin' to hope for."

"You did." I shake my head in disagreement, my fingers squeezing his. "I felt it, Bobby."

"You felt it?"

"So strong." I don't know how much he's ready for, but that kiss still burns my lips, telling me I need to feel him. All of him. The thought sends fire between my legs, my lady vibrating in anticipation of when his fingers will caress me again.

"I was hopin' maybe we just needed some time." I look at those blue eyes. *Bobby.* I see him so perfectly in this light, in this ambiance.

"Let's get outta here." He tilts his head toward the parking lot.

"Go eat your pizza, then we can go back to my place."

"Alrighty."

We walk to the restaurant. He opens the door and we go to our seats.

We're met with inquisitive looks by everyone at the table, but I don't say a word. Neither does Bobby. His hoodie draped across me says enough.

Nothing to announce here, folks.

"We are studyin' for Myers' mid-term after this." Mickey looks frustrated about it. "You took his class, didn't you, Lexie?"

"Oh, yes, junior year." I remember the class pretty well.

"What do we need to know?" Mickey rubs his temples like thinking about school has him tense. When we were growing up, he always struggled to get passing grades. I was hoping college would be easier for him, but it doesn't look like it is.

"Myers mostly takes the exams from the slides. At least he did. I'm assuming that hasn't changed." I lick my lip, tasting the memory of Bobby against them. He captivated me so completely. Trish was absolutely right. I'm already in love with him.

"Do you have your old tests?" Mickey taps the table, trying to get my attention.

"Yeah." I jump out of my daydream.

"Can we come grab them?" Mickey's chin is dipped low, his eyebrows high.

"Sure." It wasn't what I was hoping to do tonight, but I'd like to help.

19

BOBBY

$\mathcal{G}$etting to her house, I stop frozen in the doorway. All the pictures are gone.

The crucifix is still on the entry wall. Cody's cross. The last trace of him in this hollow house. Instinctively, my hand finds my cross necklace tucked under my shirt. Cody gave it to me after getting his first paycheck from Publix. I told him not to. But he said I needed one. I didn't know then how much I'd need it. This physical part of him close to my heart.

How long has it been since I offered a prayer? We grew up very Christian, especially Cody's family. But I'm not sure where I stand with faith and all that. *You haven't given me much to believe in lately, God. Are you just teasin' me that I'm gonna have a perfect moment, just to lose it all again?*

The office is cleared out. Lexie is halfway down the hall.

"What are you gonna do with the office?" I ask, but she doesn't hear me because Mick has taken over this evening. I seriously want to slug him. He's acting like he's doing me some favor. Yeah, right.

My heart pounds in my chest—because for the first time, I'm free to be with my girl. To leave my kisses all over her sweet skin. And Zac and Mick are acting like it's any other Friday night. I wish I could kick them out without being obvious. Lexie didn't exactly publish our relationship to the world.

Slow down, Bobby. We are not in a relationship...

I don't know how any of this is going to go. Fast or slow. I've fucked up so much of it already. And she still wants to try.

"Nice place." Zac has never been here before.

"I've been helpin' Lexie redecorate. Seems you like my taste." Trish stands beside him, overtly flirting.

"Oh, I do." Zac's loving it.

We all stand around the kitchen, like old times.

"You got some brownies or anythin'?" Mick rummages through Lexie's cabinets and she joins him.

God, she looks beautiful getting out a bowl and some brownie mix. Her face lights up, like she likes entertaining.

I offer to help, but she shoos me away, so I sit on a barstool and watch her. Her black blouse is billowy at the top and fitted around her waist above adorable tight jeans. She's fucking gorgeous. Not a care in the world. Just being her.

I love *everythin'* about her. Being free from my own head makes this moment better than anything I've ever experienced. All that guilt is slowly being replaced by hope.

Eggs. Oil. Water. Mix. She glances at me and I smile, so in awe that I can't fucking move.

When the brownies are in the oven, Lexie heads toward the living room. "Now, about those notes."

I'm annoyed Mick is hijacking our evening, but it's so fun to see Lexie in her element, taking care of her friends.

She can't seem to find the papers, so she flusteredly goes back into the hallway. I follow her and she gasps, surprised I'm here.

"Fuck, don't sneak up on me like that."

"Whoops." A teasing smile goes wide on my face as I step up to her, soaking in her nearness.

I still her shaking breath. My mouth caresses hers and takes it all away.

"I don't want them here," she forces out, her green eyes making me all kinds of dizzy.

"Me neither." My lips find hers again, tasting her, filling every part of her with all that I have. All I am.

"Oh." Trish stands at the doorway. "Didn't mean to interrupt."

I step back from Lex and shove my hands in my pockets. But trying to stop now is like walking off the field in the middle of a game.

The fact Trish saw us kissing brings up all sorts of worry. I don't know if I'm ready for all this. My heart pounds as reality sinks in. I don't know what I need to do. I don't know if I'm ready to really dive into this.

But why wouldn't I be?

I sigh.

"Mickey says that a bunch of us are going over to Garrison's," Trish says.

"What happened to studyin'?" Lexie asks.

"Some girl texted him, and he's gonna meet her there." Trish shrugs. "It'll be fun. You deserve a night out. Wanna come?"

"Oh, um no." Lexie rocks from her heels to her toes. So damn cute.

"You can go." I swallow. "We can go." I correct, as quickly as possible. "Whatever you wanna do." My eyebrows rise, telling her I'm serious.

"Maybe next time." Lexie gives Trish a look. Trish takes the hint.

Before long, the house is ours.

Finally.

"I wanna get to know you better. Tell me, what's somethin' you hate?" I ask her.

"Bein' lied to."

"Oh? Thought you were gonna say cockroaches or some shit."

"You wanted stupid surface answers like we're on some datin' app?" She busts up laughing. Shit, I missed her laugh.

"You go as deep as you wanna go, darlin'." I wink.

"Well, then yes, that is the answer. Bein' lied to, or secrets bein' kept from me. I just really like honesty."

"Honesty is important." I smile, trying to ignore the queasiness in my gut. There are a lot of secrets I have. We will get to them in time, I hope.

"Okay, well, tell me somethin' you want me to know." She sits on her couch, brownies on her coffee table cooling off next to vanilla ice cream. Her legs are criss-crossed, toes tucked under her thighs. Our knees brush.

"I can't believe I'm here right now." I purse my lips, noticing how fucking adorable she looks. Hair frames her face. Full lips and high cheekbones. A sweet smile glistening in her green eyes. Like she's content. Like she wants to be here, with me. Like she's happy and that makes me happy.

"You can't?" Her chin drops and she teases me with an exasperated sigh.

"Not even a little bit." I watch her and wonder if I can tell her all that is on my mind. No, not tonight. Another time. Soon. But not tonight.

She leans closer to me. Her hand brushes against my cheek and I smile. "I'm so glad you're here, Bobby," she whispers against my lips. I edge closer, taking her in a warm and loving kiss. Her taste fills my tongue as we keep kissing. I bring her close, my chest against hers. She's so soft and warm. Little tingles erupt under my skin as I lose my breath to her.

She flips my cap off and grips my hair, driving me closer to her, like we can't get close enough.

"Remember what you did when we got drunk?" Her tone is so sexy I may die.

Warmth flares through my body. Unrestrained. Working another wave of tingles all over me. I wet my lips, hoping desperately that I won't do anything to fuck this up. Imagining that scene in her kitchen I've relived a thousand times, I lean in. "Oh, I remember." My breath tickles her nose as I bring my forehead to hers. For several moments our hearts rattle, chests so close I feel her strong heartbeat against mine.

"I want this. I want *us*. Do you?"

"I want it more than anythin'." I hold her eyes, begging her to believe my words. I mean them, more than I've ever meant anything before.

She moves from her place on the couch, straddling me. "I want you to do what you did that night, again." She is so hot. I can't believe my ears.

"God, you feel right." My breath heaves at her contact, every rush illuminating my soul.

How haven't I already fucked this up?

She takes my hand and guides me under her shirt to her lacy bralette. My fingers unhook the clasps at the back. I hold her beautiful chest. Lord Almighty. I've never felt anything this soft. My thumbs work across her perfect skin. She moans as I touch, her head craning backward in pleasure as my nails scratch her nipples.

I'm not drunk this time.

I'm in control. Giving her whatever she desires. Taking care of her.

She wiggles her arms out of the sleeves of her blouse, that little black lace falling beside us. Oh, my, God. She's gorgeous. In all my fantasies, she looked like an angel. I cannot believe this isn't a dream.

My lips join my hands, coaxing her, readying her.

"Oh yes." She hums as my tongue circles her hardened tip. I suck, hard. She cries in pleasure, bouncing in a rhythm that has me writhing beneath her. Working her out from her tight jeans, it's just little black panties on her incredible body. I slide her onto the cushions, stripping down to match her in my boxers.

"Damn, Bobby." Her eyes lock on my body like she's seeing me for the first time. She lays props her head up on her hand. It's so fucking cute.

"Just wait." I raise my brows. Take my place beside her on the couch. I start at her knees. Drawing hearts with my thumb. Teasing the hell out of her. Alternating kisses and touches. So much of our skin connects as I move over her body. Our lips meet, and it breathes life into me I've never known. My speed increases, hungry for more. She matches my intensity. Hot and heavy. In a way that I sense every bit of our needs parallelling in this escape from time and space.

"Bobby." It's like a cry. A plea. A longing, dangling from her tongue onto mine.

"We can take this real slow, alright?" I push against her panties with my cock. "No pressure."

"Mmm," she moans. "I want *your* pressure."

I didn't know how much I needed to take care of her. But it's like something is mending inside of me by giving her what she wants.

This isn't just some girl.

Cody's.

My eyes press shut. Energy replaced by guilt. Foreplay replaced by a dark hole. This is harder than I thought it would be.

"What?"

"Fuck." I squint tighter. I've lost it. The whole moment is gone in one thought. I slide off of her and press my palms into my eyes, sitting on the corner of the couch.

"Bobby? What is it? What's wrong?" She sounds worried, her cheeks rosing over like she's done something wrong.

"It's not you." I push harder on my eyes. "I guess I'm not ready for this." I'm just adding to the list of things I need to beg for forgiveness. This is going great. Dream girl. Dream moment. Ruined. "Fuck, Lex. I'm–" my chest is so tight while I try to form words out of the vortex inside of me.

"Don't you dare apologize."

"No?"

"No."

I feel so broken. Useless. I can't even fuck her. Goddammit, why did I try?

"Do you want me to apologize?" Her question kills me.

"No, of course not."

"Then, it's alright."

I open my eyes to see hers, tenderly enveloping me with her care and concern. It's the sweetest thing. She straddles my body, wrapping her arms around my neck with the kindest smile I've ever seen. "We can go slow. I'd like to go slow. We need that, apparently. Neither of us know how to do this."

"It's not that I don't think you're beautiful." I grip her hips.

"I know."

I swallow the knot in my throat. "Because I do. I think you're the most beautiful woman in this world."

She smiles like her face is saying *awe*. "I was gettin' a little too nervous, myself." She slides my hands around the small of her back. Rests her body into mine. Cuddling like she belongs here. She does belong here.

"Oh, I don't want you to feel nervous." I rest my chin on her head. "I've always loved so much about you. And I've always thought you're gorgeous. It's not a line, either," I whisper into her ear.

"I don't think you're the type to spout off lines." She kisses my nose.

"I love bein' with you." My voice catches, overcome with this moment.

"I love bein' with you, too." Her body relaxes into mine, blissful caressing for as long as we want. "Thanks for givin' us a chance."

"I'm really sor—"

"Bobby." She raises her brows.

"Right." I sigh, trying to think of something better to say. "How you been? Not just tonight. I mean, ever since you got back."

"Honestly?"

"Yeah, honestly. You like honesty." I wink.

She smiles, but then lets out a long sigh. "It's been a lot to be here." There's a heaviness in her words that makes it all worse that I haven't been there for her.

"I've been an asshole."

"Yeah, you have." She looks away, but not for long, popping her lips when she returns to my eyes. "I don't blame you, though."

"You don't?"

"I figure you did enough of that on your own."

Shit, she's so right about everything.

"I walked home that night. Punishin' myself for not takin' care of you. For leavin' even though you didn't wanna be here alone. I wanted to support you and I fucked up."

"Shh." She puts her finger over her lips. "I'm not mad. Do you know how hard this is? All of it? Every bit of this loss and heartache is the worst thing we've been through."

She doesn't know the half of it.

The deep parts of his death creep up into the corners of my troubled mind. I think about telling her. I want to. She literally just told me how important honesty is to her. But no words come out of my lips. I haven't been able to say them out loud. Ever.

I promised Cody I wouldn't tell a soul what he told me the night he died.

"We need each other. I really do believe that, Bobby."

How is she so sweet? I don't deserve this kindness. And here she is.

"I need you, Lex. But I don't deserve you. Not yet." I take her knuckles and kiss each one. There's a knot in my throat I wasn't expecting.

"But I want to, real soon, alright. Because you deserve so much more than I am right now." I take her hands in mine, kissing her knuckles because I can't stop this endearing gesture. Her hand against my lips makes my body relax in a way I can't explain.

"And what are you now?" Her eyebrows raise.

"A fuckin' mess."

"A gorgeous mess." She brings her lips to mine. "We've been over this, anyway. I don't mind messes. I paint on ruined canvas all the time and turn it into something beautiful."

"You really do."

"Maybe we can help each other paint over the past? It'll still be there, but we can add a new layer and make it into something."

"I'd love that."

"Okay, then step one–you're not a mess." She tilts my chin up because I'm staring at the ground. "And you're enough for me."

I lean my cheek against hers, blinking back the tears that want to come out of my eyes. I don't deserve even a tiny bit of her grace.

I have to get better… for her. For us.

For you, Cody.

I'll get better for you.

20

LEXIE
DECEMBER

*J*ust like I promised, we're going slow. It's good. I know we both need this. It's been five weeks since we reconnected at The Splat. He was embarrassed we stopped short that first night, but in all honesty, I was a panic attack waiting to happen. As much as I craved him, *really* diving in would've been a mistake. Neither of us were ready for *everything*. Maybe soon, but not then.

Bobby and I are cuddling on the couch, just being together at the end of a long week of classes.

I let out a deep breath, still shaking off the stress of today, and more–the inner turmoil that overwhelms my overthinking head. Being here makes me want to relax, but sometimes these thoughts run rampant and I can't turn them off.

"Somethin' on your mind?" He curls my hair around his finger.

I sigh. He's so in tune with me that he picks up on all my vibes.

"Just thinkin' about that night at the beach house our first week. Ya know, after The Splat."

"Jeez. I usually have so much more game than that." His chest tenses up under my head.

"No, no, not that." I sit up a little bit so I can look at him. "This is

gonna sound stupid but I'm a little scared of actually havin' sex again."
I close my eyes for a long time, worried that I shouldn't have said
anything.

Bobby takes my hands in his. "Scared?" His tone is kind and
somehow I don't feel as insecure anymore.

"Like I said, it's stupid." I huff hair out of my face.

"It's not stupid." He tilts his chin down, raising his gorgeous, deep-
brown brows, like he does every time he wants me to know he's being
serious. "You're scared? Do you know what you're scared of?"

Jesus, he's being so sweet with me right now. This has weighed
heavy on my heart ever since that night. I haven't known how to talk
about it. Haven't even wanted to think about it. I know I like Bobby
and I know I love when he touches me, but I don't know if I'll ever
stop worrying about it. In some ways I've been relieved we haven't
gone past third base since that night. I've needed some time to work
through this emotionally.

Looking into his eyes, I know I can tell him. I know I can trust him.

"I'm scared because I know you have a lot more experience. Not
even that, you have practice. Lots of practice that I don't have."

"Sex is about sharing. It's not about practice."

"What do you mean?" I grab my hair and twist it into a knot.

"It's not about who has practice or not. Not to me." Bobby holds up
his wrist for me to take my hair tie that he always carries around. I
smile because it's so sweet he's started wearing these so I don't have to
go looking for them to put my hair up.

I twist my hair into a bun on top of my head, whisps slipping out.

"No, it's about us gettin' to know one another in a special way. Lex,
I've had lots of hookups. You know that," he shrugs. "Everybody probably knows that." He runs his thumb across my forehead, tucking a few
of the flyaway hairs behind my ear. "But with you, baby, I want more
than that. I'm not at all worried about anythin' we've already had with
other people, because this is about *us* and *only* us."

I try to smile, but I feel so much weight in my chest–like a rock is
taking the place of my lungs and I can't get any air. "It's just that me
and Cody...we really didn't do much. In some ways I feel like I'm still

a virgin. I'm not gonna have any clue what the fuck I'm doin' and that scares the hell outta me because I don't wanna blow it with you."

"That won't blow it with me, I promise." He kisses my cheek, a tender look in his eyes as he pulls back. "Besides, virginity is a social construct."

"What?"

"It's a social construct that's bullshit. My first time was a special experience, sure. But it didn't change me like society likes to pretend it does. I'm not morphed into something different than I was before I had sex. You're still you. I'm still me. We're not chewed up bubblegum, or whatever other stupid comparisons people make, just because of goin' all the way with someone. It's an experience. Simple as that." He leans in close, holding my eyes.

"An experience." I try to let his words soak in, hoping that maybe they can offer a bit of redemption for me and the moments that went so horribly wrong with Cody. It's not just the inexperience that worries me. I suddenly feel the opposite of sexy. That I'm boring, too plain, not sexy enough. Maybe if I would've been sexier or more fun Cody would've....

"Lexie, when we make love it's about us sharing." Bobby pulls me from my thoughts before they get too dark. He's saving me. Healing me. My throat gets tight because somehow I know he's right. It doesn't matter what happened before. It doesn't matter that I have some trauma I'm still working through. It doesn't matter that I'm new to this. Or that I have far less of a clue how to be good in bed than he does.

"Sex is about giving and receiving. It has nothin' to do with how much sex I've had or how much you've had. I'm not better than you because I've been laid more times or with more people. This is about us. Only us. It's about me taking care of you. Learnin' what you like. You learnin' what I like." His mouth parts and his voice lowers. "Us sharing an intimate physical connection, like we are here and now." He brings his head to mine, his arms wrapping me in a hug. Whispering in my ear, he says, "It may not be my first time, but it's my first time with you. It will be wonderful, no matter what it looks like. I'll make sure it's just what *you* need, whatever that is."

I melt into his arms, finding that comfort he always gives. For so long I've been hurting, feeling broken, not worthy of love. I didn't know he could soothe this pain.

He holds me so close, so tenderly, that he may as well be inside of me–an intimate connection, just like he said. I feel that we are making love, just sitting here. Nothing to be scared of. Nothing to fret about. Nothing to make me worried. Maybe it would be with someone else, but not with Bobby. He's always taking care of me. Sex won't be any different.

It gives me hope that he's right. When we do go further, it will be okay, it will be safe, I will be good enough.

"You can always talk to me, alright? We never even *have* to have sex. You mean the world to me and I want to do what makes you feel most comfortable." He scratches my back, rubbing his cheek against mine. "Even if this is as far as we ever go. Absolutely no pressure whatsoever." It's so delicate, the way he touches me, the way he talks to me.

"I'm so comfortable with you. If there's anyone I could do this with, it's you." I bring my lips to his. "Thank you for bein' someone I can trust. Someone who cares about me."

"I care about you so much." He brings his lips to mine, his tongue dancing. Heat pours from me to him, kisses driving me wild with need. At this moment I think I'm getting close, almost in a place to share this with him.

———

THE DAYS GET SHORTER AND COLDER, SOUTH CAROLINA MELTING INTO deep fall. I see him when I can, but we're both swamped with class, assignments and studying, his training and my clinical hours. His engineering program is crazy intense, and it's a wonder I see him at all. Sometimes he doesn't get back to the apartment until midnight and is often out the door first thing.

Most nights are ours. I sleep in his bed with him, tangled in his legs, under the black sheets. We've yet to go farther than making out and spooning all night. I'm hungry to feel him and experience him completely. Considering everything we've been through together, I'm almost ready. It's weird, but I've never been more sure of wanting anything.

"One to one-and-a-half ratio." He hands me the measuring cup.

"I know how to make your rice." I raise my eyebrows. "How long have I been helpin' you with meal prep? Don't you think I can remember the rice ratio by now?"

"Fine, fine." A smile stretches across his face. God, I love the way he smiles.

Ten containers are on the counter while I sauté the broccoli, brussel sprouts and carrots. He's mixing up chicken and some sauce he puts on it.

The doorbell rings, and I go to get it since he's busy with measuring stuff.

"Oh, hey Lexie." It's Claudia. "Is Mickey here?"

"No, probably at the library," Bobby shouts from the kitchen.

"Oh, um, well if you see him, can you have him call me?" She isn't acting how she normally is, like something weird is happening and she's worried about it.

"Did you text him?" Bobby furrows his brow, standing beside me in the doorway.

Claudia huffs. "Nevermind." She throws her hands in the air and storms off.

"Are she and Mickey a *thing*?" I go back to food prepping. "And what was that?"

"I have no clue." Bobby lets out a surprised laugh.

"He dropped out of the athletic trainin' program." I feel bad, because I should really be a better friend to Mickey. "After he stopped showin' up for all his hours and started missin' all the exams."

"Why am I not surprised?" Bobby shakes his head. "He's never studyin'. Hell, he's never home. He's been in his own world lately."

"I don't get it." I feel a tinge of anger inside of me. So many times he's ignored me or left abruptly when I was trying to have a conversation. I've tried.

"Yeah, it's not normal for him." Bobby looks troubled.

"Totally not. I've tried to keep tabs on him. Tried to hang out with him, but he's constantly pushin' me away. And if that moment with Claudia is any indication, he's pushin' her away too. Did somethin' happen?"

"Dunno." Bobby shrugs, portioning the veggies into his containers with a measuring cup. He's so precise...like not one extra vegetable can end up in that container.

There is an ominous feeling in my stomach I can't seem to shake every time I think about Mickey. "We used to be so close. I've missed our conversations." Everything has changed. Whatever happened must be since I got back, because he was acting normal when he cleaned my beach house. "Is he mad that we didn't go to Garrison's?"

"Doubt it. Claudia went with them." There's no secret Bobby doesn't like her. I kinda wanna know their history.

I really hope Mickey's okay...but I know he's not. "He used to text and call me all the time. Kept me up to date on all that was happenin' here while I was gone." My voice is small, but Bobby catches it and stops what he's doing to look at me. Only, it's not his listening face, there's something more there, hurt?

"You've kept in touch? With Mick?" His tone confirms my suspicion, that typical velvety warmth replaced with jealousy. Far from yelling, but definitely a raised voice.

We've never fought about anything. I don't wanna start now.

For several heartbeats, he looks at me, brows knit together, nose wrinkling. My eyes travel to his tense shoulders, then back to his face. His jaw jerks out. Oh fuck...what have I said?

"I kinda hoped you shut everyone out. But it was just me?"

A throbbing hits my chest, and I lean against the wall, gripping my shirt and holding tight while my heart surges. Why didn't I text him back?

Was there something more inside of me, even then? That day when he held me after the funeral, I felt something.

My throat inflames, longing for an ice cube to cool it down. The cheap laminate floor is all I see, unable to look up.

I felt something, and I was afraid.

"I shoulda texted you back." The croak in my vocal chords makes me sound like a frog.

"Why didn't you?"

His words sting. And I can't swallow, can't take a breath.

"I wanted to be there for you. I wanted–" He shakes his head. "Forget it."

"No, tell me." I take a step toward him, the running heater hitting my face from the ceiling air vent. "Please?"

His chest fills with a long, deep breath. "I wanted you to know that I get it."

My eyes are on his, that understanding we share as clear as day. "I know you do."

"I get how hard it is. How hard it must've been for you." His face is intense, and I'm shocked that our tension has transfigured into concern.

"And what about for you, Bobby? Who's been there for you through all this?" My hand runs down his long sleeve shirt. He closes his eyes for a while, and it's like I feel his pain, like I can sense every bit of it–as if I'm in his body. His forehead rests on my shoulder, his arms wrapping around the small of my back.

There was no support for him.

I don't have to hear him say it to know, he's been utterly alone in his grief.

All those text messages were his cries for help, and I ignored them, lost in my own pain.

But not anymore.

"You're not alone," I whisper. "You never have to be again."

He needs to know why I kept in touch with Mickey.

I squint against the running heater, wishing I knew how to say this. It's not something I've told anyone besides my sister and Cody, but I want Bobby to know. No secrets from me, and no secrets from him, this is the way it needs to be. I want him to know everything I have to tell, every bit of my story. Even my scarlet letter, my dirty little secret, my mark of shame. This is a new feeling, because I've never *wanted* anyone to know.

"Mickey's my brother." It's barely a whisper, so hard to convince my throat to utter that much. I shiver at the memory of my mother's threats, but I don't have to listen to her. I never should have.

"Yeah, he's like a brother to everybody."

"No. He's *really* my brother."

Bobby pulls away, eyebrows wrinkled and confusion written all over his face. "Your brother?"

"Well, half-brother, but yes." I shake my head, hearing the pain in my voice. "Secrets have always bothered me, but we found out in a horrible way and thought it best not to broadcast. My mom slept with his dad and I was conceived." My teeth start chattering because I know I'm not supposed to speak that out loud. And I never have, besides when I told Charlene and Cody. "Mickey and I decided a long time ago that this wasn't something we wanted out on display. Between our chat and my mother's wrath, I've kept it tight."

"You're not kiddin'." His eyes look for something and I push farther away.

"I wouldn't kid about this, although I wish it were a joke." I open up his cabinet, not sure why I haven't stocked it with hard liquor for moments like this.

"Jeez, Lex. I dunno what to say." He leans against the counter, hands shoved in his pockets, the food prep forgotten.

I pull out a coke and pop the bottle cap, turning off the stove so nothing will burn. "Can we sit on the porch?"

"Yeah." We walk through the living room to his glorified slab of concrete with two beach chairs.

"What was that like for you?" His tone is caring, but there's no hiding that he's completely in shock. I was too, when I first heard.

"It's been really awful comin' to terms that *Dad* isn't my dad, ya know? Mr. Hawthorne and I aren't really related at all. Because Mom kept this secret, I've never even talked to him about this."

Bobby scoots closer, our knees brushing. "Have you thought about talkin' to him?"

"Not really. I mean, if I was him, I wouldn't want to talk about it. So awkward knowing the truth while we parade around town like this perfect happy family." I stare at the cobwebs in the ceiling. "I didn't really feel accepted growin' up. Like I didn't quite fit. Never knew why. Maybe it was my art. Maybe it was that I never really connected with my parents like I thought most kids probably did."

"Cody told me a few times that your parents weren't the accepting type."

"That's for damn sure."

"How'd you find out?" His tone is cautious, and I appreciate the concern that he shows. "You don't have to tell me anythin'." He grips his kneecaps, like he wishes he hadn't asked. "But I'm here, ya know, if you wanna talk."

My lips pull into a smile, reminding me how caring he is. How he won't overstep but wants to be supportive.

"My mom wishes we hadn't found out." I sigh, that pain in my chest that comes when I think about her, showing its ugly face. To her, I'm just a walking reminder of her infidelity…her drunk mistake. "Mickey and I hung out a lot, and she never liked it. Meanwhile, she didn't care if Cody and you and Trish came over. It was so weird."

"I remember her bein' awkward with him."

"Right? As much as she loves appearances, she sucked at keepin' this to herself. It's clear as day if you look."

"God, that's not cool of your mom."

"I know." I close my eyes, so upset with her for so many things. She has never tried to smooth any of this over with me or Mickey, and it makes me sick when I think about it.

"Was she like that with you, too?" He takes my hand, his face reflecting the sympathy he's giving me.

"I mean, she's my mom. But she's always held back from lovin' me. There are a million reasons we don't get along, but this is surely the biggest one. Mickey never had a mom, and she coulda been at least civil to him."

"Yeah, you two didn't deserve any of that."

"When Mickey's dad went to jail we were goin' through some old stuff at his place. There was a picture of his dad holdin' a baby in *my* pink blanket at a hospital. At first I thought it was just a popular blanket, but then I remembered that Granna had sewn it special." I stop talking because I don't know how to say any of this. "It looked like my baby pictures. Same hospital room. Same picture hanging on the wall behind the chair." I shake my head. "I've had that blanket forever. It's still in my closet." My eyes burn as I look at Bobby's. He's quiet, waiting for more of the story.

"Mickey was really confused and so was I. We took the picture back to my place and pulled out my baby book. It was the same goddamn blanket, same goddamn room. Same goddamn baby. We figured out that I must not really be who I thought I was. That our family didn't have any reason for me to be with his dad at the hospital, unless–" I swallow, rubbing at my throbbing throat like the words are trapped there and don't want to come out.

"Unless your dad was Mr. Checketts." Bobby holds my eyes, giving me strength to go on.

"As fate would have it, Mom walked in on us lookin' at everythin'. She blew up in rage." As hard as it was to say all of that, this is worse, the memory that burns me to my core. "I hate how she treated us. Her response was so volatile. You wouldn't believe the way she acted." My jaw just sits here and shakes like I have all this pent up adrenaline and it's only escape is through my teeth, so many unfortunate memories playing in my mind.

Bobby stands from his chair, closing the space between us. He scoops me up and holds me close, his hand cradling my head to his chest, smoothing my hair while I take long, deep breaths.

"Shit, Lex, that's so much." He rubs my scalp.

"I've never fit, Bobby. Like I don't belong in this world. Just some mistake my mom made one night." Tears sting at my eyes, and he holds me tighter.

"You're not a mistake." His voice is sure, warm lips pressing into mine. Fingers pull at the curls of my bright red hair. "Every bit of you is unique and wonderful. The fact that your mom can't see that just means she is fuckin' blind." His lips take mine in a radiating comfort emanating from his body to my soul. I drink in every sensation, wondering if this may be what *love* really feels like. I thought I had it with Cody, but this is more, this is deeper. Is it *real*?

Whatever it is, I hope to God and Jesus and the Universe that it never fades away.

21

BOBBY

"*S*o you and Lexie, huh?" Mindy and I talk privately in her office.

"Somehow, I haven't managed to scare her off yet." I shake my head. Still just amazed we're together at all.

"You feelin' any better?" Mindy texted me to come. I know it's to check in on the eating disorder shit. Most of the athletes have the after-noon off to get ready for the Christmas Gala tonight.

"Some." I really appreciate that she doesn't bring this up with my buddies around. I mean, gotta keep privacy and all that anyway, but I do appreciate that she is so professional. It's not like a strained wrist or something. It's hard enough she knows. It'd be worse if all of them did, too. Briar would become a fucking mother hen or some shit.

She takes my blood pressure and jots it down in my file.

"Did you make the appointment with Dr. Rogers?" Mindy's smile is kind.

"He's been out of town." I'm glad I told her. God knows I needed someone I could trust to get me through this. "His first available appointment is next week. Right before we go home for the break."

"Proud of you," she smiles, and it's sincere, like she's my mom or something. If only my mom could actually be there for me now.

"I wanna get better." I look at the floor because I can't handle looking at her face. So much shame fills me. I shouldn't starve myself. I shouldn't make myself heave. I know that with my logical mind, but I do it anyway. Because stuff like this isn't in my logical mind. It's in the sick part that can't figure out what to do, except keep hurting.

"How's this week been? Any better?"

"Yeah, I mean, besides finals." I huff. "Think they went alright, but this week would be a doozy even in a perfect situation."

"Dr. Brown wants to see you again after break. He suggests weekly checkups. Make sure you're well enough to play."

My heart drops to my stomach. I know I'm still down from ideal. Because "doing better" is only eating enough to survive. Not enough to take care of myself. Not with all the workouts. The little I'm eating isn't enough. I have to do better than "better."

I sink in disappointment with myself.

"Does Lex know about this?"

"God, no." My voice is a painful whisper. My airway cuts off as I think about telling her. We just started dancing into a relationship. An eating disorder is too heavy to plop in her lap. "Not yet."

"Maybe she could help, ya know?" Mindy puts her hand on my shoulder. "You don't want to tell Coach, don't want to tell your parents."

"Just you and me need to know. That's it." I grind my teeth. "I'm doin' what you want, okay? I haven't purged in weeks, Mindy. I just wanna keep this as small as possible."

"I think you need someone there for you. Can you tell Lexie about this? Or Briar? Mickey? Someone." She gestures to the file. "Because you could use some support. I know you're used to doin' everythin' on your own, but you don't have to. You woulda told Cody, wouldn't you?"

I swallow the lump in my throat and nod. Couldn't fucking talk if I wanted to. We wait, both of us just here. I've known Mindy for years. I've always mattered to her, and I know it. Cody mattered a hell of a lot to her, too. I just need to let some of this out. Free these words trapped inside of me.

"I stayed around, but man, I wonder if Lex had the right idea." I press my eyebrows, rub my forehead. "Maybe we all needed to run away." My words surprise Mindy, I can tell.

"Do you think runnin' helped her?"

"I think stayin' hurt me." It feels heavy, but I mean it. "My best friend was supposed to be playin' for the Yankees right now. And I see him in every goddamn inch of this town." I grip the strap of my backpack, tight. "But I don't really see him, Mindy. I see him dead. Everywhere." Goosebumps appear on my arms, remembering how cold I felt in that hospital the night he died. "Would I tell him about this? Dunno. But I'd at least have him to talk to if I wanted to." I pull my arms tight around my chest. I'm so cold I'm shaking.

"I miss him, too." Her voice is low and full of compassion. "It hurts."

"So much." I close my eyes and hold a long breath. The air is thick around us and I blink away wet eyes. "I'll see you tonight."

Mindy nods, her eyes wet, too. My heart is heavy as I get into my truck, slam the door and pound my fist against the steering wheel, hating myself for not just driving Cody home that night.

"I Drive Your Truck" by Lee Brice blares on my sound system. I can't stay my fucking tears. *I need you, Cody. I need you here with me. I can't do this alone. I can't do this without you.* Every part of me aches for him in a way that makes me know it'll last forever. There will never be a time in my life where it doesn't suffocate me to think of him.

Please, God. Give me some kind of meanin' in all this. Show me that somethin' good can come from all this pain. Just as soon as I think this prayer, Lexie's face comes to mind. *God, if anythin' good could come of this, it would be me helpin' to ease some measure of her pain.* And it hits me again. More firm than before. I must be strong. For her. For Cody. Because he left her behind, lost and broken. I *am* going to do everything I can to help her heal.

In the parking spot at my apartment, I take a few minutes to make sure I look normal. My eyes are a little puffy, but nothing too horrendous, so I go inside.

Lexie is dolling herself up in the bathroom. God, she's gorgeous. The curling iron molds her hair in steady bright red waves.

"Hey." I dangle from the doorframe, a smile on my lips, heart warming in gratitude. I can't believe she's really mine. That we're together. I never thought this would happen.

"Hey, love." She pecks my lips while she finishes her last curl.

"You look amazing, baby." I kiss her, taking my time to reconnect. She is everything I need. Though she doesn't know it, being here with me offers support.

Part of me wants to tell her everything. Just pour out my whole heart. But now isn't the time. I know there will be a time, but it's not here yet.

"I've been thinking a lot." She brings her body against mine. "I think I might be ready." Her eyes find mine, a shimmer of hope.

"Ready?"

She bites her lip. "Ready to go all the way. I'm not scared. Not anymore. I think I've worked through a lot." She raises up on her toes. "Maybe tonight? After the Christmas Gala? I don't know. Maybe it's not sexy to plan on it." She darts her eyes away, her cheeks turning pink.

"It's sexy as fuck, Lexie." I run my thumb across her cheek. "I'm glad you told me where you're at. We can always talk about this." I wrap my mouth around her ear, the smell of her hair spray filling my nose. "I always want you to feel comfortable." I move my head back to look at her. "Really."

The look on her face tells me that she appreciates my response. Her lips take mine with so much love. "I want to share this with you."

"I want to share this with you, too."

———

WHEN WE ARRIVE AT THE CHRISTMAS GALA, I CAN'T TAKE MY EYES off her. Everything about her is mesmerizing. Her breathtaking smile, her laugh. My skin tingles as she places an arm around my waist.

"Ready for Christmas?" Mindy smiles at me, wearing a shimmery red dress. Her husband, Jon, holds a glass of champagne. He's a nice guy. Manager at one of the hotels on Main Street.

"Oh, yes." I try not to think about our conversation, though it's so insanely hard not to.

"He's countin' down the days." Lexie smiles. "Like one of those kids with an advent calendar." She elbows me playfully and we chuckle.

"Finals go okay?" Mindy asks Lex.

"Yes, they did, thanks." Lexie looks incredible in that little black dress of hers. It's tight across her chest and hips, fishnet stockings on her legs. I can't stop thinking about what she told me before we left the apartment. I wouldn't dream about pushing her to be intimate. But I'd love for us to get there. Standing here, I think I'm ready. Really ready to be with her.

I'm doing better. My best. That has to be enough. Every time we're together, I work harder to make sure I'm in a healthy mental state. I need to be in a place where I don't tease her just to run away. I won't try tonight unless I know I can. Maybe it's time for us.

Coach Conners shakes my hand. "Anderson, good to see you." It's one of those two-handed hand shakes that pulls me in for a hug. He's a shorter guy with really dark hair and thick eyebrows. He's wearing a suit that's nicer than mine. Polished shoes. The whole nine yards.

"Lexie." Coach Conners gives her a hug, too. "Glad you're back."

A smile warms my face. *So am I, Coach, so am I.*

There's a fancy dinner and a long presentation that would be more interesting if the speaker weren't so dry. Not that I could hear a word of it, anyway. Every part of this evening melts into *her.* The way we are together. How much I have planned for our night.

I never thought this could happen. The more I think about it, the more I want her. I can't wait to *really* please her. In the way she looks at me, I sense that she's ready, too. I think. I hope. I pray.

Please, God, don't let me fuck this up, and thank you, ya know, for givin' me a chance with her at all.

———

"YOU GONNA FINALLY MOVE IN WITH ME?" I HAVE SAID THIS TO HER A few times, in teasing. We walk through the apartment door.

"I sleep here. What's the difference?" She ditches her purse on the coat rack she bought for the entryway.

"I want it to be yours." I latch the lock on the front door.

"I've been making it mine." She points to the throw pillows on the couch.

"Can we hang up a Lexie Hawthorne Original on the wall right here?" My comment makes her laugh.

"I don't think you can afford it." She giggles.

"Oh." I tickle her ribs. "What if we do one of those rent to own sort of arrangements, huh?"

She tickles me back. "You'd have to provide a down payment and two references."

"Think you can give me a chance to earn it somehow?"

"Oh, I'll give you a chance." Her lips are close to mine, wearing a seductive smile.

My heart beats faster, anticipation building in all the best ways.

"You look beautiful, tonight. This dress." I bite my lip. "Mmmm."

"Looks better off me."

Blood rushes to my ears. Like when I'm swimming underwater and there's too much pressure in my head. I know we talked about it. I'm ready. If she's ready, then I cannot fucking wait.

"Oh, I have no doubt." I suck in a breath.

She's giving me *the look*. The one I've been hoping for. The one I've been longing for. The *please, Bobby, just fuck me* look.

"I think you better find out for yourself." Her sexy smile makes me come undone. Red lipstick glistens off her full lips. Eyes shining off the dim lighting in the apartment. Her gaze holds mine as if she's looking deeper into my soul. As if she's saying *yes, take me. You're ready. I'm ready. I trust you.*

"You sure? Because we never have to."

"Yeah, Bobby I'm sure." Her fingers pull at the collar of my dress shirt. Fire surges through me. She's so damn hot. "I want you. Desperately."

"Me too." Wrapping my hands under her ass, I pull her tight against me. That pretty little black dress scrunches up her hips. Her back flush with the wall, I devour her. Kissing her deeper every second. Fast and heady, then long and slow–a pace I've ached for. Our tongues grace each other. Mouths opening wider, like neither of us can get enough.

I know I can't get enough of her.

Everything around us melts away. All I feel is an insane level of connection.

Her breath is sultry on my neck when she pushes back to catch it.

"I wanna know everythin' you want. Everythin' you need." My feet kick out of these dress shoes, rest in a pile in the corner with her heels. "We can go slow or fast or...or both. Whatever you want, alright? Let me take care of you, baby. Please?" I'm begging for validation, for reassurance that the comment about her dress looking better off and the *fuck me* look on her face were more than just a joke or a coincidence. *I promise not to rush this. I promise to make this about you. It's all about you.*

For so long it's only been sex. Just the hookup, the attempt at feeling something–anything–for another guy or girl. This is going to be so different, I already know.

"Yes." Lexie's green eyes hold mine and there is so much emotion, like if I don't give her everything I am she'll fall apart.

I've wanted you. In so many daydreams, it's gone like this. She's been the one that I caress.

"What...what do you want?" I won't rely on her to tell me because I can feel what she likes. An intuition proving, once again, we're meant to be together.

"Anythin' with you." She winks with a teasing raise of her eyebrow.

"Anythin'."

"All I want to hear is you screamin' my name," she whispers it low against my ear.

A rush goes from my head to my toes. I lift her legs around me so

I'm carrying her. Her core is pressed against my middle, warm and inviting. She plasters needy kisses on my lips.

I carry her to my bedroom and kick the door shut, locking it. My tongue dances in her mouth until she and I are inseparable. Clinging tight for more. Her body bounces on my bed. I drop my suit coat and rip out of my button down shirt, left with only the tank top underneath. Even though we sleep together, we've always been wearing something. This is the moment where I'll get to see all of her. She wiggles out of those fishnets to the glorious lace panties beneath. Arching her hips, the panties slide down and I get my first *real* look.

She is perfect. Pink, swelling.

She quivers.

Yes please, baby.

The look on her face is greedy as she wiggles her skirt up to her stomach. "Come on, dollface. Show me what you can do."

"Oh, I intend to." My knees hit the ground, giving me a better view of all that is her beauty. Oh my word. She props a pillow under her back, getting comfy. Good. We're gonna be here for a long time.

My mouth edges up her thighs. Kissing under her knees. Licking that perfect flesh of her curvy legs. Her body catches, receiving each sensation. I wrap her hips in my hands, gentle but firm. She moans, inching her perfect ass to the edge of the bed.

Lick.

I slip my middle finger inside her wet opening. "Fuck, Lex." I hum. "All for you."

My heart drops to my stomach.

For me?

Could she really be here for me?

I swallow the emotion in my throat, willing to stay in this moment, willing to give her the best night of her life.

Double lick.

My tongue lingers, exciting her. Years of practice finding meaning at last. She's already so turned on, and we're just getting started. My finger hugs her ridges as I find that little spot that makes her sing.

"Yes. Oh, yes." Her hips buckle, pressing her clit harder against my tongue. She's the best thing I've ever fucking tasted. I work into a rhythm. Give her everything I hope she'll love. My finger pulses in time with my tongue, lapping sweet juices as they tingle out of her fluttering folds.

"Yes!" She squeals, her body tight around me. Turning me on so hard I can't handle it. My cock is throbbing, needing to be inside of her.

"Fuck, yes, Bobby. Oh, fuck, Bobby." Her hands pull my hair, nails dig into my scalp. I lean back. Her face is pure ecstasy. She untucks my undershirt out of my pants and trails her magic hands on my skin.

I suck her clit until she screams in pleasure. She grips my lats, clinging on for dear life. Her head leans back. She moans with the sound of an angel. It's the best fucking thing I've ever heard.

My heart is ready to jump from my chest as I feel her clench. Holy fuck, orgasm. Already? It's a good one too...I feel it with her. This hasn't happened before. Ever. I usually just feel when I come. But man, I can experience hers with her?

With a love unrestrained, I harrow her into the deepest level of climax I possibly can. Fingers moving, tongue gliding, heart racing. It's the most beautiful thing I've ever been a part of.

I need her. Around me. Now.

"I wanna come inside." My body starves as I tantalize her through her climax.

"Come inside me."

Jeez, I want her.

Mine. Finally mine.

She trembles in aftershocks, that gorgeous chest of hers heaving like she's run a hundred laps. Sliding off the bed, she joins me on her knees. "Bobby?"

"Yes?" I search her eyes. Brace myself for whatever she may say. Though I just experienced so much sweetness with her, vulnerability washes over me. Was that good enough?

"Wow...." She kisses me. Hungry. Making out until my lips are raw and burning. "Let me do that for you."

Her hands unlatch my belt buckle. Slipping off my pants until I'm exposed before her. Her eyes go wide. Like she's pleased. A smile takes her face.

I'm so excited I could come from looking at her.

She teases. Strokes. Arouses.

Holy hell.

Her touch.

A groan escapes my lips as hers envelop my cock. So warm and wet. There's something different about her. The want and need I've longed for is satisfied. No, it's more than satisfied–it's ignited. Like this is only the beginning of what I've been waiting my whole life to feel.

I return to the first time I saw her at Shakey's standing by the juke-box, the smile that warmed her face then. Years ago, I wanted this. *I never stopped wanting this.* My throat gets tight realizing what is actually happening. To me. Today. This can't be real. I can't really be with her...can I?

Her tongue wraps my length, seductive motion that is so new. Like I'm really having sex for the first time. Because all those other times are futile now. They didn't matter. She matters. This matters.

I've always wanted it to be her.

"Lexie, oh, oh, Lexie," I scream her name while she works me into a thousand layers of passion. So close I'm holding everything back not to come. "Wait," I tap her shoulder, straining all my control not to fill her. "I want inside of you."

"I want you inside." Her voice is breathy, coming off my dick with a bit of drool. I've never been this turned on. Fumbling with my bedside table, I pull out a condom. Bite it open. Slip it over me. She lays on my bed, pulling at my shoulders, getting me to lay on top of her.

As I stretch my body above her, everything slows. My eyes find hers, filled with all the longing I've ever felt. Soon, I'll be a part of her. The closest we can be.

"Do you know how much I love you, Lexie?"

"I think so." There's an anticipation in her expression that drives me wild. Her body relaxes. Her teeth bite her bottom lip. Her eyebrows raise. A slow nod lets me know she's ready.

So am I.

I slowly slide inside of her. Feel every ridge. Become one with all her contours. She's so fucking tight.

Fireworks pulsate through me. Time stands still. Breath fills my lungs. I hold it in. I'm overcome. This can't be real. It must be a dream. As I focus on her face, I see that I'm not capable of dreaming this. I am, in reality, melting into my soulmate.

My throat tightens. This feels like coming home. Her expression tells me our feelings are the same. That we are *one*.

A single tear runs out of her cheek. I wipe it away with my lips, kissing her skin tenderly. She is breathtaking. I hold her for a second, enjoying the gentle way her breath comes against my neck. This is where I was always meant to be. I knew there was more to the way I felt. I knew I needed her.

"Jeez, Lex, you're perfect," I manage to choke out.

"So are you." Her hips rock under mine. I match her flow, her pace, her fervor. It's soft. Comforting. Exciting. A million feelings at once.

"This is unlike anythin' I've ever felt." She breathes life to all that I feel.

I brush her cheek with mine. "I love you." Listening to the language of her body, I move. "I loved you a long time ago." My whisper makes her breath catch. "I loved you a few weeks ago." My tongue tangles on her ear lobe. "I loved you then." I sink deeper into her body.

She welcomes me. A look of pleasure blooms on her face. Rosy cheeks. Wanting eyes.

"I will always love you."

"Oh, Bobby." She moans. "I love you." She grips me tighter. Moves us faster. I work with her. Together. Every part of us is together.

"I love the way you feel," I put my lips around her ear. Seal my words with a kiss. "Around me." I bring my forehead close. My lips melt into hers. "Please stay mine."

"Please stay mine." She repeats. We bounce. We thrust. We go for a long time until she's clenching around me. Ready. Waiting.

"Lexie, oh Lexie, oh, Lexie," I scream her name. "My Lexie," my groin goes tight until I'm numb all over. I'm filled with so much pleasure I can't think of anything else. Vision goes black, edging towards my sweet release.

I fill her with all the love I have in my soul.

Perfect.

Mine.

Ours.

I don't know how, but it's better than all my dreams.

22

LEXIE

*B*obby is, hands down, the sexiest man I've ever known.

I orgasmed three times. *Three.* I've never gone that many times in one round. Didn't even know it was possible, didn't know it could feel like this. Already, I want to stay here–forever.

"Wow." My heart races as he lays on his back beside me, gasping for breath.

"Wow." His head turns toward mine and there's a new smile–like he's really, truly happy. We lay, catching our breaths, enchanted by the afterglow–relaxed, at peace, more than satisfied. I snuggle into his chest, listening to his heartbeat, the heart I've come to love so perfectly in just a short time.

Pulling my hair out of my face, he caresses me. "How was it for you?" His thumb runs against my cheek, and my heart warms that he would think to ask me how my time was.

"Was it okay? Was it...good?"

I push up, pressing a kiss on his lips. "The best time I've ever had."

"Really?" His voice is unsure, lacking all the confidence I thought would be there. My God, is he really insecure about this? He's practically a sex god so I assumed he'd be cocky.

"Are you kiddin'? That was incredible. For you, too?"

"Oh, yes." Watching his eyes, I know he means it. That even though he's mentioned that he's been with several partners, something about me is special to him.

"Shower?" He stands, offering me a hand as we go clean up in his bathroom. I'm covered in sweat, waiting for the water to warm. A new bottle of shampoo is on the shelf, my favorite kind.

After I'm in the shower, he steps into the hallway for a moment. He comes back with his water bottle. "Thought you may be thirsty." The way he shrugs makes me clench under the water. I could take him again, here and now–I might have to.

I take a sip, ice cold water rushing down my fiery throat.

"Get in here."

He crowds in this tiny shower beside me, and I'm delighted to be this close again, covering his skin with kisses.

"You got my favorite shampoo."

"Yeah, I was hopin' you'd like that." His hands meet my scalp, massaging it in the water. He takes a glob of shampoo and works it into my hair, his body pressed against me. No one has ever washed my hair like this. No one has ever cared about me like this. No one has made me feel like this.

I'm breathless, losing all ability to think straight. My body responds to his every touch, the shampoo rinsing down the drain. How on earth did I live with him for a month before having all this?

His hard cock glides against my belly, inviting me to take another drink–and I want to....

I work my hands along his shaft, and it feels so long, so smooth, so thick.

He lets out a groan. "How are you so amazin'?" His lips take mine, and though they are swollen from all our kissing, I don't care. I pump him harder, faster, his cock growing in my hand.

"Press me up against this shower wall," I beg until he lifts my body with ease. He's so fucking strong, holding me comfortably while I move my hand to position him inside of me.

"I can get a condom." He sounds worried, pulling away.

"It's okay with me." I give him a reassuring smile.

"You sure?" He wrinkles his nose.

"I've taken birth control since high school. Is it okay with you?"

"Oh." Surprise glimmers on his face. "Yeah, it's more than okay with me."

"You're clean, right?" I want to double check.

"Yeah...yeah, I've been careful. Always use protection. Get tested. All that." There's his to-die-for shrug, again. "So, if you're okay with it, I'd love to with you."

"I'm clean." I tilt my head away from the water. "If you're okay with trustin' me?"

"Is that a question? I'm not even a little worried. You say what you mean," he slips inside of me. A smile comes on my face as he rocks my body. Heaven above, this is the most amazing angle. He taps so deep I tighten with each motion.

"Harder." As much as all that bedroom stuff was sweet and sexy, I want more now. I want to play. He catches my message without me saying a word.

"Harder?" His cock goes so deep while he slaps my ass. The bite is exquisite. Oh, God...I didn't know he'd play dirty. Fuck, that's so hot. If I thought I was turned on before, that level has quadrupled. I sincerely hope that the little spank was just the beginning of hours of playful sex.

"Do that again."

"I love when ya tell me what to do." He bounces me with one arm, thrusting up and down. How strong is he? He's moving me like I weigh nothing. When I least expect it, he spanks me, hard. Again and again. I'm dying of pleasure. My vision is white as I reach *another* climax.

"More?" His alluring voice edges me farther into ecstasy.

"Oh, God, don't stop."

"I won't baby, I won't." He thrusts harder, faster. I've never pulsed this hard in all my life. Never felt this surge through every part of my body. If this is what it's like our second time, what will it be like after a lifetime? I need him. I crave him. Everything he gives could never be too much.

We explode in wonder. Skin to skin resuscitation, healing from all we've been through, giving life when we once felt dead. Just me and him. The bond I'm forming, both terrifying and exhilarating all at once.

He lets me down slowly, carefully, taking so much *care* of me. I don't know if I've ever really been cared for. Not like this.

Maybe it's a good thing that I'm not with Cody...

My mind darkens, body heaving from the mental assault. The euphoria is gone, suffocated with a feeling of shame. The good I felt transforms into just as deep a level of misery. I force a smile on my face as fast as I can, trying to remove the guilt in my eyes before I ruin everything.

"What, baby?" Bobby looks at me.

Oh fuck, he already noticed.

"Nothin'." I shake my head. "It's nothin'."

"Did I hurt you?" His hand goes softly to my butt cheeks, horror in his eyes that he may have done something wrong.

"No," I shake my head harder, words spilling out of me. "No, Bobby, it's not you."

I expect him to withdraw. After hearing something like that, the moment of afterglow lost, I don't know how he wouldn't. But instead, he wraps me in the sweetest embrace. "You can tell me anythin' you need to." His words surprise me. "I'm right here."

I blink away the emotions, burrowing my face into his shoulders. "I was happy that it's you and not Cody." A sob knocks from me, and he holds me tighter. So close. I feel his pounding heartbeat against mine. "I'm not supposed to think that. It's not right."

"I know, baby, I know." He runs his hands down my back.

"He would hate me for thinkin' this."

"He doesn't hate you." Bobby pulls my chin to look at him. "He will never hate you." He says it like he knows, and somehow, I accept the words. I want him to be right. But God, I feel wrong for everything. I thought I was ready for this. But now it feels like I'm never going to be ready for anything.

Grief dissolves the beautiful momentum we've cherished tonight. I try to move on. I do the best that I can, and suddenly it all shatters. I lose the person I want to be and get trapped in the monster I despise, the one who can't make any sense of what happened and can't find a way to move on. I'm afraid this is the person I'll always be, that I'll never outlive my grief. I'll never process it, never move on–not even if I were to have a future with Bobby.

"We can figure this out, I promise." Bobby kisses me slowly, deeply, with that passion that drowns away all my pain. "We are here for each other through this." He brings my head to his chest, the warm water as soothing as his presence. "You can tell me anythin', everythin'. How much you miss him. How much your brain plays tricks on you." He brushes my cheek with his thumb, taking away my tears. "I get it. I promise, I get it. I know how hard it is." There's a depth to his words that makes me believe. He knows and understands, like no one else ever could.

"We are gonna figure this out, alright?" He holds me so close, my head against his pounding heart. "There's gotta be some way to heal."

I think maybe he's right.

———

OUT OF THE SHOWER, WE DON'T BOTHER GETTING DRESSED. WE snuggle in the bed, my skin on his. I am so comfortable, feel so peaceful.

"I've had a really nice time with you tonight." He scratches my head, plays with my hair.

"I guess I've experienced one of the infamous Bobby hookups." I lift my head up to get a look at his face while I tease him.

"Nah, that wasn't a hookup." He smiles so big I get a glimpse of his dimple. "With you, it's so much more."

"It's so much more?" My heart beats faster, craving his touch.

"Baby, I'm yours." He draws a heart on my shoulder with his finger. "Nothin' about tonight was casual. Not to me." He rubs my shoulders. "Was it casual for you?"

"Not even a little bit." I prop my chin against his chest. "Can we keep goin'?" I already want him again. Our first moments make me hungry to experience more. He's right, I don't need to feel bad about what happened with Cody. This is about me and Bobby now, a time for us. The way he held me and spoke so lovingly to me in the shower. The way our skin feels against each other. The way there is nowhere else I'd like to be.

"Please? I want you."

He gives me that *I'm touched you want that, baby* smile. I lather kisses all over his skin.

This is the beginning of something incredible.

I can feel it.

———

THE WEEKEND IS AMAZING. WE SPEND ALL MORNING TANGLED IN HIS sheets. I've never had this much sex, ever. Like, I didn't know what I was missing out on, because this is glorious. I'm getting really sore from my muscles moving in new ways.

Around noon, I throw on his workout shorts and t-shirt and we go to eat at a little diner in town. I'm starving because I've been working my body like crazy, so I order a huge breakfast with pancakes, eggs, sausage, home fries and hot chocolate.

Bobby orders black coffee and scrambled eggs. He eats them straight without ketchup; low carb, low sugar. This is funny to me, because most athletes I know eat tons to keep up with their metabolism. I don't know why he doesn't, but he looks real good, whatever he is doing, and I'm not about to be his mom about his choice of food. I offer to share mine, though.

"You can have as much as you want." I hold my fork out and tease him with a bite of pancakes dripping with maple syrup.

"Oh, baby, I've been havin' as much as I want." His tongue flicks the t sound in the word *want* with dreamy eyes, and I melt in them like they are an ocean. My pulse beats faster as his finger draws the shape of a heart on my wrist. Breath hangs in my lungs. How is he so fucking sexy?

He gives cash to the waitress after I've about licked the plate clean.

"What do we need to do today?" I ask to take my mind off of how amazing he is before I come on this public diner bench.

I'm so sore, yet all I want is to pound him again.

For a while, I wondered if I liked sex. It's abundantly clear now that it depends on the partner. Because with Bobby, I fucking love every second of it.

"Laundry." He shrugs and my heart patters in my chest because I'm falling so fast and hard that I love the way he talks about simple chores. I love everything he talks about.

Are we really together? Really? Together. Oh, I like the way those thoughts light up my insides. I like the way *he* lights up my insides. I want every bit of him inside of me right now. It's an urge I need to satisfy. And we've only just started.

"Yeah, let's go to my place and wash everythin'."

"Laundromat is fine." The corner of his lips raise. God, his smile. He looks really happy. Really, truly happy. Am I able to make him happy? A burning comes into my throat because I cannot handle how utterly perfect we are together. Who would have thought?

"Don't be silly." I shake my head. "We are not usin' any more of your quarters so long as I'm your girlfriend."

His eyes flicker in the light, a smile blooming on his rosing cheeks. I put my fingers on my lips. "I mean, if you want me to be your girlfriend." I hiccup and a little squeak comes out of my lips.

"Do you think I'd want anythin' else in this world?" His voice is so deep, so sincere, like I've triggered his emotions with my question. Those incredible blue eyes go straight into my soul as he brings my hand to his lips and kisses each knuckle. "I. Want. You. To. Be." He says each word, between each kiss, from my pinky knuckle to my thumb. Flipping my hand over, he kisses my wrist long and slow. "Mine." He looks up with the most wanting I've ever seen in those eyes.

I jump up from the booth and slide in beside him, because I cannot bear to be across the table. It's too far when I need to be with him. My body craves that oneness. I'm not whole when we're apart.

I smush onto his lap, laying a long wet kiss on his lips, not caring who can see. Cheers come from across the restaurant of people watching us.

An incandescence spreads through my lungs as I breathe in his scent. Laundry soap and Hollister cologne.

"Let's get outta here," he whispers, biting my earlobe.

"Please."

He carries me to the car on piggy back, and I giggle the whole way. "Did you get enough breakfast, baby?"

"Yeah."

"Well, good. You're gonna need your strength." He winks, setting me in the front seat of his truck.

I giggle more and think I haven't ever laughed as much as I do when we are together. God, he makes me smile. *Please, God, Jesus, Universe, let us keep bein' good to each other. Because it feels so good to have someone in my life who takes care of me.*

"When you gonna tell me how long you've had a crush on me?" I ask as his Tacoma heads to the apartment.

"I already told you." He taps the steering wheel.

"No, you didn't."

"I said it'd been a while." He smiles all cute. "I've liked you for a real long time, baby."

He kisses my hand, and I drop the subject because damn, all I can do is look at that adorable face of his and drown again. *Please, never throw me a lifejacket—I always wanna drown in these eyes.*

"You hopin' to go anywhere specific after graduation?" I know he's got his last courses scheduled for spring semester.

"Anywhere they'll take me." There's an insecurity in his voice I don't think I've ever heard before.

"Wait, wait, wait. You worried about the draft?"

"Hell, yeah." One hand grips the wheel and the other pulls on his long brown locks. He hasn't cut it since I've been back, and man it's the perfect length of just a little bit longer than shaggy style. He's not wearing a cap right now, but when he does, those adorable waves come out the bottom and it's about the hottest look I've ever seen on a baseball player.

"Coach Conners is pretty confident from how he talked last night." I put my hand on Bobby's thigh. "I'm sure they'll want you."

"There's no guarantee."

Wow, he really doesn't believe he's gonna get drafted. I think for a while about what I can say. He's one of the best players on the team. That he's so worried isn't what I expected. I just assumed he would be sure of himself. I couldn't have been more wrong.

"There's always tryouts if you don't make the draft, right?"

"Right," he shakes his head. "It's stupid. But, I always hoped I wouldda been drafted junior year. I played a good, strong season. Just wasn't enough."

"I'm glad you weren't drafted last year." I look at him, and when the light turns red, he turns to me. "Do you believe everythin' happens for a reason?"

"No."

"Well, I do. And I'm sure glad that you're drivin' me around Suncastle instead of livin' your dream just yet."

He scrunches up his lips, and I can tell that he's taking my words to heart.

"I'm glad we get to be here this weekend. Not sayin' we never woulda been. But here we are, and I intend to make the most of it." I lean my head toward him.

"We already are," he says it so matter-of-fact.

And he's right, because in his embrace I feel more love than I ever have.

And this is the beginning.

We gather up all the laundry from his place, and I smile, realizing that half of the clothes in his hamper are things I've worn. I get his sheets and towels, and we take a bit to clean up the apartment.

"Does Mickey even live here anymore?"

"Not hardly."

"Is he stayin' on the team? I'm more than upset with how little he talks to me. It's been months since I've been back, and we've barely seen him. I've been stayin' at his apartment for Christ's sake."

"Dunno. Think he is stayin' on the team 'cause I heard he switched programs." Bobby throws the hamper in the bed of his truck, tucking a towel on top to keep the clothes from flying out while we drive. "He and I have never been tense, and he won't tell me what the hell is goin' on. So, I just kinda dropped it."

"He'll come around one of these days and *finally* tell us what's up." I shake my head, acknowledging that I wouldn't know how to handle this if I was Mickey's roommate. "Good thinking." I point to the towel. "Wouldn't want to go chasing your lace panties all over Suncastle."

"My lace panties?" He gives me a confused look.

"Well they'd be flying from *your* truck." I hop into the driver's seat.

He laughs. "Guess so." He raises his eyebrows. "You're drivin,' then?"

"Buckle up."

"I'm gonna need to." He chuckles. "Probably need to go get a helmet. Or a neck brace for all the curbs you're gonna climb."

I start laughing because I find everything he says adorably funny. I thought Cody was hilarious, but it turns out Bobby was really the funny one the whole time. I can see that now. Cody played off him to enhance his jokes, like accent colors on a painting bringing out what was already there and making it shine. I remember them carrying on so much when we all hung out. It was the sound of happiness incarnate.

"You're not so bad at this." He's talking about the way I drive his truck.

"Is that a complement?"

His eyes tease me, begging me to make some quip. When I don't, he starts playing around with my chest. At the stoplight, he squeezes tight, pinching my nipple.

"Ow!" I move his hand off my boob with a playful screech. "Say you're sorry."

"Nah, I'm not gonna." He giggles.

"You hurt me," I tease, eyes alight with happiness. "Say you're sorry, now!"

"Uh uh." His smile is wide. I kiss him, and he shoves his tongue in my mouth. I bite it, and he jerks away. "Hey!"

"I wouldda bit harder, but you're gonna need that tongue later."

"Oh am I, huh? And what am I gonna need my tongue for?"

"To apologize."

He laughs–really, truly laughs, and the sound is music to my ears.

We pull into my driveway but before I can open the truck door, he takes my hand.

"I'm sorry." He kisses me like he means the apology. "I know I'm gonna hurt you." His kisses fill my mouth with wanting. "But I'm never gonna mean to. And I'll always be right here beggin' for your forgiveness. Workin' hard as I can to not make the same mistake twice." The last kiss takes all my breath, feeling dizzy from the way he steals my air. I stare into those blue eyes for so long that goosebumps wiggle up my forearms, and I shiver.

"Let's go, my li'l peach." He hasn't called me that before, but I do know that peaches are–in fact–his favorite thing on this earth. It feels really endearing that he referred to me that way.

The beach house is stuffy, so I leave open the front door with only the screen so we can get some fresh air.

"Did you think about what you're gonna do with the office yet?" Bobby hangs from the doorframe like he's gonna do a pullup.

"Yeah, I want to make it my art studio."

"That's a great idea, Lex!" His face lights up so bright I see the shimmer against his irises from the entryway chandelier.

"Can I help you move stuff around? Get it ready? All your canvas 'n such?" He steps into the empty room, apart from the furniture sitting there. "Where are they? It's gotta be heavy, right? Lemme help you."

"I would love help, actually. That would be great." I follow him in. "I want to put this desk on the other wall. Move those shelves into the other room. Have space for a few easels to always be set up so I can paint whenever I like without havin' to worry about all the setup." I wave my hands in the air, showing where everything is going to go. Passion burns at my heart as he wraps his hands around my waist from behind, bringing his lips against my neck.

"I'll help you with anythin' you want, baby."

"I know you will." I'm breathless, he bends with me over the desk, his cock pressing against my ass in the sweetest depth of desire.

"Do you have the easels here?" He nibbles at my earlobe.

"No, they are still at my parents' house."

"Oh, let's go get 'em." He pulls back like we have to go this instant.

"You wanna drop everythin' to drive over to Willardson right now?"

"Couldn't think of anythin' more worthwhile if I tried." As much as he teases all the time, he's dead serious.

"We don't need to," I whisper. "We will be there for the holidays. Can bring some back then." Spinning around, I face him. "Will you come home for Christmas with me?" I didn't know I was worried about it until the words left my tongue, spiraling in the air with all my uneasiness. "I mean, if you'd like–"

His lips take mine in long, deep kisses as he gently lifts me onto the desk. "I would love to go home, with my girlfriend, for Christmas." The smile on his face is one I haven't seen before.

I've seen his excited smile. His teasing smile. But this one, this one is different. It's a smile that tells me it means the world to him that I asked.

It means the world to me that he wants to come.

————

WE WATCH *ARRESTED DEVELOPMENT* WHILE THE LAUNDRY WASHES, then go to switch the last load into the dryer. He leans casually against the washing machine. "I oughta take you to an arcade and spend all those quarters we just saved."

"I know a better game we can play." I can't handle that he's standing here fully clothed when I'm this hungry for him. I take his hands and lead him over to the dryer, warm kisses melting into his lips again and again.

I unbutton his jeans and bend down to lick the length of his cock.

He gets so hard for me, so fast. God above, we've had so much sex in the last twenty-four hours.

I lick him for a while, his face pure delight when I glance upward. He pulls me to stand and slides down my panties and his workout shorts I'm wearing. Then he puts me on the dryer, my bare ass against the warm metal. Positioning inside of me he thrusts, my body vibrating with the shifts of the drying clothes.

"Oh," I gasp, because this feels so fucking good. He's everything I want, everything I need.

"I never knew you'd be this amazin'." I can't breathe, my hips working into his motions in a sweet symphony. Heat rushes through me and I come, spilling all over the dryer.

He smiles. "That's it baby, just like that." His face is loveable satisfaction, rocking his hips as I come again, in time with him. I've never felt this close to another human before. All I feel is him. The way he rocks, the way my body hugs him, trembling in aftershocks.

Please, can we keep doing this for the rest of our lives?

23

BOBBY

*W*e just finished the best weekend of my entire life. Everything was perfect. All about us. I didn't even check my phone.

With Monday comes all the stress of life again. My mind is racing because today is my appointment with Dr. Rogers. He happened to be out of town the week Mindy learned about my eating disorder. I got his first available appointment. And that's soon. Too soon. I am so fucking far from being ready for this.

"Told my mom you're stayin' over for the holidays." Lexie sits on the bed, refreshing Suncastle College's webpage a dozen times to see if her exam scores are posted yet. "Goddammit could they just post the scores so I can stop stressin' over them?"

"I'm pretty sure you aced them all." I offer her a smile.

"Not Clinical Eval." She shakes her head. "Dr. Riche has been hard on us all semester. I just have to come out with a B." She crosses her fingers.

"I would be surprised if you came out below that." I throw some clothes into my duffel bag and go into the kitchen for my protein powder.

Gazing at my phone lock screen, I realize it's time.

"I gotta go, baby." I lean down and kiss her.

"Where ya goin'?"

Oh, shit. I haven't told her. "I have a therapy appointment."

Her eyes go wide and her mouth drops open. She shakes it off, like she's trying to recover from the shock. "Oh, okay, I'll see you in like an hour then?"

"Um, probably. I'm not sure." I let out a deep breath, worried she will catch on to the *why* for this appointment. Don't know what the hell I'm going to do if she does. Lying to her isn't an option. "It's my first time. Wish me luck." I stuff my phone in my pocket, doing my best to act normal.

"Good luck." No questions. Thank God. Her sweet smile gives me the strength I need to get into my truck and drive across town.

The office is cold. I mess with my hoodie sleeves, pulling the bill of my cap farther over my face. What if word gets out that I'm here? Will they cut me from the team? No, no. Mindy knows I'm here. She gave me the name of this place, for Christ's sake. Coach wouldn't care, either. Mental health is important so I can play my best. I'll only get cut if I refuse to be here. Just nerves. All nerves.

My fingers drum my kneecaps through my jeans, body refusing to relax no matter how much I try to talk myself down.

The receptionist chuckles with her coworker. I don't know what to plan on, except raw emotional vulnerability. I can't do this.

I should tell Mom. I pull out my phone and text her.

Me: Gonna be in town tonight. I'll drop by after dinnertime.

I don't totally know when I'll make it into town, but I can't wait to see her. And give her shit for not returning my calls all semester.

My fingers hover over the keyboard, so many words I want to say, but can't. Mindy telling me I don't have to go through this alone. *I'm goin' to therapy because*...I sigh. Mom doesn't need to know. Hell, she doesn't get to know. You don't go months without talking and then be privy to this information.

Looking at the clock, it's only been four minutes since I finished all that goddamn paperwork. Still not time for my appointment. I've been sitting here, antsy as hell for what feels like hours.

My heart's racing so hard. I need something to calm me. Reaching under my shirt, I feel my cross necklace. I dip my head low, closing my eyes.

Father in Heaven, I'm strugglin'. I just need some help. Can you help? Please, God, make me more than I am. Strengthen me. Heal me from this pain, this torment, through Your redemption. I wanna be with Lexie. I wanna be good enough for her. I know I'm not. I need to meet with Dr. Rogers, but it's so hard. I'm fallin' apart here, God.

I pick up my head, opening my eyes to this drab waiting room. The fact that I'm *really* praying and not just sending a passing thought toward heaven shows how nervous I am.

People come and go from the waiting room. My eyes stay on my hands or my feet. Avoid eye contact. I don't want to know why they're here. What I *really* don't want is for them to know *I'm* here.

Do I look too skinny? Do I look like I'm on drugs? Do I look suicidal? Shit, I probably look like all of those things. Fucking broken. I look fucking broken.

Looks don't lie.

Not this time.

"Robert?" It's an old guy with a long white beard. Kinda looks like a mall Santa Claus, only he's fit. What am I gonna call him? Santa? Dr. Santa? Crossfit Santa. Yeah, there we go. Crossfit Santa it is.

This is my fate. My doom.

"It's Bobby." Do we shake hands? I look at him for a minute, ready but not sure. He doesn't move, he's just looking at his chart. No. Okay. Apparently we don't shake.

"Hi, Bobby." He holds out his hand. Nevermind, we do. We definitely do. Okay. Just follow his lead. I can do this. I have to do this. For her. For Cody. One day, maybe for me.

"Just this way." He leads me down the hallway to an old wooden door that looks like it was hung crooked, and stops.

Relax. I beg my body to obey, but there is no hope for me now, standing frozen in the doorway. Do I have to do this? Do I really have to do this?

Lexie's smile flashes in my mind. Her tears mixing with the shower water. I have to do this for her. For us. Because I don't know what it would do if she caught me in one of my episodes. Because *I* don't like to catch myself in them. I can't imagine what it would do to her.

"We keep the tigers out back." Crossfit Santa chuckles, trying to offset my nerves. He reminds me of Robin Williams in *Good Will Hunting*. "It's alright. The couch is quite comfortable, really."

I already feel like I'm doing this wrong. Lovely. This is just going great.

I force myself to move and earn a smile and a nod from Crossfit Santa.

The inside of this good-sized room is pretty basic. Some book shelves. An old rug he probably got the year he graduated from school, at least thirty years ago, and a leather couch. I take a seat on the edge of the cushion. On the edge, it's almost as good as me not being here at all.

The urge to run away is more tempting than a double workout. No. I have to stay on the team. I have to get over my shit. It's about damn time.

I probably don't really need this. I have Lexie now. She doesn't know what I'm going through, specifically, *yet,* but she gives me more than enough support. I can get over this without some sterile shrink writing down my deepest, darkest secrets on his notepad. What is it anyway? A magic notepad? Gonna somehow cure me? No, I'm better off on my own or with Lex.

If only Mindy saw it this way.

Shit. I have to be here, don't I? Mindy didn't say I'd be benched all season, but she didn't have to. I've been dancing around the issue, like I dance around every issue in my life. But it's time to change that. It's time to get better.

"So, Bobby, what are you hoping to get out of therapy?" He's not from here because he has a Brooklyn sort of accent.

"My athletic trainer sent me." My hands are sweating. I press them against my jeans. But it doesn't help. Denim isn't good for curing clammy hands. "So how about you tell me, Doctor? What am I hopin' to get out of this? Cause I dunno."

"That's alright." Crossfit Santa tries to exude a good impression, I can tell.

"So therapy is a little different for everyone. I'm here to help you in the ways I can." He holds my paperwork. "It's just a matter of what you would like to accomplish."

We sit in silence for a long time.

"Let me reiterate. What are your goals?" He's looking at me, but I'm looking everywhere else. There are exactly seven pens in a cup on the corner of his desk. One pen is alone, near his laptop. There's a jacket slung across the back of his office chair. Focusing, I see that there's frayed stitching on the right pocket.

I let out a sigh, pulling my hair that's shaggy beneath my cap.

"I don't have any." It's a lie. And the look on Crossfit Santa's face says he knows it. Shit. I don't usually get off on the wrong foot. Who knew it was possible to suck at going to therapy?

"Okay." Crossfit Santa looks out the window to the park right behind his office.

Come on Bobby. Show up. We are not here to play some stupid mindgame with an old man. My hands start shaking while my heart pounds in my chest. I need some air. "Can I open your window?"

"Sure."

I pull the latches and breathe in the cold breeze, closing my eyes, trying to get some measure of control. "I wanna get better, I guess."

"Good place to start." He doesn't miss a beat. "And what does better look like?"

Closing the window, I take my seat on the edge of the couch. "If I knew that, I wouldn't be here." God, I sound like a bratty kid. Something about sitting here makes me feel vulnerable, like I'm five years old.

"Let's start somewhere else then. What's something you love?"

I watch him, mouth dry, hoping he can give me something to hold onto on days when I'm sinking.

"I love peaches." It's a clear moment. A break from the tension inside of me. I know the answer to that question, even if I don't know the answer to any others.

He smiles. "I love peaches, too. Tell you what, these local grown ones are better than anything. Forget the famous Georgia peaches. South Carolina peaches are far superior."

"Damn straight, they are. My parents have an orchard in their back-yard. Fifteen trees. Well, one of them didn't do so well, and it had to be cut down. But the others are thrivin'." My chest relaxes a touch. It feels good to talk. This isn't as heavy as all the reasons why I'm here.

But then it fades, and I rub my forehead, that sinking in my gut getting bigger. "Do you even think I can work through this? The eating disorder? I want to." I press my forehead harder, worried that I can't. My biggest fear is that I'll never resolve this issue that I have. That I'll never be able to have a day when I'm healthy mentally and physically and not battling the constant push and pull that torments my mind.

"I can tell." He waits until he has my attention, the look on his face trying to reclaim the glimpse of connection we grasped a moment ago. "You want to get better."

My heart pounds in my ears. I want it so bad. But I don't know if I can. I feel broken inside. That I won't be strong enough to face these thoughts. No, it's more than thoughts. It's everything. Takes over my whole being until I'm not me anymore, I'm lost...hollow. I don't know if I can be the kind of person to pull themselves out of such a horrible situation.

The walls feel like they are closing in. My teeth involuntarily crash into each other. I want to throw up.

"I know that I have a problem." My throat catches on the words because I hate having to say them at all. Crossfit Santa looks at me, like he can see the façade I wear clearer than the Yankees cap on my head.

Another few minutes go by before I can bring myself to continue. "The first time I, you know–" I shake my head. This is so hard. So huge. It's like the biggest thing in the world to admit to anyone. "That first time, it was just gonna be once. I felt awful after. Well, I felt awful before, too. I guess that's why I did it in the first place. I didn't wanna feel that anymore."

The corner of Crossfit Santa's lip rises, offering support. "What did you not want to feel?"

"Out of control." I stretch out on the couch and feel exhausted, like I could fall asleep right now, and shut down again, looking at the ceiling. They are those gray and white tiles in a grid pattern.. I rarely sleep well, even with Lexie beside me.

"How was life for you growing up?"

"Good, I guess." I sit up because I'm not comfortable being this casual in an office.

"Get along with your parents?"

"Yeah, pretty well." I nod. "They were your average Southern couple. Spoiled me rotten as a kid. So did my grandpa, Skipper. He always had lots of fun stuff for me when we went over to his house. Lots of fishing trips out on the lake. Hiking in the hilly trails."

"So you considered your childhood to be happy?"

"I mean, happy is a big word, Doctor. But yeah. Things were fine."

"You mentioned the first time. How old were you then?"

"Sixteen." I lean back on the couch.

"What did you believe about yourself? When you think back about that time in your life."

I look at the ceiling for an eternity. The words stick to my tongue like honey in the winter. "I'm weak," I force out. My throat burns and I unzip my hoodie and take it off, wadding it into a pile beside me. "Not enough." I've never been enough. Not for an early draft. Not for Mom. Not for Lexie. Not for anything. Nothing.

Not for Cody.

No, no...we aren't gonna go there. Too dark. Too much. *Come on Bobby, think about somethin' else. Anythin' else.*

"What isn't enough?" Crossfit Santa's voice is kind.

"I'm not enough." There isn't a more true statement of myself. What is that thing Lexie is always saying? *"My truth."* Yeah, that's it. This is *my* truth. I'm not enough. Because if I was, I would've been able to do something.

"It's not all the time, ya know. This eating disorder bullshit." I rub my goosebump covered arms, unable to decipher if I'm hot or cold. "Sometimes I'm fine. Just fine."

"Would you like to talk about when you don't feel fine?" Crossfit Santa leans against one arm.

"When? Hmm. Well, it's when life's too much. I stop eatin'. First to go is breakfast. Lunchtime rolls by and still nothin'. Ignore the hunger through dinner. Keeps up for days, weeks, I lose track." I flip my cap around backward.

"You lose track?" Crossfit Santa asks for clarification.

"It's gotten easy just to skip. And then when I do eat again, I hurl it all back up. Thoughts get dark. Can't bring myself to nourish even though my apartment is filled with fruits, veggies and protein. Things I *should* be able to have, especially with how much I work out." I look at my arms, all I've worked for. My body is a well-oiled machine. Too bad I can't manage to take care of it. "Everythin' becomes off limits. Can't have it. Can't have the calories. The sugar. Nothin' but sugar-free grape Powerade or black coffee." My teeth grind, all the tension in my jaw bringing a weird pain through my head and neck. "I always snap out of it at some point. Life shifts. It gets better, and I'm back to a normal diet and all that."

"So, right now, it's too much." Crossfit Santa sets his mug on the desk. "What's too much, Bobby?"

It feels like the world is on my shoulders. That I can't carry it all. So many secrets I hold. So many lies I tell myself trying to cover up reality. So many that I don't want to unearth what *really* happened.

"My parents aren't talkin' to me." Why is this what comes out of my mouth?

"Oh?" He looks at me. "You mentioned that you did get along with them. Did something change?"

"Dunno." I grab my water bottle and chug, throat so hot, hands so cold. "I've tried callin' and they don't pick up. Mom's busy takin' care of a neighbor that broke her hip. But still...she used to call more. Hell, even Dad used to call. But we're gonna stop by for the holidays." Why am I talking about this? What the hell am I doing here? My parents have nothing to do with my eating disorder. "They say I'm just like her, ya know. My mom. They've always said that. 'You look like her, Bobby.' 'Oh, yeah, you favor her.' 'Oh, that's somethin' your mom used to do when she was a kid.' 'Oh, you work out with her? That's so cute.'" I roll my eyes. "Cute," I scoff. "Real cute that she up and stops returnin' my calls." I rub my eyebrows. "She's not normally like this. And, well, neither am I. So maybe we are the same."

"You may favor your mom, but you're not the same." Crossfit Santa seems sure.

"I miss her. And I shouldn't have to miss her. I miss way too many people, Doctor. Do you know what that's like? I'm right here. I'm the constant. The one that is always there. Yet, people don't see me. Lexie, she never saw me at all. Until a few months ago."

Shut up, Bobby, jeez. I was not gonna bring her up in therapy, that's for damn sure. Not gonna talk about her. Nope. Leave her out of this. Yet, here I go, running my goddamn mouth as if there is some magic dust in the air making me talk.

Crossfit Santa looks thoughtful. "I know what it feels like to miss people and what it feels like not to be seen or appreciated. These feelings are valid."

I guess that shuts me up because I don't have anything to say now.

He continues, "Maybe we can think of some other things to control."

"Slim chance." The tension reappears in the room. Crossfit Santa looks at his desk for a moment, like he's considering his next move. Like we are playing a game of chess, or cards. Or baseball. He's striking out. Or maybe it's me. I'm the one losing the game. I'm the one that should have a fucking handle on life. I'm the one that shouldn't need fucking therapy.

"I think I'm stuck in the past," I blurt out, because if I'm going to sit here, I may as well get to the point. "That's when it all started, ya know? The binging. The starvin' myself for days." Pain courses through me like a vibration from head to toe.

"Stuck in the past? Can you tell me more about that?" Crossfit Santa leans back in the chair, his fingers steepling over his chest.

"Just what I said, Doctor. He's here in all my memories. All the time. It's like I'm haunted, like I can't move on."

"He?"

God. I didn't know how hard it would be to say this–but my throat closes up completely, shunting any power to my vocal cords. Crossfit Santa stares at me, looking through my walls as if they don't exist.

"My best friend Cody died in a car crash six hundred and three days ago. It's been damn near two years now. And I'm still broken up about it." My insides are ablaze and my tear ducts get wet so fast I slam my palms into my eye sockets, refusing to put on a show.

Crossfit Santa doesn't say a word while I gather myself with a few tight breaths.

"I could've stopped him. I came–" I hold an inch between my fingers. "I came this close to stoppin' him from gettin' in that car that night. And I didn't." My arms go limp and my legs feel like jello. "It's like this darkness consumin' me all the time. Like I want to off myself just to be with him again. And that's fuckin' terrifyin', becasue I have a hell of a lot to live for." I can't believe I'm saying this. It will probably jeopardize any chance I have at a Major League Career, saying I've been suicidal. Mindy doesn't even know about that. I'm sure that this guy will make some note. Probably file some report with the state. Not good for the press. I might as well admit to him that I'm bi. Can see the headlines now *Suicidal Bisexual Baseball Player Ridden with an Eating Disorder, Bobby Anderson, Throws Away a Promising Major League Career.*

My palms smush my face again, every part of me wanting to storm from this office, but knowing full well it will only make things worse if I do.

"Everyone who dies by suicide has a lot to live for," he says. "Any attempts?" Crossfit Santa is serious, because he has to ask about stuff like this now that I've brought it up.

"God, no."

"Plans to?"

"No, no, it's not like that." I shake my head.

"What is it like?"

"It's when I'm feelin' really low, it's like I don't wanna be alive without Cody anymore. I know it won't help if I off myself. I don't think that's how all this works. But I wanna fade away. What I really want is to–" I go quiet while several moments pass.

"What do you really want?" There's an energy in this room that rattles me, catching every part of me off guard. Feels like I'm gonna suffocate.

I purse my lips, another wave of emotions wracking my soul. My heels bounce against the ugly rug. "What I really want is to apologize."

"Apologize?"

"It's my fault. But I don't wanna tell you all that. I wanna move on. I wanna get over this shit. I wanna be able to go to a restaurant and order whatever the hell I want and not throw it up that night. I wanna train hard and be in good shape. But not in a way that makes my athletic trainer worried so much she texts me three times a day to make sure I ate somethin' and that I kept it down." The words stumble over my tongue like I can't say them fast enough. "So you wanna know what better looks like, Doctor?" My voice is getting louder with each word. "Better is when I can fuckin' eat again, every day, and not have to force myself to not ram my finger down my throat. I wanna get over all this." I'm yelling now, but it doesn't phase him. He lets me feel. Shit, I've never said any of this.

"How long have you felt this way?"

"Suicidal? I don't know." My nails bore into the fabric of my jeans and I focus on the bookshelf behind Crossfit Santa. There's a bunch of thick, old-looking books that I can't quite make out the titles for.

"Wanting to be with your friend is a longing that many experience after losing a loved one, Bobby." His words settle in the air, and I want to believe them. Want to believe that I'm not broken or messed up. Not alone. But that desire feels distant, like I can't reach it even if I exert all my effort from now until forever.

We were supposed to have forever, Cody. I should be watchin' you on television playin' ball. Goin' to see broadway shows like Spider-Man: Turn Off the Dark*, starring Reeve Carney, with you on your days* *off. Workin' our thumbs raw on our controllers playin' Diablo all night long.*

Shit, this hurts. All of it hurts. All the time. All the fucking time.

"You said you want to apologize. Can you tell me more about that?"

I look away. The clock on the wall ticks. *Tick. Tick. Tick.* It sounds like a sledge hammer, destroying the walls I've worked so hard to build.

"I should've been there with him. I should've saved him. If I could've kept him from that accident. If I would've talked to him longer, he wouldn't have been at the wrong place at the wrong time, and he would still be here with her."

"Her? The Lexie you mentioned earlier?"

Tick. Tick. Tick. The rhythm of the clock brings peace this time, calming my racing thoughts. *Tick. Tick. Tick.* I twist Lexie's hair tie around my wrist. When I get out of here I'm buying a watch so I can have this calm with me everyday. Like my cross necklace and her hair ties. I need to be able to wear things that bring comfort. It helps. Something concrete. I need more things that are concrete.

"Yep, Lexie. She's my girl now. But she shouldn't be." It feels so heavy coming from my lips. I didn't expect any part of this to be easy. But I also didn't know what would make it hard. It's that sharing of myself that makes it so much. Things I never speak to anyone else come sliding out of my mouth, like when I slide into home. Natural, but uncomfortable at the same time. As if my brain has been waiting for its chance to work through the issues.

Somehow, I talk through my fifty-five minute session. Crossfit Santa deduces that I am ridiculously hard on myself.

"If someone else was in your situation, would you be this hard on them?" His question makes me think. If this *were* Cody, I would have grace for him.

"No." It's barely a whisper.

"Seems that you're very hard on yourself. I've seen you play baseball. That dedication is very helpful on the field. But there needs to be a way for you to shift into a more comfortable headspace. A way for you to reframe the pressure into a mentality that helps you have faith and grace for yourself." Crossfit Santa goes into an analogy but I'm still hung on his last statement.

The clock says it's time to go. This ticking brings peace. I feel calmer watching the second hand. *Tick, tick, tick.*

"Maybe you can take some time to think about that." He stands from his chair and shakes my hand. "Good to meet with you. I look forward to our next appointment."

"Thank you." I gather my things and go.

——————

Since I was gone for a while, it's already time to head to willardson. Wish I had a moment to catch my breath.

"Ready?" Her sweet smile greets me, arms wrapping around my waist, hugging me close. Lips meet mine, thirsty to be filled. But I feel drained. Like I have nothing to offer her.

Did I ever?

"What?" She holds me at arms length, the smell of her cinnamon perfume filling my nose. "What's wrong?"

I want to be with you, but I don't know how. Right now I don't know how to be with myself. Feeling overwhelmed, I sit on the bed. She comes up beside me.

"It was a lot." I debate telling her why. No, that won't help. Mindy's wrong about this one. Telling her will only make everything harder. The last thing we need is for her to be conscious about my food choices. I'm already concerned enough for both of us. Let me get this under control. Then maybe I'll tell her. Yes, then. After I've figured it out.

"I thought it might be." Her hand rubs between my shoulder blades. "You talked about Cody?"

I nod.

"I'm glad you went."

"I'm not. Jeez, does therapy always open up a big ol' can a worms?"

"Yeah, I think it does, actually. Good to go through those worms though, figure out which ones you wanna keep and which ones you need to let go." She leans her head on my shoulder for several heart-beats. "I went to a grief counselor for a little bit. Helped a lot."

"I have a lot to sort through." *Come on Bobby, just tell her.*

It's on the tip of my tongue when her phone alarm plays some annoying song.

"We gotta go." She takes my hand. "Mom's expectin' us for dinner and she goes psycho if we are late. I'll drive. We can talk about it on the way, okay?"

"Okay." Only, I don't talk about it. Too many thoughts go through my head, making it ache as I recall every second of that appointment.

———

SHE STOPS FOR A COKE AT THE MCDONALDS. "WHAT DO YOU WANT?"

"Nothin'." Couldn't put anything in my mouth to save my life.

"One large Coke." She shakes her head to the music playing while we wait in the drive-thru. After she pulls out of the parking lot, she sips as we drive.

We're fifteen miles down the road before we say another word. I'm still on pins and needles, like my body can't calm down. This is not a good way to feel going into my first dinner at the Hawthorne's, as Lexie's boyfriend.

Shit, I need to relax.

"Do you like your therapist?" She glances my way.

"Yeah. I mean, sure, he's fine." I strain to swallow. My mouth is so fucking dry.

"Did your mom ever call you back?"

"No, I'm assumin' she's busy with stuff for the holidays." The excuse is forced, and I wish I believed it. But since Mom didn't bother calling me for my birthday or Thanksgiving, I'm really fucking angry. I know Mrs. Harris needs attention, but this is bullshit. She hasn't had *any* time to call me?

"You've called her several times. You'd think she'd text back, at the very least." Lexie wrinkles her brows.

"I can't think of a time in my whole life when we've gone this long without an actual phone call. We are the type of family that actually talks to each other. Makes it even weirder."

"That is weird." Lex focuses on the road. "I try not to talk to my parents."

"Yeah, that may be my new approach." I shake my head. This is so strange for Mom and Dad. Good thing I'll see them soon so I can figure all this out.

"I remember the cookie exchanges your mom always used to host. We'd come back with platters full." Lexie pops the lid off her Coke and pours a few ice cubes into her mouth to chew on.

A smile pulls at my face. I loved the times that our families all got together.

"Have you told your parents about us?" I ask.

"Yep. Have you?" Her eyebrow raises.

I rub my forehead. "No, not in the few and far between conversations we've had."

"Oh, right."

"It's a little unsettlin'. I don't know if they are just extra busy or what."

"We're all busy."

Her words bite my insides. I'm empty. The weight of my therapy appointment and this conflict covers me like a blanket of fire, singeing my skin.

"I'm sure it's fine." She gives me a smile.

I hope she's right. I'm worried that it's not going to be the picture-perfect holiday from years past. It already isn't.

Enough of the heaviness. I work to shake it off. Optimism is everything. Good vibes only. I'm about done with all this stress.

———

PULLING UP IN LEXIE'S DRIVEWAY, I SEE THE ESTATE. MY PARENTS ARE well off, but hers are in a whole other tax bracket. Her dad made it big in the bank law business. I think her family came from money, anyway.

Makes my heart ache for Cody's family. Pain wraps around my tight throat wondering if they are still in debt from the funeral. Grief flows through my system and on top of all the other heaviness, I can't breathe. Vomit comes to the back of my throat. I swallow and it burns a trail back into my stomach, acid lingering on my tonsils.

"Maybe I should have you drop me at my parent's place? I don't want to impose on your family." I run my tongue over the roof of my mouth. So fucking dry.

"Don't be silly." She gets her backpack out of the back while I grab the duffel. "Mom is fine with you stayin' over."

"You're sure?" I eye her.

"I don't want to be here without you."

There is a weight to her words that makes me worry. What has her homelife been like? Mick is her half brother. Her mom treated her like she didn't want her. What is Mr. Hawthorne like? She has his last name, but that may or may not mean he accepts her.

She unlocks the door.

Meg, their maid, pulls her into a big hug. I remember Meg from when we hung out here as kids. She's worked here since before I was in junior high.

"Where's Mom?" Lexie steps back from the embrace and cleans her shoes on the greeting mat.

"She is finishing a call with the country club." Meg smiles.

Their home is stunning. Something you'd expect to see in a Southern Living magazine. Pristine marble floors. Large hallways with arched walkways. A grand staircase with gold trim.

Famous paintings hang on the wall. None of 'em are ones Lexie painted. Jeez. She wasn't kidding when she said she didn't feel like she fit in with her mom. How hard is it to display your daughter's prized work? My parents made the whole living room a tribute to me playing ball.

My eyes scan the visible walls, hoping maybe I've just missed it. I could pick Lexie's style out of a gallery. But these? Not one is even close to how she paints. I wish that her parents cared more about her. If this was my house, my daughter's work would be all over the halls. Lexie's paintings are good enough, too. She's an amazing artist.

"You remember Bobby?" Lexie gestures to me.

"Oh, yes." Meg shakes my hand.

"Baby girl?" Mr. Hawthorne steps out of his home office.

"Hey, Dad." Lex rises up on her toes to hug him. He smiles big and pulls her close for a hug, like he's missed her a lot. Seems they get along just fine. She's really only mentioned things being tense with her mom.

"Bobby." He shakes my hand. "Good to see you."

"Mr. Hawthorne, you as well." I match his firm grip with my own.

"Bobby's stayin' over. Did Mom tell you?" Lexie brushes a strand of hair out of her face.

Butterflies flutter in my stomach, not having a clue what her dad is going to think about this.

"Oh, is your home life still in shambles, Bobby?" Mr. Hawthorne's face is serious while I wait for him to crack a joke. The longer we stand there, I realize he's not teasing.

"Dad!" Lexie gasps, bringing her fingers to her lips. Her eyes dart to mine and I give her a frazzled look.

Shock plays on my face. My cheeks are burning hot. "Shambles?" I try to play it cool, but my pulse throbs in my veins.

"Lexie." Her mom rushes down the stairs.

I welcome the distraction. I don't know what the hell he was talking about. Shambles? Terror squeezes my insides. My frustration and worry turn to near panic and total confusion.

Lexie and her mom hug like nothing's wrong. I know otherwise by the way that Lexie's smile doesn't reach her eyes. Whatever Mrs. Hawthorne did that day when Lexie found out about her birth father likely caused a permanent wedge between them. It's sad, but I can see it.

"Bobby and I are goin' up to my room." Lex takes my hand. I carry the duffel up the stairs.

"Don't be too long," her mom calls after us.

"Okay, Mom."

"Meg has lasagna in the oven."

"Got it." Lexie sounds annoyed.

"Dinner is promptly at six!" her mom calls, louder.

"We understand!"

"God, my mother." She lets out an exasperated sigh as we get into her bedroom, childhood pink coating the room, like a cotton candy machine blew up in here.

"Pink?" I run my hand against the pastel textured wall.

"Gotta make sure I stay their little princess."

I shake my head. "They don't have a clue about you, do they?"

"Never cared to find out." She tucks the suitcase on the top of her dresser. "I'm sorry about my dad. I don't know what he's talkin' about."

My stomach tenses so tight. "I need to figure out what's goin' on." I pull out my phone and dial mom. It rings to voicemail. I call again. Same thing. Try Dad. No answer.

My mind spirals into worse case scenarios. What the hell is wrong? Some trouble with the house? Their health? Money? Shit, I don't even know what kind of trouble they could be in. This isn't Cody's family I'm talking about. His family was a shit show running a marathon all day every day. But mine? Nope. A normal, well adjusted, mostly functional family.

Until they stopped talking to me.

Oh shit.

The reality that something is horribly wrong consumes me. As if today wasn't overwhelming enough. I'm here at the Hawthorne's trying to look like a good boyfriend. Just dumped my whole fucking soul in Crossfit Santa's office. Now *shambles*....

Holy hell how am I supposed to handle all this?

I want to go get in the car and drive over there. But I can't. Not with how Lexie's parents are. That would ruin any good impression I'm capable of making.

I don't even know if my parents are at home.

Shambles.

"My dad says a lot of shit. He's probably just over exaggerating." Lexie must be sensing my inner terror.

"Am I that easy to read?"

"Your face is all red." She leans up and kisses me, like she's trying to give me comfort. "It's gonna be alright, okay?" Her fingers fix my hair. "I don't know what Dad meant."

"I wish I did." My heart races as I pull off my shirt.

"Here." Lexie gets her yellow dress and my button up out of the suitcase. "Try not to worry 'til we know what's goin' on, alright?" She steps closer to me, her hands on my back, drawing me tight to her.

I force out a breath. "Okay."

———

THEIR DINING ROOM IS BIG ENOUGH TO FIT THE WHOLE BASEBALL TEAM. The clink of silver forks against fine China is the only sound. We dressed for dinner, because here, that's what you do. Lex's yellow dress hugs her in all the places that I refuse to stare at with her father looking.

I dish up a small serving of the lasagna. About a quarter cup. Thoughtful portion.

"Oh, take more than that." Lexie's mom grabs the serving spoon from my hand and dishes up a heap that covers my plate. She doesn't understand that I'll pay for it later. I could've handled a little bit, but not this much.

I keep waiting for them to ask me stuff like most families do when you bring a fella home. Or at least, what I've watched in movies. I guess I've never been in an actual dinner-with-the-parents situation, until now. But they don't. They don't say anything. Tension builds in the air like fog after a bad storm.

"Well, Bobby, how's the team lookin' this year?" Mr. Hawthorn breaks the silence. Thank God.

"It's lookin' great." I smile and nod. "Coach Conners has us workin' hard already."

"Glad to hear it. I mean, last year it fell apart toward the end of the season. But you boys really pulled it together." He holds his fork out, like he's punctuating his thoughts. "Reminds me of–" Her father talks about some case he's working on and I zone it out, shaking in my skin needing to get home.

Focus, Bobby, focus.

I gotta keep up appearances now that I'm the boyfriend. Mom always said I was good with people, so it's no trouble to get them to like me. The feeling may never be mutual. I don't like anyone who isn't willing to take care of my girl. She isn't hard to take care of. Her mom barely tries at all.

Cool it, Anderson. Not like you need to drive a wedge between you and her family so soon.

Her dad may be a good person, but he doesn't do enough to support her dreams.

I hope she's ready to tell me more someday. I want to hear all her stories. I want to ease all her pain.

Will she ever be ready to hear about mine?

The grandfather clock in the corner ticks. *Tick. Tick. Tick.* Just like the clock in Crossfit Santa's office. I try to find that bit of calm.

Her dad's monologue drones on and no one competes with it. Her mom looks tired. That kind of tired that makes me think she's listened to his stories for too many years. Like, if it wasn't for the money, she wouldn't still be married to him.

But hey, they stayed together after Lexie's mom slept with Mick's dad, so there must be something there. Even if it is just money.

Shambles.

My stomach sours as I recall her dad's words. It's hard to eat this lasagna. I want to eat. Each bite is a battle as it enters my mouth. I don't taste, because I'm too worked up trying to make myself swallow.

My hand shakes. I have to do this. Have to get better.

I stare at the food on my plate. My body will not tolerate all the shit I'm forcing down. Just three months before season, too. Can't have this. High carbs. High fat in the ground beef. Too many calories. Not good for me. No, I can't have this.

I feel so weighed down. All the things Crossfit Santa said to me in therapy. All the heaviness of being here with her parents when I still haven't seen mine. All the tension building inside of me.

I covertly check my phone under the table. No fucking reply.

Thanks, Mom.

24

LEXIE

I wish I knew how to help.

Bobby's shutting down. I see it in every moment of this dinner conversation. The best thing is to finish the meal and see if we can go to his parent's house. Part of me wants to confront Dad and ask him what the fuck he was talking about. But I won't do it at the table. And I certainly won't leave Bobby alone with Mom to go talk. She can be a ruthless viper when she wants to be. He's dealing with more than enough already.

I feel his pain and distress as if it's my own. Being this connected to someone is new and strange. I've had empathy, sure, but this is a whole new level. Bobby is often the life of the party, the entertainer, the one making everyone else at ease.

Right now he is anything but. Even though this is basically a meet-the-parents moment. *Let me do somethin'...let me be there for you. Please?*

Dad tends to exaggerate, but the word 'shambles' could be a hundred different bad things. Hell, it could mean anything from him destroying Dr. Anderson in a game of golf last week and keeping the teasing up through Bobby. Or it could mean the Anderson's house burned down, leaving the ashes of their peach trees to be devoured by worms.

Better to not assume anything until we have the facts.

I reach out, brushing aside the long cloth that dangles from the table to hold Bobby's hand. My eyes find his and I smile. Then I look at his plate. Fuck, he probably thinks he needs to eat all that. I'm sure he's panicking about how it's not on his diet.

I wait until no one is looking, and scoop most of the lasagna onto my plate.

His eyes find mine, a silent *thank you* written in those perfect blue irises. I love Meg's lasagna, so it's a win-win. I know it meant a lot to him that I took it off his plate. He has so much on his plate right now: coming down from a crazy semester, our new relationship, baseball coming up, whatever *shambles* meant. Extra lasagna is the last thing he needs to pile on top of his proverbial plate.

We'll figure it all out, Bobby, I promise. I wish he could read my thoughts. Tomorrow will be better, once my sister gets into town. She and Paisley will take a lot of the attention off us.

Bobby finishes his last bite and rubs his forehead. I stuff a few bites in my mouth, but it really was too much for me.

"We have a couple errands to run." I stand with my plate in my hand.

"You haven't even eaten." Mom scrutinizes my plate. "Sit back down and finish."

"I'm good, see." I take two bites while I'm standing.

"Alexia Marie Hawthorne, sit down and finish your dinner," her tone is rash.

"We're goin'."

Mom raises her hands toward the ceiling with a *why me?* expression on her face. She dips her head down and massages her temples.

I feel that pull at my insides, wishing things between us were better. I don't know if they ever will be. She needed someone more "high-society" to be good enough for her. Not my tattoos and bright red hair and artist soul.

She never really wanted me.

Just a mistake.

I walk around the table and give Dad a kiss on the forehead good-bye. "See ya, Daddy."

"I'll be workin' a lot while you're here. We have dinner at Meadow Ridge tomorrow night." He wipes his lips with a napkin, and goes for his red wine.

"Yep, plannin' on it." I nod, remembering how to get to the country club where we spend every Christmas Eve.

After we clear our plates, we get into my car, and I see Bobby's shoulders relax. He sits a little straighter. Color returns to his cheeks, and air fills his lungs like he's taken his first breath all evening.

"Jesus, my mother." I curl my hands around my stomach. "We can get a hotel if you don't wanna stay here."

"It's fine. If you're okay?" He puts his hands on mine.

"Yeah, I'm used to it." I try to smile, but man I hate how Mom treats me.

"Thanks for takin' some of the lasagna." He rubs my knuckles.

I shrug. "I've got you."

We make it halfway to his parent's house when we stop at a red light. His hand starts trembling under mine.

"Hey now, it's alright."

"Somethin's wrong, Lex." He let's it all out like a gust of wind in a storm. "And I dunno what it is, and I dunno what I'm bringin' you into, and I dunno if it's gonna be okay or not."

I struggle for words to say. "Whatever it is, we are doin' it together." I squeeze his hands, feeling so cold beneath mine–like he's been covered in ice.

He's holding his breath, and I keep driving. *Please, Bobby, let me inside. Let me support you. It's all I want.*

The porch lights illuminate Bobby's sweet Southern home. It has a circle driveway, white pillars going from ground to roof. White shutters and gingham window treatments in each window. The house has *not* burned down. I just hope that means that Dad won against Dr. Anderson playing golf.

I kill the engine and walk up to the front door with him.

He jingles the handle but it won't budge because it's locked. Bobby knocks a few times, then stuffs his hands in his pockets and leans against a pillar like he can't stand on his own.

We wait for several minutes, and I wonder if it's time to leave. Maybe they aren't home.

"Do you have your key?"

Bobby reaches in all his pockets, frowning while he rolls his eyes. "Probably left them on your nightstand when we were changing for dinner."

"We can go get them and come back," I offer.

"If they're home, they'll answer." His voice is lower than normal and he clears his throat.

My heart aches for what he's dealing with.

The door slides open and his mom gasps. She's a tall woman who is perfectly fit, with deep brown hair. A nightgown falls off one of her shoulders as she readjusts, pulling a silky bathrobe tighter around her waist.

"Bobby." Her arms come around his neck and I have a chance of hope that maybe everything is alright. I don't think either of us need any more heartache right now.

"Lexie?" She comes around me in a quick hug, pulling back before I have a chance to wrap my arms around her. Looking at Bobby, he smiles and nods.

Is she upset? I can't quite pick up her vibe.

"Come on in, honey, it's freezin' out here." She runs her hands down her arms against the chill. We come inside, sliding the door shut behind us. We slip off our shoes in the entryway. A pile of mail sits on their entry table with a few of the envelopes open and the contents sticking halfway out. Boxes stack up against the coat closet door, like it's holding it shut.

In the living room, red rooster throw pillows are stacked haphazardly in the corner of one sofa. A dozen candy bar wrappers, an open cracker box—with accompanying crumbs—and a half full glass of water collect dust on the end table. It's not a lot of clutter, but it's more than I've ever seen at their house before. It always used to be really clean.

"Can I get you a cup of coffee? Wine? I think we have some apple cider in the back that I can warm up. Are you stayin'? Gonna need your room? And the guest room, maybe? I didn't make any real holiday plans, but I'm sure we can come up with somethin'." Bobby's mom keeps talking like she's nervous.

"Where you been, Mom?" Bobby's gripping his knees for dear life while we sit on their fabric sofa with black and white plaid squares. He observes the room and gets up to fix the pillows. Then he puts the garbage off the end table in the trash. "You been sick?" There's no masking his concern.

She opens her lips to say something and stops it before the words come out. "How about that coffee?" She goes in the kitchen, and Bobby follows her there. Torn between where I need to be and where I am, I stop and think about what may be going on.

I force a breath, looking around their living room, doing my best not to eavesdrop. It has everything you'd expect. Only, it's changed too. There aren't the family photos on the wall. The big recliner, where I often saw Dr. Anderson reading when we came over, is missing. Come to think of it, a lot of this room has changed. Are they remodeling? Where is Dr. Anderson? I force a breath as my stomach cramps with worry. Bobby's mom is here, she's alive, I'm sure whatever is going on will sort itself out. Right?

One thing hasn't changed. All the baseball trophies and posters hung on the main wall. Their pride and joy, prominently displayed. I can tell how proud of Bobby they are. Bringing myself to the mantle, I look at a bunch of old baseball photos. Bobby and Cody as kids, always together.

My heart tightens, and I swallow the lump forming in my throat. Hopefully they won't be in the kitchen talking too long because I really don't need to stay here drowning in yesterday. The graveyard of my happy memories.

25

BOBBY

"Why are you here with Lexie Hawthorne?" Mom's voice is a faint whisper as she starts up water for the coffee. Dishes take over the sink. What a mess. Well, not that much of a mess, but for Mom it's more than she'd ever tolerated when I was a kid. In all my life, there have never been dirty dishes piled up.

"Why haven't you returned any of my calls?" Things feel so tense. I've fought with Mom, sure, usually about small stuff. Not about big stuff. This feels big, and I don't even understand why. I don't know what the hell we are fighting about.

My head is spinning. She hasn't been answering my calls or texts. We show up, and she acts like nothing is wrong. Everything is wrong. Garbage overflows from the can. Sticky stuff and crumbs cover the counter.

"I called you back."

"Yeah, weeks later." I grab a rag and wipe off the counter. Leaning against it, I reminisce on all the times I leaned here talking to her as a teenager. Cody and I both begging her for a ride to GameStop for the newest video game, or bugging her while she cooked dinner, going over college applications and talking about my plans to follow Cody to play professional ball.

I'd do anything to bring him back right now. So we could both talk to Mom about this and not just me.

"Wanting to be with your friend is a longing that many experience after losing a loved one, Bobby." Crossfit Santa's words come at me, and I swallow a wave of emotion. It's been such a long day. And I've got a feeling it's gonna get much longer.

"You can't expect me to just call you back all the time. I have a life too, ya know." The level of accusation in her tone makes me wince like when I got in trouble as a kid.

"It's just fine for you to have a life, but you cuttin' me out of it is recent and you know it." My teeth grind at her defensiveness. "You missed my birthday, Mom."

"I sent a package." She dumps grounds into the Ninja Coffee Machine from her measuring scoop. "You still haven't answered me." She gives a level stare. "What is Lexie Hawthorne doin' here, with you?"

Heat burns at my eye sockets. *If you woulda returned my calls I woulda told you...*

"I'm not blind, Bobby, and I don't think this is a good idea," she puts the canister of coffee grounds back in the cabinet.

"Why? Because you're afraid of her parents? Her dad just referred to my homelife as 'shambles.' Somethin' goin' on between y'all and the Hawthornes?" My heart rate skyrockets at the thought. Lexie and I have overcome so many obstacles, already. The last thing I need is a Stark and Lannister debate between our households, like a living version of "Game Of Thrones."

"Heavens, no. It's because I'm afraid of you bein' with her for the wrong reasons." Her hands are on her hips, an exasperated huff working it's way out. "I've seen this happen with other couples, and I will not watch you take advantage of that sweet girl because you miss Cody."

Shit.

"I'm not with her 'cause I miss him." My jaw ticks, front teeth clashing so hard I feel pain. "I'm with her because I love her. And I would have told you all that if you would have replied to my *many* messages. Jeez, Mom."

"Love her?" Mom's face transforms into the one she always scolds me with. "How are you supposed to know that you love her? He's been gone less than two years and you're datin' his survivin' partner. Do you really think this is a good idea?" Mom's whisper is so faint you couldn't hope to hear it more than a foot away.

My veins turn to ice. "How can you ask me that?" The words are harsher than they should be, but she is not going to bring up what I've been working so hard to forget.

"What do you want?" her eyes meet mine.

I want you to accept my choices. I thought you and Dad could handle that.

"I wanna know what the hell is goin' on." I swallow so hard it hurts my throat.

Her eyes flicker. She bites her lip before her gaze darts away from mine. Then she's back with a smile plastered on her mouth, trying to hide whatever the hell that was.

"Wait." My heart is pounding as I connect a missing puzzle piece. As much as the house is filled with a mess, it's not filled with any traces of Dad. The shelves in the front room didn't have his books. The furniture in the room was rearranged to remove his favorite recliner. I turn to the wall behind the kitchen table. Their wedding picture, that has hung there forever, is gone.

My body goes cold. No, this can't be it. They woulda told me. If they split up, they woulda told me. Emotions fight to be recognized. I push them down.

She's just redecorating. That's why there's a mess. She's moving shit around.

Only looking at her, I see guilt. I have to ask her a question that hurts just to think about. With a deep breath, I force the words, knowing that she will not offer this information willingly. If she was going to, she already would have.

"Where is Dad?"

Color drains from her face.

I can't fucking breathe. "Mom?"

The longer we stand here, the worse I feel. She's giving me shit when there is something going on. Any shred of a healthy relationship we may have had just shattered like a baseball through a window. Every part of me wants to go get in Lexie's car and drive away. But I have to know. I have to know about those 'shambles' Mr. Hawthorne mentioned.

"Where the hell is he?" My voice is loud. She jumps. Shit. I don't usually shout. Even when I'm mad as hell, she's my mom and deserves respect. I hold a trembling breath in my lungs, pulling at the collar of my shirt. Lexie is at the doorway of the kitchen. Double shit.

I hold Mom's eyes, pleading for some sort of answer.

"Your Dad walked out a few months ago."

The words register, and at first I think I heard her wrong. I must've heard her wrong. Only her face matches exactly what I think she said. There's sadness there. Loss. Grief. I understand those feelings. Better than I wish I did.

"...a few months ago." Bile rises up the back of my throat, anger coursing through me with each heartbeat. How did I go so long without so much as a returned phone call? They were splitting up and didn't bother to tell their only son.

I grip the counter in both hands to steady the spinning room. "When the hell were you gonna tell me?" My voice is too loud, I know it is, but I can't stop it. I can't believe what I'm hearing. My knees turn weak, refusing to hold up my body.

"Look, Bobby, it's not because I didn't wanna tell you. Part of me was hopin' he would come back." She crosses the kitchen and stands too close, trying to pull me into a hug. I jerk my shoulder away from her and pain flares in her eyes.

This is one of those moments I can feel is going to be important as it plays out in front of me. But I still can't stop myself from making some terrible mistake. Like there isn't any choice besides a mistake. No way out; all nonviable options.

"How could you?" Is all I manage to say before I storm out of the house, passing Lexie as I go, slamming the back door.

I go out into the yard, lighting up the beautiful landscaping and orchard. Storming into the shed, I get my baseballs and go between the many rows of peach trees. Their peach trees. The ones Mom and Dad planted together. Raised together. Just like they raised me.

I wind up and throw. My ball slams into the wooden fence. Again. Stings reverberate through all my muscles. I throw harder and faster. The box at my feet is the ammo to my rage. I throw. Again. Again. Again.

She didn't tell me.

Dad left.

Dad left months ago, and she didn't tell me.

He didn't tell me.

Neither of them bothered to tell me.

I must not matter to them a fucking bit.

I stare at the last peach tree in the row. The ground beneath it. My body quakes, remembering. I wanna forget. I just wanna forget. My throat burns. Fucking tears glide down my cheeks. *How could you do this to me, Cody? How could you leave me here alone?*

So much pain about what happened years ago combines with the reality of my broken family. A burden I've been bearing long before it had a name.

All the days I felt this pressure, this strain. I hoped I was overreacting and that nothing was going wrong. But this is enough to shatter anyone in the best of circumstances.

What would you do if you were me, right now, Cody? Just go with it? Pretend everything is damn fine? Because it ain't. It's far from alright. I need you here, and you're fuckin' gone.

I storm to the fence with my empty box and pick up every last baseball. The fence is splintered and cracked where I hit it. I shouldn't be ruining their property. I shouldn't be doing any of this. But I am.

Who splits up and doesn't fucking tell their son?

Parents shouldn't hurt their child like this. It shouldn't feel like my soul is being ripped in half and lit on fire.

It ain't right.

26

LEXIE

I stand in the kitchen, watching Bobby storm outside.

His mom covers her face with her hands, stifling sobs. I'm probably the last person in the world she'd want to offer her any sort of comfort, but I cross the kitchen, anyway.

The coffee maker beeps, a carafe full of an amazing smelling vanilla roast done brewing. I get some mugs off the rack and pour, going to the fridge for creamer. Keep going, keep moving, get through this. There isn't creamer, so I go for the almond milk and pour a little in my cup. I stand by his mom at the counter, offering a sympathetic smile.

"I don't know how much you overheard." She wipes at her tears.

I'm not sure how to answer her, not sure what's appropriate to say. Instead of addressing her question, I direct things back to Bobby. "He's been really worried about you." I guess I strike a chord because her face fills with brand new tears.

Mrs. Anderson is a personal trainer at the gym on Main Street. I saw her at the baseball games growing up and she would say hello. Our families sometimes attended events together. She always invited me to the end-of-the-season parties she threw, and the Christmas parties, and Halloween, of course. Every year she went all out for Bobby's birth-

216 | MARISSA J. GRAMOLL

day. She also threw big parties for Cody's birthday, stepping in as the best friend's mom when Cody's mom couldn't.

Another woman enters the kitchen, coming toward Mrs. Anderson. "Who is here?"

"Bobby." Mrs. Anderson shakes her head, bringing her fists up to her eyes.

"Come here." The other woman pulls down Mrs. Anderson's fists, bringing her in for a hug.

"He didn't take it well." Mrs. Anderson holds the other woman close. Is this her sister? Bobby's aunt maybe?

"I know, love. It'll be alright." The other woman kisses Mrs. Anderson for a long time, like a good, hard kiss.

Oh, oh, boy, not a sister. Not a relative. A lover. A girlfriend or something. I feel like maybe I need to turn around or go find Bobby, be anywhere besides where I stand.

Am I watching this? Am I really watching this?

After convincing my frozen feet to move, I sit at their kitchen table stirring the almond milk into the coffee. I take a gulp that burns all the way down my throat.

No wonder Dad said 'shambles.' Yeesh. Though I am one hundred percent supportive of everyone being free to love who they love, I can see why this sorta thing wouldn't go over well in our small, Southern, super conservative, Christian town. Fuck, I cannot imagine the gossip that's been circulating, and I have no clue how Bobby and I didn't catch a lick of it. Word spreads like wildfire around here. I'm surprised it didn't get all the way to Suncastle yet. This kind of gossip is exactly what made Mom so mean to me and Mickey. *Never tell a soul, Alexia Marie.* The memory of her words makes me shudder.

"I'm Nira." The woman holds out a hand, and takes a seat beside me at the Anderson's kitchen table. She must not be from around here because there isn't a bit of twang in her voice.

"Lexie." I shake her hand, noticing her long, black, fake nails. The woman is beautiful–stunning, even. She's got really nice boobs in a tight shirt and perfect cascading lush blond curls down her spine.

"Nice to meet you, Lexie." Her body is even more toned than

Bobby's or his mom and being surrounded by all of them makes me feel like I'm at a fitness expo.

Pretty soon Bobby's mom comes and sits down with us. We all endure the silence for a long while.

"School goin' well, sweetheart?" Mrs. Anderson asks, pretending nothing happened.

I'm in so much shock, I just take another sip of coffee. "Yeah, school's great."

"Are you and Bobby–" Mrs. Anderson starts, and I jump in before she says anything more.

"Yeah." I sip more coffee. "Been together for a few weeks, now."

"Oh, um, I'm surprised." She taps her not-fake nails on the table-top, contrasting with Nira's.

"You're the one surprised?" My eyebrow raises; Nira chuckles. As awkward as this moment is, I actually kinda like her. The longer I sit here, the more reality sets in, and I worry about Bobby. Maybe I should go check on him. Or maybe he just needs space.

His mom left his dad for a woman…and didn't bother to tell him when the whole town probably knows.

I take a long look at his mom, grinding my teeth to keep from giving her a piece of my mind. *If I was Bobby's mom I woulda fuckin' told him. Disgraceful, Mrs. Anderson. Disgraceful. Well, I guess you aren't Mrs. Anderson anymore are you? Probably not.*

The door swings open. Bobby comes in, covered in sweat. He glances at his mom and Nira for a minute, face unreadable, carrying a big ol' box of baseballs, heading directly for the front door. "I'll be back to fix the fence tomorrow."

"Have a good night." I manage, rushing after Bobby. He's already outside, putting the balls in the backseat like they are a new baby. His baby. Or a baby version of himself. Like an inner child, the last thing left to hold on to after his family life fell apart.

He gets in the driver's seat, and I hand him the keys.

We go through town, missing the turn to my parent's house. Street lights shine with their holiday wreaths. It's getting late and pretty dark.

After a while, he takes us toward the mountains. I guess he's heading toward the Elerish Mountains and I'm right.

Parked at the top of the mountain road, windows rolled down, I look at the marvelous view. I can see the whole town. The air is a little cold, but I'm comfortable with my dress and sweater.

"You wanna talk?" I bite my tongue because that is probably not what he wants. Come to think of it, he's barely even told me about his therapy appointment. After seeing all that, I'm acutely aware of how he doesn't like things being kept from him. There's an ache in my gut that only gets worse the longer we sit here. Meg's lasagna sloshes around like its liver and onions, instead of my favorite meal.

He slams his palm into the steering wheel. Then his forehead. "How could they?"

I look at him for a long time, wishing I knew how to help him navigate through such a shock. I've only seen the Andersons as a happy couple, the type of people that would kiss under the mistletoe in front of everyone at the holiday parties. Every time I saw them, they were in love. Were they just pretending? Or maybe it was real, but now it's changed.

"Did she tell you why she didn't explain sooner?" I put my hand on his shoulder.

"No." His looks dazed. "I mean, I knew somethin' was up." He massages his temples and rests his head on the steering wheel for several minutes. "I can't believe this."

"Me neither." I sigh, wondering if he's ready to hear this next bit. "Your mom is with that other woman. Like with *with* her."

He clicks his tongue. "She should've told me. She should've told me months ago. This whole damn time." He lets out a huff. "I'm not mad at her for splittin' with Dad. Hell, I'm not even mad about her bein' with that woman. This may sound crazy, but if she feels this way then who am I to question it?"

He's so understanding, even after such a low blow.

"But she shoulda fuckin' called me back and told me at least some of this, goddamnit."

"They definitely shoulda told you."

"Yeah." He blows out a long breath. "I'm gonna call Dad. See if I can at least tell him Merry Christmas or somethin'. I bet this whole situation it tearin' him up somethin' fierce." He leans his head against the headrest.

"Yeah." I put my hand on his. "I'm sure he wants to see you."

"What happened when I went out back? Did you, ya know, talk to her and shit?" He tilts his head up just enough to see me.

"She cried for a little while, and then the other woman showed up and they kissed."

"They kissed." He moves in his chair, leaning back, and stares at the city in front of us for an uncomfortable period of time. "You wanna go on a walk? I could use some air."

"Yeah."

We get out of the car and take one of the trails, the moonlight enough to light our way. Our hands intertwine. I remember coming here as a little girl, on one of the rare times Dad didn't have to work. Something about being with these trees, with this man I care about so much, makes my heart dance.

"I always thought my parents had it, ya know? That love of a lifetime. That one and only. The happily ever after and all that shit." His voice is heavy. "I guess I didn't really know."

"It's hard to ever know what goes on between two people." I squeeze his hand.

"Ain't that the truth." He seems so defeated, and I worry he's somehow blaming himself for what happened with his folks.

My heart pounds in my chest, because I've been wanting to talk to Bobby. So much got pulled out from under him, and I won't keep more secrets. "I need to tell you somethin'."

"Anythin', you know that, baby." He slows down to look at me.

"Well I don't even sorta like this, so I have no clue how you're gonna feel." I shake my head. "Because you need to know. Well, I need you to know. It has haunted me day and night. But I need to say this, I need you to hear me. With Cody..." my throat clogs up, and I don't know if I can go on.

"It's alright. Whatever you need to say." His eyes are kind enough that I dare to hope he's ready to learn this.

"With Cody, we were far from perfect. There was so much goin' wrong. Right before the accident I didn't know if we could stay together." The burden I'm trying to release quadruples in size, taking life from my chest, making it hard to breathe. I don't feel better. I feel worse. "It was so much of a struggle and I was tryin'. Really, I was tryin' so hard." My lungs collapse on themselves, horrified that I've betrayed Cody and that I picked tonight of all nights to tell Bobby.

"I know." Bobby doesn't sound the least bit surprised.

My heart batters my insides. Oh God, how much does he know? They were best friends. Fuck...did Cody talk about our sex with him? Or rather, our lack thereof?

"I'm so embarrassed." I close my eyes, bringing my palm to my face.

"Oh, Lex." His tone is so caring, pulling my hand down to kiss it. "I know you're conscious about it, but I'm not judgin' you. Not even a little bit."

I squeeze his hand, trying to believe him.

"How much did Cody tell you?" A darkness spreads through me. I never knew what to make of it then, and I definitely don't know what to make of it now. Bobby showed me just how good sex can be. What Cody and I did was like a failed attempt.

"We talked some. Cody had a lot of shit he was workin' through. I know that none of it was your fault." He wraps his arms around me. I hold him, trying to let go of this heartache. Cody telling Bobby isn't something I'd even considered. I thought this would be news to Bobby. But it's not. He's known this whole time.

Even though he knows, Bobby doesn't think any less of me. So often I think less of myself. Bundled inside his embrace, I feel as though nothing could ever hurt me as long as he's here. Maybe Bobby can teach me how to give myself more compassion.

"I know the relationship was really hard for both of you." His hands bring me closer, no space between us.

"You do?" I listen to his heart, feeling raw and exposed, my soul naked before him. "All I want is to love you. We've both been through enough–" my words are cut off as Bobby presses his lips to mine, under the moonlight.

I kiss him, gripping his hair, pulling him tighter to me because I've never been this close to someone. Not like this. With Bobby it's there, that physical and emotional bond between us. The way that I feel at home in his arms; safe and accepted.

This need to be loved forces me forward, clenching onto him, holding on for dear life. *Don't leave me. I can't handle life without you.*

"I'm here, baby. I'm right here." He holds me like he can read my thoughts. His warmth floods me with comfort. "I want to be here. I want to be with you." His words shake the center of my soul.

Holy fuck. I don't know how I'm always shocked, but I am. He wants *me*. I thought I knew what it felt like to be wanted. The longer I spend with Bobby, the more it becomes clear that I had no clue. I felt needed with Cody. Cody *needed* me to take care of him, to be there, to not judge him for all the shit he'd been through. But maybe he didn't really want me. Because this feels fucking different, in every way. That Bobby would give anything to keep me. That he wants *me*. Not just some girl.

I think back to all those girls Bobby's slept with and how worried Trish was. I was right, that was waiting for me.

He wanted me.

The thought is so incredible I melt into his embrace. I'm not just me anymore. I'm one with him. There's no separation between where I end and he begins. There's only what we are, together.

All my life, I've wanted *this*. I cannot breathe with him this close to me, each kiss building on the last one. Breath holds in my chest, the love between us reaching a new depth.

His head moves backward, putting space between us, leaning to whisper in my ear. "If you don't wanna talk about everythin' tonight, we don't have to. But please know that we will. Because I'm here for you, alright? There's nothin' you can say that is wrong. Whatever you feel, I wanna know," he steps back, holding my hands in his. Bobby's hands are freezing cold so I bring them inside of mine and work to warm them up.

"There's so much I need to tell you." I'm staggering from the withdrawal of his body against mine, blowing hot air onto his chilly fingers.

"I know." He sees me, the real me, standing before him with all of my flaws. Thoughtfully, he smiles. "I have a lot to tell you, too."

I raise my eyebrows. What could he possibly have to tell me? Does it have to do with what Cody said about our relationship? I don't even know what he's referring to.

His mouth presses into a thin line. "Can we agree to be patient with each other? Work through stuff one step at a time?"

"Always." I kiss him with the depth we enjoyed just moments ago. "I'm relieved you're not mad. I just...it always feels like I'm betrayin' him when I think about how much was goin' wrong between us."

"Believe me, I know the feelin'." He shivers, shaking all over. Worried, I feel his forehead for a fever. No, of course not. He's just cold, like he often is.

"Let's warm you up. I've got some blankets in the car." I hurry to grab the black checkered picnic blanket I always keep in the back and spread it over a grassy patch off the side of the road. He's right behind, carrying an extra large fluffy purple blanket I bought freshman year at Suncastle–for times like these when I found myself outside on cold nights.

We cuddle under the clear, starry sky. He holds me, snuggled in my fuzzy blanket, hands rub my hair, massage my scalp. I trust his every touch, knowing he could lead me anywhere, and I would follow. So tender, so deliberate, so exquisite. "You take such good care of me."

"You're the one that went and got me a blanket." He tickles me under my ribs.

I laugh, swatting him away. "But you take care of me in so many ways."

"I need to take care of you, baby." The longing in his tone drives in deeper the truth that he *wants* to be here. "I can't change what happened. Everyday I wish I could. But we can't go back. We are here, right now, and all I want to do is hold you," He brings his lips to mine. "I want to kiss you." His tongue goes deep. "Can I do that? Please?" His voice is smokey, promising. He frames my face in his hands and a rush sizzles through me.

"Yes." I'm breathless from his kiss.

He cuddles into my chest, both of us looking at the stars. "I've liked you for a long time, Lexie." Head on my heart, he soothes me.

"You keep sayin' that, and I keep wonderin' how long. You gonna finally tell me, or what?"

"Okay, okay, I'll tell you." He burrows his head into my chest. "Since I saw you at Shakey's that first time, when we all went out after the junior high baseball opener."

"Since then?" We must've been twelve.

"Oh, yes."

"Then why the fuck didn't you ever ask me out?" A funny feeling spreads through me thinking about how we get along so well, how he feels like home.

"I shoulda. Guess I was worried if you liked me or not. Then, by the time I got up the courage...it was too late."

"I'm not sure it was too late." I play with his hair. "You shoulda."

"I was goin' to." He shakes his head. "I was goin' to right when Cody did."

"Well you coulda–"

"Coulda what?" He sits, stretching his neck until it pops. "You and I both know that when y'all got together, that was that." There's a hint of something in his tone. "But I liked you then, and now," he leans in for a long, sweet kiss. "I feel like we were meant to be together, maybe even all along. Like this is our special chance." His voice is tight. "Because, Lex, the more time I spend with you, the more I fall in love with you."

There's a pain in my heart that doesn't know if I can really believe it. The part that wonders if there is any part of me that is truly worth loving, if I'm worth anything at all.

"You mean everythin' to me." He kisses me with a yearning that immerses me in the depths of his soul. "There is so much about you amazes me. The longer we go out, the more I see to love." He pauses long enough for his words to sink deeper into my cells. "Like the lasagna. You didn't have to do that." He raises his eyebrows in a way that tells me these things come from deep in his heart. "You're doin' your best. You're always doin' your best. And you don't have to be. You could be mad at everyone. You have every reason to be mad at your family and your obnoxious mother. But I see you here tryin' to make the most out of a tough situation and it inspires me to get a handle on my own shit."

"I can't believe you think that about *me*." Here I was worried about how he was handling everything, but somehow he's focusing on what would build me up.

"How could I not?"

His eyes find mine, the look so genuine it melts me.

"Do you know how incredible you are?" He kisses my skin under my collarbone.

"How incredible?"

"There aren't even enough words." He loops his thumb under the sleeve of my dress, whispering to my body with his skin, drawing a heart. "We both have a lot of pain." He holds me delicately, and it's like my soul sings with happiness, like our souls sing together. "You don't let that pain destroy you. And I'd love for you to teach me how to do that. Because shit, Lex. I don't have a clue."

"I think you're doin' better than you think." And I mean it. "A few months ago, I didn't know if we could be together."

"Me neither. You've always been too good for me. But I'm glad it happened. Real glad."

I think about his words for a moment. "You thought I was too good for you?"

"Yeah, Lex, I think you're perfect. You've always been perfect. Even with everythin' you and Cody went through. I mean, he's no picnic to be with, I know. But you've always been awesome. Like there's so much good about you, it's just kindness incarnate. You have a beautiful soul."

It's what I need to hear, though I didn't know that until he said it.

The pain in my heart liquifies, because I believe him. Everything that happened with Cody and me, it wasn't my fault. It isn't my fault. I can be free. I truly did the best I could. Cody did too–and maybe in some beautifully broken way–that can be enough.

Bobby's arms go under my back, bringing me into the warmth of his love. "You have never done anythin' wrong here, baby. Alright?" He kisses me. "You deserve all the love there is." The most insane connection comes with his words.

I think this must be what people are talking about when they say *making love*, because I feel loved. He's brought me to another planet. Another reality. I relax into him, our bodies so close.

Please, God, Jesus, Universe, let me feel this way for the rest of my life.

27

BOBBY

EIGHT YEARS AGO

*W*e are alone here. My parents are at work. The yard is ours.

Cody and I sit under my favorite peach tree, the grass still a little wet from the sprinklers. We just finished our afternoon shift at Publix and walked back to my place, as usual.

Our wrappers litter the ground around our feet. Gustafson Farm chocolate milk. Pizza flavored Pringles. Peanut M&Ms. An empty box of Chinese takeout from the Publix deli. I always grab dinner and pretend I can't eat it all so Cody gets some food before he goes home. My paychecks go to a savings account for college. His go to keeping the lights on at his place since his old man doesn't take care of them. I can buy him dinner.

This is our favorite place, the tree at the end of the line, closest to the back fence.

Cody's upset about something but he hasn't told me what yet. I can fucking tell. Our whole shift he was acting weird. Not happy. Mad about something. Or confused maybe. I don't know. Was hoping that if I started talking, he would. Usually works.

"You wanna go to the mall Saturday?" Maybe I can coax out some-thing. Anything. "Meet up with Mickey, Lexie and Trish?"

He only shrugs.

I let out a sigh, the air so heavy I can sense it. *Fine, I'll just ask you straight out because you aren't givin' me any other choice.*

"You alright?"

"No." He rakes his hands through his blond hair and pulls at the roots, that frustrated tick we both do all the time.

"I could tell, man." I can always tell. I hear a few cars drive on the road behind my house. Still nothing from Cody.

"Well, what's wrong?" I give him a little side hug because it looks like something's really getting to him. He winces and moves away. There's a huge scrape peeking out of his collar. I squint my eyes a little bit, trying to see past the fabric of his AC/DC shirt. "Did you hurt yourself?"

He swallows, nodding. "I fell at the junkyard helpin' Uncle Rick."

"Lemme see." I slide up his shirt. He winces as the fabric catches near his neck. My eyes go wide. Scrapes and bruises everywhere the fabric covered, purple and blue. Scars, too. God, it looks like he was run over by a truck.

"Cody," I gasp. "You should get this looked at."

He scoots away, fixing his shirt, covering it up.

Something tells me this wasn't an accident. He was lying. I know he was lying. I try to think if he has any bullies. Any enemies at school. Someone who would want to hurt him.

"What happened to you?" My mind races to the worst. Is he in some kind of trouble? Sure there are assholes at school, but this looks more serious. Shit, I don't even know who would do this.

"You have to drop it, alright. I don't wanna talk about it." He hangs his head.

"You want some ice or somethin'?" Jeez, it hurt me just looking at it.

"It's fine. Was a few days ago. Doesn't even hurt anymore." Cody shrugs it off.

"I can go real quick for the ice, it'd just take a second." I have to do something.

"Forget it, okay? Just drop it." With the back of his hand, he flicks away a tear.

God, what happened that would make him tear up in front of me? We haven't cried in front of each other since Kindergarten.

"You just embarrassed, or what? Why are you lyin' to me?" A heaviness settles in my chest, mixing with a little bit of anger that he hasn't told me about this "accident" until now.

"I said drop it." His tone is cold.

"I'm worried, okay? Looks like you're hurt. And if you're not safe, I need to know."

"Bobby, lay off." His tone is harsher than I've ever heard it.

We sit there while Cody stares at the back of the house. I don't think he's ever lied about anything before. But he's never shown up hurt before; at least not without a detailed explanation of whatever caused the injury.

"Life sucks, ya know?" Cody sounds so broken. He's looking at the grass, shoulders hunched over. I hurt just watching him. Even though his life is shit, he's normally in good spirits. He's always larger than life, taking things in stride. But whatever this is, it's broken him.

Shit, what happened?

"Life sucks." I lean against the tree trunk looking at the sun shining through the leaves. Wind hits them, and they crackle. Squirrels scurry around. Birds chirp. Peaceful afternoon in the orchard. I don't know what to do.

He's so goddamn stubborn sometimes. Wish I could at least get him some ice. Thank God we aren't in season. He couldn't play like this. How'd he manage to go to school and work?

"Here, this'll cheer you up." I stand, looking over all the sparse peaches, searching for the best. There's only about ten left on the branches this late in the season.

"Why ya pullin' peaches off? Your mom has bowls full inside."

"But these are the best ones. The ones kissed by the sun all summer." I hand him one and smile. *I just want you to feel better.*

He holds it, keeping his eyes on me. They are kind and searching mine, but for what, I don't know. He takes a step in. "You can tell me if this isn't okay, ya know that, right?" His breath tickles my neck as he brushes hair behind my ear.

Why is my heart pounding so fast?

"If you don't want this, tell me." He's so close my head is spinning.

"Want what?" I honestly don't know, but this feels like a crazy rush.

Another step closer and his chest is against mine. My breath is stuck in my lungs.

He drops the peach to take hold of my hand, fingers intertwining with mine. One eyebrow raises in question, "I wanna kiss you all summer." His tongue runs across his top lip, then he bites the bottom.

My cock grows. Oh, hell. I look at the ground.

What is happening?

"Look here." He tilts my chin up, to focus on those perfect blue eyes. Teasing me. Coaxing me. Needing me. My cock perks into his, so hard.

I've seen him, how good he looks. Of course I've noticed. Of course I've had a crush on him since the beginning of forever. Of course I never thought we'd do anything about it.

My heart surges faster and faster.

I want to do something about it.

Desire fills me to the point that I'm terrified. I had no clue he had any feelings for me beyond friendship. He's never shown the slightest indication.

"You do?" I choke, teeth chattering. His thumb runs along my knuckles, looking at me with a longing I've never seen before. The pounding of my heart blocks off my ability to hear anything. Roaring silence, like when I sit alone and I'm trying to soak in the moment but I just hear a loud hum. Only the hum isn't there, it's just my heart, because the silence is so loud.

I want this?

I swallow, my knees like Jello. He's *still* holding my hand and something about it feels right and good. Kiss me? For real?

I've never been kissed before.

I know I like being with him. Cody's my best friend. Always has been. I stumble when I pull back my hand, tripping on a root and falling on the ground.

Shit.

I go to sit up, but his face is over mine, framing it in his hands, the peach forsaken on the grass. My heart beats faster and faster. His lips meet mine, lush and warm.

A storm goes off in my chest, that silent hum overtaking me.

Cody pulls back, a grin across his face. "Did you...you know, did you like it?"

No words can come out of my throat, but I don't have time anyway because he's kissing me more. Lots more. And I do like it.

I like it a lot.

Pretty soon he's laying on top of me. When he pulls back, I put my hands gently around him, careful of the scrape. I study his expression. I've never seen a smile like this on his face before.

My God, has he always been this attractive? Yes, I know he has. But I never thought I'd get this close. My body gets really excited, and I can't control it. I've touched myself, sure. But no one else ever has.

He's unbuttoning my jeans. Holy fuck, holy fuck, holy fuck.

And I don't stop him.

I don't want to.

It feels nice.

It feels *right.*

"You okay?" He's breathless, eyes smiling brighter than I've ever seen him, so much contrast to what I saw before. His heaviness is replaced by excitement. He's eager, hungry.

"Yeah, yeah, I'm okay. Are you okay?"

"I think I love you, Bobby." He licks his hand and starts stroking my dick.

Oh fuck.

Sparks sizzle through me on contact. Oh shit, that feels good. How long has he wanted to do this? Am I supposed to touch him back? Kiss him more? I don't even sorta know what to do.

Faster than ever, I come. Probably shoulda held back. But man, watching him touch me, it does something to my heart I've never experienced.

"Wow, Cody. That felt amazin'." I'm gasping for breath. He uses the grass to wipe his hand then zips up my jeans like nothing ever happened.

Wait? Are we done? Is it all over?

He stands, helping me to my feet.

"We can't tell anyone." He puts a finger to his lips to shush me.

"Of course I won't. I won't mention it." My eyebrows wrinkle. "Probably a good idea. Well, I mean, the guys on the team probably won't be cool with it."

"Not just the team. No one can know, okay? My dad told me it's wrong. He believes all those Sunday School lessons. Unnatural, unholy, all that shit. So don't tell, alright? It's bad, what we just did. Our secret." He glances over his shoulder like he's making sure we are still alone. One more kiss comes from his lips to mine, making me feel more alive than I've ever felt.

I've always been conscious, wondering if it's okay that I like guys and girls. Cody's just shown me that it's more than okay. It's perfect.

"Remember. No one can find out." He raises his eyebrows.

"Oh, um, alright." I'm still catching my breath.

"Promise?" He's being so intense. His hand clutches my shoulder so much it hurts.

"That's my throwin' arm." I wiggle away. "You don't have to be so heavy. I won't tell, I swear."

"Okay." He takes a breath and his smile's back. "I gotta go, alright?"

I try to pull him in and kiss him, but he resists putting his finger over his mouth like he's telling a little kid to be quiet. As he runs home, I long for more.

How could that possibly be bad?

———

A FEW DAYS LATER HE'S AT MY HOUSE, EATING PRINGLES AND PEANUT M&Ms with me after school. I ask Mom to make sure she buys them because I know he doesn't have any at home. He doesn't have much regular food at his house, much less snacks. We live three streets over, and it's a different side of town. He's never had enough, so I share as much as he'll let me. Ain't right that I have everything I want when he goes without.

"Are we gonna do that again?" I have to ask because I've been dying to know. I don't like the idea that we need to keep a secret, but I won't do anything to hurt him, ever, even if that means keeping quiet. He's probably right, too. All those folks teaching lessons at church don't take kindly to *this.* Mom has a *Love is Love* rainbow sticker inside her wallet, so I know she's accepting. But it's inside her wallet on purpose. People in our town condemn anything that isn't *straight.* It's a big part of why I've never gone out with anyone. This is a good thing to keep secret.

"I mean, do you wanna have a turn?" I'm sure I don't sound sexy enough. I don't know how to sound sexy.

His face lights up in a huge smile and it does something to me. Fucking tingles *everywhere.*

"Yeah, I'd really like that. But what about your mom?"

"She'll be at work for a while. Let's go upstairs." I take his hand and pull him up to my bedroom, locking the door. For a minute I look at him, because I can't believe this is happening. He stands close to me, like he did at the peach tree. The smell of him comes into my nose. His lips meet mine, soft, tender, the taste I've craved. Salty from the Pringles. Sweet from the peanut M&Ms. He presses me against the door and I feel like I'm in a really good movie.

"I'm glad you want more. I hoped you would." He brushes my cheek with his thumb. "Gosh, Bobby, I was so scared I ruined every-thin' between us."

"Ruined everythin' between us? Hell, no. You made it even better."

He gives me a smile, letting me know that it meant a lot, what I just said.

"I wanna play around with you, Bobby." The way he draws my name makes the world melt away. "Cover you in kisses." His cheek caresses mine, our chests close. His touch is making me crazy.

"I want you, now." I kiss him, sucking hard on his bottom lip.

"I hoped so." He slips my shirt over my head and steps back to look at me, really look at me. I hold my breath, suddenly insecure. But that melts away when I see the look in his eyes. He's seen me shirtless a hundred times, but not like this. Not like he wants me.

He steps closer and the air between us is erotic, the hum of need filling my ears the way it did by our peach tree. My heart races as he traces my nipples with his nails. A bite of pain and pleasure as he scratches my skin. His mouth takes mine, biting my bottom lip and driving me over the edge. I'm so turned on. I'm dizzy at his touch. I'm dying to know what he feels like inside of me.

He unbuckles my belt.

"No." I take his hands, holding them tight in mine. "It's your turn."

"I want you naked."

"O-o-okay." I can't talk. I can't breathe. I can't do anything but feel the tingles all over my skin. He wants to see *me* while I give to him. It's so fucking romantic. Jeez, he's making me fall fast and hard. There's nothing I'm gonna do to resist it.

Our clothes fall to the floor in a heap. Placing both my hands in his, stepping into him, I can't breathe. Skin on skin. Pure and warm. He feels awesome against me.

This is a time to make him feel as good as I did. I haven't stopped thinking about it since.

I lay beside him on the bed and brush his blond hair behind his ear. Just like I love playing video games with him and playing baseball with him, I love doing this with him.

I *love* everything about him. Always have.

"You comfortable?" I ask, ready to move pillows, get another blanket, anything.

"So comfortable." He's got one arm behind his head, eyes never leaving mine. I lick my hand, like he did the other day, and stroke him.

Holy fuck. He's in my hand, like he belongs here.

"Mmmm," he purrs.

I lay between his legs, bringing my mouth to his cock, kissing. He's silky smooth against my tongue. I open wider, letting him fill me. He's perfect. I want him.

A warmth fills my chest as we share this moment. Gliding. Tasting. This feels incredible. It's everything I want.

My breath hitches. There's something so beautiful about being with him here, like this.

I move him in and out, pleasuring the hell out of his tip. Flicking my tongue around him. Faster. Licking him makes me so hard, desire making me want to go all the way. Hoping we do, soon. Wanting more. Giving him more. Promising to give him everything.

He groans and the sound is heaven.

Lapping his length, enveloping him in my mouth and pumping with my hand. He is mine. I am his. Nothing else matters. We matter. This matters.

Am I in love with him?

I look up to see what he thinks. There's a big ol' grin on his face. I guess I'm doing this right.

"Oh yes, Bobby. I knew it'd be you. I just knew it'd be you."

———

THE NEW DIABLO CAME OUT. I DROVE CODY TO GAMESTOP TO GRAB it, since I just got my license. We've played all evening. Mom ordered some pizza. It's basically perfect timing because there's no school tomorrow. We can stay up as late as we want.

Cody and I have been together, secretly, for a while. Almost a year. Acting normal until we are at my house alone. Sharing these moments in the dark. We've gone all the way, several times. Two teenage boys figuring it out together. And holy hell, have we figured it out.

Didn't know what love could feel like, until Cody. It's been really nice to hold him, to touch him, kiss him. His kisses are incredible. He's always been my best friend. Feels like everything is just deeper now. It's so natural to be with him.

"Can you to do somethin' for me?" Cody tosses his controller on the carpet, fiddling through his backpack.

"Sure, what is it?" I set down my controller.

"I need you to keep this safe, okay? Don't let anyone see." In his hands is a journal. "Your mom's not the type to go snoopin' in your room is she?"

"No, no, she's not." I hold the journal and flip through the pages. It's all recent dates. Awe, my eyes catch some of the stuff we did together. I made it in his journals.

"Don't read it in front of me." He snaps it closed. "Just keep it safe."

"Oh." I swallow because I feel so weird when he bosses me around like this. If it was anybody else I'd tell 'em to go to hell. But I listen to him. I wanna listen to everything he has to say.

"There's somethin' else too. You're probably not gonna like it, so take a deep breath or find your zen or whatever other stupid shit you're into."

"Meditation?" I hardly think it's stupid, but alright.

"Yeah. You ready?" He's being so intense.

Where is this coming from?

"Yeah, I mean why wouldn't I be?" My defenses rise because he's never talked to me like this. I have no clue what is coming.

"I'm straight now. We can't–" he trails off.

"You're straight now?" I whisper because Mom's home. "Cody, you're not straight. We've had tons of sex and you love it. You're at least bi."

"I'm straight now." He sets his jaw. I wait for him to go on, but he doesn't.

My throat gets really hot. "But what about us? Don't you want to be with me?" I'm not sure why I'm pleading for more. I sound pathetic. But holy hell, this hurts.

"I know Bobby, I know. But it's time to move on. Shoot straighter." He holds his hands out like he's an arrow or some bullshit.

"Did I do somethin' wrong?" I'm all choked up but swallow down every bit of emotion.

"No, no, you didn't do anythin' wrong." Cody looks away from me. "It's not you at all."

"What are you sayin'?" I clench my fists. "If I didn't do anythin' wrong, then why would we stop? I don't understand." And it's the truth. How can I wrap my head around what has been our relationship? Maybe he didn't mean any of it. My pulse races like I've run for miles. "Was this all some joke to you?"

"No." He's getting angry. His voice is loud. "This was not a joke to me, Bobby I swear to God it was not a joke. I love you. But we are breakin' up. I can't be with you anymore." He's gripping my collar, pulling me close to him. The nearness assaults me. All I want is to melt into his kiss.

"Why then? I haven't told a soul."

"This ain't about you, okay?" He stands up, shaking his head. Before I know it, he rushes down the hall, hides in the bathroom, and shuts me out.

My head hurts trying to think about what the hell happened and what I'm supposed to do about it.

He's in there for a while, so I go and lay on my bed. My sheets smell like him. I hug my pillow. It's crushing me, ending this small thing we've been doing. What we've been building has been stopped too soon. Like I was on a bus, but got off several miles early and have to walk the rest of the way. Alone. In a thunderstorm.

I shiver, swallowing the knot in my throat, trying to calm my pounding heart. I feel like I got beat up.

Then he's there, saying, "Hey."

I wish he would come lay by me, but instead he sits on the edge of the bed.

"It's better this way, alright?"

I feel robbed. Cody is the one that I listen to. But I don't have to listen to this. I don't need any part of it.

"It's not better." I sit up on my elbows. "I don't know how you do a one-eighty like this unless you're somehow repulsed by me or somethin'."

"It's not about you." He palms his eyeballs. "Dang it Bobby, if it was you, I'd tell you. But trust me, it's not." His hand goes to my leg, thumb caressing below my kneecap. Shocks work through me as I fight the urge to swat him away, because I want his touch so bad, even more now that he says I can't have it.

"Please, I have to do this. And I know it's hard to understand, but trust me. I've got to be straight now and have a girlfriend."

"Oh? And who is that gonna be?"

"Lexie Hawthorne."

Fuck. No. God, no. Why her? The only crush I have.

I didn't know I could possibly feel worse in this moment, but shit, I do. It's like someone took out all my organs and I'm floating hollow inside my chest cavity.

"Lexie? Really? You think she'll go out with you?"

"Oh, I know she will." His hand is off my leg, leaving me alone in my mess of emotion.

"How do you know that?"

"We went out last night."

"You already went out with her before breakin' it off with me?" I feel like I'm falling. He's going out with the only girl I care about. How am I supposed to make any sense of this?

He ignores my question, off in some la-la land. "She is so damn sweet."

Yeah, I know, Cody…shit…I know.

"I told her we can go get ice cream tomorrow. Wanna come?"

"No thanks." My mouth tastes like I've been chewing on tar.

"Cody! Cody, your dad's here!" Mom shouts from downstairs.

His countenance collapses, shoulders slumping, fear in his eyes. "Fuck." It's barely a whisper, but I heard it. We are told in Sunday School not to swear. I don't give a damn, but Cody's mouth is as clean as a bare of lye soap. His dad getting here made him say *fuck*?

He gets off the bed. "See ya."

"Wait." I grab his wrist.

"I gotta get."

And I see it, red eyes filled with feeling. All that we've shared, all this time, that he just went and threw away.

He doesn't want me anymore.

Maybe he never did.

28

BOBBY
NOW

"*L*ook, I'm sorry about everythin'. Can you give me a chance to explain?" Mom sounds sincere since I decided to answer her call. The first time she's dialed me in months. I'm looking through the Hawthorne's kitchen for anything that is not a million horrible calories of artificial shit. I'm still sour. But I can't stay mad at Mom. Hopefully she has some good fucking explanation.

I sigh. "I need to come fix the fence, anyway."

I leave Lexie at her parent's house and go to Home Depot. I still remember the color of paint from the many summers it was my job to paint the fence. Cedar Wood.

With the supplies in hand, I knock on Mom's front door.

A woman opens it. The house is a mess still, nothing like when I was growing up. The change is as jolting as seeing the woman my mom left my dad for. I'm still in shock, though I don't want to be. I want to be okay with this. Nira didn't do anything to deserve my rudeness, so I make a point to keep that hidden inside.

"Hi." I put a smile on my face. It's not genuine, but I'm trying my best to be open-minded. Maybe in time, I can understand. But now, well, now I'm fucking mad about it. *Keep it to yourself, Bobby.* I don't know her at all, but I feel like I've seen her on Instagram. Wait. "You're Nira Hofstettler?"

Why didn't it dawn on me last night?

"I am."

"Oh, shit. Well, I've seen your stuff. Great stuff." I set the paint and supplies near the entry table. Unencumbered, I shake her hand with both of mine, nestling Mom's Christmas gift under my elbow. "I follow all your food-prep recipes. Oh, and that ab workout you did last year." Am I really nerding out over my mom's girlfriend? Never thought this would happen. It feels all sorts of surreal. She's one of the top body-building influencers in the country. I've been following her for years. Briar got me into her posts. Crazy to see her in the flesh. Crazier that I didn't realize last night. Just goes to show that I was not thinking straight.

"Your mom has shown me a lot of clips of you playing ball. You're not so bad yourself. Must really apply my videos." She looks me up and down until I blush.

"Yeah, they're good shit." I smile and it feels good not to hate her, like I thought I might.

"I know your mom's been busy." She leans her head toward the kitchen and heads that way.

I follow. The smell of cooking comes through my nose. On the table is a better spread than Jesus had at the Last Supper. Protein pancakes. Tons of eggs. Lean turkey bacon. So much fruit it looks like we live in the tropics.

"I fucked up, and I'm sorry." Mom holds her hands out with a plate. She's wearing her Suncastle Knights apron that I gave her my freshman year, on the first Christmas I came home.

Now I don't have a home to come home to. I hold my breath. I'm not going to be mad about this. I won't do that to her. In my hands is a wrapped cookbook I got for her this year. "You may already have it."

"Awe, thanks honey." She sets it on the counter.

"You didn't have to do any of this." I give her the hug I refused to give her last night. Feels good, like maybe I can forgive her sooner than later.

"I know I didn't. Now go eat." She puts her hands around my thin waist and I worry she'll ask about the twenty pounds I've lost that I didn't really have to lose. The muscle disguises a lot of it, sure. But I don't want her asking. I'll get it under control. She doesn't need to know. She doesn't inquire, and I don't tell. Mom is a bit of a health fanatic, herself.

At the table, I pour some sugar-free syrup on my pancakes. This is so much better than what they have at Lexie's house. I managed to grab a banana this morning but everything else was processed, fatty, sugary shit. No, thank you.

"My mom makes incredible healthy food. She's perfected it like an art," I rave to Nira.

"I know she has." Nira winks at me and I think about how many people pay serious money for a photo op with her at conventions. And I'm having brunch with her because she's with my mom...

I'm glad I can eat what I want here and not worry about it. Mom taught me half of what I know about nutrition. She's always been really supportive of my food goals.

Hey, I'm eating. I'll have to tell Crossfit Santa about this. Can't wait to text Mindy.

"Thanks for brunch." I start to stand, but Mom takes my hand.

"Well, I'd like to explain what happened." She has a sad expression on her face.

"Nira happened." I keep a smile on my face, trying to be as respectful as possible.

"I loved your father. I really did," she sighs.

My heart breaks a little bit, because I notice that she said *loved* instead of *love.*

"But neither one of us had what we really needed." Mom pinches her lips together, like it's hard to say this. Nira puts her arm around her and pretty soon Mom is smiling again.

She looks good. I wouldn't expect her to look this good when she just went through a separation months ago. But she does. She looks *alive.* I see something there that I didn't before. Was she always unhappy with Dad?

I swallow, the acceptance I started to feel evaporates like a puddle in the sunshine.

"Where's Dad now?"

"He moved downtown." Mom glances at the table.

"Did you tell him I'm here?"

"I haven't talked to him since he left. That's why I didn't tell you. I didn't know what he felt about everythin'. I didn't want to add any more pain to him or you. Now I see that was wrong of me." Mom sounds heavy, and her tone adds pain to my chest.

I feel the lump in my throat grow because I know exactly what this feels like. All too well.

"I'm happy for you." I take her hand in mine. "I know it's not easy, and you did what you needed. I'm glad for you. For both of you. Welcome." I glance at Nira. "I mean it."

Mom has tears in her eyes and wipes them away with the back of her hand.

"You didn't tell me you had such a sweetheart for a boy," Nira says to Mom, pulling her close.

"I do have a sweet boy." She shakes her head. "My sweet bean."

"You haven't used that one since I was eight." I chuckle.

"Yeah, cause you made me promise not to. Wasn't cool enough to call you in front of your friends."

"It wasn't." Nira chuckles.

For a second, it feels nice. But then I think about how Dad used to be the one sitting here and how that will never happen again.

"I'm gonna get workin'. Thanks for breakfast." I clear my place, then go out to the back fence. I destroyed it. The shredded fence pieces lay like the broken pieces of my soul, dying on the grass.

I set the supplies down, but that blasted peach tree stares at me. The last one on the row. Our tree. My hand goes to my cross necklace. I take cautious steps toward the trunk and reach out my hand to touch it.

I feel that tremor. It stops me, still as a statue, because I wasn't expecting it now. Or ever. I never know when it will come or what I'll do with it.

You're here, aren't you? Still with me. I swallow. *Always with me?*

My feet stand right where I did all those years ago, feeling him come toward me.

I fuckin' miss you. I want to scream the words. *You weren't supposed to die!*

I crumble to the ground, because I can't handle all this. I bury my head in my hands like his body is buried under dirt. "It wasn't supposed to go this way, you know that?"

That night when he came to my apartment, the night of the accident, he wanted me to be with him. I've never let myself really think about it. I've tried to forget a million times. I've wanted to forget what he did to me. That he left me for Lexie. And he didn't even love her right, when I would have. All that time. He took her and I couldn't have either one of them. All I wanted was to love him. To be with him. Or to love and be with her. But I couldn't have either one.

"You took that away from us!" My body quakes, trembles working through me. "We never even got a fuckin' chance." I curse this world. The one we live in where it's not okay to be gay or bi or anything that isn't straight. But we aren't straight. We've never been straight and we'll never be straight. The world needs to open its fucking eyes.

People like Cody's dad that beat the shit out of him for loving me. I can't take it anymore. The torment rolls through me because I haven't allowed myself this fantasy. The one where Cody lived. The one where we had a chance. The one where we could've let our relationship be more than teenage boys hiding silently in the dark.

I still want to love you in the light of a thousand sunshines. In the eyes of a million people kissin' you on national television after winning the world series. I'd come out for you. I'd take our love out of the darkness and put it in the light.

I don't know if I'd still be with him or if I'd have been with Lexie all those years ago. I'll never know. I can't know.

But I know this. I love Cody. With all my soul I love what we had, no matter how brief and painful. I love it. I'm glad he kissed me under this tree. I'm glad that I could give him his dreams, his fantasies. That I could, in a very small way, be the lover he wanted. Even if we couldn't keep it.

Instead of stuffing it down deeper in my heart, I embrace it now, under *our* tree. Embracing my darkness. I try to lie to myself. Try to remember something different because it hurts so bad to recall what is real.

I'm coming to terms with my loss. My best friend. My lover? I hug the tree and pretend it's him.

I think about how that first time felt. I miss him. Shit, I miss him.

It's like being in a dark tunnel with no way out. That grief that I'm supposed to be going through holds me prisoner. Stuck, still stuck. Always stuck?

Hot tears pour out of my eyes. It's not fucking fair. It's not okay that he died. It's not okay that I'm the only one that knows where he was that night. That I'm the reason he was in that car. That I'm the reason he's gone.

The floodgates open. I don't want to be trapped in this prison. I need to be free, to be whole.

To be his.

A hand comes on my shoulder, and I flinch, because I think it's Cody, but Cody is dead.

"You and Cody sure loved this tree." Mom puts her arms around me, not saying a word for a bit. I'm a blubbering mess.

"You cryin' about Cody or about me and your dad?" She lets out a sad chuckle. "That's a stupid question, isn't it? I'm sorry honey. Doesn't matter what you're cryin' about. Heaven knows you're welcome to more than a few tears with all the last few years have been like."

"It's not fair." I force a shaking breath.

"No, it's not."

I wipe away my tears with my hoodie sleeves.

"Wow, you really did a number on that fence." She eyes the wrecked wood.

"You split up with Dad and didn't tell me."

"Also true."

I really want her to say something to me that makes the hurt go away. Like when I was five years old and she got a bandaid for my scraped knee. But there is no bandaid for this. And no matter what she could say, it wouldn't diminish the anguish. Nothing will. This is my battle. My torment. My loss.

"I'm sorry I was rude about Lexie."

"I didn't plan any of this, Mom."

"I know you didn't." She tilts my chin to look at her, like I'm five years old, and I really do wish there was a bandaid.

"I want to make sure you're not with her because you miss him." Her tone is serious. "She'd never deserve that."

"No." I let out a sigh. "I think I should've been the one with her this whole time."

"Maybe so." Mom looks thoughtful. "I didn't need to make you feel worse last night," she repeats, "and I'm sorry. I know it's already been a hard couple years."

I purse my lips. "Yeah. It really has."

"Nira's got some mimosa's if you're interested? Sugar free juice."

A smile cracks through the stone anguish I was stuck in. "Thanks."

I go and finish the fence, coming inside and cleaning the paint off my hands. Nira and Mom are giggling. I'm glad to see them happy.

That's really what this is all about, isn't it, Cody?

Being happy.

A wave of insecurity rushes through me. I haven't told Lexie enough. When do I tell her this?

I worry I'll never find peace from the past. I worry that maybe my mom is right and I'm with Lexie for the wrong reasons.

But I'm trying. That's all anyone can do. Try.

———

"How is it I miss you when you're only gone a few hours?" Lexie welcomes me into her house with open arms.

"I missed you, too." I spin her around like she likes. She smiles so big.

"Are you going to try and go see your dad?" We go out to their back porch. The mountains spread from the view over the lake. They have the best view in the county.

"Yeah." I pull out my phone.

Me: Hey, I'm in town til next Tuesday. Can we get together?

It takes a while, but Dad replies.

Dad: Get drinks tonight at Merkley's?
Me: What time?
Dad: 7
Me: K.

"We are gonna get drinks tonight. Does that work? What's your family got planned?"

"Nothin' tonight. I think Charlene is gonna go shoppin' with me. Get coats for Cody's family." Lexie's sister got into town sometime when I was with Mom and Nira.

Mom and Nira.

If they stay together, does Nira become my stepmother? I lean on the patio furniture. Just a few more days and then we get to go back to normal.

"Do you think we should go to the cemetery? Or Cody's house?" Lexie clenches her hands a few times then shakes them out like she does when she's nervous. "See his parents?"

I close my eyes. Cody's house is the last place I'd want to go. I'm mad at them.

"What?" Lexie takes my hand in hers. "You're closing up. What is it?"

I grind my teeth together. So much anger needs a place to go. It's all too much.

"You said you hadn't seen them since the funeral. I thought you'd jump at the chance." She's trying to communicate but I really don't want to talk about this.

"I'm plannin' to keep it that way," I say, a little too harshly.

Lexie flinches, pulling her hand from mine. She gets up and walks to a chair farther away from me.

A cramp goes off in my stomach. Fucking hell, I don't want to have tension with her. I wish I didn't hurt her. I cannot let my anger explode at her. Not today. Not ever.

"I'm sorry, baby." I wanna reach out and touch her, kiss her, make it all better. It won't work.

It's too much to make it better in one moment. Maybe too much to make it better at all.

She's looking at the water. Elbows on her knees. Like she wants to keep her hands far away from mine. I deserve that. With a deep breath, I move from my chair and sit beside her, swallowing the anger down enough to avoid an outburst.

"We can go if you'd like. There are a lot of reasons I don't wanna see his family, but if you do, I'll be there for *you.*" My chest aches at the thought.

"I know you weren't close with his parents."

That's the understatement of the year. I let her leave it there, because I'm not ready to go into all that. Last night I destroyed my parent's fence. What would I do if my emotions got unhinged at seeing his father? Apparently I haven't processed any of this shit.

That ache in my chest spreads. Each breath burns. Like I'm drowning. So much pain that I've never dealt with. Can I ever deal with it?

"There's somethin' you're not tellin' me." Lexie looks at me with sadness painted all over her face. When I don't reply, she turns her body farther away, putting all the space she can between us.

I feel like I'm dying without her connection. We've never fought about anything. This adds a layer to my torment. I sink deeper into my ocean of despair.

She walks in the sliding glass door without taking my hand.

Lex microwaves leftover lasagna. "You're not gonna eat?"

I don't think I could if I wanted to. "Ate at Mom's." It's not a lie. I will not lie to her.

Silence rings in my ears. Without her nearness, I feel lost. That feeling terrifies me. Like every time I've felt lost on the baseball field since Cody died. I haven't felt this way with Lexie since we decided to be together. But man, it's here. And, it's fucking miserable.

Am I supposed to talk to her? Make up? Give her space? *God, please help me not fuck this up. I can't lose her too.*

There I go. Praying again, wishing I knew how I felt about the big man upstairs. I'm mad at him...I'm mad at everything. All those stupid sermons about how sinful it is to have "same sex attraction" because they can't even say the term gay in those holy walls.

It's not how you really feel, is it, God? Can't you love me for who I am? Regardless of who I love? The God I believe in wouldn't treat anyone with so much hostility. God is love, isn't He?

"I think I need to go to Cody's house. Last year I bought some things for the kids. Winter coats. They probably need new ones now. I am gonna text his mom for the sizes. See if Charlene and I can pick them up while I'm out shopping." Lexie breaks the silence of my God debate. "I don't feel right that I haven't talked to his mom since last year. I don't know how to do any of this." Her tone is so heavy that it hurts me. I'm supposed to support her, but right now I have nothing left to give.

"I know you're goin' through hell. Maybe it's not a good time. I can go by myself if you don't wanna be there." She clenches her hands. "I just hate knowin' that I'm here in town and not doin' anythin' to see her."

"You wanna go tomorrow? Christmas Eve?" I'll do it for her. I'll do just about anything for her.

"Yeah." She eats the last bite of her food. "We have dinner at the country club. Can swing by right before that."

"Good idea." Hopefully we won't be stuck at his parents' house for long.

———

I ARRIVE AT THE BAR WHERE DAD TOOK ME FOR MY FIRST BEER AND give them my ID. He's sitting at a corner table with a bunch of appetizers in front of him. I'm not late…he went overboard. Typical of him. Show up early and order everything they've got.

"Hey." I take off my hoodie and hang it on the wooden chair. Dad stands and gives me a hug that's so tight it almost suffocates me.

"Missed you," he says before letting go.

"Missed you too."

"Here, eat up." He pushes all the food toward me while I slide my chair in.

Food. Calories. Junk. Sugar. I should eat it because Dad went to the trouble. But I can't. Because if I eat it, I'll make myself heave. I'm trying not to do that right now.

I could vomit in the bar bathroom before I head to see Lexie.

No.

I'm teetering that line that I hate. The one where I don't want this, but I can't seem to stop myself. It's a particular kind of hell. Like this winter vacation.

"You like these ones, right? The barbecue ones." He rearranges the plates until the wings are closer to me. Makes me miss Lexie because she *loves* wings.

"Ya' don't have to buy my love, Dad. You've already got it."

"Oh." He drums his knuckles on the table. "Yeah, of course not. I, well, I'm sorry that we are meetin' up like this and that I really haven't been there." He shakes his head, looking at the decor hanging on the walls to avoid my gaze.

"Not a big deal." Maybe a lie, but Dad's down low enough, I don't need to kick him lower. The heaviness in his eyes tells me that he's been down for a long time. I know what that's like.

"Oh, it's a big deal. And I should've handled it better." He looks down at his plate.

If there was ever a question where I got this need to be so hard on myself, it's sitting right across from me.

"You know what, can we talk about somethin' else maybe?" I eat half a barbecue wing. Jeez, this tastes good. A horrible-for-you-chicken-wing may be heaven on earth. I want them all. No. Just half of one. Not enough to alter my calories. Not enough to have to do anything drastic. I can have one beer and half a wing. Maybe the plain celery sticks.

"You gonna spend Christmas with your mom?" He eats a mozzarella stick lathered in ranch dressing.

I used to eat ranch dressing. Used to love it.

"No, I'm spendin' it with Lexie's family, actually."

"Lexie Hawthorne?"

I try to gauge his response, but it's hard to tell. "Yeah, she's my girlfriend."

"Oh." His eyes go wide. "That's great son. She's always been a sweet girl."

"Yeah." A smile grows on my face. I lean back in the chair. Thank God he took that well. Mom didn't. Jeez, I never want to think about that conversation ever again.

"You're takin' good care of her?" There's that stern look he puts on when he's pretending to be the intense type.

"What do you take me for?" I scoff. "You know how you raised me."

"Oh, I think I can take very little credit for who you are." He shakes his head. "I know, I know, gave you all those lessons in bein' the Southern gentleman everyone deserves. But man, Lexie. Wouldn't have guessed you'd be with her."

He's happy now, a total change of pace from when I arrived.

"You and me both." It feels good to talk. I nibble on the wing.

"There's a whole platter here, don't need to be shy. I'll order more." Dad gestures to the food on the table.

"I'll take some home for Lexie." I smile.

"Oh, good thinking. I'll order a box to go." He waves over the waiter and puts in an order for later.

"You doin' okay with everythin' Dad?" I lean back in my chair, wiping sauce off my finger with a napkin. "Does Skipper know?" I think about all the summers we spent out on his boat.

"Doin' okay? Yeah, I mean. I can't change any fuckin' part of it now, can I?" He empties his beer and waves for another. "Skipper, no, I really haven't felt like makin' this announcement. I kinda hoped we could fix it after a break from each other, but word on the street is she's moved on."

I feel crushed with him. Because man, how do you tell people that your marriage fell apart this way? In Willardson? I can't imagine.

"Is that why you didn't tell me?"

"Didn't tell you?" He looks shocked. "Fuck, she didn't?" He drops the mozzarella stick into the cup of ranch. "I thought for sure Mom told you months ago."

Months ago. I swallow hard, the room spinning around me. I'm queasy, ready to heave that half a chicken wing.

"So you just learned?"

"Last night."

"Dag nammit." He slams his fist into the table and we get a few looks from people nearby. Bringing his hands to his lap, he nods to try and calm the crowd. "Son, I had no idea. I should've told you myself. I thought for sure Mom woulda called you up first thing." There's a heaviness in his voice, and I hate it. He's always laughing. Always joking around. It's like splitting with Mom sucked the joy out of his life.

I've always loved my dad and looked up to him. Never in my life has he looked this broken. The beers keep coming, and we sit together until almost midnight. The fact that they didn't tell me is a big sore spot right now, but a good night like this makes me think that maybe I can forgive them someday.

"Oh, here." He gives me an envelope and I open it up to find a wad of hundreds in there. "I knew you wouldn't cash a check, and well, your mom always had your account info so I haven't given you much lately."

"Oh, I'm alright. You don't need to."

"I'm always gonna take care of you, Bobby, 'til you're really established on your own." He smiles. "Skipper did that for me, and I'm doin' it for you."

It warms my heart to know that he and his dad are close like I'm close with him.

"I really am sorry that you didn't find out about your mom and me."

"Dad, it's okay. You've already apologized ten times."

"I know. I just–" He sighs, his shoulders sagging toward the ground. "I don't know how to do any of this." He holds my eyes and there's so much sadness.

"We're gonna adjust." I shrug. "Nothin' lasts forever, right?" I quote his life mantra. "And with God all is possible."

He cracks a smile. Always had a soft spot for things about faith.

"I'm proud of you, Bobby. You know that?"

I don't know why the words affect me so much, but they do. I've been so confused with his and Mom's behavior that I haven't known what to make of it. "It feels really good to hear that."

"Then I'll tell you a thousand more times."

29

LEXIE

 e took Charlene's car so Bobby could take mine to meet his dad.

The mall is always nuts this time of year, but I don't care. I've got to get the coats for Cody's family. A funny knot works its way up my throat. The only relationship I've been in during Christmastime was with Cody.

Dear God, Jesus, Universe, is it always going to be this hard?

"So, Bobby, huh?" Charlene was bound to bring him up sometime, and here we are.

I flip through the clothing rack. "Yeah." There's no hiding the smile on my face. Thinking about Bobby lights my heart up, just like the Glo Worm caterpillar I used to cuddle with as a little girl at bedtime. He's my comfort, keeping the darkness away.

Cody's mom texted me sizes for the kids, so I'm picking through what's left over from overzealous holiday shoppers. Charlene is a big help, her golden curls bouncing as she pulls hanger after hanger across the circular racks.

My niece, Paisley, is at home helping Mom decorate an extra Christmas tree she kept in an upstairs room, out of the way. Heaven forbid anyone see a tree decorated by a child. That simply isn't done in a house like hers.

"But why? I mean, isn't it hard to date his best friend?" Charlene means well, but questions like this sting the bit of insecurity I haven't quite worked through.

I would love to keep lying to myself that there could never be anything wrong with me and Bobby. But the truth is I have no idea what I've gotten myself into.

That passion of his is all kinds of wonderful, but sometimes it makes me scared I won't be able to really give him what he needs. Am I enough for him? Is this a joke that we're even trying things? I'm wondering if I will just wake up from this dream.

I don't know, and I don't like when so many around us seem to think this is a horrible idea. I know him because of Cody, but I love him as himself just like there was never a connection between them at all. One day, I won't naturally compare them, I hope. And as long as I can learn how to do that, I have faith we will be fine.

"It's hard." I sigh.

"Then why are you doin' this to yourself?" Her honesty is usually a good thing, but it's rubbing me all kinds of wrong today.

"You're one to talk." It's a low blow, but I use it.

After I say that, she stays quiet. My sister walked out on her husband, Jethro, right before her daughter was born, so I know she is well-acquainted with the harder path one can take.

"Bobby's worth it, alright?" I find her eyes, knowing that she won't stay hurt for long. We agreed a long time ago not to hold back, even when it's hard to share our truth. Mom kept so much from us. When all of their secrets unraveled, including that I'm not Dad's biological daughter, and a lot of Mom's money was obtained in ways we find unethical, we promised we wouldn't do that to each other. It was why she left her ex-husband. He lied to her. And it's why I can never be with a liar. It's too painful to be with someone who isn't honest.

"I feel good when I'm with him. It's like we were always meant to be." I put a coat into the cart for Cody's sister, Anna Mae.

"You sound like a chick-flick." Charlene is next to me, pulling one for Abigail.

"Just 'cause you're jaded as fuck doesn't mean I'm not entitled to my perfect romance." I chuckle.

"Is that what you have? A perfect romance?" She rolls her eyes.

"Yes, actually, I do believe so." Most of the time. All the time, when I can shake this sense of worry.

"Alright then." She takes a deep breath and fiddles with her blond curls. She got Dad's hair, and I got Mom's.

I was blessed to favor Mom and actually look like I belong to the family until I started dying mine bright red.

"I'm not gonna fight you on what makes you happy." She takes my arm in her hand. "But be careful, Lex."

"I don't remember any of this hesitation when I went out with Cody."

"Yeah, because I knew Cody was genuine with you."

"One day you'll know Bobby is, too." I put another coat under my arm. "He's a good person. All I want is for you to give him a chance." We head to another section of the store.

"Isn't that what I'm doin'?" She takes a hoodie off the display rack and hands it to me. "Get this one for Bobby. Blue is definitely his color."

I smile, because she's right. This perfect navy and bright blue striped zip up is what he would wear. We leave the men's section, heading toward the boy's section for Cody's brother, Toby.

"You ready to see Cody's family tomorrow." Charlene pulls a coat off the clothing rack and then puts it back, realizing it's the wrong size.

"I haven't talked to them since last year. Holidays can be the worst time." I find a better coat, pulling up the note on my phone to double check the size. Toby should be in a bigger size by now, I woulda thought. Nope, my phone lights up the right size. He isn't growing enough if it's the same size he needed last year.

"Yes, holidays can really suck." The sadness in her voice makes my heart hurt. Our losses have been different, but losses nonetheless.

"Do you ever talk to Jethro?" I've been wanting to ask, and now feels like the best time.

"Not much." She sighs.

"And you're better off without him."

"Always will be."

After we finish shopping, we get home and find Paisley sleeping on the sofa, her head in Mom's lap. It's adorable to see her all cozy, but it also stings because Mom didn't cuddle with us much. It's sad that so many people make better grandparents than parents.

Charlene carries Paisley and her special blankey upstairs to one of the many guest suites.

"Is Bobby back yet?" I ask.

"Haven't seen him." Mom clicks off the TV.

I wonder if we're gonna hang out and spend some time together for once, but she stands up and goes down the long hallway toward her room–without so much as a goodnight–just like so many other times when I needed her to be there for me.

I swallow hard because bringing Bobby home matters to me, and she's acting like it couldn't be less important. I don't know what she thinks about him.

I go upstairs and lie on my childhood bed with the big bedframe custom made to look like a castle for mom's little princess. *Some princess… you never talk to me.*

I pull out my phone and tell Bobby I'm here. But I don't send the text, since he's standing at the doorway.

"Hey, beautiful." He smiles.

"How's your old man? Did y'all have fun?"

"He's okay." He takes off his shoes and locks my bedroom door. "Yeah, it was real good, actually."

"I'm sure it's been a hard few months. People don't know how hard divorce really is, but I remember with Charlene, it was really painful."

He lays on the bed beside me. "I don't want to ever be that close to someone to tear them to shreds. Like what's the point? I'd rather be single than do that to someone." He whispers. But then she shakes his head. "I didn't mean it like that. Not about us. No. Sorry. Jeez." He gets up on his elbows and looks at me. "I'm takin' it real hard, the shit with my parents. Guess I'm sayin' stupid shit now."

"I know, love. It's okay." I kiss his lips, because I'm not mad that he said that. It's terrifying to really be that close to someone. As much as I love being with him, I know we aren't there yet. "I'll be here, when you're ready to love me that way. I really doubt we'd end up like your parents or my sister. I mean, I don't know the future. But I have this feelin' we're gonna be alright." I watch his eyes when I say those words. They are so sincere that I feel amazingly close to him. His lips melt into mine, diving into all the love that I've ever known. He cups my chest in his hand and touches me with so much wonder.

Every time we are together, he does this. I'm enchanted in a way I cannot explain.

30

BOBBY

ALMOST TWO YEARS AGO

I think about it sometimes. The way he left me. I never really got a straight reason why. He wanted to have sex with me. Then he told me we had to stop. It broke me in half. But I went with it.

I guess I don't feel good about it because I'm the one being left behind. He's spending time with her when he *was* spending time with me. We hang out, but it's different.

I never should've let him touch me. I don't like it, but I kinda regret ever having sex with him.

The thick feeling in my throat reminds me that I don't actually believe that. I loved every moment we had together. The intimate ones and the non-intimate ones.

I don't know why I didn't get more information from him. But I didn't and I can't now. It's been too long. All of this runs circles in my brain like I'm a hamster on a wheel.

It's pouring rain. The door of my apartment bangs repeatedly. I look at my phone. It's 2 a.m. Mick probably dropped his keys somewhere and can't get in. Again.

I move my laptop with psychology slides from my summer class onto my nightstand, then hop up. Mick's bedroom door is open, and I can see he's asleep in his bed. I don't know who's at the front door then, but they're banging harder now.

"Bobby? Are you home? God, please be home." Cody's voice echoes through the cheap wood. *Cody? The hell?* I open to his knuckles, red from all the banging. He's soaking wet from the rain, a white t-shirt hugging all the places I shouldn't look at.

"I can't do this." He's upset and slams the door behind him.

I search his breath for alcohol, but don't find any. He's not drunk. Why is he at my door at 2 a.m.?

"Hey, quiet, unless you want Mick to hear." I latch the lock on the door. He looks fucking terrible. I lower my voice. "What's goin' on?"

"Bobby, I just. I can't. I can't anymore. I thought that I could, but I fuckin' can't." He's gotten a lot more relaxed with his language since going to college.

"What are you talking about?"

"She–" He rakes his fingers through his hair, pulling tight. "It's not her. You know." He points his finger at me. "You know exactly what it is, though."

Oh, God. My stomach drops like I'm free falling. My heart hits against my chest harder than the rain outside.

His eyes devour me with need. I gulp. He slams me up to the wall, his body flush with mine, his erection pressing into me. Closer than we've been in years. Wrapping his hands around the back of my neck, he brings me into a kiss. I jerk back, banging my head against the painted sheetrock.

"No." Shit, my eyes sting, holding back tears. I feel how hard he is. I *want* how hard he is inside of me. Fuck, I can't let myself feel this way.

"I never should've let you go." His eyes are fire, burning with that same desire as they did when we were seventeen.

"Then why did you?" All the feelings pent up inside of me come rushing out.

"I didn't want to."

"Then why did you?" I repeat, throat tight with so much pain. I shiver, my body fighting against the chill in the air and the waves of anxiety rolling through my body.

"Because I thought he'd hurt you."

"Who?"

His eyes roll. "How long we been friends?"

"Since church daycare when we were three." There's not a time in my life I don't remember knowing him.

"Remember the scrapes and bruises? I told you they happened at the junkyard." He looks ahead. "It wasn't from the junkyard. It was my old man. He's fuckin' psychotic. Do you know what he calls me?" His eyebrows knit together.

"What?"

"Forget it."

"No. You're tellin' me." I inch closer.

"He calls me diseased. Told me he was worried about me. About my mental well-being. That if I liked guys somethin' was wrong with me. A defect. A devil. Then, when he thought he figured me out, he beat the living shit out of me." His eyes gloss over.

"Did he beat you anyway or just because of this?" My chest collapses on itself. *God Cody, I coulda helped...coulda done somethin', anythin'.*

"He beat me anyway, usually when he drank a lot."

I can't imagine what that would've been like. My dad has never laid a hand on me, even when I deserved it. My throat is scratchy and dry, but I have to know more. "When did this start?"

"A long time ago."

My body shakes. I should've pushed him harder to tell me this years ago.

"What about your sisters? Does he—"

"No, he doesn't beat them. I don't think. He's obsessed with respectin' women and shit. But my little brother—" his voice trails off.

"Is your brother okay?"

"I don't know." Cody hangs his head. "I've been tellin' Mama to do somethin'. Anythin'." Cody slams his fist into his other hand. "We were never good enough for him. Like he expects perfection that's impossible. He's not as hard on the girls. I've always hated it." Cody scoffs. "He thinks I'm the one messed up in the head." He lets out a laugh, but it's sinister instead of jovial.

I feel sick. My dad got mad a few times, but I can count on one hand when he was anything other than reasonable. I know things were bad for Cody. But hearing it all out loud, I feel fucking blind and stupid for not doing more. I knew he went hungry a lot. That's why I insisted on buying him food. But I didn't know this.

"But when I got a girlfriend, he stopped."

"He stopped beatin' you when you had a girlfriend?" This feels more like a nightmare than reality.

"He's got issues."

"Clearly." We sit there for a while. But I still don't understand. "If he beat the shit out of me, I couldn't handle–" Tears rush down his cheeks and he stifles sobs behind the hands covering his face. Fuck. "I couldn't handle the thought of what he may do to you."

You stopped bein' with me cause you thought he'd hurt me *if he found out.* My eyes burn. My heart beats erratically against my ribs.

"So you got a girlfriend." I'm piecing together what I don't want to understand.

"Yeah, I got a girlfriend."

"Wait. You never liked Lex?" Confusion turns to anger, real quick. "How could you do this to her?" I have so much fire in my chest contrasting with the cold all around me. "She doesn't deserve any of this." I won't bring myself to ask the next question: does she know?

"I thought that if I could love anyone, it'd be her. And I do. But not like that. I tried. I'm sorry, Bobby. I never should've done any of this to her. Or–" His voice catches. "Or to you."

The heartache I've endured sizzles under my skin. He's sorry. I knew he was, that's how I stayed friends with him. He's my best friend. Even though he destroyed me with how he broke things off in high school, I still love him. I still care about him. I still want him to be happy. Shit, I didn't expect an apology.

I've never seen him this broken, leaning against the front door like he couldn't hold himself up if he had to.

"I put you through hell and I hate myself for it." He sinks to the ground. "Do you think you'd ever be with me now?"

I swallow, worrying I won't be able to force my acidic saliva down, sitting beside him on the ground.

"You have a fiancée, Cody." Why I'm choosing now to be the voice of reason is beyond me. He just tried to kiss me. It's what I've wanted for years, and I'm telling him no.

"I'll break it off with Lex. I have to anyway. You don't wanna know how awful this is. I wanted to love her as a woman. I just don't. I'm fuckin' gay, Bobby. I kept tryin' to suppress it. Have enough faith to make God heal me from this. Make me straight. But it didn't work. None of it worked. All this time," he grabs a wad of his hair, the strain of years of torment evident in how hard he yanks at the strands. "All this time, I've just wanted you."

Vomit jumps up my throat. This whole goddamn thing makes me sick.

"God doesn't need to heal you from anythin'." My eyes burn. We aren't accepted at church, or in baseball, or our small hometown. "If there is a God, they love you as you are."

He needs to hear this. I just hope my words sink in.

This is why it felt so good when we touched. It was what he really wanted. I'm not surprised to hear he's gay. But jeez, what has he been doing to Lexie all this time?

"You've been with her for *years*." I hold his eyes.

"I know that."

"She thinks you're gettin' married." I rub my eyebrows, a headache forming behind them.

"I know that."

"Why did you fuckin' propose to her?" Another shiver works through me.

"I don't fuckin' know."

"What about your dad? Cody, I wish I would've known. You didn't have to go through that alone. You never should've gone through it at all." I am his best friend and it took this long to tell me? Those bruises, those scrapes. His dad did that. Never shoulda happened.

He looks ahead, frozen, like it's too hard to talk about this.

"I'm here now, alright." I put my arm around his shoulder.

"Do you even want me?" His eyes are raw. It does something inside of me that I'm not ready for. We are older now. This *could* be something. I hold him tight, hoping he can handle what I'm about to say.

"Cody, look, I can't answer that when you're with Lexie. You two need to figure all of that out before you even think about me." I force a breath. He's already hurt her enough. I won't add to her pain. Won't let him cheat on her with me. Hell no.

"I've never stopped thinkin' about you." Cody squints his eyes tight.

My stomach cramps. I haven't either.

"I'm so pathetic." He presses his hands against his eyes.

"No, you're not. Okay? You're not. You have a shit dad who didn't accept you for who you are and now you're stuck pickin' up the pieces of all the things you tried to do 'right' but couldn't. It doesn't do anyone any good to inhibit themselves from being who they truly are, and loving who they truly love."

He leans into my shoulder and cries so hard his whole body shakes. "I fuckin' love you Bobby."

"I know you do." I hold him tighter. *I'll be your strength to get through this.* "I love you, too." I keep holding him, my heart doing backflips inside of me. After a while, his sobbing slows.

"Hey, does Lexie know where you are right now?"

"No, we got in a fight. I stormed out." He's embarrassed. Oh shit, how often does this happen?

"Alright, how about you go home and talk to her? She's probably worried about you. Lemme know how it goes." I help him up and wrap my arms around him. "I'm glad you told me. It's gonna be okay, alright?"

"I do love her too, ya know?" He's always been crazy protective of her. Wouldn't let me take a look at her without giving me shit. He does love her. Just not in a romantic way.

"I hope you do. She's fuckin' amazing. Go take care of her. Hell, maybe you two can work somethin' out. Whatever happens, I'm here for you."

What he needs most right now is hope.

"Thanks, Bobby." He hugs me again for a long time.

I don't let go, because I didn't realize what was happening. All this time I felt rejected. Cody always refused to talk. I didn't know about his dad. I knew something was up, but I didn't know what. Dammit, I should've known. It makes my stomach knot. I hate that I couldn't save him from that. It's a new kind of pain. Because this had nothing to do with me. All those days when I wondered why I wasn't good enough for him, something very different was happening.

"You okay to get home?" I'm suddenly worried that he's not. It's late and he's been dumping his soul on my cheap apartment carpet. Another story for these walls to tell.

"Yeah."

I feel funny, like maybe I shouldn't let him go. But I didn't smell any alcohol on his lips. I'm tired, too. Funny thoughts go through my head when I stay up this late. So much for getting any studying done.

"You're out of that hell hole now. And if I know anythin' about Lexie, she will talk this out with you if you let her, alright." I'm not awesome at relationships, but I feel like I could write a book about all I know about Lexie.

"You're great Bobby. I needed you. Thanks for bein' there."

"Always, okay? Always." I hold him for another minute, the feelings I've stifled still alive. "Text me when you get home." I unlatch the door and take off my hoodie, handing it to him. "Stay warm out there, okay?"

"I love you." He wipes another tear off his face. I pull the hood over his head. "And I love her. I need to talk to her."

"Yes. Tell her. She deserves to know, from you, alright?"

"Alright."

I watch him head out to his car, rain falling on my hoodie with each step.

———

I'M ASLEEP WHEN I HEAR THE BUZZING OF MY PHONE AGAINST MY nightstand. Blinking awake, I see the notifications. Ten missed calls? All of them are from Lexie. Oh, shit, did he hurt himself? Did he tell her about him? About us?

I click open the voicemail. Her message is jumbled through weeping. "Bobby, get over here. Peterson Memorial Hospital. He's–he's already gone."

31

BOBBY
NOW

*L*exie and I spend the morning making holiday treats with Charlene and Paisley. Don't know where her parents are. Guess holiday family time with everybody isn't their thing. Jeez, this makes me miss what holidays were like growing up at my house. We had everybody over on Christmas Eve. My grandparents, aunts, uncles, cousins. Mom and dad *both* in the kitchen with all of us cooking all day. Not this year. Probably not ever again.

"You alright?" Lexie notices me deep in my thoughts.

"Yep." I force myself back into the moment. Shit this is hard. I'm still in shock.

After a while of trying, I'm able to focus on the here and now. Charlene helps Paisley roll out sugar cookies while Lexie and I whip up some frosting.

"Sing time, Mommy." Paisley pulls on Charlene's shirt.

"Oh, you need to show Auntie Lexie your dance, don't you?" Charlene pulls up her phone and connects it to the kitchen speaker. "This is the cutest thing ever." She tells us.

"We Will Rock You" by Queen fills the kitchen.

"Paisley is this your favorite song?" Lexie walks over to Paisley's barstool.

"It's the bestest song." Paisley drops her cookie cutter. "I gonna be rockstar!"

"You already are a rockstar." Lexie taps Paisley's nose. "Well how do I do the dance moves?" She is so cute with her niece, I can't handle it.

"Like this, Auntie Lexie, this!" Out of sync, Paisley tries to clap and stomp to the music, almost falling off her barstool.

"I don't know how, Paisley. You gotta teach me." Lexie lifts her up and sets her on a clear area of tile.

"Clap." Paisley shows.

"Stomp?" Lexie demonstrates.

"No, clap be first. Clapping the first one," Paisley corrects.

"Oh, okay. Yeah, show me." Lexie pretends she doesn't know how.

"This!" Paisley is laughing and singing, doing her best off beat attempt. I chuckle until the song is over and Paisley begs her mom to put it on repeat.

"We gotta finish these cookies." Lexie puts her back on her barstool, where every few minutes Paisley stops everything to stomp and clap.

I give her lots of extra sprinkles when it comes time to decorate.

The cookies are for Cody's family.

I'm not ready to go to his place.

―――――

THE AIR GETS HEAVIER WITH EACH STEP I TAKE FROM THE CAR TO THEIR front door. I can't hardly breathe. The yard of their trailer is unkept. Old baby playsets reek of mold. An ancient car has weeds growing around the tires like you couldn't drive it out of there if you needed to.

Beer bottles lay haphazardly on the corner of the rotting porch, covered in mud like they've been sitting there a while. The roof is dipping in the middle like it's gonna fall down. They've jimmy rigged a two-by-four standing up like a column to keep the whole thing from collapsing. We have to walk around it to get to the front door.

Looking at my shoes, I see that the wood has a lot of water

damage. There's a bunch of bricks and duct tape in the corner, like they are fixing to repair this porch. Only it's covered in dust so you can tell that project never quite happened. Other random stuff covers the porch, like they don't have enough room for it in the house so they put it out here.

Lexie offers a smile, but I'm so amped up that I can't relax, even with her support. My breath is stuck in my lungs. I can't do this. It was a horrible idea to come.

Cody's face is everywhere. The shadow of the man he once was, and the ghost he now is, traipses around my mind like I'm in the Haunted Mansion.

"Do they know we are comin'?"

"Yeah, I texted her." Lexie holds the plate of cookies, and I carry a box of coats she wrapped up pretty.

How can they not afford coats?

Judge not, Jesus said. Judge not. I sigh. If only I was good at that one.

I wish I knew what Lexie hopes to accomplish here. I haven't brought myself to ask.

My throat tightens around thick saliva. *What would you like me to say to them, Cody?* I feel out for his tremor, that little connection I love that we share. But I'm hollow. Like he doesn't want to be here either, even as a ghost.

Anna Mae answers the door, TV blaring in the background.

Wow, she's grown up in the last several years. She'd be about sixteen now, I think. Her big brown eyes are the same and she's still skinny. Noticeably beautiful, despite the worn out clothes she's wearing. Awe, Cody's old Willardson High Baseball shirt. Damn, the fabric is getting threadbare. Hand-me-downs, from years ago. Shit, does she have anything that's just hers?

I wonder sometimes why they had so many children when they weren't in a position to care for them. Cody was the oldest of eight. Eight.

I want to pull out all the cash in my wallet and give it to them. They probably don't have gifts for Christmas. Lexie is trying to change it, and I find that beautiful. We can do more. I'm sure they could use more than just coats. The thoughts of anger mixed with the desperate desire to do something to help tumble over each other. Each thought leaves me more anxious than before. Is it too late to give them a better Christmas?

"Is your mama here?" Lexie keeps her face bright, though I sense a bit of sadness. Maybe she wishes Anna Mae gave her a big hug or something.

"Mama!" Anna Mae yells, but I don't know why. The trailer isn't even a double-wide. It's three small rooms with old furniture and a bunch of kids and animals, all of whom don't have enough.

"Y'all come on in." Anna Mae yanks the door, but it's hard to open all the way because something is behind it. "Sorry." She steps aside and we slip through the crack. Several big dogs come running at us.

"Shoo, get back. Eliza, take the dogs to the bedroom." Mama Jones comes toward us. She's wearing her work uniform for Shakey's. Gonna work the Christmas Eve shift. Man, these years have not been kind to her. She looks a decade older, hair that used to be blonde turning grey. Losing a child this young must age a person something awful.

Eliza shoos the dogs away so we have a place to stand.

"Lexie." Mama Jones smiles. "Good to see you, sweetie."

I set down the box and take the plate of cookies so that Lexie can give her a proper hug. They hold each other for some time and when they let go, both of their eyes are wet. Makes me choke up, just seeing it.

"Here, we brought you these." Lexie passes the cookies and Mama Jones has Anna Mae take them over to the kitchen.

"And these are the coats." Lexie tilts her head and I give Mrs. Jones the box.

"Oh, Lexie, thank you. You didn't have to do this."

There's no Christmas tree, so Mama Jones hands the box to Anna Mae.

"Do you wanna sit and chat a minute?" She gestures to the living room.

It smells horrible in here. Dust, cat pee, and other unidentifiable odors waft into my nose. I know they try to keep the place clean, but between everyone living here and the animals, there's no hope. Five of the kids squish on the couch, old brown fabric bleached a splotchy orange from the sun.

"Turn that off!" Mama Jones yells over the TV. It's one of those old box TVs from long before the days of flat screens. It is a color picture, but there's static lines running up and down in horizontal chaos.

One of the kids gets the remote and clicks it down. Suzy? Josie? I've forgotten her name.

"Go out and play in the yard; make room for our guests. You remember Lexie and Bobby. They brought some cookies." Mama Jones point's at the back door.

"Cookies?" Two of the girls jump up and ram into each other running to the kitchen.

"Ma, we was watchin' that show." Suzy–I think it's Suzy–gives Mama Jones some lip.

Mama Jones points to the big painting of Jesus on the wall, a reminder of trouble coming for disobedience.

"Yes, Mama." Suzy takes the remote and turns the TV off.

"You can watch it later, now get." Mama Jones moves around some boxes of junk to create a walking path to the sofa. She fixes the crocheted blanket on the back of the couch. She moves a pair of muddy boots and a damp towel off the cushions. "These children." She shakes her head. "Well have a seat, would ya?"

I sit on the couch, hands on knees, hoping I don't get some weird disease from what is lurking within this fabric.

"Good to see you, Bobby." Mama Jones forces a smile, but I know it's gotta be hard to see me. I represent everything her son doesn't get to have.

"Look at you, all grown up." Her hand opens and closes near her mouth, tears pooling in her eyes. "I'm sorry. So sorry." She takes a moment to gather herself.

I've already outlived Cody and I'm only twenty-three. Ain't right. None of it's right. Wish it wasn't my fault.

"Did Lexie tell you she was comin' over and you wanted to come along or?" Mama Jones messes with her fingers in her lap, sitting on a pile of laundry on the couch smushed against the opposite wall.

My heart bumps hard against my chest as I wonder how to talk to her about *us*.

"Yeah." Lexie holds her hand on mine and I guess that's enough.

I appreciate her being the one to say something. I don't think I could talk right now to save my life.

"Now, Lexie, you didn't need to go and get us new coats. Kids still fittin' just fine in their coats from last year."

I glance at the couple of kids still in the room. Their coats from last week are inches up their arms and tight across the chest.

"I can pay you for them." Mama Jones pulls out some wrinkled one dollar bills from her pocket. "Just tell me how much."

"Oh, no need." Lexie sounds so sincere it makes me fall even harder for her.

"Sure have missed you, Lexie." Mama Jones looks so sad. She's always looked sad. How can a miserable life become worse? Losing a child. That's how.

"Sure have missed you, too." Lexie is a picture of strength beside me. She wears this heaviness with more courage than I have in my being.

An uneasiness rests in the air. My nerves tickle me, wondering if Cody's dad is coming through the door and what I'd do if I saw him. I avoided him at the funeral. But I don't know if I could hold back now.

"Ever since Kevin went to prison, I've just been workin' all the time. I thought we were already in tough shape, but man, things can always get worse." Mama Jones looks at her scuffed up shoes for a moment. "It'll turn up though, one of these days. You know, Cody was always dreamin', always tellin' us there was good times comin'. I guess we all just have to hold on to that."

"Mr. Jones is in prison?" I raise my eyebrows. The news brings relief. But also guilt. How can I be glad someone is in prison? But I am. Damn that monster and all he did to Cody. My hands clench. Breath hangs in my chest. Jeez, I am not over this at all.

"Yeah, a few months ago." Mama Jones looks at her shoes again, and I don't press.

Doesn't matter what he got arrested for. Lord knows he did all kinds of things that weren't keeping the law. I only know a little bit. But man, if Mr. Jones ain't here, that means Cody's mama is alone to provide for them. Looking around the trailer makes me feel awful again. Yankees salary coulda bought his mom and siblings a nice place, easy.

I hate what I see. No one helps them. Not even all the *Christians* we went to church with.

Mama Jones and Lexie make small talk, but it's just background noise, I'm too lost in my own world.

Cody's kid brother, Toby, is in the corner of the room, sitting on the floor beside the Old English Sheepdog. His toy looks broken, and he looks mad about it.

I get off the couch, gaining the attention of all the animals. I have to shoo them away before my nice pants get covered in slobber.

I kneel beside Toby. "Can I take a look?"

Toby jumps back, scared of me.

"It's alright, I used to be buddies with your brother, Cody." I hold a smile while he's avoiding my gaze.

After a minute, he sets the toy in my hand and I fiddle with it. He stares at the ground.

Toy wasn't hard to fix. I had a dozen of these when I was a kid. The wheels like to get off kilter, but I was able to adjust them pretty good. "Here, should work now."

He still doesn't look at me. Jeez, what has this kid been through? My heart hurts. *How would you help him now, Cody?* The kid needs his brother, someone to be there for him. But no one is here. I'm nothing more than a stranger. Cody and I hung out alone or with our group of friends. We didn't invite his kid brother.

Guilt smothers me like a blanket in a sauna. I could've been there for Toby years ago. Could've shown up for him every weekend. Taught him how to play ball. But I've just been avoiding the whole family. I haven't been there when they needed Cody. He can't be here, so it needs to be me stepping in for him. Selfishness pulls at my heart. I shoulda been there for all of 'em.

"Well, we won't keep you. Merry Christmas." Lexie holds Mama Jones in a hug for a long while again.

"Glad you're still playin' Bobby." Mama Jones brings me in for a hug.

"Hope life gets better real soon." I try to smile. "There's good times comin'." I quote Cody, debating what more I can say. "Maybe one day you can have a fresh start." I swallow, hoping I haven't said too much. It's not my place. I barely knew Mr. Jones. Maybe he's a good person who just has a lot of issues. I don't know.

We cross the yard back to Lexie's car. I get her door for her and look at that old trailer. My thoughts spin all the way to the country club parking lot.

"How was it for you?" I ask Lexie, because she hasn't said a word and that ain't like her at all.

"Hard."

"Yeah." I swallow that thick feeling still overtaking my throat.

"I'm glad we went." She's smiling, but I know that it's work to keep happy after that.

"I wanna do more." It's a whisper, barely audible, leaving my mouth.

"Me too." She parks the car.

I kiss her, melting into the sadness we both feel. "I hate what they are goin' through."

"I know." She lets out a heavy breath, making me want to take all the pain away.

"Let's get more gifts for the kids. You think that would help?" Of course it would help. Anything would help.

My chest tightens thinking about Toby. I can't let go of the way he couldn't look me in the eyes. So much fear. This kid lives in terror. His life is hell. Thank God Mr. Jones is in prison. Toby's been through so much. I've gotta help them somehow. "Let's get them Christmas gifts right after this. I'm sure the Walmart is still open."

"Perfect." Her hand rubs the back of mine. "Great idea." She kisses me, drawing me into her tender sweetness. . "Such a void of his life, bein' gone. Not at his house when he could be helpin' them like he always did."

"Such a void." My eyes get wet. "I shoulda been there. I shoulda drivin' him home, made sure he got back to the beach house. This is all my fault." I squint my eyes shut, a warm tear escaping before I can stop it.

"No." She grabs my hand with both of hers. "No, this is not your fault."

"He came to my place, Lexie." My jaw trembles.

"What?" The shock on her face kills me. She never asked. I never offered.

Time for the truth.

"That night, he came to my place. It was late and it was rainin'. He was upset. I shouldn't have let him drive home."

"The night of the accident?" She leans closer, hanging on my every word.

"I swear he wasn't drinkin' or anythin'. I thought he was okay to drive. I coulda' gone with him or somethin', anythin'." Shit, this hurts. I pull at the collar of my Christmas sweater. "It's like I knew, Lex. I felt it. Somethin' was wrong and I shoulda stopped it. It should be him in this car, goin' to your parent's country club, not me."

If Cody was still here he would be able to help his family. He'd be playin' for the Yankees, bringing home truckloads of presents on Christmas. Maybe he'd help his mom feel safe enough to leave Mr. Jones for good.

"Hey." She wipes my tear away with her thumb. "This is not your fault any more than it's mine."

"It's absolutely not your fault." I shake my head, taking her hands in mine. Not an ounce of blame for her exists in my mind.

"He and I got in a fight that night. I bet that's why he came to your place. It's my fault as much as it's yours." She starts trembling, tears coming out of her eyes.

I can't breathe. It's too hard. "It's not your fault. I promise it's not your fault." I bring her close and we cry together, just like we did on the day of his funeral.

"Even if you had some feelin' how were you supposed to save his life? Feelin' somethin' can mean all kinds of stuff. It was an accident." She pulls back and we wipe each other's tears.

Her words sink deep into me in a way no one else's ever have. A glimpse of healing.

I don't know how she hears something so horrible and still shows me compassion. *How do you do it, baby? How?* I force a breath, wipe away all the tears and look out the window for a while. Maybe she can handle the whole story. *Please, Cody, help me know when to tell her the rest.*

32

LEXIE

"*G*lad that's over," I sigh. Christmas in Willardson was enough for me to know I never want to move back there. The last night we were at home, I tried to talk to Mom about our relationship. She got mad at me and I dropped it. Typical of her to avoid any hope of resolving our conflict.

"Hey, we survived the holidays with both of our dysfunctional families." Bobby smiles as I park in the spot outside the apartment.

"Somehow." I take an armload into the apartment. Eminem blares from the stereo, startling me.

Mickey's eating a bowl of cereal at the table, propping his phone against the jug of milk. I would've thought this would be something I saw often since I've been living here, but it's the first time.

"Hey." I drop my armload of stuff on the floor. "How was your Christmas?"

"Bobby's truck is here. But he's not. Your car is gone. Hmm, how does that add up?" Mickey's looking at his phone while he talks. Eventually, he glances up. "You're really with Bobby, then?"

"Yeah." I smile. "Jesus. Why haven't I seen you at all lately? Are you doin' alright?" I bite my tongue because I don't know if he's ready to talk. "You dropped out of the program."

"I switched majors." He says.

"But you've been here years already. That doesn't make a lick of sense. And where have you been?"

"Where have I been?" He's angry. "I've been runnin' myself dry every goddamn second of every goddamn day." He stands, rinsing his bowl. "I thought when you got back you'd finish school and move on. But I never thought it would be with *him*. I swear, Lex. He's not a good boyfriend. If he isn't already, he's gonna cheat on you. "

I close my eyes for several heartbeats. "Now how would you know that?"

"How would I *not* know that? Has he told you about everyone he's brought home? He is a player. And I'm not talkin' about baseball."

"It's different with us." I clench my hands at my side, hating this confrontation, wishing Bobby would hurry up and come in so he could clear things up.

"Different?" Mickey laughs. "He's just puttin' on a good show."

"If he is, I'll figure it out." I huff hair out of my eyes.

"I just thought you'd be smarter than this." He puts the cap on the milk, taking it to the fridge.

"We used to be close, Mickey. Used to talk all the time. I thought maybe my *brother* would be there for me durin' one of the hardest times of my entire life. Thought that maybe my *brother* would tell me why the fuck everythin' is wrong in his life." I swallow, throat tight. "Seems we were both wrong."

His face displays eleven kinds of hurt. "It's been a hard time for me, too."

"Then quit shuttin' me out and let me support you."

"It ain't that easy, darlin'." He pulls his backpack over his shoulder and grabs his keys. "I wish it was." He bumps shoulders with Bobby on the way out. Bobby turns to look at him, but Mickey just huffs away, mad.

"Why won't he just tell me what the fuck is wrong?" I sink into the couch. A sour feeling spreads through my insides.

Bobby sets the duffel on the floor and comes to sit beside me. "I'm not sure."

"Do you know why he's so mad at you?"

"Um, well, I slept with Claudia." He swallows. "The best I can come up with for how he's actin'."

"Oh?"

"Over the summer. We both got drunk at Garrison's. I shoulda said no. Mick's had a crush on her but never done a damn thing about it." He leans his head back on the couch, looking at the ceiling. "They weren't together, but he freaked out about it as if they were."

"So he thinks you're gonna cheat on me?" I try to think through all this but it doesn't make sense. "Y'all were such good buddies. Now he acts like he hates you."

"I'm very much against cheatin'. I'd never dream of doing that to you or anyone else. But I never shoulda slept with Claudia. I've regretted it and stayed away from her since the last time. It was just the hookups. I've hated that Mick refuses to talk it out with me. He told me to stay away from you, when you moved back."

"Jesus." I let out a breath. "He's always been overprotective about me. There's no reason I can think of why he wouldn't be okay with you, Bobby. I mean, I'm not surprised you slept with Claudia. And it's not a reason to hate you. Like you said, they weren't together. You weren't cheatin'."

"No, I make sure they are single before I'll agree to a fuck." He sighs. "There's gotta be more goin' on with Mick. I have no clue what. But there's gotta be somethin'."

A knock comes at the front door. "You expectin' anyone?"

"Maybe." His voice teases me and he does that to die for shrug as he heads to the door.

"Oh, hey, Miss Lexie." Briar waltzes through the door, wearing his Suncastle Knights cap and hoodie. "You both have a nice Christmas?"

"Good enough, I guess. We are glad to be back." I realize I'm still shaking out of drama with my mom and seeing Mickey here, with my tone so heavy. "Did you?"

"Oh, yes. My mama makes the best gingerbread." He nods his head.

"I know we already exchanged gifts." Bobby says.

I look at the butterfly Vans he ordered special for me. Every gift we gave each other was thoughtful.

"I don't need anythin' else." I show Briar my shoes. "Look, he got me these."

"Nice." Briar leans down to get a good look.

"Doesn't matter if you need anythin' else." Bobby smiles. "Briar agreed to help move some stuff around in your studio. You ready?" Bobby offers his hand to help me off the couch.

"Well thank you." I smile at Briar, then at Bobby. My heart patters in my chest. He surprised me with this. What he knew would mean a lot to me. After all that tension with Mickey, it's exactly what I need. *How do you always take such good care of me, Bobby?*

―――――

WITHIN MINUTES, THE THREE OF US SQUEEZE INTO THE FRONT SEAT OF Bobby's truck with all my art stuff in the bed.

"Alrighty." Bobby claps his hands and tells Briar the plans for the room.

He remembered everything I said that night when we talked about it. It's all I can do to keep tears from coming out of my eyes.

Briar and Bobby make quick work of things, moving furniture around, giving me the studio of my dreams.

"You didn't have to." I rise on my toes, grabbing Bobby's hoodie and pulling him close to me.

"'Course I did, baby."

I kiss him, bringing my tongue to dance on his lips until they part, welcoming me inside. His tongue goes against the roof of my mouth, exploring my teeth. I grab his ass and hug him tight to me, quivers vibrating between my legs. Pulling away, I'm breathless. "How are you so perfect for me?"

"Because we belong together."

―――――

WE TOOK BRIAR OUT TO DINNER AS A THANK YOU, THEN DROPPED HIM at his apartment.

After parking in the driveway of the beach house, we head inside. As beautiful as my studio is, I feel that creative block–worrying that I'm not ready for this.

"It may be hard, painting again for the first time." Bobby brings me close, wrapping his arms around me with that soothing presence that has only become stronger the more time we spend together. "And it doesn't have to be today. It can be whenever you're ready."

"No, I need to." I swallow a wave of emotion, so many memories filling my mind.

The canvas calls to me. My hand runs over the edges of my easel. I prep my palette and start painting. My hands shake, and I take a deep breath.

"I'm right here." Bobby sits beside me, squeezing my knee. "You got this."

"I do." I take the brush to my pallet, trying to convince myself I can.

Each stroke appears one at a time. If it was anyone else looking over my shoulder, I'd freeze. But Bobby has the opposite effect of most people. He makes me feel more confident, not less.

I cover the canvas, letting my brush take me wherever we need to go. There's a brokenness inside of me as I paint. Like this is a way of grieving. Cody helped me paint. He believed in me. Now I can't even tell him how much he meant to me.

Keep going, keep moving, get through this. A butterfly takes life from my strokes. Another and another, until the painting is complete.

"It's beautiful, Lex." Bobby wraps his arm around me.

"I did it." A tear rolls down my cheek. "That felt really good. Like gettin' a piece of myself back." I bring my lips to his.

"Why do you paint butterflies? I've always wondered."

"I guess they stand for somethin' to me." I look at the canvas, all the butterflies extending from one corner to the next. "Butterflies emerge as their true form after lots of struggle being trapped. I just feel that in my soul."

"You've emerged after being trapped." He smiles. "You've emerged into yourself despite never having support to do so." He grips my hand. "Nobody would guess how hard you have it from looking at your *perfect* life. But it's never easy to grow up on the outside of your family, never feeling like you belong or that you'll be good enough. That's a special kind of torment. And you've overcome it in so many incredible ways." His words bring a warmth through my body, knowing he sees me and believes my challenges are real. He's never once treated me like a spoiled rich girl, like so many other people have throughout my life.

"Cody helped with that a lot. He made me want to paint, even when my parents didn't approve." I sigh. "If not for him, I wouldn't have painted nearly as much in high school." My throat gets tight. "And if not for you, I wouldn't be dreamin' of art school right now."

"I don't believe that for a second." A glimmer shines in his eyes. "You, my butterfly," he takes my hand and kisses each of my knuckles, "would've found a way past every obstacle, past every cage, emerging just like these wings and finding your way to fly, all on your own."

A tear falls from my cheeks, dangling at the bottom of my chin, and he kisses it away. "I'm so glad you're here." I sniffle, forcing a shaky breath from my lungs. "Oh, I almost forgot to tell you." I shuffle in my desk drawer and pull out the printed application for a dozen art schools.

"What are you lookin' for?"

"This." I hand him the papers. "I'm going to make sure I have my portfolio ready to apply...as soon as I'm ready."

The smile on his face is new, one that seems to say how proud he is that I'm moving toward my dreams.

"When we were at your house, I saw how little your folks have been there for you. It's pretty goddamn remarkable that you've done all this despite them." He holds me close. "You're inspiring Lex. Anyone who hears your story will find faith in themselves. Faith to become the butterflies they need to be. To break from their cocoons, because you have."

"I wanna be free."

"You are free." His dimple catches my eye.
"I'm not yet. But I think one day I can be."
"To me, you already are." He brings his lips to mine.
My heart swells at his words. "You mean the world to me."
"You are my world."

33
___

BOBBY

FIRST GAME OF THE SEASON

I wake up holding Lexie, both of us wearing nothing. Jeez, I can't believe how fulfilled I feel with her in my arms. I didn't know love could be like this.

Yesterday was our three month anniversary of getting together. Mindy cleared me to play, proud that I'm making changes. I've been going to see Dr. Rogers twice every week and I'm starting to feel okay about going to a psychologist. I try to keep in mind the things he tells me. I'm starting to feel better.

When Briar and I worked out this week, I ventured a look at the scale. I've put on five pounds, closer to my weight before I dropped last summer. It's not much, I know. But it's big for me. I'm holding on tight to that hope.

I thought when I saw Dr. Rogers, he would want me to be more responsible. But he thinks that I'm too hard on myself. I guess I'm starting to see the ways that he's right.

Lexie snuggles closer to me. The others who've slept over don't usually hold me this close. But man, Lexie does. It's like we're glued together. This queen size bed could be a twin and we'd still have extra room.

She blinks and stretches, a yawn emerging in the morning light.

"Mornin' baby." I bring my lips to hers, enveloping her with the longing I've always felt.

"I'm so excited to watch you play tonight." She rolls on top of me and my cock presses into that sweet belly of hers, as she rests her head on my chest. She's warm. Gentle. Feels like home. My home.

"I'm so excited you get to be there." My lips kiss her hair, fingers scratching her scalp the way she likes. "Love you so much, my butterfly."

I still can't believe we're together at all.

"I love you." She lays on my chest. Beneath her sweet little face is a horrible pain that I worry may never go away. My heart hurts from what Cody did to her. It hurts that he didn't care enough about my relationship with him to share it with his fiancée.

It's on the tip of my tongue like a canker sore, uncomfortable every time I try to ignore it and flaring up whenever it comes to mind.

I've thought a million times about how to phrase it. I don't want her to regret their relationship. We've talked a little about my previous partners. But not about Cody. I promised him I wouldn't talk about it. It's a thousand colors of complicated.

I take a deep breath.

"Nerves about the game?" she asks.

I wish. Instead of answering, I stroke her sweet back. Her skin is warm against mine. My heart races, wanting her. I could fuck her several times every day and still want more. Some days we do, and if there is a heaven, that is where both of us ascend.

She is my heaven.

Her mouth meets mine, body delighted. Everything about her is ecstasy. I eat her up. She turns upside down, giving my mouth access to her as she licks my cock. Goddamn, that's my favorite. She tastes so good. We go for a while, until I grab her and flip her over so I'm on top. She licks harder, faster.

"Gimme some," she teases. My fingers are hitting her sweet spots, her body clenching against me as I pleasure her into oblivion. She pushes off and flips around, descending on my erection from on top. She breathes in the sweetness we both feel whenever I'm inside of her.

Her breath huffs hair out of her eyes as she settles in around me. My eyes are locked on her, smiling at how complete I feel with her. It's so fucking cute the way she looks after she's been licking me. The way her cheeks rose over. The way her eyes are all big, and those sweet eyelashes beg for more. The way she sets the pace and I follow. *You do whatever you want with me, baby. I'm yours.*

She starts out slow, all the right sensations blooming in my chest. I like when she's on top because I get such a good look at her face. She bites her lips as her core sucks me deeper. I thrust to her rhythm. *Anythin' you want, baby. From now until forever....*

"Lexie," I whisper. "Lexie." I thrust harder. "My Lexie." I scream her name. Her favorite thing since our first time. My heart expands. Like the language of our souls combines in a chorus of angels singing.

And she is an angel, singing. Loud screams of pleasure. "Oh, oh, yes!"

I don't care if the whole world hears her. *Sing, my baby, sing.*

She picks up the pace, faster, harder. Warm liquid seeps from her clit and she holds her breath, on the cusp of all I'm about to give her.

She's not expecting it, but I roll her over, because she loves when I tap from on top.

"Yes!" She grips my shoulders, clawing at them with her nails.

She is so hot. Her climax triggers mine and I go as long as I can while she levels through all the pleasure she can take. I catch my breath, but not for long, moving faster and harder to give her another one.

"You don't have to," she whispers.

"'Course I do, baby." The corner of my lips rise as I give her another one. As many as she wants.

When I know she's finished by the way she pats my shoulder, I lay beside her. We catch our breath, covered in sweat.

"You're so perfect for me." She brings her lips to mine. "I didn't know I could have more than one orgasm until you, Bobby."

"You didn't?" I shouldn't be angry at Cody, but I am. If he never had good sex with her in three years, then I'm more upset than I realized. When he and I were together, it was awesome. I hate to think about how much Lex probably blamed herself when their sex life was hell. My heart feels like a rotten peach thinking about that.

"What?" She pulls a long strand of hair out of my eyes.

"Lexie, there's a whole world of pleasure for you and I'll be damned if you don't experience every bit of it when you're with me."

34

LEXIE

"I'm gonna start breakfast." Bobby pecks my lips, stumbling into boxers on the off chance Mickey is home.

I lie naked in our sheets, catching my breath. *Wow, he is somethin' else in the bedroom, that's for damn certain.*

Every time I think I can lose myself completely in this relationship, a nagging fear pulls at my heart. I wonder when the shoe will drop, bringing our fairy tale to an end. Nothing this passionate, this intense, can last forever.

A relationship is about more than sex. Of course it is. But there's a connection I get when I make love to Bobby that I didn't know was possible. Here we are three months later, and I'm still in awe. I never had a single day with Cody that was as intimate as one day I've shared with Bobby.

Cody took a while to get comfortable having sex. I'm honestly surprised we did it at all, with all the religious beliefs he held close to his heart. Bobby's kinda an Easter and Christmas going sort of Christian. I think he believes in God in a pretty casual way. Cody, on the other hand, couldn't get enough of Jesus. Sometimes we'd go "too far" and Cody would spend hours on his knees praying for forgiveness. Pretty sure Bobby doesn't even have the thought cross his mind. Sex isn't *sin* to Bobby. Cody couldn't relax while we fucked to save his life.

At the time, I thought it was normal to not hook up in high school. I didn't mind so much. I was a virgin anyway. I'd waited 'til I was seventeen to really have a boyfriend. What was another few months until I lost my virginity? We liked to be together, and it was enough for me.

I wondered sometimes if I needed to date other people, but I liked him a lot. Loved him a lot.

He was the first person who really supported my art. I loved painting with him. Cody would sit there with his Brandon Sanderson books while I made love to the canvas instead of him.

It worked, that gentle rhythm. I thought it was enough, I really did. There was no way for me to know any different.

But now that I've been with Bobby, I see that I was horribly wrong. Being with Cody was like a sprinkle of rain when Bobby offers me a hurricane.

When Cody would come, that was the end of it. Never thought twice about if I needed more. And fuck, I did. Every time, I did. I think I orgasmed once with him, ever. Most pleasure was done on my own. We'd touch ourselves and Cody preferred that. But I didn't. I craved connection, craved pleasure from his hands, from his lips, his cock.

"I'm hopin' in the shower," I call to Bobby.

"I'll join ya, just a sec." He must be fiddling with the coffee machine because I hear it beep. Warm water washes the sweat off my skin, and I remember the first time Bobby held me against this shower wall.

"Hey, baby." He steps in beside me.

"Thanks for startin' coffee." I kiss him and move out of the water so he has a chance to get warm while I shampoo my hair.

"I put on some oatmeal, too." He grabs the soap.

"Sounds great. Need a good breakfast today." I smile.

His body glides against mine, the soap so foamy against his skin. Slippery. Wet. Warm.

"You've gotta stop looking at me like that, or I'm never gonna make it to class."

"Like what?" I tease.

"You can't do that, baby." He squeezes me close to him, gripping my ass, hard–just like I love. "Uh, uh. I won't have it." He pretends to scold me.

My clit trembles.

"We don't have the time."

"We have all the time we need." I'm dizzy, lips meeting his and more fireworks exploding in my chest than at the lake on the Fourth of July. His tongue wars with mine, a battle I never let him win. I slam him against the cold tile of the shower, my hands clutching his hair.

He's all I've ever wanted.

There's no shoe to drop. I'm his Cinderella and the butterfly Vans he got me for Christmas fit perfectly.

———

THE BASEBALL OPENER IS FIXING TO START–THE TIME OF YEAR I LIVE for. The air feels different, *excited,* as if the trees themselves know what's coming. I make it through all my classes and grab a quick snack before getting things ready in the training room.

The boys look perfect in their jerseys, several of them passing through to grab stuff from the training room before the game. Bobby is with them, his batting gloves tucked in the back pocket of his tight gray pants.

"You have a good day?" He lifts me up and swirls me around between two of the exam tables.

"Yeah, you?" I love that he could care less who sees him being affectionate with me. Good lord, I love it so much.

"Well this is the best part." He plants a kiss on my forehead, so much anticipation running through him. "I gotta run."

"See ya soon, baby." I take a good, long look at Bobby walking down the hall with the other guys. I'm with the hottest one on the team, that's for sure. My lady clenches thinking about how good I did him earlier, giving me an orgasm aftershock just from the thought of our sexy morning.

"You have the coolers loaded up?" Mindy walks into the training room with her kit. I swallow down my arousal, cleaning off the tables that just had baseball players on them.

"Yep, ready to go," Jae says.

"You meetin' us there?" Mindy asks me.

"Yep."

Jae is driving me there, and I'll come back with Bobby.

There's a funny ache in my chest, because when I did work baseball, I assumed I would be working one of Cody's games.

I swallow an unexpected wave of grief, clenching my fists and holding my breath until it passes. But it doesn't. It's too strong.

Mindy heads out the door.

"I'll see you out at the car," I call over my shoulder to Jae, and rush to the bathroom, making it to the stall before I start crying. Fuck, I was not expecting this. Using the cheap one-ply toilet paper, I dab my eyes hoping to keep the little makeup I'm wearing from smudging.

Keep going, keep moving, get through this. Forcing air into my lungs, I push back the tears. After a few minutes in front of the mirror, the only sign of tears is the redness on my cheeks.

Walking out of the bathroom, I keep my gaze down to avoid questions from wandering eyes. But I run flat into a purple and grey uniform. It's Bobby, thank fuck.

His arms are around me and I turn my head to keep his purple jersey free of my smudging foundation.

He pushes my shoulders back and gets a good look at me. "You been cryin', baby?"

I suck my tongue to keep more tears from falling down.

"C'mere." He wraps me in his arms.

The tightness in my chest relaxes within his support. So much is broken about where we are and what we're doing. But I'm embracing the broken and sitting in the ashes of the life that burned twenty-two months ago.

"I just–" I squint away more tears. "I always thought that when I worked baseball, I'd be workin' *his* games." I bite my lip, my body buckling as if I would collapse to the ground if Bobby weren't holding me up. "But he's not here." Every part of me aches, the pain so palpable in every cell, every muscle. "It's so stupid. I wouldn't have worked his games anyways since he got drafted. It's so stupid. I shouldn't be fallin' apart right now."

"Shh," he brushes hair out of my face. "Cody's here." Bobby gives a slight smile, the pain I feel written all over his face. "He's right here." He taps his chest with one hand and mine with the other. "He'll be on the field out there with me tonight, alright? And he'll be right there in the dugout with you."

"I just wish–" I can't go on because I'm crying again.

"I know, baby." His voice catches. He's right here with me, in our special, mutual hell. "I know."

After a moment he pulls back and messes with a chain tucked under his jersey. The cross necklace he always wears.

"When we were sixteen." His voice is thick. "Right after we both got jobs at Publix, Cody took me to the dollar store and bought it with his first paycheck." He moves to put the necklace around me.

"No, you wear this all the time, I can't take it from you." I didn't realize Cody gave it to him, and now it means so much more.

"Tonight, you need it more than I do." He kisses the cross and tucks it under my polo. "You were the best fuckin' thing to ever happen to him."

"No, Bobby, it was you." I hold him, trembling. "I didn't mean to do this. Not on openin' night. You don't need to worry about me right now."

"Stop," he lifts my chin so I'm looking into those wonderful blue eyes. They're a little fogged over.

Oh, fuck, I made him cry.

"I was thinkin' about him anyway."

"You were?"

"'Course I was." His eyes wander to the big clock on the wall.

My limbs are stone, too heavy to lift, stuck to the ground with the weight of the past. The pre-game warmup starts soon and we have to go, but my chest tightens so much it hitches at my breath. I suck in, waiting for air to hit my lungs, pulling and pulling until it finally catches so that I can relax a bit.

I hold the cold air, thankful for a true inhalation of his scent of laundry soap and cologne. My lips come to his, kissing, tasting, escaping.

I take his hand in mine and kiss each knuckle, pausing between each one. "This. Is. Your. Luck. Tonight."

His face is a big smile.

I kissed his catching hand, on purpose.

Maybe everything really will be okay. Bobby is my real life knight in shining armor. My *Suncastle Knight.* The thought makes me smile and I feel hope smothering my doubt. He's done it again, healed a little bit of my anguish. Cody can't be here, but Bobby is. I'm so glad he's here with me.

35

BOBBY

*O*peners are always perfect. I feel familiarity of the field lights on my back. The last time I'll play an opener on this field. Nostalgia washes over me, warming my heart like how the field lights are warming my skin.

We've run some practice drills. Stretched, warmed up, gotten ready.

Butterflies in my stomach, I'm up to bat. The first one is foul. The second one is ball.

I think I see Cody throwing to me. God, I'm in another dimension right now. *Head in the game, Bobby. Head in the game.*

I've been keeping down enough food that Mindy's letting me play. I'm in my element. My home. The place where I belong. I only get one opener as a senior, ever.

Focus, Bobby, focus.

The ball connects with my bat with a perfect *chink*. I run to first before they get my Texas Leaguer, the ball landing just beyond the infielders and too far from the outfielders to catch.

I hang out here while Tate bunts, getting me to second and him to first.

While they aren't looking, I steal third.

The crowd goes wild. *There we go...back in the game.*

"Jesus Christ," Northwestern's third baseman mutters under his breath.

I give a smile, taking my lead off while Ethan hits me home.

Back in the dugout, I get water, smiling at Lexie who is fixing the tape on Dexter's wrist that he sprained last week in practice.

At the bottom of the inning, we head to the field.

"Make it count." Zac throws me his cocky smile, heading to first.

"Make it count," I echo our motto we say every game.

The rest is a blur. My heart is not here, though I'm trying. *God, Cody. Why are you on my mind so much? Huh?* I shake my head. *I know, I know. I'll probably always be thinkin' about you. Especially here.* I swallow thick saliva.

I catch a couple balls. Hit a couple base runs.

We win five to none.

"Good game." We all shake hands with the other team.

"Good game," they say back.

"Good game." Keep shaking. All the team crosses in front of us and I see *him.* The guy I hooked up with a long time ago, at a hotel in San Diego when I was on a family vacation. He smiles and nods. I do the same.

"Good game." I shake his hand, and he moves down the line. I'm always nervous if I look too long. Don't give them anything to look at. I force a breath. He has as much to lose if he told on me as if I told on him. There's an unspoken rule between us. No names, no relationship. If we happen to run into each other, we happen to run into each other. Nothing more. Never was gonna be.

Lexie's cleaning up the dugout. It's adorable how much she cares, memorizing the needs and preferences of everyone on the team. There are always students in there to help out but I've never seen any with this much love of the game. It's fucking precious. I cannot wait to get her home.

"You looked great out there." She steals a quick kiss, hefting a cooler of ice.

"I got it." I take it from her as we walk to the parking lot. "I'm amazed you can carry this when it's full." I throw it in the back of Mindy's truck.

"Ha! I can hold my own, you know that." Lex winks, putting the first aid kit next to the cooler.

"You absolutely can." I bring her close for a hug, my hands sneaking into her back pockets.

"Great game!" Some people shout as they pass us. I step back, seeing Cal and his mom coming over to say hi. Cal's wearing Suncastle Knights gear. Wouldn't be surprised if he plays here for college.

"You looked great out there, Coach." Cal smiles wide.

"It's gonna be you out there very soon." I pat his shoulder.

"With a lot of thanks to you." Cal's mom yells to be heard over the noise.

I shake my head, happy they come to watch. "No, no, he's the one workin' so hard."

My dad is in the parking lot, leaning against his truck until he spots me. He walks like a fish swimming up stream to meander through the crowd leaving the stadium. There's a big, proud smile on his face, his purple Suncastle Knights cap on his head.

Didn't know he was coming.

"I'll see you next week, alright?" I nod to Cal and his mom, then push toward Dad with Lexie's hand in mine so we don't get lost among the people.

"Well this is a surprise." I give Dad a huge hug.

"Wouldn't miss it." He holds me tight. "Can I take you for a cele-bratory beer?"

"Yeah, if Lex can come." I send a smile her way, noticing how fucking cute she always looks. Damn, I got lucky.

"'Course she can." Dad nods to Lexie.

"I gotta run by the trainin' room, but I'll meet you there after." Lexie kisses my cheek.

"Yep, let's go over to Happy Brews." Dad offers.

I grab my keys and hand them to Lexie.

"Sounds good." Lexie hurries back to the field to check in with Mindy and Jae.

Dad waits in the athletic building parking lot while I change out of my uniform and cleats. I put my new watch on my wrist, a small reminder that I can find moments of calm amidst the storm constantly raging in my mind. I leave my cap in my locker, taking a second to fix my hair in the mirror.

"Party at Tate's place?" Zac puts his arm around my shoulder.

"My dad's in town so I'm goin' for a beer with him."

"Next time." Zac heads to his locker.

I hurry back to Dad's truck.

———

WE CATCH UP FOR A BIT, SITTING AT HAPPY BREWS, UNTIL LEXIE GETS here and orders a strawberry margarita. I steal a sip before my IPA comes out with a bunch of mozzarella sticks and wings.

"They have really good wings here." Lexie licks barbecue sauce off her fingers.

"You think *everywhere* has good wings." I wink. Since we've been dating, everytime I ask where she wants to go, it's always somewhere with wings, and/or cheese bread.

"That's because wings are basically the best food ever." She grabs another.

"You're not wrong there." Dad tips his beer in agreement.

A heaviness clouds over me as I look at the platter. My brain calculates the calories against what I burned at the game. Shit. I stop myself. The numbers make it worse. I look at my watch, mentally thinking the ticks of each second. Find my center. Just like the clock in Dr. Rogers office. *Tick, tick, tick.* Relax.

I can eat them today...probably...hopefully....

Yes.

"How've you been, Lexie?" Dad asks.

"Great." She pats the napkin on her lip before talking, all proper like. Her leg is close to mine, all cozy in this booth, foot wrapping around my ankle under the table. Being with my dad seems to make her nervous. That'll pass, because he's a genuinely nice person. All the kindness I have is mirrored from what he and Mom taught me.

Mom…

It occurs to me that I won't see my parents together again except if they are both at an event for me. Mom and Nira are on a cruise right now. It hurts me that they missed the game when Mom usually comes to the opener.

"It's nice working baseball," she goes on.

"Oh, I'm sure it is." Dad is genuine. I love that about him. Dad's always been supportive of me and I know he will be there for her, too.

"I still feel bad, Bobby, that you didn't know about your mom and me. I thought she would've told you, and well, I was mad at the world." He plays with the ranch on his appetizer plate.

"I know how that goes." I sip my beer down, enjoying the evening. I shouldn't have this. Thoughts are getting dark. No. I clench my toes. Baby steps…just like Crossfit Santa says. I can do this.

———

WE FINISH AT THE RESTAURANT AND WALK DAD TO HIS CAR. "GOOD TO see you."

"Let me know if y'all come down to Willardson, and we'll meet up. I'll try to get here for a few more games." He gets in his truck.

"Your dad's really nice." Lexie clicks her buckle.

"Yeah. I'm glad he came." I get in my seat and kiss her soft lips. My heart races the longer we kiss. "You doin' alright darlin'?" I brush her hair out of her face. "I know it was a rough night."

"Yeah." The corner of her mouth perks up. She unhooks my cross off her neck and puts it back around mine.

"I loved being there. Have always wanted to work with the baseball team. You helped a ton, in the hallway." Her face is a little flushed like she's embarrassed. "But I couldn't stop thinkin' about him."

"Me neither." I swallow hard. I need to tell her. The more time we spend together, the more it eats away at me. I'm torn between two horrible choices. Usually, after a win, I ride the high. But I'm not feeling any part of it.

Lexie plays with my hair, pulling me from my thoughts. "I'm not gonna see you much tomorrow. I've got a huge event they roped me into workin' because Jessica's lead is out sick."

"We can get dinner after if there's somewhere you wanna go?"

"Wings and Things." She smiles. "That'd be nice."

"I'm beginnin' to think you love wings more than you love me." I tease, tickling her under her ribs. Everytime I ask where she wants to go, that's what she says.

"I do not," she gasps, flicking my hand away. "But I think you'd taste good covered in ranch dressing."

I let out a much needed laugh. "You think I'd taste good covered in ranch dressing, huh?"

"We will just have to try it." She winks. "How else am I gonna know otherwise." She giggles.

I cannot wait to get her home.

———

THE NEXT AFTERNOON, I PACE IN CROSSFIT SANTA'S OFFICE.

"Feeling tense, Bobby?"

"Yeah." I stop to look at him.

"Tell me about your week." Crossfit Santa has his clipboard and a cup of coffee on his desk.

"Good. Started baseball and my dad came down to the game. *And,* we went out for some food, and I didn't throw it up."

"That's great." Crossfit Santa leans back on his chair, smiling. "How are things with Lexie?"

"Last night I couldn't sleep. Lots of nightmares. Kept dreaming that Cody was here but then waking up and remembering he wasn't. Then I dreamed that Lexie got hurt. It's like I know I'm hurting her, even in my subconscious. I have to tell her." My chest feels tight and I sit back on the couch.

"Hurting her?" He watches for a minute.

"I need to tell her some shit, and I don't know how." I look at the ceiling wishing I wasn't in this position. I've been with her for *months* and haven't begun to tell her what she needs to know. "It could go a lot of different ways. I'm not ready to lose her, but I'm afraid that is exactly what will happen if I tell her."

"It could go a lot of different ways. But you *want* to tell her."

"Yes. That night when my mom was there with her new girlfriend, I knew I couldn't keep it from Lexie anymore. I try to forget what happened. I try to pretend it didn't happen. But really, it did." I get hot from talking. My eyes feel swollen. Hurt from the moment and lost in the dregs of the past, swimming in murky puddles of all that could have been so different. "I wish it never happened." My voice is low and probably the most honest I've ever been. "And he fuckin' died, Doctor. The whole damn thing tore me up like my insides went through a runnin' disposal. I'm not in a place to heal. And I'm not in a place to hurt Lexie more."

"If you were her, would you want to know? At this point in your relationship?" Crossfit Santa takes a sip of his coffee and sets it back on the desk.

"If I was her, I would've wanted to know on day one." I rake my hands in my hair. "She doesn't even sort of know." I burrow the back of my head into the couch, wringing my hands. "I keep askin' her if she knew what Cody told me. Wishin' that Cody woulda been the one to tell her all this."

I stand from the couch and pace beside his coffee table. "It shouldn't be me explainin' his secrets, Doctor. Do you know how fucked up that is?"

"How fucked up?" He mirrors my words.

"It feels like both choices are wrong. That what I'm doin' is a mistake by Lexie and that if I do tell her I'm betrayin' my best friend."

"You feel you'd betray Cody by telling her the truth?"

"He made me swear not to tell a soul." I squint hard and squeeze my palms into my eyes to keep tears from coming out. "But do you know what else?" I sniffle, pointing my finger at Crossfit Santa. "He also made me promise to stay away from her. And then he fuckin' left us here." I clench my teeth, worried I may say too much. Not even Dr. Rogers can know what really happened. He can know there are secrets, but he can't know what kind. Too risky.

"Do you think if Cody could talk to you now that he would feel the same way?"

"No." I flick a tear off my cheek. Fucking feelings.

"Do you think he would want you to be happy?"

"Cody'd want both of us to be happy." I stop pacing and collapse into the couch. "Only, I don't think it's what is best for anyone. Keepin' his secrets." My palms bore so deeply into my eye sockets that when I move them away the room is blurry. "I have to tell her, Doctor. I'm gonna lose her, but I have to tell her."

I feel horrible. Like every part of my insides is getting crushed. The thought of not being with her is the worst thing I can feel, next to how bad it hurts that Cody's gone. I've gotten a taste of what life is with her. Living without her is going to be hell. But I won't make her stay. Not when I've kept this from her. It's not right. She deserves better.

"Are you sure you're going to lose her?" His tone is kind, like he understands my torment, and I'm thankful that Mindy sent me here.

"It's a big possibility." The room is still and cold. I think about how so much of our relationship is woven on lies and secrets.

Her face comes to my mind. The way she feels against my chest. The sound of her giggle when I'm cracking jokes. The way she takes time to pick out things at the store. But it isn't for me. I'm broken by things that neither one of us can ever fix. "I've been a horrible boyfriend."

"How so?" He leans on his knees with his elbows.

"This ain't a foundation for trust." I grind my teeth. "She already has such a breakable heart. Her parents aren't worth her trust. Cody lied to her as much as I have been. She won't want anythin' to do with me."

The truth lays in front of me on the table like a lost game of baseball. I played my best, but at the end, there's nothing I can change. What has happened, has happened. All I can do is try better next time.

There won't be a next time with her.

"Seems you're making a lot of decisions for Lexie. Maybe you ought to talk to her about it."

"I can't be with her," I whisper.

"What's that?" Santa leans closer to me, his rolling chair up against the small coffee table.

"I can't. We never should've done this. I was horribly and completely wrong."

———

My heart is heavy as I go into my apartment. It's time to meet Lexie for dinner but I can't bring myself to go.

I sit on the floor, crumpling in the same spot where Cody poured out his soul to me. Tears run down my face like a faucet that won't switch off. Only I don't want to switch them off. I want to feel this. I want to grieve him without pretending it never happened. Because it fucking happened. Every last moment of his life that I was with him, happened.

I should've told you not to go. I should've had you stay over. I should've been with you. This was supposed to be the two of us, Cody. And now I'm too beat up to be with her. There's no healing from this. Not if I went to years of therapy. I'm too broken. I'm too fucked up. I can't handle being here with her, knowing that there is a mess inside of me. That I'm only with her because you're gone. She deserves someone better, Cody. Someone better than me. Better than you.

I grab a fist full of my hair and tug, grateful for the grounding sensation of pain. I hold my breath. I don't want to be here anymore. I want to slip away. If I close my eyes long enough, can I fade into eternity?

I haven't been alive since you died. I haven't drawn breath since you sputtered out your last bloody one.

There is no healing. There is no peace.

There is no way for me to be with her.

There never really was.

36

LEXIE

*W*here the fuck is Bobby?

Working all day has me worn out and ready to climb into bed. I broke down and ordered wings thirty minutes ago. They were cold before I decided to go ahead and eat a few, expecting him to walk through the door any second.

Something feels wrong.

I've texted him a dozen times. We went out with his dad last night, and he doesn't like going out much, it seems to make him on edge. Probably the crowds or the noise or the calories. Maybe I should've changed plans and he could've popped spinach leaves into his mouth like they were potato chips.

I hope he's alright.

When I went to grief therapy, they called this hypervigilance. Since Cody died in a car wreck, I'm now afraid that anytime Bobby is late, he has also died in a car crash.

I force a breath. He's just late.

Frantically, I text him again.

Me: You ok?

I wait for a long time, sipping from my second glass of lemonade, bouncing my eyes from my phone screen and the restaurant door. Bobby's glass of water is misty, a fat drop of condensation rolling down the side, ice cubes mostly melted.

The waitress has checked on me three times. I've been here an hour and a half. About to leave and drive the streets looking for him, he walks through the door. A smile pulls at my lips, but doesn't stay.

He looks horrible. As he gets closer, his eyes are puffy. His skin is pale. Walking to the table, he doesn't say a word.

Nerves bubble in my stomach while I stand and give him a hug, but he barely hugs me back. Did I do something? I can't think of anything. The air feels wrong, like something bad happened.

"Hey, how was your day?" I try to keep conversation light, knowing that won't help and wishing I knew what would.

He had therapy right before this. Some days digging up everything feels like it does more harm than good. I've been there. The only way through shit like this is by making it worse to make it better.

"Hey," he's looking at the wall behind me, his voice horse. "Lex, I, um," his words go flat. "I need to tell you somethin'."

"Yeah, of course." I slide my hand across the table to hold his. "Is everythin' okay?"

"After dinner." He doesn't tell me if everything is okay, and that worries me even more. My mind wanders through worse case scenarios, not sure what on earth this could be.

"Yeah." I try to smile, but it all feels so heavy.

"I can't do this." His voice is so quiet I strain to listen, and then question myself twice, wondering if I heard him right. He rakes his hands through his hair and pulls harder than normal. Since he got here, he hasn't looked at me once. His eyes are on the table. Then they're back on the wall behind me.

Just fuckin' look at me, Bobby.

"Can't do what?" I tap my fork on the edge of the wing platter.

He's in his own world where all I can do is wait until he's ready to open up and let me back inside.

"We can go home. I know we went out last night and you don't like crowds and loud restaurants–"

"It's okay." He looks up with so much pain in his eyes it kills me. My feet tap the floor, worried about whatever is going on and how long it will take him to unravel it.

The world sways around me while I try to adjust to this sudden tension. I don't do tension. I avoid it like the plague. It is a plague, because I'm physically ill whenever things get like this.

"Did somethin' happen?" I bring my hand to his.

He forces a long breath. "Yeah."

Looking deeper, I see that his eyes are red.

My heart thunders the longer we go without words.

He doesn't touch the food I ordered.

Why won't he eat?

He won't even eat the salad I ordered for him without dressing. I thought he was driven. Now I'm wondering if all this is unhealthy. No, he just eats extra healthy, that's all. He's just having a rough night.

"It's okay, baby. Whatever it is, it's okay." I let out a shaking breath, the tension around me seizing every ability to function properly. I wave down a server and get takeout boxes and the check.

His head is in his hands, the salad bowl in the middle of the table, I've never seen him *this* upset.

"We can come back for your truck." I offer to drive.

"It's fine. It's just been a long day."

"That's alright." I take his arm but he's quick to hug me. My mouth hangs open as he jets to his truck. No kiss hello. No kiss goodbye. So late getting to the restaurant without any explanation.

What the fuck is wrong?

Still in the restaurant parking lot, I sit in my car for a while trying to figure out this hell of a night. For the first time since we've been together, I wonder if he wants me to come over. He *did* say he needed to tell me something after dinner. Of course he wants me to head to the apartment. An ache blooms in my chest and the longer I sit with it, the worse it hurts. What isn't he telling me?

I force myself to turn the car key and drive across town. My thoughts are so focused on him that I can't recall a single detail from the drive over, almost as though someone else had been driving. When I open the apartment door, he's sitting on his couch, elbows pressed into his thighs, head in his hands.

"I'm not much company tonight," he sighs, looking at my Vans butterfly print shoes.

"It's fine." I put the food in the fridge and notice it's empty of his normal food prep containers. It's been a crazy week for both of us. I should go get some groceries, give him some space. Maybe when I come back, he'll be over whatever the fuck is going on.

I take a deep breath and lean against the wall. This is every kind of uncharted territory. I can't say this is a fight, but it feels tense like maybe we are about to have one.

"I can't do this." His voice rings in my mind. What was he talking about?

I sit beside him on the couch and wait.

"I'm not okay right now." He stares at the carpet by the door.

"How can I help?" I put my hand on his back, drawing hearts and butterflies against his hoodie.

"I need to tell you somethin' that I wish I told you a long time ago." His voice cracks and he clears his throat.

"Anythin'." I take his hands in mine. "Whatever it is."

"It's not good, Lex."

His voice worries me, icing on the shit cake of this night.

"Tell me." I plead, surprised how desperate I sound.

"First, I need to tell you somethin' else." He swallows so loud it echoes off the thin walls. "I have loved loving you. Ever since junior high, Lex. I've loved every part of you. Your laugh could play in my ears a million times and I would never get sick of it. And I hope that one day, you'll have even more love than I can give you. Because you deserve it, Lex. You deserve all the love there is." His voice drops off.

This either sounds like a breakup or a proposal, and I don't know what warrants either conversation. "What are you talkin' about?"

"I loved you when I couldn't have you. Just like I loved him."

Bobby bites his lower lip and his jaw quivers. "Both of you were a constant reminder of what I couldn't have."

"What are you referrin' to?"

He looks at me for a long time but I don't know what to think. "Wait here."

A moment later, he returns with a notebook. He sits by me and thumbs to a bookmarked page, well loved, like he's read it a hundred times. But it's not his writing. It's Cody's.

My heart hits against my chest so hard it sends a throbbing pain through my lungs.

"I thought I had all his journals."

"Not this one." Bobby's voice is soft, heavy. "He gave it to me the night after your first date and made me swear never to share it."

My eyes glaze over the sloppy writing as if my heart doesn't want to know what it says. What secrets did Cody possibly have that made it so hard for Bobby to tell me?

He felt so right in my hands. Like we were supposed to touch each other. One second we are just hanging out under the peach tree and then I'm kissing him, tasting him. I always knew there was something there. Something between us that I had to figure out if it was real. It was so real. The realest thing I've ever felt. We went so far under that peach tree. I thought that it was just me. I didn't know he'd be okay with it. But fuck, he was. It was so amazing I can't even explain it. I was flying, Seeing him so happy.

It takes a minute to really believe what I'm reading. Feels more like he wrote this as fiction, but I know he only wrote journals, swearing one day he'd publish a memoir about his rise from a trailer park into a baseball star.

This is not the Cody I knew. My throat burns, my insides feeling dead and dark. What else don't I know?

"Please tell me he was workin' on a fictional story." The words stay in the air between us.

Bobby looks like he sinks lower into despair. His eyes squeeze shut. "No. It's not fiction."

"He gave this to you to keep his secret?" There is a war going on inside of me that I can't fathom. "He told you, but he never told me?" The truth rattles my soul, everything around me shakes. First my fingers, then my toes.

I've never been jealous of him and Bobby. They were best friends. But he told *him* when he didn't tell me? Cody liked guys? Trembles that I can't control reek havoc on my body. I look at my hands. Stop shaking.

"Lex, he didn't have to tell me." Bobby's eyes are sad. "I was there. I'm the *him* that he wrote about."

Lava pours through me. It's sudden, this change, wracking my being and making it into something vile and ugly. *I was there*, he said.

"You and he–" I can't go on, but I don't have to. Bobby's nodding his head slowly. Yes. He's nodding his head yes. Oh fuck. No…this can't be.

My body rages. Cody was into guys, and he never told me. He was *with* Bobby and never told me. I close my eyes.

This can't be real.

And after all this time together, Bobby never told me either.

37

BOBBY

I didn't want it to go like this, but there was no good way to tell her. Just like I thought, it's an earthquake shattering any foundation we had. I feel every bit of her simmering rage so much that she doesn't need to say a word. I've always been empathetic. I feel things, all the things.

Cody, man...how could you keep this from her? I wish she already knew and I wasn't the one explaining it. I'd hoped maybe she just pretended it didn't happen, like I do. But the look of pure shock proves that she didn't have a fucking clue. We were good at keeping it to ourselves. For better and worse.

She should've known this months ago.

She should've known this years ago.

You made me tell her, Cody....

My anger knows no bounds watching the girl I love fall apart because of things he and I did. I'm hollow inside. Ruined. The death that absorbs my insides flares it's hideous fangs, like some monster from the underworld coming for me.

"Do you regret it?" Her words shake me in a way I didn't expect, jolting me away from the underworld and into this moment.

"Regret bein' with him? No. I only regret that he broke up with me and wouldn't tell me why." I need to tell her that part too. Shit. I can't. Not right now. I knew she wasn't ready for this. Could she ever be ready for the rest?

"You said he gave you this journal the night after our first date."

"He did." I nod.

"Then when was all this between the two of you?" Her tone is beyond agitated. I knew at some point we'd get in a real fight. I just wish it wasn't about *this*.

"Right before." The truth spreads pain through my head. Every bit of me sinks into a vortex of despair with no hope of coming free in one piece.

"Right before?" Her voice is loud. I jump back. I've never heard her yell before.

"Yes. Well technically we were *still* together when he went out with you the first time. But then after goin' out with you, he broke everythin' off with me." I try to stay calm, but I don't know how.

"Wait? He was *with* you when he went out with me?" It's almost a scream. "You and Cody were *together* when I went out with him, and neither of you ever told me?"

"Lex, I hoped he had." I work my hands through my hair and scratch my scalp until it hurts. It isn't hard to bring the pain with how sore my head is after all the times I've pulled my hair today. But I need this sting to keep me from doing something drastic, like punching a wall or throwing baseballs at a window.

I hate to God that I said any of this. I already want to take it back. To give healing instead of pain. This wasn't a good idea. Being with her was never a good idea.

I close my eyes, knowing I don't mean that. It was so good to be with her. Every moment of us was everything we both needed.

Now I've gone and ruined it all.

"Well, he didn't." She shakes her head, pointing her finger. "You knew he didn't." Her tone is a word that I've never used to describe her: hostile.

"That night in the shower I told you he'd only been with me."

Anger pours from her every word. "Why didn't you tell me right then? How could you not tell me?"

"This isn't what I wanted." I clear my throat, willing to get any semblance of words out of it. "I didn't want you to be mad at him, or hurt. It wasn't okay. Not one bit of him bein' with me and then goin' out with you was okay. He cheated on me to be with you. Why do you think I hate cheatin' so much? I know what it feels like."

The words feel wrong. It's all so wrong. That's why I pretend all the time that we were *just* friends. That's why I've had so many one night stands, trying to convince myself that sex means nothing. She means so much. *Please, Lex, just let me explain....*

"Cody was far from perfect. But that first date was all the cheating lasted. He broke it off with me right after. And then I wished—" tears sting at my eyes and it's hard to go on. "I wish that I woulda told you that first night when you came back to town, but the thought of you questioning your relationship with Cody isn't what I ever wanted."

"What did you want?"

"You, Lex." I clench my teeth. "I wanted to take care of you and to be with you and to finally tell you that I've been in love with you for years." I thought I'd feel guilt for betraying Cody, but I don't. I feel nothing but pain, everything wrapped up in how hurt I am that I'm hurting *her.*

Her brows pinch over her nose. "I trusted you. I told you how hard it is for me to trust people. How hard it is for me to be able to give of myself. You knew." Her eyes are hard. "But I didn't know any of this."

"Please, don't blame me." It comes out before it should, before I think of what to say. "Don't you think I blame myself enough, already?" Like a volcano erupting, the words rush out of me, scalding her the longer they sit on her perfect soul.

"Do you even like bein' with me? Or was I some cruel joke to both of you?"

I feel queasy. Light headed. This is what she thinks? My hesitation only hurts us, I see it in her face. That's what I thought Cody was doing to me.

"Cruel joke, Lex? No." I lean closer, but she pulls away. "You were never a joke."

"I'm pretty sure I am, because if what this journal says is real, then I've now gone out with two gay guys who like playin' tricks on me."

"It's not like that." I blink my burning eyes, hard.

"Then what's it like, Bobby?" Sarcasm laces her tone as if she wouldn't believe me if I told her.

"Now, that's not reasonable and you know it." I'm matching her energy in a way that comes so naturally, even when we fight.

"Not reasonable? You waited until I'd been fuckin' you for months to tell me you were *with* my dead fiancé."

She's trembling all over, and I resist the urge to scoop her into my arms. I knew this wouldn't go well. I knew it, and here I am doing it anyway.

Wishing I could change the past kills me. I have so much regret. Seems like I'm always doing the wrong thing.

I brush her arm with my hand, but she pulls away even faster than before, as far away from me on the couch as possible like I'm poison oak. Like she has to stay away from me. I am poisonous to her. It's surprising she's still sitting here at all.

"Cody told me the night he died that he's gay. He tried to be with you but it didn't work. But I'm not gay." I sigh. "I promise I'm not gay and if I were, I swear to God I would own it right now. Despite the stigmas and confusion, I really like guys *and* girls, sexually. I've known I was bi ever since I was twelve years old." My heart rattles in my chest, the silence filling my apartment in a way that feels empty.

She raises her eyebrows.

I stare into her eyes and hope for a bit of understanding. "You're it for me, Lex. All the guys and girls I've been with, they weren't you. You're the one I want to be with." My face gets hot. I swallow hard, hoping these tears won't stream down. "He hurt me, too. It tore me up so bad when he broke up with me to try to be straight. Now, I wanna come clean to you. I hate that I don't know how to not fuck everythin' up. There's no way to know what to do here."

"You could try tellin' the truth."

"I am." I lick my dry lips. "I'm not lyin' to you about bi. And I'm sorry I didn't tell you to begin with. I haven't told many people. Most of the guys I've been with don't even know my real name, okay? It's the biggest, deepest, darkest secret I have. Baseball makes comin' out next to impossible. If we kept goin' out like this, I woulda told you regardless of Cody. Hell, I shoulda told you day one." I look at the front door, the past haunting me more with each breath. No, not now. This is already hard enough. "Are you mad about that?"

"Am I mad about you being bi? Hell no."

Her voice makes me sure that she means it, giving a tease of relief. At least she's okay with that.

"What I'm mad about is that I didn't know about you and Cody. That I didn't know this about Cody at all."

I watch her, and here it comes, her walls tumble and she's completely vulnerable in front of me. Tears pool in her eyes. She swats them away in rage. "Because it sure as fuck hurts."

"I know." I've already slipped up in so many ways. "I know it hurts." I watch her cry for a minute, cautiously taking my hoodie off my shoulders. I drape it across her back, hoping to give some warmth. She's shaking really hard, and I hate being so useless in her time of need. I want to hold her. I want to fix this. But she doesn't want to be touched. I hate that. Hate knowing I caused it. Grasping for anything I could say to mend this mistake, I force a breath.

"Every moment of what we've shared has been completely real for me. I love you. I loved Cody. I love you both. Always have, always will." My voice catches as her eyes find mine. "I know you're angry. I know it was wrong of me to wait so long to tell you. I didn't want to hurt you."

"Then why did you?"

I have no answer. This is eerily like the conversation I had with Cody.

She stands from the couch.

For a second I see it on her face, that war of not knowing whether to stay or to go. My eyes beg her to stay, beg her to let me explain. But not a single word finds its way out of my mouth. My heart splits as she walks out the door and closes it with a solf click. Like she's too mad to even show her anger.

Adrenaline courses through my veins. I won't let history repeat itself.

I run to catch up, place my hand on her shoulder.

"Please, can I just drive you home?"

"What?" She spins to face me.

"It's stupid, I know. But, please. I shouldn't have let him go home alone that night, and I'm gettin' all these flashbacks right now." I'm gasping for breath against the cold February night. Tears burn at my eyes. I blink them back as hard as I can. "At least let me follow you and make sure you get home, alright?" My voice is raspy, arms folded against the chill.

"Just–" She squints, flicking away more tears. "Just leave me alone." She purses her lips.

Not wanting to push, I let her go.

I'm just the same. Haven't learned a goddamn bit.

Hours pass as I sit on the couch, frozen in time. Numb from what happened and unable to accept it, no matter how hard I try. I'm disconnected from reality. Can't grasp it. Hell, I can't even get up.

I haven't drank water in hours, or eaten dinner yet. Mindy texted me and I lied that I went out to eat with Lexie. It's easier to lie than to eat.

I really am just a good for nothing liar, aren't I? I lied to Lexie. The only woman I've ever loved.

It's easier to hate myself than to help myself. I need the pain. I need the darkness. I don't deserve anything better.

I've clicked my screen a hundred times looking for a text or a call I know won't come. *Please be home safe. Please tell me that you're home safe.* I want it to light up with a call from her. For her to come back over here, to say something, anything. If she didn't ask me to leave her alone, I'd be at her place now begging for forgiveness.

Me: I'm sorry.

I send her the text, staring at Cody's journal until my eyes throb, not knowing why I told her at all. It was a horrible idea.

Bile rises up my throat and I go to the bathroom, vomiting what little there is in my stomach. Somehow it feels good and right, so I keep it up. Let it all flow out of me. Calories I don't have to spare. Calories Mindy will notice are missing. Calories that would disappoint my parents. That would disappoint my athletic trainer, my coach, my team. My girlfriend. No, I don't have a girlfriend anymore.

One less person to hurt.

I heave again and again. Sore muscles, raw throat, tight jaw, pinched nerves in my shoulder. The insane amount of heartache and the pounding in my head that won't stop.

I've lost control. I don't feel like myself. I'm a shadow of the man I wish I was. The one who doesn't hurt people. Who doesn't disappoint people. Who has enough faith to heal himself with God's grace. Who doesn't hurt *her.* She's already been through so much. I was supposed to help her heal. But I'm not that man and now, I'm not her man.

I never deserved to be.

Hot tears run out of my eyes. I press my forehead to the cold tile floor.

I've never been enough for her, never been what she deserves. It's better this way. Nausea hits, a sudden lurching in my stomach. Acid erodes my throat on it's way out. Purging everything out of my system.

I've missed the way it feels.

It's my horrible indulgence.

Tonight, I welcome it.

I won't tell Mindy. Won't tell anyone. My little secret.

The only one I have left.

38

LEXIE

" *nger is a secondary emotion. It's the one to cover up whatever deeper feeling there is. Like our brains can't handle the reality, so it masks it with anger. Because you feel in control when you're angry. And sometimes that's all you need."* My therapist told me.

I speed all the way to the beach house wondering if I'll get pulled over.

I called Trish, and on the third attempt she answered.

"Can you come to my place? Now-ish?"

"Yeah…" She's always been the kind of friend that will drop everything when I need her. And tonight, I need her.

I should be crying. Instead, I'm enraged. Anger flows through me like a rushing river, washing away any sense of reason.

Every time I think I finally know who I am and where my life is headed, things are upended. I thought I was the daughter of both my parents. I thought Cody and I would get married and start our own family. Lies. It was all just fucking lies.

Who even am I? What is real? What is left of me after all of this falling apart?

It's not just a breakup. It's so much more painful than that. I thought I belonged there. With Bobby. I thought I was finally safe. Lies. All just fucking lies.

Cody pretended to love me. But this isn't love. Keeping something so fundamental about himself a secret is the opposite of love. I thought I belonged with him.

And then, oh, then, I allowed myself to think I belonged with Bobby.

I'll never belong anywhere. I never have. It's all a lie.

The house is dark, covered in shadows of Cody. I storm past my studio because it hurts too much to see all that Bobby did to make it the perfect art space.

I don't live here. I haven't slept here in months. Bobby's apartment was my home. Bobby was my home. Cody lied to me. Bobby kept secrets from me. My only value to my parents is my propriety.

My throat throbs as the shaking returns. I have to keep moving to get through this. I go to the boxes with all of the old memories that Cody left behind. I have to find answers for myself, because there is a huge fear wrapping tendrils around me that all of this was right in front of my face and I didn't see it.

"Our eyes fill in all the things we cannot see." It's a medical phenomenon that Dr. Riche has told us about in class many times. *"The eye beholds something, but if it's an incomplete picture, it will fill in the rest."* I suppose that is why they say that perception is everything. I swear to fuck that the Universe and God and Jesus want me to know that right now, because I've been so off in all my perceptions.

Was it always there and I was just blind? I have to know.

I was blind about Bobby liking me. Blind to my family growing up. I must have been blind about the two of them, too.

They were intimate? That passage runs through my head on repeat. Cody *loved* being intimate with Bobby. And Bobby misses and loves Cody. They were lovers. Truly, completely lovers. Probably closer than Cody and I ever were. It hits with so much weight that I hug my arms, bracing against the pain. My heart feels weak, like it's gonna forget how to keep beating. Emotions mix together, overwhelming my head with a buzzing euphoria, like I'm floating in and out of conscious awareness.

I close my eyes, pressing my hand to my heart. *Keep going, little heart. We will get through this, somehow.*

I work to ground myself in this moment, looking around the room and trying to remember the coping skills my therapist taught me. Being present is a must in order for me to sort through this.

Have I been a fill-in to their romance? The warm body they both wished was the other person? It tears me to shreds, like a wet newspaper–each new piece of information ripping at the stuck together pages as they peel apart. Thin, fragile and heavy at the same time. The damage is done. It's irreparable, too far gone to recover.

To Bobby, I was just Cody's memory. He couldn't be with Cody anymore. Guess I was the next best thing. He used me. I thought we were helping each other through grief. That we could heal those wounds. But I didn't know what his wounds were. I didn't know.

He didn't tell me.

I wanted to have a boyfriend that loved me. Now, I feel so used and so worthless.

My parents didn't want me. My fiancé didn't want me.

Did Bobby?

His touch haunts my skin as I shed his hoodie into a pile on the floor, releasing his scent into the air. Damn that laundry soap and Hollister cologne. My throat seizes as I suck down a sob. I don't want to be here, around these memories, around anything that belonged to either of them. But I have to. I have to know the truth. Maybe something can ease this burden and cleanse this pain.

I don't know if that's possible.

I go to the boxes, ripping them open without care. My finger burns with a papercut as I pull out journal after journal, cheap notebooks that Cody loved to write all his thoughts in. The ones that cost a dime during back to school shopping, because he couldn't afford real journals.

I get lost in these pages, countless entries about his family and

baseball, when Cody and I started dating. I stop at the first mention of
Bobby, a deep breath preparing me for what I may find.

*Bobby came to dinner with us. I've missed him so much. Wish I could
talk to him. Wish I could tell him the truth. What really happened. I feel
bad about what I did. Will he ever forgive me? He hasn't even wanted
to hang out. How can I blame him? What I did hurt me like crazy. I bet
it hurt him worse. How could I? I'm sorry, Bobby. I just wish I could
tell you I'm sorry.*

It's all there. Right in front of me. It's funny how you can see
something so differently once you get a new bit of information. Once
it's viewed through another lens everything looks different, it's all
more clear. It was there all along. I keep reading.

*Lexie looked amazing tonight. I caught Bobby looking at her and lost
my temper over it. I didn't mean to, but I raged at him. Maybe I'm just
like my messed up father. Bobby's really pissed cause I went too far.
I'm lashing out at him and he doesn't deserve it. I told him never to
look at my girl again. But really, I wanted to say something different. I
wanted to tell him I'm sorry. I'm so freaking sorry.*

My body quakes. Why was he so protective of me when I didn't
have anything to give him? My insides burn. He wasn't protective of
me. He was jealous that Bobby was noticing *me* and not *him*. Fuck.
The hurt goes so deep it feels like an endless vortex pulling me–calling
to me.

I love you both. Always have, always will. Remembering Bobby's
words makes me hurt worse. Was he lying then, too?

I shouldn't have stormed out on Bobby that way. It wasn't right of
me. So much of this is all wrong.

"Hey girl, I'm here!" Trish lets herself in, bringing a bottle of wine
upstairs where I'm surrounded by scattered papers and pictures.

She sets the wine on the nightstand and ditches her purse to the floor with a clunk. Her eyes go wide while she scans the littered room. "What the hell is goin' on here?"

"I walked out on Bobby. We broke up, I think. I don't even know." I sigh into my hands, a quiet scream emerging from the back of my mouth.

"Oh, honey." Trish pours us both a glass.

"I don't know what I was thinkin'." I blurt out, the wine burning my raw throat, removing the thick feeling I've endured the last few hours.

"You were thinkin' you felt somethin' for him."

"It was all a lie." Words come pouring out of me, and before I know it all of our story is with Trish. I can't believe I've said it all. My heart aches with a pain I've never felt. Hot tears race down my cheeks. "I'm a fuckin' idiot. How did I not know any of this? It's all here, Trish. All of it. Every last word. Cody wanted to be with Bobby."

"Jesus," Trish drinks a sip. "I did not see this one comin'."

"You and me both." I go to my bed and scream into my pillow. After replacing my pillow, I dangle upside down to let blood rush to my head.

"Did Bobby tell you why they wanted to be together but Cody chose you instead? There has to be a reason." Her words barely enter my ears as I fight the exhaustion of the night. A glimpse of hope, that there may be a reasonable explanation, goes past me like a gentle breeze.

"Bobby didn't give me any sort of reason." Not that I gave him much of a chance.

"Well, did he at least explain why he waited until tonight to tell you?"

"No." I shake my head. "How did we not know Bobby is bi? How did we not know Cody was gay? We were all such good friends." I was so wrong about them.

"I always thought Bobby was a player, but never thought twice about Cody being gay. This is a huge shock. Damn them for not even givin' us a hint. I can't remember ever wonderin' about them."

I flip right-side-up. "Me neither. Fuck, we were blind."

Trish looks at me, wrinkling her brow. "You know, it shouldn't matter."

"It doesn't." I sigh, leaning against my headboard.

Cody's stuff sits on the nightstand. As much as I tried to purge him from my house, something made me leave it there. His Bible catches my eye and I run my fingers over the worn leather. Church isn't usually a safe place for someone to be gay.

"I just wish I would've known. Because it's horrible that Cody never once told me. I didn't want to wonder. I just thought our sex problems were all the Jesus stuff. You know, the 'save yourself for marriage' thing. It was so confusing. One minute he'd wanna be all pure, and then the next he'd tell me we should move in together." It hurts to remember him praying, begging for forgiveness, hours on his knees. Probably praying to become straight.

"Must've sucked to be that religious while trying to figure out your sexuality." Trish sets down her wine glass.

My stomach drops. "Cody had so much fuckin' heartache already."

"There has to be a reason, Lex. Did you even ask Bobby why he's tellin' you now?"

I swallow more wine. "No."

"I hate to play the devil's advocate here, but I think that he's probably got a reason. Probably a good reason."

"I'm angry." I shake my wine glass at her. "No. Not angry. Do you know what I am?"

"What?"

"Hurt. So damn hurt I can hardly breathe"

"Of course you are." She wraps her arms around me.

"How could they?" Tears fall from my body, shaking heaves. The emotional wall that kept me from these feelings crumbles, offering a liberation from this hell.

"I don't know," Trish soothes.

"Am I just that hard to love?" My words are difficult to understand while I'm talking and crying at the same time, like when a little kid throws a fit.

"No." She pulls back and moves my hair out of my face. "This is not about *you*. It's about them. Cody wasn't straight with you." She chuckles sadly. "Straight–like honest, not straight–like heterosexual. Well, technically both. Anyway...." She shakes her head. "But Bobby had every reason to tell you the truth if he really wanted y'alls relationship."

Her words make it all hit harder and another wave of tears seep out of my eyes.

"I thought Bobby wanted me." I cry into her shoulder. "He just wanted Cody."

———

I WAKE UP A FEW HOURS LATER, MY HEAD POUNDING WITH EXHAUSTION, stuck in an endless looping of thoughts refusing to let me rest. Trish is sleeping on the other half of the bed, the wine bottle we both emptied hugging the edge of the night stand.

Going downstairs, I find my canvas. Bobby was so excited for me to have my own art studio. I thought he was taking care of me.

I need to do something. Something more than thinking the same thoughts over and over again. The canvas stares back at me, waiting. So, I paint.

Emotion surges from every brushstroke, finding its way out of me and onto my forming creation. What I'm drawn to paint isn't something I understand. As the canvas fills in front of me, I'm brought to tears. Because without wanting to, I'm painting a picture of the three of us, together. In the photo that I absently reference, on the wall in front of me, I'm in the middle. It was one of our summer beach trips. But I paint it differently. Now Bobby is in the middle.

He always has been.

39

BOBBY

APRIL

*I*t's Cody's death anniversary. Two fucking years later and I'm just as broken as the moment it happened. Maybe more broken. Can this get worse with time? Because it has.

Before I only had him to miss. Only had him in the dark of night. Only had him to haunt my every nightmare.

Now I'm grieving both of them. Never should've been with her in the first place. It's too hard to be with her when I can't be honest. My whole life is a secret. Every part of who I am is shamed and ridiculed in our society. Every part of who I am is lost inside.

She can't be with me.

I won't have her go through the pain of talking things through. We can never be the same again. I don't even know where to start, how to talk to her, how to talk at all. The voice I wish I could've used my whole life has been silenced in a million little ways. From the porn I'm supposed to watch or not watch, to the way I can't wear anything with a rainbow on it in public. Society took my voice, and I knew it from an early age. If I want to be accepted, I have to pretend I'm not who I am. Simple.

So I kept secrets.

Secrets I didn't even tell the one person I care more about than anyone in this entire world. Why didn't I tell her I was bi? It's such a foregin concept to tell anyone. I've only told Sam, and that was after years. In time, I would've gotten there with Lexie–even if Cody and I never had sex. Just sucks that she needed it sooner than I was able to give it.

I wish I could trust myself to really talk to her. But I can't. We are a bad combination. Maybe I need to be with someone who could care less about secrets. Someone who has their own.

No.

I need her. And I lost her.

But today isn't about Lexie. It's about my loss that happened seven hundred and thirty days ago.

It's about you, Cody.

I'm lying on the pitcher's mound, stars covering the night sky long after everyone else left practice. Clay and sand dig into my nails. I want to bury myself here like people bury themselves on the beach under sandcastles and longing. If I'm underground, can I be closer? *Please, God, can't I just be closer?*

It's your death anniversary, Cody. Brought you all the best. Mama and Papa Gus always made chocolate milk right, didn't they? Pizza-flavored Pringles. Peanut M&Ms.

I pop one in my mouth and stare at the starry sky above me.

I feel ya, Cody. I feel ya right here.

My hand is on my chest, the pounding of my heart raging harder the more I feel. The more I desire him. The life we never had. The one we will never have.

I never stopped thinkin' about you.

My fingers find his necklace under my jersey and edge over the metal. There was no salvation for him. Not even in death. I hate that he suppressed who he was. I hate that he hurt Lexie because of it. Most of all, I hate that the moment he was gonna finally have the life we wanted....

A jingle comes from the gate.

"Hey man, I saw your truck." Briar stands above me, appraising the snacks and my position on the mound. "You alright?"

I think about sitting up. About standing and gathering all this shit and going home. But it's like the life is sucked out of me. I can't move.

"Two years ago today, isn't it?" Briar sits beside me and before I know it, he's lying here looking at the stars. Joining me in my grief. I love that he knows what day it is. Means a lot to me that Briar is here. I don't want to be alone. If things weren't so shitty with Lex, I woulda done something with her today. Or if Mick hadn't up and decided he hates me, we could've all done something. We could've invited Trish and gotten our high school group together.

"Two years too long." I run my hands through my hair. Shit, this hurts. Everything hurts.

"He was the Goose to your Maverick."

Briar's deep voice rings in my ears. The Goose to my Maverick. The peanut to my M&Ms. The light to my darkness. He was everything. I lost everything.

Wish I could just bring you back or go ahead and join you in heaven.

"You like *Top Gun?*" I grip another handful of clay, clinging onto anything in reality to steady me in this moment. The past beckons to me, calls to me. Not a bit of fight left in me. Only a prisoner. Always a prisoner.

"Oh, it's a classic." Briar's face lights up like it's one of his favorite movies. It probably is, he's a huge movie buff.

"Yeah, a classic." I sigh. "Really I was the Goose to his Maverick."

Cody was the one going places. The one who knew who the hell he was. I still have no clue who I am or how to be what I want to be. No purpose. I should be the one gone.

"Well Goose is the one that dies. Plus, *you* are the one that has Tom Cruise's hair." Briar chuckles.

"You're not wrong there."

"You sharin'?" He reaches his hand into the Pringles can and stuffs about twenty chips in his mouth, as crumbs fly everywhere. "How's my Cody impression?"

I lose it laughing. Jeez it feels good. Cody was always stuffing his face. Briar remembers. Oddly, this makes me miss Mick. We used to have good times like this. Feels like I'm destroying every friendship I ever had. Cody was the glue that held us all together.

"Nope, hold up." Briar gets the chocolate milk and chugs, then puts the empty bottle on his baseball cap. He stands slowly and while balancing the bottle on his head, does a little dance. A stupid dance like he's some mix of a cowboy and a ballerina. This moment is perfect.

"There ya go." I sit up, clapping my hands as Briar continues dancing. "Couldn't have done a better impersonation myself."

Briar dips low a bow before taking a seat next to me.

I'm not alone. He's here, trying to make me feel better. We are still again. Quiet.

"Are we really gonna do this? Get drafted? Quit playing on this field where we are kings to become the bottom of the line again?" Briar lets out a nervous laugh. "Man alive, I never thought I'd be good enough to even be in the runnings."

"I can relate." I click my tongue. "Coach Connors told me he's sure."

"Oh, I know he is." Briar reaches around me and gets some M&Ms.

"Why don't I feel confident? Do you feel confident?" My stomach cramps thinking about it. Just a little bit longer before we will know for sure. Before we see if it's just a dream or actual reality.

"Nah, it's more surreal. I mean, we've always wanted this." Briar hands me the bag of M&Ms.

I eat a handful. "Always."

I think about being a little kid and watching games on Dad's lap. Watching those players moved something inside of me. That stirring is still present whenever I think about it. For as long as I can remember, this has been the goal.

"Cody told me what it was like. Told me it was more nervous energy than he'd ever had. Like the insane drop of a rollercoaster. And that was just from the phone call." I rub my eyes. "God, I wish he coulda actually played with them."

"Life ain't fair. I mean, you grew up with him. Cody had about the roughest beginnin' known to man, and then to win the baseball lottery, basically, and then not get to play."

"He was gonna write a book about it. Inspire people in rough spots, tellin' 'em they can do anythin'." The excitement in my heart turns to bitterness. "Does it ever get better, Bri? You still miss your brother?" I bend my knees, leaning over my folded arms.

"Better?" He stares at home plate. "I don't know if better is the word. It does change, though. Sometimes it'll still hit me hard. And other days it's just that dull sadness. I'm glad he had the life he had. I wish he was still alive." Briar sighs, looking at the lights. "Maybe part of your heart heals. Or maybe it just gets more used to the pain." He stands, offering me a hand up. "But either way, they are always gone."

"And we are still here." My tongue feels thick, looking at the snacks. A memorial to my best friend. Shit, I miss him. I miss everything we may have been. My hands clench up, trimmed nails boring into my skin. I close my eyes, trying to stop my emotions from taking over. Before I know it, Briar wraps his arms around me.

"I'm glad you're still here." His voice is soft, caring. The same thing Sam told me.

I don't expect to fall apart, but I do.

Briar just stands there with me, holding me tight.

A few tempered breaths calm my shaking body. "I'm so fuckin' emotional."

"We all are," Briar says. "People pretend not to be, but we all feel shit whether or not we show it."

I step back. "This Cody grief is bad enough. Then, on top of that, I fucked things up with Lexie."

"I noticed." Briar adjusts his cap, a thoughtful look on his face. "You know what? I'm gonna have you over for a Monte Cristo right now. You can tell me the whole thing."

"It's past midnight."

"Don't care. 2 a.m. sandwiches taste better anyways."

"You know what? Sure." I gather up the snacks, giving Cody's memory one more quiet moment.

———

We get to Briar's apartment, and he puts on some country music.

Briar pulls a bunch of stuff out of the pantry and fridge. "Here, you smush up the Capt'n Crunch." He hands me a baggie and pours some of the cereal inside.

"What is this you're makin'?"

He stops, looking stunned stupid. "You're jokin'." His eyebrows go so high into his forehead that I can't see 'em under his hat. "Come on, man. You haven't had one of these?" He scoffs. "That's unforgivable, right there. That's what that is. Just smush 'em up good. I'll take care of the rest."

Crushing the crumbs, I behold everything that is Briar singing and mixing around shit in his kitchen.

"You know after baseball, I'm gonna open up one of those diners. Like right next to an airport somewhere. One of those open all night sorta things."

"Are you?" We sit at the table with some weird version of a fried, cereal covered sandwich. He puts a bunch of ranch dressing on the side of my plate.

I've eaten well all week. I can eat this.

"Mama's recipe." Briar smiles proud.

"Homemade ranch, huh?"

"Oh yeah." He pours a big glass of sweet tea for both of us.

Fuck it. I'm eating some fried sandwich covered in pancake batter and Cap'n Crunch, drenched in ranch dressing. I force a breath. As long as I'm consistent, I can eat less healthy things sometimes. I can do this. I have to do this. Another deep breath. Another bite. Chew. Swallow. "Hey this ain't so bad."

"Gonna serve them all night at Briar's Skyline Diner. You watch," Briar shakes his finger in the air. "So you gonna fix stuff with Lexie or what?"

I choke on the sandwich, coughing for a sec until I recover. "Fix it with her?"

"I'm pretty sure you're her soulmate and shit. So yeah, you gonna fix it?"

I look at the movie posters hanging on the kitchen walls, not meeting his gaze. "Don't think I can."

"Well, maybe at some point, you can at least try."

"Yeah." I let out a long breath, knowing she's worth the world to me. If there is any way to fix all this, I want to.

40

LEXIE
MAY

*T*ime passes in horrible regret. I want each day to get better. Instead, it gets worse. I miss Bobby. I miss us. The way it was so natural to be together. That we were in the relationship of my dreams before everything changed. I thought that, several weeks later, the rock in my gut would soften. But it has only gotten bigger.

It's hard to focus in class and work each game, though I avoid him as much as possible. Lots of folks have asked me why we aren't together, and I don't have an answer.

I try not to look at him, but he's all I see. The torment eats away all my resolve, at every practice and every game, every hour I'm in the training room. He's having a good season, breaking his records. But man, I'm not. I'm living in a nightmare.

I don't know what to do besides keep moving. Wrap wrists. Stretch out shoulders. Make ice packs. Fill up water bottles. Rehab Zac's knees. Massage Ethan's back after it has a heat pack. Act like a robot, because my feelings hurt too much to let me do more than the basics. Stay numb so that I can function. Maybe it's good to learn how to do this. I need to keep my emotions from getting in the way of my job.

Bobby isn't in the training room much and, when he is, it's to see

Mindy. They are always in the back office talking privately. Fine. They can both hate me together.

"It didn't work out with Bobby, did it, love?" Jae wipes off the last table before we leave for the night.

Even though he's the hundredth person to ask, he's the only one I care to talk with.

"It's a long story." I shrug.

He walks with me to my car, and I drive him to his place.

I stare at the rundown dorms. A few people cluster in the corner, having fun on a Friday night. "I thought that it was the most beautiful thing in the world, bein' with him."

"So why'd you stop?" Jae asks these questions in a way I don't mind. Having this conversation feels good, like all this bottled up emotion is being set free.

I sigh. "It wasn't what I thought it was. I couldn't handle bein' there when I knew that he'd been keepin' somethin' big from me. It hurt too much."

"And this bit about not being with him? Does that hurt less?"

"Not in the slightest." I let out a chuckle, more sad than funny. "I thought that Cody cared about me. But it wasn't real. None of it was real."

"But with Bobby?" His question makes me think.

Maybe there is a way to separate Bobby from Cody, looking for the truth behind my naive perceptions. Moments with Bobby run through my head, the way I felt with him. It *was* diffcrent with us. I was happier than I've ever been.

"I hoped it was." The words hurt coming out of my lips, because I realize it's true.

"Do you think it could be again?" Jae holds my gaze for several heartbeats.

"I don't know." Usually in a breakup, friends say to move on, get a good fuck and rebound. But Trish and Jae, some of my closest friends, are supporting me to figure out if this *could* be mended. Mental note...figure out if they are right.

"Seems there's at least a slight chance if your immediate response isn't 'no'. Maybe that's a good place to start." He smiles, getting out of the car. "You'll figure it out, love." He leans on the open car window. "I'll say this, though. When you were together it was the best I've ever seen you and Bobby, so if it really was bloody real, then I would do whatever it takes to get that back. Because I know a connection that strong is near impossible to find." He shakes his head, pulling his backpack over his shoulder.

I watch him go, wondering if I could give Bobby another chance. Would he want to after what I said?

At the first real test, I ran away. I failed us.

How could it have been real if it was founded on a secret? The moment the thought enters my mind, I know it's far from the truth. We were real. Every relationship has challenges. Two imperfect people can't hope for anything close to perfection. But it felt so perfect. Was that part real? Everything that wasn't the past. Our present. Is that real?

So fucking real.

Our truth.

My truth.

———

AT HOME, THE JOURNALS AND PHOTO BOOKS REMAIN IN A MESS ON MY floor. I take a deep breath and look at them one more time. Going to our dresser, I pull on that same shirt that I wore that day when Bobby held me crying–Cody's AC/DC shirt.

It was Bobby's strength that I borrowed that day, wasn't it? I remember feeling so lost. So alone. I needed his strength to teach me to keep going. It turned out, he needed it more than I did.

A groan escapes from deep inside me, my anger turns back on myself for not seeing. Instead of trying to understand, I shut down. The truth pulls at every insecurity. It's colored me from believing anything. But maybe, just maybe, both things were real.

Is it possible that Cody really loved me and that Bobby really loves both of us?

I pull the shirt tight near my chest, the pain so palpable it could be a heart attack. Is it possible that I can be in love with both of them, even after knowing the truth?

I'm scared of getting hurt. That just like my parents, Bobby will keep telling me lies. That he will keep things from me forever.

He might.

I've replayed our fight a thousand times. Replayed our relationship a thousand times. Every part of me felt the things I longed for with Cody and never had.

It was fucking real.

I know that with every part of my soul.

I fall asleep curled around the shirt, waking less than an hour later. The next few hours I toss and turn, wondering if I need to go see him, or if I need to call him, or if I need to let the Universe and God and Jesus handle it all. I don't know the answer; maybe there is no answer.

I breathe in the pain and hold onto it tight, like I don't know how to feel anything but pain anymore.

When I was with Cody it was pain for all the hard things in his life. Or it was pain for me and the times my parents lied, putting their needs above mine. I've been hovering beneath their control for so long.

I won't hover beneath anyone ever again.

Bobby convinced me I don't have to live the life they want. *My butterfly* he called me. The one who gets to be free.

I stare at our ceiling, hoping I'm finally in a place to learn the truth.

I wish you would've told me, Cody. I wish I would've known.

With Cody, it was so wonderful and so hard to be with him at the same time—a constant pull of what he wanted to be and who he was. Now I know why.

My heart breaks for him, because he never needed to try so hard to be with me.

I ache, knowing that Bobby is such a good lover. *He must've been good to you, too, Cody. But you chose to be with me.*

Tears I don't expect run down my face. I don't talk to Cody much. It usually hurts more than I can bear—but right now, he's the one I need.

Bobby told me that the reason he finally let go, the reason he was able to try with me was because he felt like it was okay with you. Well,

Cody, did you put us together? You left us both here. And if Bobby still feels this close to you and feels like you want us to be together, then maybe there's still more to all this that I need to figure out. You want us to be happy, don't you?

That thought feels beautiful. I've always believed in an afterlife, and though it's hard for me to feel close to anyone who has passed on, I like to believe they're watching over us. Like guardian angels waiting to earn their wings by helping those they left behind.

Is that why you put us together? So we can be happy?

I was with Cody because he believed in me. I was so starved for that sort of acceptance. We were so young, and I'd never felt accepted by anyone else. It all feels like a mistake, now. But he wasn't a mistake. A beautiful disaster? Yes. But not a mistake.

Bobby is a beautiful disaster, too.

He didn't want to hurt me, he said so himself. Our story isn't one that has a playbook.

Pain blooms in my chest because I was so hard on Bobby when I left his apartment that night. He's so hard on himself, too.

It feels silly that I can't be with Bobby over a lie–or rather, a secret–when so much about being with him is what we both need. I suppose he didn't really lie to me, I was just missing a lot of the story, and blaming it on him.

It feels better, realizing how much of me wants to be with him. That soothing memory of Bobby washes over my skin, the way he held me in his arms, the way I felt safe and at peace with him. This is a bump in the road, but it doesn't have to be our ending. Maybe we don't have to get back together, but we can reach some sort of resolve.

Forgiving him will take time, and I'm worried. But I'm ready to try again.

Because like Jae said, something this real is almost impossible to find.

41

BOBBY

MAY - END OF THE SEASON

These last nine games have flown by. Seeing Lexie is the worst kind of torture I've ever endured. Of course, she's professional. Acting normal. Like nothing happened.

She's a good actress, too. If I hadn't lived it, I wouldn't believe it even affected her.

At Briar's, I thought maybe I could fix things with Lexie. But the more I think about it, the more I realize I can't. I'll just hurt her more.

She's resilient, but I can see the pain in her eyes. Pain I put there. The eyes she tries to not let me see. I was a fucking idiot not to tell her sooner. No, not an idiot. Selfish. I didn't want it to end, and the longer I waited to tell her, the worse it got.

The space from our relationship makes me sure that we weren't in a place to be together. I sure as hell know I wasn't. I'll never regret what we had. The moments we shared will always be some of my favorites. But I'll leave them there. As memories.

After winning the game, we all go out for a team dinner at one of the local barbecue places reserved just for us.

Mom is on another trip with Nira. Hasn't shown up to a single game. It's silly, but the little boy inside of me longs for her to be there, cheering me on.

This may be the first time in her life she feels fulfilled. I know what's that like, because well, I've been missing that too. Lexie was all the fulfillment I could ever hope to attain in this life. And I fucking ruined it.

I'm heading to my truck when I see her. Lexie.

Shit, I'm all sweaty right now, my hair's a mess under my Yankees cap. I literally just threw on shorts and a shirt up after taking off my uniform. She looks amazing despite working so hard at the game. Of course she does. For a second I want her, but I shove that as far away as I can. That swelling in my throat wants to swallow me whole.

"Hey, Bobby. Can we talk?"

I stop in my tracks, unable to breathe. She wants to talk. Jeez, not now. I want to, but I can't. Sorting through all the hurt hasn't gotten me anywhere. I can't fix things with her until I work on myself.

I take cautious steps toward her, my heart stuck in my throat. Her arms wrap around me. That touch. She feels like home. My body lingers in her grasp.

No. I can't. We can't talk.

"Remember what you said, back at Christmastime on our hike?" she asks against my shoulder. "Can we agree to be patient with each other? Work through stuff one step at a time?"

It would've been nice if she could have said this the night I tried to tell her about my secrets. Now, it's too late.

It takes every bit of power I have to push away. "Please, don't." The words emerge from my lips, a hoarse whisper.

"Bobby." She looks into my eyes and I lose ability to see straight. All of the things between us are a tangled heap of confusion and pain. "I know I treated you like fuck that night. I wanna make it better. I miss you."

I stand frozen, blood racing out of control. Timid, like she isn't sure if it's okay, she holds me in the sweetest embrace. Her presence is everything I've been longing for. If there was any doubt in my mind how I felt, I know now. I'm still in love with her. Like magnets, we are drawn together. I can't break myself free. I'm lost in time and space of all that we were.

Several heartbeats later, she takes a step backward. "I just needed some time to think and process all this." Her eyes are hopeful. "But I wanna know why. Why didn't you tell me sooner? Look, I wasn't in a place that I could hear you that night in your apartment, but I am now." She looks excited, like she's really wanting to just jump back in. "Sorry." She smoothes my shirt. "I should've asked before I did that, I just needed to hug you." Embarrassment makes her cheeks blush and it's the sweetest fucking thing.

I needed to hug you too, Lex. I wanna say to her, but I can't.

I force a long breath, hoping to find some measure of control.

"To answer your question, I promised him I would never tell a soul." It comes out raspy. "And I haven't. Not once. Until you."

Her eyes are shining with unspilled tears. "I'm sorry for what I said."

"Not as sorry as I am." My throat burns.

"Why did you tell me now?"

"Because I couldn't bear keepin' it from you anymore." My body gnaws at my broken heart, realizing just how much she hurt me by not letting me explain.

"I overreacted. Even Trish and Jae—"

"Shit, Lex. Did you tell them?" Worry courses through my head to my toes. I never thought about who she may tell. "Cody didn't want people to know. And I can't come out, not with baseball." It's a whisper, because shit if a teammate walking to their car overhears. Briar doesn't even know. The potential headline comes to mind again. *Suicidal Bisexual Baseball Player Ridden with an Eating Disorder, Bobby Anderson throws away a promising Major League Career.*

"I know you can't." She hugs her body, a defensive tone taking her voice.

"I've been *very* careful not to let it get public that I've been with guys." I'm whispering quieter now, backing behind my truck, worried about getting caught.

"I told Trish, but not Jae." Her eyebrows raise. "I wasn't doin' it to blow your secret. She won't talk."

"You told Trish?" I feel sick, like all that food is gonna come right back up. After all this time of being cautious, it just slipped through my fingers. I can't untell a secret.

"I needed someone to talk to."

"It could've been me, Lex." My insides erode because now she and Trish know a secret that I was never supposed to tell. Not just Cody's, but mine. "I haven't even told my Dad how I identify, for Christ's sake." It's hard not to yell. I'm so fucking angry that she tossed out something I've kept with such care.

"I wasn't ready to talk to you. You know how much I hate secrets. How much it strangled all the breath from me to see what you shared in that old journal of his." Her voice is raised and a few people look over as they walk to their cars.

"Shh." I put my finger on my lips. "Jeez, you wanna talk, fine. But don't you dare draw attention to us in this parkin' lot." I curl my toes into my shoes.

"Okay," she whispers.

With a measured breath, I continue. "I didn't wanna tell you at all. I didn't want this to hurt you. For you to regret what you and Cody had. Maybe if you woulda known how he felt, it wouldn't have hurt you so bad." I hold the back of my neck. Most of the team has left. I glance around to make sure we are alone. It's safe to talk. "When I figured out I was bi, it took a while to know if it was okay. So many people told me it wasn't. Like the people at church. Hell, our school teachers. Society told me it wasn't acceptable. It told me to stifle these feelings and keep them deep down where they can't lead to *mistakes*. But I still felt the way that I feel. I wasn't sure if I was good enough to ask you out, Lexie. Wasn't sure if it was okay how I felt. You asked why I didn't. That was a big part of it. If it was wrong of me to be bi, then I wasn't worthy of goin' out with anyone."

I look at her face for a moment. There's compassion in her eyes. It helps me to see this. I really didn't know how she felt.

"I'm sad you've gone through so much." One side of her mouth lifts up in a sympathetic smile.

"I'm sad I've gone through it, too. I'm even more sad that a lot of people have it worse. It's fucked up." I flip my cap around backward, needing something to do with my hands. "After a while, I knew it was okay with me. I accepted who I was. Cody helped me figure that out. That love *is* love and however I felt and expressed it didn't make me less of a person. I realized that this is all social pressure from people who don't understand."

"You're right." She's hanging on my every word. "I hate that this is so hard."

"But people treat you different when they know. You're not you anymore. You're somethin' messed up. Like they are afraid to be around you or to talk to you. It's an insane stigma. It wasn't how I wanted people to view me. So I knew I could keep it secret. I could be bi to myself, and love and accept that part of who I am. But no one else needed to know." Air fills my lungs, finally getting this off my chest. "It's all kinds of complicated for me to talk about it. But I've wanted to. I always planned on tellin' you at some point. I just didn't know when or how." I stretch my shoulders. "I wish with everything that I am that Cody coulda been up front with you. But he wasn't. He left me with this mess."

"I'm glad you told me." She takes my hands in hers. "And I am sorry, I'm not sure what to do. I'm ready now, maybe we can–"

"No, we can't. Okay, Lex? We can't." It takes all my strength to pull away from her. My body is burning up, like an addict without my fix. I'm glad I could talk to her, but being in a relationship isn't an option. "We can't be this to each other. We are only gonna keep hurtin' each other. I don't know how not to hurt you. I am so fuckin' broken right now. You have no idea." I can't let my fight with the world become her fight. I can't let her nurse me through my eating disorder. I can't be her project. There's too much wrong with me that would just hurt her.

"I want to have an idea. I want you to tell me what you're feeling, what you're goin' through. We are both broken. You know that. We need to help each other heal. I felt more healing with you than anythin' else. I just didn't know how to handle the truth. It was everythin' I didn't want to know. My biggest fears that I wouldn't even consciously acknowledge to myself. It took time to unravel everythin'.

But I'm crazy about you, Bobby. Remember all those sweet moments we had?"

"Is it remembering if you never forgot?" I swallow. No. I don't want to give her hope. I don't want to confuse her. Shit, I just don't want to hurt her. "I'm crazy about you, Lexie. But I have so many secrets."

"More secrets?" She gives me a look that says she is horrified at the prospect. Like maybe what I already told her wasn't the worst of it.

I put my hands on her shoulders. "You need someone who doesn't keep things from you. And clearly, that isn't me."

"It is you, Bobby. You're the one I wanna be with. Our time apart has proved that more than anythin'. Can't you see? Can't you feel this?" She brings her cheek to mine. "I need you."

Why does this have to be so hard? I swallow, missing the nearness of her skin, knowing that I am about to go without.

"I wish I was what you needed." I push around her and get into my truck because she won't have to do much to change my mind and make me stay.

I try not to look back, knowing it will destroy me, but I do anyway.

She stands, stunned stupid, arms across her chest. Tears running down her face.

My mind spirals down a dark path, each mile I drive away from her. Every part of me begs to turn the car around. To fix what I broke and to mend the heart I promised not to harm.

I should go talk to her. She wanted to talk. To give us another chance.

But I don't turn around. I keep driving. Down the highway, to the batting cages. The world passes in a frenzy, like it's mocking me for my pain.

Batting cages are about to close, but I don't care. I need these few minutes. Hitting my aggression out from every ball pitched to me, I hit hard, again and again and again until sweat lines my body.

I did this. I did all of this. It's my fault. She wanted to fix it. And I left her there crying. She should never cry because of me.

All I do is hurt people. Disappoint them.

I hit ball after ball, only stopping to refill the machine.

I'm so thirsty. My body is weak, my muscles on the verge of collapse. I imagine what Dad would say if he saw me like this. What Mindy would say.

My aggression boils past any healthy level as I hit ball, after ball, after ball. I need to hear the *chink* of the bat. Need to watch each ball fly.

I have so much inside of me ready to explode into a million pieces.

Why didn't I let her talk? Why did I wait so long to tell her? Why does it feel so good to hurt myself?

My thoughts have become a broken record, but I can't turn them off. I collapse to the ground, slamming my back into the chain link fence.

"You did this!" I scream at Cody. "You made me feel accepted. You made me feel loved. Then you left me so broken! When you gave me a little bit of hope that I could have you back, you shattered me in pieces. You did this to me! And you didn't tell her. How could you not tell her?" My voice squeaks with how dry it is, how loud I'm screaming. This scratching burn feels like the worst case of strep throat. "How could you leave me behind like this? I don't want to live here! Not without you! Not without her!" I throw my hands in the air. "You broke both of us! And I thought we could be together. Me and the only girl I ever cared about. But I fucked that up so bad. I fuckin' hate you for leavin' me this mess." The words flow out of me. So much I need to say. All this time, these words have grown roots in the darkness of my soul, where I refused to even think about what happened.

I said it, what I've held inside of me, the hate for what he did. The burden I've carried all this time. Everything feels so messed up. So lost in the darkness. So stopped from progress. So stuck, every part of me is stuck.

"Hey, it's after hours!" someone shouts, coming out of the office. They rattle the fence.

"Sorry. I'll go." I pick up the gear and head to the fence gate, noticing the place is empty.

"Oh, hey, you're number five aren't you? Bobby Anderson? Third baseman for Suncastle College?"

"That's me." I don a fake smile, the same one I give to all my fans.

"Oh, well, feel free to stay as late as you like." He gets a big grin on his face. "I know you usually use the provided facilities, but we sure do like havin' any of the Suncastle Knights perfectin' their talent at our cages."

"I appreciate you not bein' angry with me." I nod, graciously.

"Would love to know I'm helpin' you play better." There's a pride in his eyes, that same pride that so many people show us. Suncastle loves our team. It's a special gift to be on a good team, and in moments like this, and I know it.

"I'm sorry, comin' here right as you're about to close, it's not right of me. My old man would be ashamed if I was still under his roof. I do apologize." And I mean it, so much fury got the better of my actions. I need to stop letting this happen. Find a better outlet.

"Oh, no, not at all. You consider this an open invitation." He fiddles around in his briefcase, pulling out a marker and a ball. "Would you mind signin' this for my son? He's a huge fan. I take him to as many games as I can. Whenever the schedule allows us to be there."

"Sure, I'd be happy to. What's his name?" I've signed a few handfuls of balls, especially for boosters and a couple of my Tiny Knights.

"Tony."

TONY, KEEP YOUR EYE ON THE BALL,
BOBBY ANDERSON, #5

I blow on the ink of my scribbles and hand him the ball. "Here ya go."

"Oh, he is gonna flip over this. Thank you so much. And good luck! End this season with a bang."

"Thank you, sir. I plan to." I give him a big smile and go to my truck as if nothing in the world is wrong.

Only everything is wrong.

I know I shouldn't do what I'm about to do. My brain is at war with itself. A million thoughts holding me prisoner. I was doing better, getting over my eating disorder. Taking care of myself. Trying so hard to do all the right things.

Trying too hard.

It's all too much. I'm in the place of overwhelming grief and duty that drives me to do destructive things.

I've hurt so many others. I deserve to hurt, like they do. It's only fair.

Mickey isn't home. He's never home. So he won't hear me.

I kneel on the bathroom rug and plunge my fingers down my throat until I heave.

Sweet relief.

42

LEXIE

I gave him a chance. Right?

Everything glosses over as I put my paintbrush to the canvas, painting through tears. I should be going over practice questions for my certification exam. But all I can do right now is paint. The part of myself that Bobby helped me get back. Only I don't feel whole. I feel as ruined as this incomplete canvas. The broken pieces of my soul fill me with an anguish I cannot shake.

My heart aches, thinking about all the things he told me about being bi. I hate he has endured so much pain, that this world is so cruel. Our small town had no place for him. It took him months to tell me. I didn't respond well when I wish I could have.

He left me.

Just like I left him.

Are we this wrong for each other? It was only a few months that we gave this a try. Only a few months of thinking that he may be the one for me. Only a few months of dancing around what loving Bobby Anderson may be like.

I think back to Christmas, to the gifts we gave to Cody's family. About holding him on that mountain top. He wanted me to know that it wasn't my fault.

He told me that Cody had been with him that night when he died.

No, no, I cannot think about that night. I fight the memory, but it comes with full depth.

"Don't you want to make love to me?" I screamed at Cody. "You tell me all the time that I'm beautiful and sexy but you won't touch me."

A chill goes through me as I remember the way I spoke to him.

"I'm not any good at this." He covers his face with his hands.

"Then learn how." My tone is cold.

"I can't learn how!"

He left in the pouring rain without a coat, leaving me naked in our sheets where he refused to take off his clothes.

It's all so clear now. Every bit of what he was. Every bit of how my pressure broke him. I was so blind.

A million times, I've forced this memory away. Told it to stay locked up so that it can't haunt me. But it still does. It haunts me every day, because the last words I said to him are the words I never would've said if I only would've known.

Why didn't you tell me?

———

I'M LYING IN MY BED, WONDERING HOW I GOT SO LOST. ALL THESE feelings are so much more than I know how to navigate.

I love Bobby. I really do. It has pulled my heart apart every time I've seen him. Torture to feel that half of my heart is away from me.

I deserve this, after the way I treated Cody. Fuck, I haven't handled any of this very well. When Bobby mentioned more secrets, I felt on the verge of an anxiety attack.

What would it take to trust him? What would it take to have him give us another chance? I swallow against my inflamed throat. It rips my soul to know that I need him, but he's not with me.

I debate going over to his place. But I won't go where I'm not wanted. This stings a lot, because I wonder if Cody really wanted me.

Can anyone ever want me?

I sit on the floor and look at Cody's notebooks again. The only piece of him I have.

When I've been looking through all this, it's been all about him and Bobby. But now, I'm looking for something else. Trying to change my lens enough to see the whole picture, instead of allowing my eyes to fill in details.

Speak to me, Cody. Tell me what I need to know.

And in his words, it's all here, too.

Cody loved me.

He loved us both.

It wasn't a lie or a sick joke. He loved me the best he could with all he was battling inside. *I wish you never had to try to force this. I wish you coulda been gay and free to love who you love.*

My heart hurts, because I understand. He wasn't allowed to be himself. Even Bobby can't come out unless he wants to risk his career and the way everyone sees him.

I would've never been caught in the middle of them if they had felt free in the first place. Why can't they be free to love who they love?

I know that I want this for them, for everyone who cannot be free in the world we live in today.

The pain in my heart morphs into something so beautiful, because I realize that I'm not mad at Bobby for being Cody's lover. I'm happy that he was. I'm thankful that he could be there for Cody the way he longed for, even if the relationship didn't last. *I'm glad you got a little bit of time with him. I wish that things were different. Because you woulda had a beautiful life together if you coulda been allowed.*

I feel the sweetest relief wrap around me. Cody and I loved the best way we knew how. We tried. We did our best.

"He could never hate you," Bobby had said. And Cody doesn't. I feel that in the warmth going through me now. I'm filled with peace and hope that everything will be alright.

Bobby told me he loved us both. He never treated me like a second choice. I think he and Cody may or may not have worked out. But somehow, I think Bobby and I really could.

I'm hoping Bobby just needs time. I force a breath, hug my arms tight. Our love is worth fighting for, and I'm going to keep on fighting until he sees all that we can be.

43

BOBBY

THE LAST HOME GAME

I pull on my jersey, feeling like it weighs a hundred pounds. I have no strength. No will. The excitement in the locker room is palpable, but I'm barely present.

Standing in the dugout, my head is pounding. Black coffee sloshes in my gut, the only thing I've kept down in about a week. This is shitty timing. Ate just enough over the weekend to keep my weight level to pass my doctor's appointment on Monday. Then I purged. Depleted my system, and just kept going like I couldn't stop. And I couldn't. I've heaved every fucking day this week.

Last night I fell asleep on my bathroom tile until I woke up enough to climb into bed.

Been lying through my teeth to Mindy, to Crossfit Santa, that I am doing fine. I never meant to lie. But I can't stop. I need help, and I can't let myself get it.

I've fucked up everything that mattered to me. My own stupid choices. But I'm not giving up my last game.

Mindy looks at me a little too long. "Feelin' okay?"

"Yep, I'm great." I smile and nod, putting on a convincing show. When she moves on to check another player, I relax.

We remove our caps, placing them over our hearts, listening to

"The National Anthem" play like a farewell hymn. Cleats strut out onto our home field for the last time.

"Make it count." Zac throws me a cocky smile heading to first base with his number three jersey.

"Make it count," I echo. Man, I'm gonna miss playing college ball.

I feel numb playing, but I still try. I'm not really here, in this moment. Feels like I'm watching life in slow motion, too weak to stand and run. But I do. Somehow I do. Playing the best I can for the last game I'll ever play on this field .

Lexie is here. I nod my head at her between innings, looking into those gorgeous eyes and wishing I was the man she deserved. The man that would've told her the truth sooner.

The sun beats down on my skin, drying it and stretching it tight, making me regret not putting on any sunscreen. I'm so dehydrated that there are fuzzy spots in my vision. At the next break, I'll grab a drink. I should probably rest a minute, but I'm not gonna. This is my last college game and so help me, I'll play.

"Drink more. It's crazy hot." Mindy hands me and several other players Gatorade, but I don't feel like drinking. It's not sugar-free.

"You alright, Bobby?" She looks at me even longer than she did before the game. I passed all the checkups. I did what she wanted, most of the time.

"Doin' fine." I give her that smile I give my fans.

"You sure?" It's a whisper and a couple guys look over.

Just tell her, Bobby. Sit out. Get a snack. Do somethin'.

Instead, I nod. Game is half over. No use telling her now. "I'm alright."

"Got tape?" Zac taps Mindy's shoulder.

"Yep." She takes him to the first aid kit.

Jeez, I shouldn't lie to her. But this is *my* game and I'm not putting it at stake. I have to be out there. I sip down half of the bottle and set it on the bench before we go out to the field. Maybe the sugar will be enough to curb this headache.

My body hungers for nourishment. I've pushed harder than I should, skating this dangerous line. The one where I know I'm being fucking stupid but too lost to do a damn thing to get myself out of this hole.

I'm at third base. My home. My last game. I thought I would feel nostalgic but I don't. I feel lost. Ruined. I ruined everything. *Cody... why am I such a fuckup? God, I wish you were here to tell me it's all gonna be okay.* Because I need someone. Anyone. I'm utterly and completely alone, without a soul to turn to and take this pain away.

My eyes wander to the dugout, to the purest love I've ever known. She was more to me than anyone ever has been. I'm so mad at myself. She thought our relationship was some "sick joke". Our relationship was made up of me being incredibly selfish. *I'm sorry, Lex. I'm really sorry.*

How much I miss Cody makes my throat seize up, like I'm on the verge of breaking down. How many days? I can't remember.

Did I really stop counting?

I should be sweating with how hot it is, but I'm not. It's like I'm too hot to sweat. Black dots float in my vision. The crowd is cheering as Conrad winds up and pitches. I know it's loud, but I can't hear anything. The black dots get bigger until I can't see around them. I'm woozy, wishing for something to hold onto to steady me.

Oh shit, not during a game.

I really did go too far this time.

I shouldn't have heaved last night. Carb loading woulda been better. I knew I shouldn't. Couldn't stop.

My vision stays dark for too long. Reality melts into a weird inner space, like everything is surreal and hazy. It's a bit like I'm floating, but somehow extra heavy at the same time. Like when I step out of a swimming pool after being there for hours.

Gravity gets extra strong like it's sucking me down. Or maybe some invisible force is pushing me to the ground and I'm too weak to fight it. I get really dizzy. It's hard to breathe. I pull at my collar trying to get in some air.

Something's wrong.

I've had bad moments before, but nothing like this. Vision comes back but not for long. Feels like I'm in a dream.

Am I dying?

Can I be with you Cody? Can I slip away? Between this over-whelming pain, I get a break. Hope spreads through me. I can be with him again. I can leave this world behind. *All I want is to be with you.*

Through this heavy floating feeling, I wonder if it's really it for me. Have I met my end? My demise? For a heartbeat, I worry about my folks. I worry about Lexie. But then I'm not worried anymore. Instead, I feel peace.

Worry is replaced with a calming comfort that everything will be alright. That whatever happens now, there is meaning in it. I've lived the life I was meant to live and I can die here on the baseball field.

I get to be with you, Cody. A hot tear runs down my face as I remember the look in his eyes right after we'd kiss. The warmth of his skin against mine. How I felt when I was with him. *We can finally be together.*

I hear the ball connect with the bat. I lift my glove, try to reach for the fly ball. I'm so out of it.

The ground tilts upward. I grab at the air looking for something to hold me up. A horrible pain explodes in my chest, but I barely feel it as the world goes totally black.

Let me go home.

To you.

44

LEXIE

Oh, God...No!

We run out on the field. That ball must have knocked the wind out of him. But he's not moving.

Oh fuck, he's not moving.

A million possible injuries flash through my head. I saw that ball. My legs are heavy as they sprint every step. I can't get out there fast enough. He's still not moving. I thought by now he'd be shaking this off.

He's not. He's out cold. *Oh, God....*

I thought it hit his chest, not his head. Why is he passed out?

Why didn't he catch it?

These are the moments we train for. The ones that *really* matter. The ones that can make someone live or die. This is life or death. Life or death for *Bobby*. He isn't moving.

I look for breathing. It's there. Thank God, it's there. But it's too labored. Doesn't look right, like he's fighting for life.

"Jae, call 911." Mindy is at Bobby's side, checking for a pulse. "Rapid, thready, and weak."

My heart feels like it stops. I'm in a stupor, too shocked to understand what is happening. His skin is red and feels hot, like a pan straight out of the oven. You'd think he'd be sweating but there isn't a drop on his skin.

Heatstroke.

"We need to cool him down." Mindy says, "Let's get him off the field."

Coaches bring a stretcher over. There's the EMT that works the games. They jump into action, helping Mindy.

Bobby's *still* not moving. *Wake up. Come on, wake up. Please, please wake up.*

Mindy stripps off his jersey and there is a huge bruise forming on his chest where the ball hit. She palpates the area. Probably shattered ribs. But that wouldn't knock him out. *Syncope, passing out, is a symptom of heatstroke.* Learned that freshman year.

"Get the towels wet." Mindy tilts her head. "Get me the hose. We've gotta cool him down, now."

I'm taking off more of his clothes while Jae is on the phone with emergency telling them where to find us and what happened.

What *did* happen?

Mindy moves fast and something about it is so beautiful. No, it's not beautiful. It's comforting. Mindy knows what she's doing. She can help him. *Please, just help him.*

"Get me a tarp." Mindy says, messing with the hose they brought over. Everyone's shocked. Everyone's worried. I can feel the tension from the seats. The game has stopped. The other team's athletic trainer is over here trying to help.

"Let's dump the ice water from the coolers, then go to concessions and get more ice," Mindy instructs, and some of the players run off to get it. The crowd watches.

"Lexie! The towels," Mindy yells. I shake out of this frozen state, overwhelm and worry mixing in my gut. I dip rags in cold water and dab them all over his skin. It feels like hot leather, not the soft warmth I'm used to. I know him. I've held every inch of him. This is beyond wrong. *Wake the fuck up, Bobby. Come on.*

Mindy's messing with a tarp and the hose. "Get him over here."

A couple of the players help move him to the makeshift ice bath. Tate pours the ice water. Zac helps spread it around. Mindy holds Bobby's head up, cold towels all over him. The tarp holds water like he's in an icy puddle.

Mindy takes out her thermometer. "Temp is 105.7. Mickey, did he get drunk last night?" She looks at Mickey but he looks as shocked as I feel. His eyes meet the ground, refusing to answer.

"Lexie, do you know anythin'?"

"N-n-no," I stutter out. Temperature 105.7 repeats in my mind. Dangerously high. Holy fuck. Holy fuck. Holy fuck.

"Mickey, you *live with him.* Did he do anythin' last night? Does anybody know? Zac? Ethan? Briar? Who knows? Anyone know?"

They shake their heads, shame coloring their expressions. We all wish we knew more. The players are a mix of worry and concern.

"He went home after practice, I think." Zac's sitting right next to Mindy, trying to help.

"No, he went somewhere after. Saw his truck parkin' at the apartment a little later than I got back." Briar dips the towels, dabbing them on Bobby's chest. "Looked fine, though."

Bobby's *still* unconscious. Oh fuck. How many minutes has it been?

Too many.

He shouldn't be out this long, even with heatstroke. *No, no, please. Don't let this happen. Don't let this happen, God. Please.*

A siren.

I'm transported in time to when I heard sirens the night of Cody's death. No. Not again. Please, not again.

Another EMT and a paramedic come out to the field.

"Suspected heat stroke, Bobby Anderson, age twenty-three, six foot one, about a hundred and sixty-five pounds, temp 105.7 last check. Rapid pulse–weak and thready, labored breathing. Baseball impact to the chest at third base." Mindy rattles off details while the paramedic puts an oxygen mask over his nose and mouth.

Mindy looks at her watch. "It's been eight minutes since the impact and he hasn't come to. No known medications. Drank some Gatorade about half an hour ago. Anorexic-bulimic–in treatment, but possible relapse."

The EMT jots down everything while the paramedic works on an IV.

Anorexic-bulimic rings in my ears. He can't be. No, this can't be real. He woulda told me. I know he woulda told me.

"Veins are collapsed, likely from dehydration." The paramedic tries a few more spots. "After we get some cold saline, we're gonna stay here till we get him cooled down."

Mindy nods, doing what she can. "Are his parents here, Lexie?"

I look into the stands for the section where his dad always sits. "Don't think so." Fuck, I wish I knew. Wish he woulda talked to me. Fuck, he's been going through all this and didn't tell me.

He's not waking up.

I stare at his body that looks more lifeless than it should. "Hang in there." My teeth chatter, hands freezing from the cold water? Or worry? I'm not sure.

Finally, they get a vein. The saline drips as I sit near Mindy, brushing hair off Bobby's forehead that is still so hot, shocking my skin. *Hang in there, baby. Hang in there.*

The EMT puts a cooling blanket over him and takes vital signs.

After a few minutes, his temp starts coming down. Thank fuck.

"Let's transport." They get him on a stretcher and roll him out through the front gate. Security keeps guests from getting too close.

I want to ask if I can come with him. My heart shatters knowing that I can't. We aren't together anymore. My heart wants to beat for him. I struggle to exist knowing that he's fading in the back of that ambulance, without me.

"If anythin' happens to the other players, text me." Mindy takes my hands. It's her responsibility to stay with a player at least until his parents arrive. Especially after an emergency like this. "I'll have Jessica come as soon as she can." She jogs to the back of the ambulance and climbs in.

The world spins around me. My body shakes. I try to have faith, but I can't.

"Back we go." Jae puts his arm around my shoulder and leads me to the dugout. *Please Bobby, just wake up. Just be okay.*

Everyone cleans up the tarps and hose to get the field back in working order. They return to the game like nothing happened.

So much happened.

Anorexic-bulimic? My teeth chatter harder. I sit on the bench, trying to take a breath that my lungs won't allow.

How did I not know?

All the health food and bottles of supplements. All the times he refused to eat anything. All the times he was cold, like his body didn't have enough circulation–another symptom of an eating disorder.

I didn't know. How did I live with him and not know? I must be fucking blind.

Another secret he's kept from me.

I feel like I'm sinking, lost in the dark depths of an ocean.

"It's alright." Jae pats my shoulder. "They got him quick, he'll pull through."

Empty promises. He can't possibly know if he'll pull through.

"Anorexic-bulimic. Did you know?"

"No." Jae sighs. "I'm sure that's something kept discreet intentionally."

"Come on Lex, Bobby's been purgin' for years." Mickey wipes sweat from his brow.

I jump at the unexpected sound of his voice.

"You knew." I glare at him, blood racing through my veins. I want to strangle him. "Where have you been? For him and for me? You walked out on us while he clearly needs you." I'm exploding, and he leans back on the bench, cool as a winter day.

"It's when Bobby's stressed out." Mickey shrugs. "We all have our things."

Anger floods me, weighs me down, because I should've known. I should've seen the signs. I should've helped him. I've studied all about disordered eating in athletics. I've written abstracts on sports medicine articles. I've given presentations. I *should* have known.

I lived with him, and I didn't see it.

"Well his *thing* is somethin' that people die from," The snark slithers from my tongue.

"I already told you. We all have our things." Mickey's voice is intense, repeating again like it's all he will ever say, and it jars me in a way I don't expect. Almost like he's defending himself.

Tears burn at my eyes. How could Mickey know and not do anything?

How could Bobby keep this from me?

The thought is like a dam breaking in my mind. I wanted so much to have him be honest with me. Transparent with me. I hoped I could trust him.

If I had an eating disorder I would've told him. If I had been intimate with our mutual friend, I would've told him.

But he never told me. What else has he not told me? I hate myself for being so selfish right now, but that is what I feel. Maybe it's the only way to cope with the shock.

My head throbs as I watch the players.

Buzzing in my pocket pulls me away from the game. I dare to hope it's Mindy.

Jessica: On my way.

I sigh.
Another buzz.

Mindy: Send me Bobby's parents' info.
Me: Is he ok?
Mindy: Working on it.

I rush to the kit, pulling out a worn notebook with tons of player forms. Flipping pages, I find Bobby's sheet and type out the contact numbers for his mom and dad.

———

THE MOMENT I'M FINISHED WITH EVERYTHING AT THE GAME, I GET IN my car and speed all the way there. By the time I finish all the post game responsibilities, it's been almost two hours since the impact. *Please, God, Jesus, Universe, let me not be too late.*

This is a nightmare. I vowed to never set foot in this hospital again. Peterson Memorial Hospital is all too familiar. This parking garage. This old elevator that leads to the main floor of the emergency wing. This place makes my body shake with each step.

Mindy sits in the Emergency Department waiting room.

"How is he?"

"Stabilizing."

I feel like I'm able to take my first breath. "It was heatstroke, then?"

"Oh yeah." Mindy looks exhausted, like the life has been sucked from her. Hospitals aren't good places for her either...she was rushed here with her miscarriages.

"Looks like he was already depleted, though." She plays with her nails like she needs something to do with her hands.

"You told the EMT he has an eating disorder?" I hate the words coming out of my mouth.

She lets out a long sigh. "Yeah."

The word stings. She knew when I didn't. It drives these wounds deeper, when all I wanted to do was leave them alone to heal.

"I just wish there was somethin' more we could've done." Mindy fiddles with her hands.

There's that weight. The one I've worried about. The one that makes you concerned that you aren't enough because truthfully, you aren't. Heat stroke is preventable. But she was making everyone hydrate. I saw her.

"He was okay before he went out for that inning." Maybe it's the denial talking or maybe it's because I know too well what it's like when someone blames themself for a situation.

"Bobby's never okay, Lex."

My head spins at her words, because I know they are true. He puts on a strong front. Always working hard. Always performing. But he's not okay.

"He's never okay." It's a stark whisper, like I want to make the words anything other than the truth.

"No. None of us are. How could we be after what happened to Cody?" She stares at the Emergency Department desk. "That's why I don't get why you left us all here." There's a catch in her throat, and I'm reminded of all the times I saw her and Cody in the training room. "We all miss him. We're all so torn up about what happened. I wish you would've turned to us for healing instead of runnin' away. We need each other."

Every part of me unravels. I can't breathe.

"Is that why we aren't close anymore?" I wait until she looks at me. "Because I've been rattlin' my mind tryin' to figure it out." There's an anger I shouldn't have in my tone.

She is my lead. I can't talk back to her. It means risking my recommendation and could still strip me of my place in the program, just before the certification exam. And right now I don't even care.

"You think I ran away and left all of you behind?" I clench my fists. "Did you ever think for one second that this had nothin' to do with you?" Tears come rushing out of my face and I can't stop them. "And I know you sure as fuck don't approve of anythin' between me and Bobby. And maybe you're right, because I didn't know about his eating disorder, and it's one more thing on a long list of things I didn't know about. So maybe I did need to run away. Maybe I needed to get the fuck out of this town and leave every bit of it behind. Because now that I've been back for months, not a day goes by when I don't think about how it's a mistake for me to be back here, without Cody."

I expect her to yell at me, to argue, to threaten to cut me from the program. But she doesn't.

She wraps her arms around me.

45

BOBBY

I blink, opening my eyes in an unfamiliar place.

Where am I?

I feel awful. Like I'm not alive. Maybe I'm not. Maybe I've slipped away. Maybe I'm watching life from the other side.

Cold air rushes through my nostrils. Breathing. No, no, I'm alive.

What happened?

Big white ceiling tiles overhead. It takes a minute, but I remember things in broken fragments. Like trying to remember a dream first thing in the morning.

I was playing ball and then....

Oh shit, I'm in a hospital.

Jeez, I feel like hell. Wait, I've been in a room like this before. When Cody died. Someone's hand is on mine.

Lexie?

Machines are all over me. Beeping. Cold running in my veins. Is it medicine maybe?

"Wh–" I start to speak, but my throat is so dry I cough and swallow before trying again. "What happened?"

"You're awake." Lexie jumps, standing over me. "Oh my God. Bobby." She kisses my forehead. "Fuck, you terrified us."

Her green irises are shadowed to the point they look dark and heavy amidst the bright lights. It kills me to look into her eyes and see all the hurt there. "You've been cryin'."

"You gave us all quite the scare." She sniffles and wipes her tears away with the back of her hand. "Eating disorder?" It's a whisper. She coughs like she's clearing her throat, but I hear the pain she's concealing.

There's a weight in my chest, like an anvil, planting me deeper into the depths of this horribly uncomfortable bed. "I shoulda told you."

"I know." She grabs my hand tighter. "I'm just glad you're awake." Her lips pull in a tight smile, like she's trying to be strong. Shit, she is so incredibly strong.

Mindy stands next to her. "How you doin' Bobby?"

"Not so good." My hand goes to my chest. The ball took me out. That fragment of memory fits into place.

A nurse comes in and introduces herself as Julie. "We got your blood work back, and your electrolyte levels are all over the place. We're keeping you overnight for observation. The doctor has ordered an echocardiogram. He wants to check your heart." She talks to me about eating disorders and that I need to get help. After a while, she leaves a bunch of brochures for recovery centers on the tray table and goes about her business.

Dad stands in the doorway. He's wearing scrubs, like he didn't have time to change after surgery before he rushed over here. There's a look of shock on his face. He must've heard all that.

Oh, God.

I brace myself for all the disappointment that's gonna come. I feel exposed, like I'm laying here naked before the world. I close my eyes, overcome with how angry I am for letting my eating disorder go this far. I shoulda done better. It's one thing when it's just my problem. Now, I've made it everyone else's problem.

"I'm gonna see if I can find a Coke machine. We will give y'all a minute." Lexie kisses my fingers, and she and Mindy walk past Dad and out the door.

"Son." He sits beside me, taking in all the machines I'm hooked up to until he finds my face. "I came as fast as I could. Are you alright?"

"I think so." I try to be strong, but I know what's coming. He is not gonna handle this.

"When did it all start?" His eyes aren't judgemental, instead they are full of concern. "How long you been goin' through this?"

A lie is on the tip of my tongue. I could pretend it just started. I could make up something good that would be less upsetting.

No. No more lies. No more secrets.

I'm in a fucking hospital, for Christ's sake.

I don't want to tell him. Feels better when he doesn't know. Feels better when no one knows. Feels best when there's nothing to know.

If there was ever a time for total honesty, it's now. For him. For Lexie. For myself.

I can't let this happen again.

The fact that I'm laying in a hospital bed means this has gone way too far. I need help. I hate to admit it, but I can't ignore this anymore.

"Started when I was sixteen. It was Cody's birthday party that Mom threw for him. You remember that?"

The look on Dad's face makes my chest hurt. A single tear slides down his cheek. He must be so ashamed that I'm broken, that I didn't have enough faith in God to heal me from this vice. For my whole life, he taught me to be a man of faith. To be someone who was strong. I don't feel strong. I feel everything but.

"I'm sorry, Dad," I choke out.

"No, Bobby. You have nothin' to be sorry about, do you hear me?" He's as serious as I've ever seen him. His fist presses against his nose. Like he can't believe it. His voice staggers. "I'm just sad that for the last seven years, you've been carryin' this all alone." He clenches his jaw tight and lets out a sad breath. "All this time. On your shoulders. Alone. That's the saddest thing." His glossy eyes find mine. "I can't imagine how hard this has been. You've been in hell, without anyone there to help."

We sit for a while, neither of us saying a word.

"I shoulda been there for you, Son. I shoulda known." He holds his head in his hands.

"No, hey, you didn't know." I close my eyes tight. "I didn't tell anyone."

Not even Cody.

"I know, and that kills me, Bobby." He clears his throat. "You didn't have to bear this alone. Not on top of everythin' you've already been through." His voice is so low and choked up that I know he means every bit of this concern. I was always a good kid. The kind you don't worry about, much. But this worries him. I can see it.

This perfect picture I've tried to create shatters, pieces too disintegrated to ever repair.

I'm sick.

Broken.

And there's no way to fix it now. No way to change that I'm in a hospital bed, explaining to Dad that this has gone on for years without him even having a clue. And he doesn't know half of my secrets.

"Hello." Someone enters with a wheeled machine and sets it up. "I'm Lance, your ultrasound tech. I'm here to set up your echocardiogram."

Dad watches intently until the procedure is done, his eyes dancing on the reading because he knows what it all means.

"I'm Dr. Johnson." A doctor comes in and evaluates me. He and Dad talk for a bit. I'm so exhausted I tune it out, not able to focus on the words.

When the doctor leaves, it's just me and Dad. I squint my eyes against how much this hurts. Dad is a cardiac surgeon. And my heart ain't working right, because I've been starving myself and puking up calories I can't afford to lose.

"I've fucked everythin' up." I sigh, staring at the ceiling tiles.

"None of that." Dad puts his hand on my shoulder. "This is not your fault. Don't you get it?"

I want to, but I can't. All I hear is my voice of self doubt saying that I've caused everyone so much trouble.

It's all my fault.

Everything is my fault.

"Eating disorders are not because of somethin' you did wrong." He looks at me for a long time. "I'm scared to overstep right now, but I gotta ask. You wanna get some help? I'll pay for you to go to a recovery center."

"I've been goin' to therapy. Mindy's been doin' a ton. Meetin' with team doctors and everythin'. I just—" I look down at my stomach. "I let it go too far. I was doin' better but then, I dunno, I just fell apart." Defeat presses harder in my chest.

"Would you like to try somethin' different?" Dad takes my hand in his. "Whatever you need." There's a depth in his tone that tells me there are no bounds to what he would do for me.

And then there's a knot in my throat. "I don't want to do this anymore, Dad." Tears burn my eyes. "But I don't know if I can stop." My chest heaves as I try to catch my breath. "I don't wanna do this."

"I know you don't."

"I didn't mean to." It hurts so bad to cry. "I don't think I can get better."

"I know you can." Dad squeezes my hand. "You can do this. You can." His eyes aren't holding shame or anger. How does he still love me after all this?

"Can I help take care of you? Will you go?"

I consider his words. It would mean missing the championship. Or maybe I can arrange to go after. "I'll go."

Dad looks relieved, and I know it'll be worth it.

"Mom's not gonna take this well."

"No, she won't." He looks at me like he's worried he said the wrong thing. "But you don't need to worry about that. The focus is all on you and gettin' whatever you need."

Realizing he means it makes all of this somehow bearable.

"Yeah, I'll go. I'd like to go."

"You can get through this." A smidgen of a smile comes to Dad's face. "You're not alone anymore."

THE HOSPITAL MOVES ME TO A ROOM FOR A NIGHT OF OBSERVATION. Lexie comes back with a peach smoothie, taking the recently vacated seat by my side. Mindy, Dad and Lexie have taken turns in that spot since I've woken up, never giving it a chance to get cold.

"Here's your phone." Lexie sets it in my hand. There's a bunch of notifications from Sam messaging me.

Sam: I couldn't sleep so I pulled up the game. You passed out? I just saw.
Sam: Are you ok?
Sam: Fuck, Bobby, are you ok?
Sam: You're not answering so you better not be dead.
Sam: Do. Not. Be. Dead.

I scroll through all the messages and type a response.

Me: I'm not dead.

Their reply comes up quick, like they've been sitting with the screen open, waiting for a message from me. It's around 9 a.m. their time. Hope they haven't been up all night fretting.

Sam: Mate, you terrified me. Couldn't find any news clips with updates or anything. Just that bit they showed with the ambulance hauling you off. What happened?
Me: Heat stroke.
Sam: You better now?
Me: At the hospital...but I think I'm gonna be fine.
Sam: You best be. Can I do anything?
Me: No, but thanks.
Sam: Glad you're ok.

———

A BUNCH OF THE PLAYERS STOP BY BEFORE THE NIGHT IS OVER.

"You scared us out there," Briar says.

"Mindy had to go and make a slip n' slide stat." Zac chuckles. "Tryin' to freeze you like a fuckin' popsicle." There he goes, pretending he's funny.

"I'd say I missed your stupid jokes, but I'd be lyin'," I chuckle.

"You're just lucky we still won. Hendricks about lost his shit when he had to go in for you." Briar shakes his head.

"I'll bet he did. Fuck, guys I shouldn't have let this happen." I keep repeating this over and over, but it doesn't make me feel a lick better.

"We're just glad you're okay," Coach Conners squeezes my shoulder and Coach Denson sets flowers on the table.

"Flowers? I'm not dead yet, Coach." I raise my eyebrows.

Everyone laughs.

"And thank the angels for that!" Coach Denson whistles.

They stay for a little bit, reliving the game, giving me all the highlights. This definitely isn't where any of them want to be tonight. A sterile hospital room instead of a party or a night out celebrating. I've ruined their plans. One by one, most of the guys head out. Visiting hours are almost over.

"Does everyone know?" I wince at the thought. "I mean, you had to tell the paramedics I'm guessin'?"

"Some of the team probably heard." Mindy replies. "But we won't release anythin' public that you're not okay with."

"Phones are already ringin' off the hook. We've gotta be careful here, so close to the draft." Coach Conners tells Mindy.

"You think I've blown it, Coach?" I sit up on my elbows, getting closer to him and Mindy.

"Blown it? No. You think you're the first? You're not even my first tricky case, Anderson. We will release a statement about heatstroke." Coach Conners nods. "I've talked to the team, too. Unlikely anyone will leak it out."

"Yes, leave it as heatstroke." Mindy turns to me. "My athletic trainin' students, who overheard some of the details, will keep this confidential. You aren't goin' to have to explain anythin' to anyone you don't want to."

"If you're well enough, we'd still love to have you for the championship." Coach Conners puts his hand on my shoulder, looking at Mindy with a question in his eyes.

"Depends on how you're doin'. But yes, if you're feelin' up to it, Bobby." She nods.

"I'll do my best." I shake his hand goodbye.

"I know you will." He smiles. "Take care of yourself."

"Thanks, Coach."

Dad and Mindy go over the recovery options with me. After some searching, we find one that looks like it'll fit in my schedule, after the post-season. I can go there for four weeks, after the championship. It's heavy, but I know it's what I need.

A nurse comes in to get my vitals. Besides feeling fatigued, and this horrible guilt for putting those close to me through hell, I'm doing alright.

"I've got surgery in the mornin'. You gonna be okay if I come back tomorrow afternoon? Hopefully, around the time you get discharged," Dad looks at his phone.

"Yeah, I'll be fine." I bob my head.

"I'll stay with him, tonight," Lexie offers. "If that's alright with you, Bobby?"

"Of course it is." I find her eyes.

"That'd be great." Dad smiles at Lexie before he turns to me. "You call me if you need to, alright?" Dad holds my shoulder. "I'm just a couple hours drive away. Anythin' you need, call. Even if it's three in the mornin'."

"I'm okay." I muster the best smile I can.

"See ya tomorrow. Thanks again, Mindy." He nods to her. Lexie gives him a hug goodbye and then he heads out the door.

"I'm gonna get goin' too, Bobby." Mindy gathers her bag.

"Thanks, ya know, for savin' me and all." My throat is thick knowing she rescued me. "For everythin'."

"I'm glad we got you help. Glad you're doin' alright now. I'll check in with you in the morning." She walks out the door.

Knuckles strum on the door. "Come in," Lexie says.

Mick pushes the door open. A weight comes over the room as he enters and takes a seat on the chair next to Lexie.

"Didn't think you'd come." There's fire in my voice. I'm sick of the shit. We used to be buddies. The best kind of roommates.

"I'm leavin'." He's talking more to Lexie than to me.

"Leavin'? What about the championship?" I sit up a little.

"Claudia's pregnant."

Shit…is that what's been taking up all his time?

"Last month's rent is on the counter at home." He stands.

"Where you goin'?" Lexie asks.

"I'm not really sure yet." Mick rubs his forehead.

"Well, congratulations," I force out.

Lexie stands and gives him a long hug. "Will you keep in touch, at least?"

"Donno." He heads toward the door but comes back. "I'm gonna try livin' at Uncle Dean's for a bit. If you're in Willardson, lemme know." He sounds deflated. The person we all knew is lost and gone. With a deep breath, he heads for the door again.

"Mick, wait," I say.

He hesitates.

"Good luck." I try to sound sincere, fighting against all the shock after finding out he's leaving and Claudia is pregnant.

"You'll need it as much as I do." He shakes his head.

Lexie goes around the bed and gives him another long hug, whispering something in his ear.

"Like I said, we all have our things." Mick sighs and shakes his head, like it's a relief to have it out in the open.

"Dude, you can still play. There's no reason you can't still play with a baby on the way." I sit up a little bit so I'm closer to him. "Think about Dexter and Conrad. They both have little ones. Their wives just bring 'em to the games."

"The pregnancy's not goin' so hot for Claudia. I wanna be there for her as much as I can." There's a sadness in his voice that makes me feel like hell for not being there for him. I had no idea about the baby or any of this. I guess I coulda tried harder to fix things with him.

"Oh man, I hope it gets better for her real soon." Lexie puts her fingers to her lips. "Gotta take good care of my little niece or nephew in there. And their mama."

"It's twins." Mick's face lights up a little bit. Makes me happy for him. He's already trying to be a good dad. "Boy and a girl."

"Oh wow!" Lexie throws her arms around him again. "Well you have to keep me posted more than you have been. If we can do anythin' for her, for you?" Her eyebrows raise in question.

"We got it for now. I just need to take care of her." He heads toward the door again.

"Mick!" I get his attention.

"What?" He turns.

"Take the stereo."

A smile comes on his lips. The first time he's looked at me without hatred. "Nah, that's your stereo." He chuckles.

"You paid for half. Take it." It's small, but I know how he loves music and this will mean something.

He nods. "Now get over your shit and take care of my baby sister, would ya?"

"Baby sister? Um, excuse me, we are barely six months apart." Lexie rolls her eyes.

Mick points to me. "She's spent enough time in hospitals. You gotta stay out of them from now on."

"I'm plannin' on it." I shrug. God, it feels good that he's giving me shit like he used to.

"See ya." He waves. And then he's gone. Proof for the millionth time that anything can change in the blink of an eye.

It's just the two of us. Me and her and these beeping machines. "Can I hold you?" I squint my eyes shut. "Shit, stupid question. You're probably not ready for that. It must be these pain meds or somethin' makin' me act weird."

"No."

"No?" I search her eyes, unsure what she means.

"You're not actin' weird. I wanna hold you, too." She gets off her chair and snuggles beside me in the hospital bed. Just like that, I feel a million times better.

"I had no idea about Mick." I pull the blanket over her.

"Me neither. Guess it makes sense though. If they were tryin' to keep stuff quiet about the babies. That's why they were stayin' aloof so much." She settles her head on my chest, careful to avoid where the ball hit me.

I fall asleep with her and it's the best sleep I've had in ages.

When I wake up, Lexie calls in an order for dinner. Pretty soon there's a tray of food in front of me. I need to eat. I know I need to eat. Shit, it's so heavy.

Lexie takes my hand in hers, "Hey, it's alright." She brings her forehead to mine. "I'm here." Her thumb goes to my cheek. "You're not gonna be alone ever again."

"That's what my dad said." I swallow, hoping she's right, hoping I won't push people away anymore. "I didn't mean any of this to go so far."

"You may have gotten heatstroke anyway. And that ball might've still hit you." Lexie's being so strong. I hate that I've done something that makes her have to be.

"I was way depleted, though. That's my fault."

"We start where we are." Her smile gives me just enough hope to keep going.

"What about us? You don't have to be here. Shit, you don't even have to give me the time of day." I move the food tray out of the way so I can be closer to her, leaning my face to hers. "I kept things from you. That is somethin' you hate."

"Are there any other big secrets I should know about? Like is my mom actually your aunt and we're secretly cousins? Or you're really adopted from Russia or somethin'? Because if there are any more secrets, now would be a good time to tell me." Her eyes are teasing, but I know part of her means it.

I chuckle. "This is the last secret. I don't have any left. Cody and I were together. I have had an eating disorder since I was sixteen. I've slept with lots of people, both men and women and my friend Sam who is non-binary. But ever since you came back to Suncastle, you're the only person I've even wanted to sleep with, so I have no idea why Mick thought I would cheat on you. I've been cheated on, and it's not my style." I think of some other things that I know will keep the mood light. "My middle name is Grant. My favorite number is five. I've always wanted to tour Europe and settle in California or Florida or somewhere nice and hot because I'm always cold." I let out a breath. "There. All my secrets." I give her a big smile, watching her reaction to see if she can try to trust me.

"No more secrets." There's a glint of hope in her eyes.

"No more secrets." I kiss her knuckles.

"I was so worried I lost you." She intertwines our fingers. "We are gonna have to figure everythin' out. But for now, I just want you to get feelin' better." She pulls the tray back over to me.

I rely on her strength to eat every bite.

46

BOBBY

$\mathcal{I}$ t's been almost a month since my hospital stay.

It doesn't just magically get better, but I am working as hard as I can to keep from the lows. Dad brought a bunch of groceries over to my apartment. Things I can eat when we aren't on the road with post-season.

Mom and Nira came to graduation. They were worried about me, but didn't stay long. Nira keeps a busy schedule, and Mom goes with her to all her events.

After my weekly visit with the team doctor, I go to see Mindy in the training room.

"I am almost back to my normal weight." I hand Mindy the slip of paper with the doctor's notes.

"That's great, Bobby." Mindy smiles. After I got out of the hospital, she has been checking in with me even more than before. But I'm doing what I need to. Motivated to keep playing. Motivated to stay the hell out of the hospital. Motivated to heal.

"They checked out my heart again. Doctor's not worried. Just says keep it up."

"That's good news. Dr. Rogers says you've been meetin' with him twice a week now. You and your dad made arrangements for the recovery center." Mindy reads over the notes. "You feelin' up to the trip, tomorrow?"

"Yeah." I nod, nerves in my stomach. She told me I couldn't play if I wasn't in a good place. But I am.

"Any vomiting lately?"

"Nope." And it's true. "Honest." I sigh. "It's a lot, but I'm doin' it."

"I'm proud of you." She takes a sip of her coffee.

I settle into the chair next to her. In a way, I look forward to our little check-ins. I don't resent her for checking up on me anymore. I'm just thankful she's here to help. It's okay to need help. I'm learning that.

"I know I scared everyone. I didn't mean for it to go that far. I just–" I look down at my shoes. "Bein' in the hospital spoke loud to me. I don't ever wanna go back there. I don't ever wanna dip that low." I look at her desk. "Do you know other athletes that have gone through this?"

"Yes." Mindy doesn't miss a beat.

"Do they get better?" I'm afraid to ask, but I feel like I have to know. "Will I be able to get over this?"

She nods. "There's no doubt in my mind. You want to get better. You're gettin' the help that you need. And you're already improving." She puts her hand on my shoulder. "Remember that you can fight this. You just keep on fightin'." Her eyes are kind, full of the care I've experienced with everything big and small over the last five years.

"I'm gonna miss you when the post-season is over, Mindy." I stand and give her a hug. "I really appreciate you savin' my life. Bein' there for me through all the ups and downs."

"You'll have to come back someday. After you live all those dreams." She winks. "Get some good sleep tonight. I'll see ya tomorrow."

I head to my car. I have bags to pack. Then, on the road again.

———

EVERYTHING IS GOING AWESOME. WE DID WELL IN REGIONALS AND Super Regionals. Better than last year. Now we are heading to The College World Series, in Omaha.

We pile into Coach Conner's hotel room to watch the MLB Draft. It's like the best TV marathon.

My phone buzzes with an unknown number. I step into the hall.

"This is Bobby Anderson." My heart is racing wondering if this is *the* call I've been waiting for.

"Hey Bobby, this is Zayne Bicksbee, regional scout."

"Oh, hello, Mr. Bicksbee. What can I do for you?" My head spins. This is exactly who I wanted it to be.

"We are thinking about signing you in the third round if you'd sign for–" He gives me a number and I can't believe my ears. More than what I was expecting. Woulda signed for half that.

"Yes, sir." I don't hesitate. Cody was right. It's like a huge drop on a rollercoaster.

"Thank you for your time."

"Thank you, Mr. Bicksbee." I swallow down my shock as I click off the phone. I'm feeling weak and lightheaded as I sink down the wall to hug my knees. My hand slips under my shirt to find my cross necklace, rubbing my thumb over the baseball lines etched into the metal.

Hey Cody, I don't know if this was you or not, but if it was, thank you. I feel it's only right to offer a prayer while I try to breathe.

"Oh, hey." Lexie's voice registers in my ears and I look up. She sits her adorable little ass next to me.

"They want me. They really want me." I rub my forehead. "I just got off the phone with a regional scout."

"Of course they do, love." She brings me in for one of the sweetest kisses we've ever shared. "I knew they would."

After several minutes of sitting in the hall to calm my nerves, we go back into Coach's room.

"Gimme the Doritos, will ya?" Zac reaches from behind the couch. The bag crinkles and he crunches them with his mouth wide open.

"Shut it, I'm tryin' to hear." Ethan eyes Zac.

"Shhhh–" Briar puts his finger over Zac's lips, then points to the screen. "Ladies and Gentlemen, Bobby Anderson." Briar sounds like one of those sports commentators. I'm about to give him shit, but then I look at the TV.

My picture. Holy hell. My picture.

"The Los Angeles Angels select Bobby Anderson."

The words don't quite register. Really? Is this really happening? My name just got called. Mr. Bicksbee wasn't kidding.

A shiver goes through me as my stats flash on the screen. *Los Angeles Angels....* I can't believe my eyes.

"Congratulations, baby." Lexie's lips are on mine for several heartbeats. It warms my heart that she's sitting right here with me.

"Well, look at that. You did it." Zac puts his hand on my shoulder.

"Of course he did." Briar starts jumping and hollering. I stand up. Everyone hugs me and pats me on my back. My heart soars with every kind of excitement there is.

Cody's face flashes in my mind. There's that tremor. I feel it. Here and now, he's close.

"I knew you could do it. I knew you could make it."

Briar gets a call. Before the night is over, he's drafted by the New York Mets.

"We did it." I give him a huge hug.

"I'll just have to see you again on the field." He smiles.

"I look forward to that."

47

LEXIE

*M*y flip flops slap against the stone floor in the entryway of Hawthorne Estate, a home that has never really been mine. Every cell in my body wants me to turn tail and run, but I plant my feet harder into the ground.

I have to do this, for myself.

"Oh hey, baby girl." Dad steps out of his office. "What are you doin' here?"

"Can we go to Shakey's?" My heart patters in my chest, knowing I haven't asked to go there with him since I was a kid. I don't want to talk here. I need to be somewhere else. Somewhere that Mom can't overhear.

"Is that you, Lexie?" Mom steps onto the landing, phone to her ear. "What? Did you forget somethin' for that art studio the Anderson kid was settin' up for you at Christmastime?" Her scorn is evident in her tone as she puts weird emphasis on the word *studio*.

My teeth grind in my mouth. The Anderson kid. Jesus, he has a name. I look at Dad. In all these years I haven't asked for much, hardly anything. But I'm asking now, completely unsure what I will do if he says no. "Please?"

"I'll get my coat."

His driver pulls the Cadillac around, and we ride in the backseat together. "Didn't get to talk to you much at Christmastime, darlin'. How you been?"

Falling apart.

"Just finishin' up with baseball post-season."

"Did you get that interview set up with Aberdine?"

A few weeks ago I got an email from him about an opening in one of the minor league baseball teams in Florida. He'd been able to pull some strings, through his connections, to get me a job down there.

"No, um, I have other plans." This is harder than I want it to be. I swallow, wishing to get it all over with. Once I tell him I'm leaving, he can make whatever plans he needs to, and I can wash my hands of this life.

"Other plans? Still baseball right? Well, I do know a few people over in Memphis. I'm sure we could arrange you workin' one of their teams. Maybe in the collegiate level."

"Dad, I don't want to do athletic trainin'."

"What do you mean?" His face falls. "We just put all that toward your education, sugar."

"And you didn't have to. Mom insisted I finish my degree, and I have. You don't have to pay for or connect me with anyone else."

The words fill the air between us for several heartbeats while I wait for what he may say. Goosebumps sprinkle my arms. I scratch and rub them, trying to give these nerves something better to do than itch.

"How long you felt this way?"

There it is. That disappointment. The *oh, Lexie, of course you have to go into sports medicine...we won't have it any other way.* Only, that's not what he says. "Is it because of the accident?"

"Cody's or Bobby's?" It's strange that that question is relevant. How did I end up dating two guys that are so similar?

"I meant Cody's. What happened to Bobby?"

"Didn't you see the news?" After the hospital, it made the front page in several papers. "He had a heatstroke at a game."

"Is he alright?" Dad actually sounds concerned.

"Yeah, he's doin' okay now."

"I didn't even hear about it," he takes a moment to digest the information. The driver parks at Shakey's, and we go inside. I look for Mama Jones, but she must be off.

"Large hot fudge sundae, for my girl." Dad looks at me for approval, and I nod. "A vanilla shake and a large onion ring." He pays, and we wait at the counter until the food comes out, then take a table in the back, beside the jukebox.

"Is wanting to quit athletic training about Cody, though? Because the more people I talk to, the more say that staying on with your plans is vital, even after losing someone close to you."

"It's not because of the accident." I stir the hot fudge down the sides of my sundae cup. After a moment, I clench my hands together mustering up enough courage to tell him more. "For a long time, I've wanted to go to art school. And life is teaching me that all we can live for is *today*. Cody never got to live his dreams. But Daddy, if I have anythin' to say about it, I'm gonna live mine. You can sell the beach house or rent it out, or whatever you want to do. But I'm not going to put a hold on what I need any more."

"The beach house?" He wrinkles his brow. "You could've sold that at any point, darlin'." He sips his shake. "It's in your name. Remember when we went to sign all the paperwork?"

"What?" I feel stupid. Memories of that day come to mind, with the piles of paperwork. I remember signing it. But then Mom took me out and told me that none of it belonged to me. She said it was all just a formality to sign the forms so I could legally live there as my own landlord.

I believed her.

Dammit.

"Oh, yes. Beach house belongs to you. Always has."

"But I don't understand. Mom said that you couldn't sell it because you'd lose out on too much profit. She told me I had to stay there. Told me I had to finish my degree."

"Oh, no, darlin'. It's always been yours. I have twenty-three properties in Hilton Head. Just bought this one in Suncastle so you and Cody didn't have far to go for class." He shakes his head. "Wasn't about the investment so much as takin' care of you. The value has increased quite a bit over the years. You're welcome to use that money however you wish. I wasn't going to leave you to fend for yourself after college." He takes another sip. "You didn't think that, did you? What's the point of all this money if I don't take care of my own?"

"But I'm not your own," I say it out loud for the first time.

Something changes in his face, and he looks at me for a long while, setting his cup on the red shimmering diner table. "You've *always* been my baby girl." He sets his hand on mine. "Have I ever done anythin' to make you think otherwise?"

I think about growing up. He often worked, and I rarely saw him. After I found out about my true parentage, I thought it had to do with not wanting to be around me. But maybe, he was just busy with work. I blink, dumbfounded at the revelation. He considers me his?

"But Mom slept with Mr. Checketts."

He scoffs. "I am well aware of when and who your mother has slept with. Doesn't mean I don't love you as my own." He reaches across the table and covers my hand with his. "Lexie, you matter to me. Who was there when you took your first steps? Not Mr. Checketts. Me. Who stayed up until 3 a.m. making that pickle costume you had to have for Halloween when you were seven? Mr. Checketts? No, it was me. Who held your hand all night when you had pneumonia and couldn't sleep alone? Who remembers the name of your favorite stuffed animal? Daisy is still up in your room, by the way. You may wanna grab her before you go and leave South Carolina for good."

There's a knot in my throat.

"Lexie, darlin', your happiness matters to me. And if you wanna become an artist, do it. Sell the beach house. Move wherever you want to live." He lets out a sigh. "I'm sorry you worried about this, baby girl."

His eyes are kind, and I see the man I've barely known all these years. The one I assumed didn't want me. I try to say something but I can't. Tears pool in my eyes.

"Your mother has made a lot of choices over the years. She has her own unique relationship with the truth. I am not surprised she told you things to make you stick around. Has nothin' to do with Mr. Checketts or the other affairs she's had."

Other affairs? My chest tightens. "You mean, you knew and still wanted to keep me?" I always thought I was just an accident. A mistake. For both of them.

"I'd been beggin' her to have another little one. I had planned on it bein' mine, but when she finally got pregnant, I was just as overjoyed to have my last baby, like I knew you were waitin' to join our family and I wasn't at peace until you were here."

I drop my spoon. "So no part of you thought I should just be thrown out of your life?"

"Thrown out of my life? Hell, no." He rubs the bridge of his nose. "Had no idea you worried about this." He leans closer to me. "Believe me when I say that I love havin' you in my life. You have a place in my heart as if you were my blood. Because to me, Lexie, you are."

A new feeling spreads through my chest. Belonging. I feel like I belong.

48

BOBBY

"That was so amazin'!" I relax into the passenger seat of Lexie's parked car after we get back from Omaha.

"What a way to finish your college career." She smiles wide, killing the ignition in the parking spot at my apartment.

"You wanna come in?" I try not to get my hopes up, but there's nothing I want more than to spend some time with her.

"We haven't talked about us much." She scratches her nose.

"You've been incredibly supportive and patient with me." I think about the craziness of the hospital and life afterward. "I've been workin' on myself a lot. Tryin' to get over all my shit. I am so sorry for what I've put you through."

"You don't have to be." She looks at me for a long time. "When are you startin' at the recovery center?"

"Next week." Time has really flown by. I can hardly believe I'm already here. "I'll be there for a month."

"Can I come visit you there?"

"I'd like that."

ON MY COUCH, IT'S JUST LIKE HOW WE SAT THE FIRST TIME SHE CAME over. "There's more I need to tell you," I swallow. "I've been keepin' so much from you. None of it was right. When you wanted to talk, I pushed you away. It was wrong of me, too."

"You don't need to apologize any more." She raises her eyebrows, her knee brushing against my thigh.

"But I do." I take a deep breath. "I don't want to cause you any more pain, so I need to tell you the rest of the story."

I tell her everything I remember about the night that Cody came to see me. The night he died.

"You weren't a sick joke to either one of us. I had a crush on you before Cody asked you out. But he didn't know that. He was sincerely tryin' to be straight with you. And I know you meant the world to him." I laugh because God, it feels good to say the whole thing. No more secrets. Nothing between us anymore. "He loved you, Lexie. He told me so himself, even that night."

"He did?" Her voice is choked up.

"He did." I put my fingers on her chin and bring her close to my lips, the closeness of everything we've both missed. "He loved you, Lex. I promise I'm not makin' this up." I take a deep breath, soaking in how she's receiving my story, my truth. "I think if there hadn't been the accident, he would've told you all this. And I'm sorry that I haven't been able to tell you until now. Because I wanted to. I really did, but it felt like I was betrayin' him. It's stupid, I know–"

"It's not stupid, Bobby." Her lips curl up in a smile. "It's beautifully loyal."

"I sunk really low right after the accident. I've never been able to talk about it. Then I realized how wrong I was to keep it all from you."

"Of course you sunk low." She kisses me. "It breaks my heart that you and Cody coulda had a life together." She brings her head to mine. "I'm sad you lost your love."

"But I didn't." I bite my lip. "I've always wanted to be with you. I don't know what woulda happened with me and Cody." I kiss her, my tongue melting into her lips. "But I know what's happenin' with me and you. My love is right here." I take her knuckles and kiss each one. "And I'm sorry for all the pain I've caused you."

"We don't know how to do this life thing, do we?"

"Not even a little bit." I focus on her eyes, those beautiful green glimmers of light. "But you're not mad?"

"I was." She straddles me, our bodies touching in that way that I've craved. "But I'm not anymore."

"You're not?" The words almost hurt coming out, the question filling me with longing. Maybe she's truly forgiven me.

"How can I be mad at you?" She rests her body into mine.

This connection fills me with all I need.

"You've got the other half of my heart beatin' in your chest." Our noses dance against each other. "I told you a long time ago, we need each other." She licks her lips, bringing them tenderly to my mouth. "I'm scared of trustin' you. I'm scared I won't be able to really trust anyone." She pulls back to look into my eyes. "But this feels so right to me. Does it feel right to you?"

"So right." I hum against her ear.

"Then I wanna try again."

"Me too." I squint my eyes, overcome by the moment. "I love you, Lexie."

"Always have. Always will." She kisses me, bringing comfort like a bowl of peach ice cream on a hot summer day. I don't know how she does it. How she takes me as I am and lets me love her. My sins are not the kind that many could forgive, but she's holding me and offering relief.

"I'm gonna get better. Keep workin' on me. Be in a more healthy place for us."

"I'll be there to help this time." She grips me tighter, her arms becoming my sanctuary, protecting me from the danger of myself.

"Are you scared of bein' here with me, ya know, if I have a relapse?" It's my raw fears given life through my words. I've worried what it may do to her now that she knows. "Because most people don't just get better, I don't think. Even with the recovery center and therapy, it's a long road ahead. I'll probably be fightin' this for a long time.

Maybe my whole life. But if it scares you–" My voice shuts off, not sure I can face losing her again.

"No." She shakes her head. "I'm not afraid at all." She brushes the hair out of my face. "I'm amazed by you."

"Amazed?"

"Yes." Her lips purse. "You're so fuckin' strong."

"I don't feel strong." A million emotions take up space in my brain, and not one of them is strength.

"I know you don't. But that's all I see." She brings her forehead close to mine. "And I'll keep showin' you until you can see it for yourself."

———

AS FUNNY AS I FEEL BEING AT THE RECOVERY CENTER, IT HELPS TO know I'm not alone. That everyone here has been through something similar. This is a new kind of support I haven't felt before.

I don't know why I was never able to tell anyone about my eating disorder. Maybe I should've. I felt so much shame for it. But I'm working through the shame.

I realize this is a part of my story. A part that I want to overcome. A part that I want to learn from. To grow from. I'm not there yet, but maybe one day I can be more honest about this on a larger scale. Maybe one day I can help other athletes that are challenged with this. Maybe one day there will be a purpose to my pain. Because I know the darkness. And if I've learned anything about darkness, one of the best things that can be done is to sit with someone else going through it. To join them in their hell and help them know that nothing lasts forever.

I hit a low. Rock bottom, as they call it. Those nights I fell asleep on the cold bathroom floor felt so helpless. But nothing is ever truly helpless.

I'm getting the help I need. I'm doing the work.

For myself.

49

LEXIE

The beach house went under contract in six days. I sold most of the furniture and rented a little storage unit for the things I want to keep and am not ready to move across the country.

One final walk through the house brings a wave of emotion. I sit in the corner of *our* room, holding my knees to my chest.

This isn't goodbye, Cody. I blink back tears. *I love what we had. I love you. If there's a heaven, I hope you're finally free.* I sit here with his memories, one by one filling my mind with all that we shared. I'm not sure what I need to feel, so I breathe everything that comes. Being still feels right. Giving myself a moment is healing a little part of my heart.

Mental note...keep letting myself feel my feelings.

With a glimpse of peace, I descend the stairs.

Trish waits by the front door, taking down the final thing I left on the walls: Cody's cross. "You want me to put this in storage?"

"No, I think Bobby will want it. I'll ask him." I take it from her and set it with my last box of things to go in the car.

"You have to tell me everythin'. Video call me at least every few days." Trish wraps her arms around me. "I'm gonna miss you, girlfriend."

"I'm gonna miss you. But I'm sure I'll come visit for the holidays." I have to look forward to seeing her again or I'll fall apart with this goodbye.

She adjusts her purse strap. "You're goin' to get Bobby today, right? Is he doin' better?"

"I think so. I can't believe it's been a month." The time has flown by, filled with all the details and arrangements we've made. Bobby will be so surprised when I show him everything. The thought sends butter-flies clamoring in my stomach. I've worked everything out for my dreams and he's going to be a part of them, if I have anything to do with it.

"Yeah, you've been workin' your pretty little ass off." Her smile is genuine and sad at the same time. "Too bad California is so far away."

"Just means you have to come for a Cali beach vacation."

"Bikinis are packed and at the ready." She smiles.

I take one more look in the front rooms. Everything is out of this house. Looking at the stairs, I remember Cody.

"Babe, you forgot this!" I throw his hoodie down the stairs. "It's gonna be chilly!"

He stands on the third step and I rush down to kiss him. His lips on mine, his arms around me. "Love you." He taps my nose with his.

I feel him close, he's here, with me. Telling me it's okay to move forward, telling me he forgives me for our fights.

I forgive you, for everythin' too, babe. We did the best we could, and all we have is now. I imagine him saying.

Zac's truck pulls up in the driveway.

"Gotta go." Trish pulls me close for one more hug.

"Me too."

"Give Bobby a hug for me." She pulls me close one more time, and then hurries over to Zac. He kisses her and runs around to get her door.

They drive away. I lock up my front door, for the last time. This house was always mine, and now I'm moving on, doing what I need.

What Bobby and I both need.

———

ON THE DRIVE TO THE RECOVERY CENTER, I FIND MY MIND IN A VERY contemplative state. It's hard, knowing Bobby kept so much from me. I'll need a while to really heal from everything. So much of my life has been shrouded in lies.

But I believed him when he told me there won't be any more secrets between us. With the whole story laid out in front of me, I see why he did what he did. It still hurts, and I need to work through that in a healthy way. But I feel really good about us. About where we are going. About how we can get there.

I'll always regret that I missed this. That during the time when he was really at his lowest I was adding to his heartache instead of supporting him. But I know that's not fair. *"We all live and learn."* My therapist said. I'm here for him now, and I swear I'm never going anywhere.

My life is like a painting I have to keep working on. Each brush-stroke, each lesson, adds depth and layers to what is already there. It doesn't always work out the first time, sometimes I have to come back with a fresh perspective. Bobby and I have had to paint over a lot of hard memories, but in my mind there is so much potential here. Our relationship is worth every bit of learning and layering it takes

Getting off the freeway exit, anticipation swirls in my heart. Every time I'm with him, I know he's the one I want to be with. The one I want to share my dreams with, my life with.

My thoughts go to when he asked to hold me in his hospital bed. It made my heart soar, because I wanted that too. Holding him, being with him, talking to him, it all means the world to me.

I throw the car into park at the recovery center. The acceptance letter burns a hole in my pocket. He doesn't know I have it. I run across the parking lot to the front doors.

I don't want another second to pass without him.

Bobby's standing in the lobby wearing a button up and jeans, his hair peeking out of his Suncastle baseball cap. My mouth waters. I've missed him so much.

My arms wrap around him and hold. He is home to me. All the problems in the world melt away when we are together.

"You look good." I take his hands.

"I feel good." He really does look better, so much better, healthier than he has in a long time. "Thanks for comin' to get me."

"Are you kiddin' me? I wouldn't be anywhere else today." I hold his eyes, replaying his voice in my mind. "All checked out?"

"Yep, I'm ready." He smiles, nodding to the staff at the front desk. I've come to visit every week while he's been here. But this time, it feels so good to be leaving with him. Bringing him home. To *our* new home. I'm not sure he will approve of this bold move, not sure if he's ready for it, but I hope so. If not, I'll give him all the time he needs.

We load his stuff in my trunk, next to the box from the beach house.

"You cleanin' out some stuff?" He eyes Cody's cross sticking out of the box.

"I have some big news. First, this surprise." I pull out the envelope and hand it to him.

"Laguna College of Art and Design?" He reads the return address aloud. "Lex?" His eyes go wide. "Is this what I think it is?"

"It *is* what you think it is." I squeal, grinning.

"No way! But Laguna...that's in–"

"California," I shriek.

"Shit, that's...you're comin' out to California with me?" Shock plays on his face, like he's piecing it all together.

"There is nowhere in this universe I'd rather be." I step closer.

"I've been dreadin' what I was gonna do across the country without you. It's been drivin' me crazy, worryin' about flyin' back here to see you whenever I could. I knew it wasn't gonna be enough." His tone is so sincere and I can tell that he's been worried about this.

"You were gonna fly back here to see me whenever you could?" I guess I shouldn't be surprised, but I am. We hadn't talked about what was gonna happen next, both of us just focusing on him and his recovery whenever I came to visit. My heart swells, because fuck, he wants this relationship as much as I do.

"You're it for me, Lexie." His lips take mine, lingering for several seconds, exploring my mouth with his tongue. "If you'll have me, I want to be yours. Really, truly, yours."

"I want you." I bring him into another kiss, longing for everything we were, everything we can be. My body responds to his, the way I've craved. "I love you."

"I love you so fuckin' much." He picks me up and swings me around in circles in the parking lot. "How'd you pull all this off? I thought you were gonna work some teams first while you saved up. Not that you need to, I'd be happy to pay for it once I get goin' with–"

"Major League ball," I cut him off, a huge smile on my face. "It's really sweet of you to offer to pay for it. Thank you."

"I'd give you everythin' I have to my name, especially if it meant you pursuing your dreams." He is being sincere and it makes my heart sing.

"Well, you don't have to. I had a nice long talk with Dad. I told him everythin'. You wouldn't believe the conversation we had. Turns out the beach house was always mine. Anyway." I let out a deep breath. "I sold the beach house and got all my ducks in a row. It's time we both go and live our dreams, isn't it? Together, if you wanna be?" I give him a serious look. I need to know if he wants to really try again. "It's real close to where the Los Angeles Angels play."

"Oh, baby." He brings me in for the sweetest, most tender hug. "This is incredible."

"We did it, love. We got through all of our own obstacles and here we are." I kiss him, melting into his lips, feeling the closeness that fills my heart with love. "I'm so fuckin' proud of us."

"Are you kiddin'? I am so fuckin' proud of you." He shakes his head. "Art school. Lex. I'm so thrilled for you to finally get to go."

"It feels really good."

"It really does." He brings his lips to my forehead and I know that he shares every bit of my happiness. We are moving forward, together.

After we get in the car, I hand him my phone. It's pulled up to the check-in email. "One more surprise."

"Plane tickets?" He raises his eyebrows. "Wait, this says today."

"It's just a little weekend getaway. Figure we both need to be there in person, then come home and wrap everythin' up here." I'm shaking from excitement. He doesn't know what I have planned. I cannot wait to show him. "We have a couple hours to get to the airport." I wink. "Let's go back to your place. I'll help you pack."

———

THE WHOLE FLIGHT HE TELLS ME ABOUT THE RECOVERY CENTER. I TELL him about Dad, still getting used to the fact that he accepts me. That he always has. It feels so good to be with Bobby. So perfect.

After the plane lands, I arrange a car to take us to the little place I found about halfway between Los Angeles and Laguna beach.

"Where are we?" Bobby slings his backpack over his shoulder, standing in awe.

I hand him the house key. "Come check it out."

He is hesitant, but unlocks the door. Inside are mostly empty rooms, with endless possibilities. A fresh start. A place for us.

"I put down a deposit to rent this house for the next year, and I wondered if you wanted to move in with me?" Goosebumps line my flesh and my heart beats faster. *Please say yes, Bobby. Please, say yes.*

"Jeez, Lex." He wraps his arms around me. "You really did this?"

"I did." There's a smile on my face that fills my being. "I told my mom it was time I make it on my own in the world. Do what I need. What *we* need."

He spins me around in a circle. "I'm so proud of you, baby." He stops spinning, holding me tight to his chest. "Can I stay here with you? Please?"

"I was hopin' you'd say that." I rub his shoulders, then pull back. "Look, I have somethin' to show you."

"You've got one surprise after another, don't you?"

"Yeah, well, it's about time we get a break from shit, isn't it?" I take his hand and bring him into my art studio. On the main wall, in a beautiful display with a light directly on it, is the painting I did of the three of us, Bobby in the middle.

"You painted this?"

I hear the emotion in his voice.

"So we can all be together." I pull him close to me.

His arms grip me so tightly. "It's incredible, Lex." His lips come to mine, a tear slipping out of his eye and onto my cheek. "Just like you."

Part of me knows we are gonna be alright. And I can't wait to see what our future brings.

50

BOBBY
SEPTEMBER

*T*angled in sheets, we collide. The sweetest love I've ever known. Things just keep getting better. I don't deserve any bit of this, but I have it. God, do I have it.

"You're it for me." She whispers against my ear.

"No, you're it for *me*."

My kisses drive her deeper into the best pleasure we've ever felt. She hums as we climax together. Always together. I collapse onto her, holding tight as we breathe heavy.

We've made a home together, started a life together. I still miss Cody every day, but I don't feel as trapped by the past. I'm working toward closure. Toward letting him go.

No, it's not about letting him go. It's learning where he fits now. And I know the answer. It's on the other side, reminding me every day that I can do this. That I can be the person I want and need to be.

That I am enough.

And I'm finally starting to believe him.

THE END

ACKNOWLEDGMENTS

"It takes a village" keeps going through my mind when I think about my book journey. It takes a village to raise a child, and it takes a village to publish a book. So many of my friends and family have supported me in a million small ways. Each of those ways has given life to me and this book.

A Game Like Ours started on a notebook with a pencil when I was in high school. Even then, I dreamed of the day when I would hold the finished work in my hand. As a teenager, I knew I needed to prepare myself for this book. I wanted to perfect my writing craft and one day give this story everything it deserved. Being here now, knowing that this book *has* become even better than my plans for it, feels amazing.

Special thanks to my Josh, who teaches me what love is. You have gone above and beyond to support me in making my dreams a reality. So many hours you cheered me on. Through so many heartaches you have been by my side. You read my first draft and my last. I love you, baby. Thank you for giving me so many cute romantic moments in real life, fueling my creative energy to write books like this.

Thanks and accolades to my editors Deanna Young and Karin Salisbury who helped shape this novel into what it is today. Thank you for your thoughts and eyes on this manuscript. For being the polish I need.

Deanna Young, thank you for being my critique partner, my listening ear, my sounding board, my soul sister. I am so very thankful for you showing up for me. For being who I need in my life. So many times you have helped calm my storm. You haven't judged me for the absurd anxiety that has taken me hostage, instead you have held my hand.

Karin; the creator of Thought Provoking Thursdays. Thank you for the butterfly necklace, a gift to me and Little Marissa. She didn't get what she needed as a child, but she is getting it now–in large part thanks to you. We've been through so many ups, and so many downs, but I wouldn't have life any other way.

Jenn Jackson, I love you. I'm so happy that for that brief snapshot in my life we were neighbors and then became lifelong friends. You are one of the most incredible women I have ever known. You raise me up as we grow together.

L. Steinworth, who is incredibly cool. Really though, you have been one of my best friends through all the ups and downs of publishing. The ups and downs of surviving narcissist abuse. The ups and downs of being a creator. Liz, thank you for the hair dye. For the avocado. For the cover. For the format. For the feedback. For holding my hand through this daunting journey. Your friendship means everything. Shoot True.

Huge, huge, HUGE thanks to Ashley and Scott Knapp for being my real life Bobby and Lexie in so many ways. I love the way that the cover and promo photos turned out. I am forever thankful to both of you for making my dreams a reality in such a magnificent way. I've been dreaming of this book cover since I started this book when I was fifteen years old. Seeing it come to life with the two of you is better than I could've imagined.

My incredible team of Alpha and Beta readers, some of whom include: Laura Phillips, Melissa Ivers, Danielle Hill, Rachel Mitchell, KM Rives, and Jessi Phillipson.

Julie Soper, who loves me for who I am. Julie, you have no idea what your constant support has done for me. That whenever I'm feeling down, I can come to you and you remind me that I am ready for this path. For helping me know about the hospital scenes. For always telling me to invest in myself. Thank you for being you and for sharing that with me.

Keri Sandford, for knowing who Bobby is, even before I did. Having you in my life is one of the most precious and unexpected things. I love that we connected and that we have bonded over so much. You brighten my life in a million colors. Thank you for being my constant in a sea of shifting friendships.

Eris Marriott, I thought I was *your* editor, but really in a lot of ways you became mine. So much of your feedback helped me make this book a work of art. I love our many writing sprints and conversations. The support you give me. The deep and real conversations we have.

Brandon Martinez, thanks for being there for me, kiddo. I loved chatting with you about workouts and what Bobby would have on his counter. Thanks for being one of my early readers. When you published your book, it really told me it was time for me to publish mine.

Christy Miller, I love you. I love the chibis and our virtual hot chocolate time. I love that you're so real with me. I love that we are writers together.

Matt Buckley, it is celebration muffin time.

M. Jae Cooper, for being the first to read my book start to finish. Your enthusiasm got me through many dark days that followed the first draft of this book.

Cameron Asbury, thank you for being my sensitivity reader and helping me shape the scenes with Bobby and Cody. Your thoughts and suggestions, as well as support, helped me so much.

Erika Zimmerman, my longest known friend. I love that you knew me as the little girl with the notebook. You were the first person I called on our home phone to tell you I finished my book. Really, you were one of my only supporters. You've read my fantasy book. You've read A Game Like Ours, even when it was littered with mistakes.

You've always believed in me. Thank you. After all these years, I'm glad we are still friends.

Katie and Pete we miss you. Even though we are far away, you have shown so much support for this book. From the video chats, to asking for a link, to pre-order, I love and appreciate all you do for me.

Tyson and Catie Williams, every time I've mentioned my writing you've been excited for me. It means a lot to have your friendship and support. We miss you guys.

Melanie Atkins, we've had so many important conversations over the years. So many friendships have come and gone, but you've always been here for me. I appreciate your friendship and enthusiasm as I continue to live my dreams.

Byron Lane, when you said "keep going" it kept me going. I was at a pivotal point in my writing career, where after years of writing and learning how to write I wasn't sure if I was up for it all. Something happened in my personal life that made it so I was ready to set my book aside, again. Instead, I listened to you. It gave me what I needed that day, to take the next step. One step at a time, I got this book ready to publish. Thank you for always, always, always encouraging me. You're a gem of a person. I'm forever grateful for you.

Emma Scott, for being you. Your books inspire me. You inspire me. I'm so glad you're in my life.

Steven Rowley, your books make me laugh. They make me want to write. They make me think about things in new ways.

Stephen and Madalyn Batman, thank you for asking my baseball question! I appreciate you making sure that my details were accurate.

The Captain. I appreciate you, your hype and your babytalk voice. Thank you for the macaroni and cheese packages, among other things.

My Therapist, Kim Fernandes, thank you for the many sessions of helping me work through my past so that it no longer hinders my future. So often you talked me through the trauma that told me I wasn't good enough to write the book, and the backlash I got after the fallout from circumstances that rapidly spiraled out of control from a fellow writer. I appreciate your perspective about writing about Bobby's eating disorder and helping me have confidence in myself as a writer.

Our sessions built me up so that I was able to make this book what it needs to be.

Dr. Mick Lynch thank you for answering my many questions about an athlete with an eating disorder. Thank you for sending resources. They were very helpful.

Reeve Carney, your music has played on repeat through my kitchen and my car. Though you don't know me, you mean so much in my life. Your songs bring comfort and hope to me that I don't feel any other way. Thank you for being such an inspiration.

200 Rogue Fantasy Writers, the first writing community I really felt a part of.

And always, thank you to my angel on the other side, Jeff. You got me out of my personal hell. All of the life I have now would be drastically different, if not for you. I wish so much I could read my book to you. I don't get to do that, not the way I would like to. But you are still there for me every moment, helping me live my dreams. I'm so glad I'm here. And I'm so glad you helped me get here.

ABOUT THE AUTHOR

ENCHANTING SEDUCTIVE
REDEMPTIVE ROMANCE

Lover of stories since before she could walk, Marissa has always had a passion for creating characters and worlds. Learning to read was a challenge, so she learned words by writing them–taking her notebook everywhere and asking total strangers how to spell. Since then, a laptop has replaced her trusty notebook and her stories have evolved into novels.

Marissa lives in Texas with her husband, two children and an endless collection of David Bowie hats. She enjoys reading in the sunshine, with a big bottle of chocolate milk and music playing in the background.

facebook.com/authormarissagramoll

twitter.com/MarissaGramoll

instagram.com/marissajgramoll

Made in the USA
Middletown, DE
07 June 2021

41366739R00250